Bound by Chaos

Bound by Chaos

G M Hutchison

CONTENTS

First Printing, 2025

WELCOME TO BOUND BY CHAOS

Well, well, well.

Look who wandered into **Bound by Chaos**.

Curiosity—a dangerous thing.

But sexy of you.

Let's get one thing straight:

This book?

It is **not safe**.

It is **not sweet**.

And it is *definitely* not tame.

It's hot.

It's dark.

It's crawling with dangerous men who will absolutely ruin your life—and you'll thank them for the privilege.

OFFICIALLY UNOFFICIAL WARNINGS:

Graphic sexual content that will make you blush, sweat, and possibly question your life choices

Reverse harem energy—because *one* man was never going to be enough

Violence, blood, trauma, and enough red flags to start a national parade

Dirty talk so filthy it should come with a warning label

Possessive men who would kill for her—and already have

Knife play. Gun play. Power play. All the plays.

And a heroine who doesn't need saving—she **is** the storm

A NOTE TO MY DARLING GRANDMA:

Close the book.

Walk away.

Go make yourself a cup of tea and pretend you never saw this.

Because unless you want to read about your granddaughter getting metaphorically (and occasionally *very literally*) pinned to a wall by morally grey men with dangerous hands and even dirtier mouths?

I beg you—spare us both.

BUT FOR THE BRAVE:

If you're into:

Being seduced, ruined, and emotionally wrecked

Enemies-to-lovers—but with knives, trauma, and kisses that feel like war

Men who snarl, bite, and *definitely* don't play fair

A heroine with rage in her heart, blood on her knuckles, and a mouth that could cut diamonds

Then congratulations, sweetheart.

You've just found your new obsession.

This isn't a love triangle.

This is a damn pentagram.

And it's about to get messy.

Read it. Regret nothing.

Hydrate. Lock the door.

And for the love of chaos, *do not read Chapter 38 at work.*

Unless you enjoy HR meetings.

WARNING: This Book Contains Mature, Explicit, & Excessively Questionable Content

While it's packed with filth, fun, and morally grey chaos goblins you'll absolutely fall for (despite your better judgement), it also contains scenes and themes that may be triggering for some readers, including but not limited to:

Violence, bloodshed & creative injuries
PTSD, trauma responses, and emotional spiral gymnastics
Extremely explicit sexual content (including kink elements: dominance, knife play, power play, choking, spanking, and enough tension to snap steel)
Threats of sexual violence (not between love interests)
Kidnapping, captivity, restraint & "oops, you're chained again" moments
Mentions of past abuse, grief, and loss
Unhinged emotional breakdowns (hers, theirs, and yours)
Language your grandmother would exorcise you for
Spice levels that require hydration, a snack break, and possibly a therapist
Toys. Yes, that kind. Used creatively and often.
Morally grey, obsessive, possessive, alpha men who do not believe in "personal space"
Thin walls. Everyone hears *everything*. Again. And again.

This book is for readers 18+ who enjoy their romance dark, their danger feral, and their emotional damage fully marinated.

Please take care of yourself while reading.

And if at any point you whisper:

"Oh no... but also yes."

Congratulations — you're exactly where you're supposed to be.

For the girls with blood on their knuckles,
sass in their veins,
and the audacity to choose themselves—even when it burns.
And for everyone who's ever whispered,
"Maybe I'm the problem,"
with just the *tiniest* smile.
This one's for you, chaos goblins.

"She wasn't built for glass slippers and happy endings.
She was forged in fire, stitched together with scars,
and kissed by chaos until she stopped apologising for the way she burned."
— Unknown (but probably un-medicated)

1

Rain, Metal, Silence

Riley

Safe & Sound – Taylor Swift ft. The Civil Wars

We were soaked—utterly, hopelessly drenched—as we bolted down the muddy trail, slipping on wet leaves, rain hammering down like it had a personal vendetta. My boots squelched. Hair clung to my neck. My jacket sagged under the weight of a hundred buckets. Agatha was right beside me, determined to beat me to the car.

"Last one there sits in the middle!" she yelled, breathless and smug, surging forward with all the bratty teen energy in the world.

"Nice try," I snapped, pushing harder despite the stitch in my side. "You're the middle child. Embrace your destiny."

Behind us, Sophie slogged along like a tiny rain-soaked goblin, hood in her eyes, arms swinging. "This is the worst vacation ever!" she howled. "My socks feel like slime!"

The car loomed ahead, parked awkwardly at the edge of the gravel lot like a beacon of warmth and dry sanity. I charged forward—only for Agatha to dart in front of me at the last second.

"Move!" I shouted, hopping a puddle and shoulder-checking her. She shrieked, elbowing me in the ribs.

"Back off! I called window!"

"You didn't call anything!" I growled, yanking the rear door open.

Sophie beat us inside from the other side, climbing into the back like a gremlin with a mission. "I'm sitting here!" she declared, already buckled by the window. "I get car sick, you know that!"

"Yeah, yeah, Princess Puke gets her throne," I muttered, half in the car, half still wrestling Agatha.

"I'm not sitting in the middle!" Agatha shrieked, her soaked ponytail whipping me in the face as she shoved past.

"You're fifteen! You'll survive!" "You're eighteen! Sit in the middle and grow up!"

I wedged myself inside, knees smashed against the back of the front seat, shivering and furious.

Agatha finally collapsed into the window seat, smug as hell. I was left crammed between them, cold and squashed. The car door slammed. Rain hammered the roof like a war drum.

Mum slid into the passenger seat, breathless. Dad got behind the wheel, shaking rain from his coat.

"Riley," Dad warned, sharp. "Act your age."

Mum gave me the look. "You're the oldest. Stop acting like one of them."

I bit the inside of my cheek, arms folded tight. The car was humid, full of wet clothes and tension.

Agatha smirked, nudging me. "Don't," I warned. She did it again. I shoved her. Sophie groaned, head back. "Can we please just go before I throw up?"

That was it. I twisted toward Agatha, ready to snap. She was already grinning, spoiling for a fight.

We were soaked. We were stuck in a fogged-up car. Halfway through a miserable vacation. None of us knew this would be our last normal moment.

The windshield wipers groaned. Screech-thud. Screech-thud. A grating, stubborn metronome.

"You're such a brat," I snapped. "You're being unfair!" Agatha shot back, voice rising.

Screech-thud.

"Both of you, stop it!" Sophie whimpered, barely heard over the rain and wipers.

Screech-thud.

"Enough!" Dad barked, twisting to glare. "Do you ever shut up?" Mum muttered, fingers pressed to her temple.

I turned away, arms tight, staring into the storm. Screech— Headlights. Blinding. Close. A semi's horn bellowed.

Dad yanked the wheel. The car jerked. The wipers screamed as we spun. Time slowed. The weightless lurch of fishtailing.

Sophie's inhale turning into a scream. Agatha clawing at the seat. The rain—endless—marking the inevitable. Screech—snap. The wipers froze mid-motion.

The tree came out of nowhere. Crunch. Metal shrieked. Glass exploded. My world collapsed in a single, ragged breath.

Silence. Rain blurred the glass. Still pounding.

Then—Sophie's cries broke through. I gasped, blinking at the warmth trickling down my forehead. My fingers came away red.

For a moment, there was only ringing in my ears. My breath came in ragged gasps. My body felt both weightless and impossibly heavy.

Rain slapped my face. Wait. The roof—gone. Peeled back. Jagged metal curled like claws. Wind howled through the wreckage.

My fingers gripped the wet seat. Cold reality tore through the fog.

Sophie was still crying, trembling beside me. Agatha— A breath hitched. Agatha wasn't moving. Her body twisted, limp. Blood at her temple. Her eyes—vacant.

No. No, no, no. Sophie couldn't see this.

With numb hands, I reached for her, pulling her close. She clung to me, sobbing into my chest.

Wind howled. Rain roared. The seat belt dug into my ribs as I twisted, every inch of me aching. Shouts rang through the storm. Flashing lights. I turned, blinking through rain and blood— The front of the car was gone.

Not crushed. Gone. Mum's seat—twisted metal. Dad's side—mangled, unrecognisable. They weren't there.

Bile rose in my throat. My whole body shook.

A hand gripped my shoulder. A voice—urgent. Unfamiliar. But all I could do was stare at where they should've been.

Rain pounded me. My arms locked tighter around Sophie. I wouldn't let go. Then—hands. Rough. Strong. They ripped her away.

"No!" My voice cracked as I lunged, but my body failed me. Pain flared. But I barely felt it.

Sophie screamed, clawing for me. "Riley!" I fought. Weak. Wild. "Let me go!" I choked out.

Someone spoke, calm. Words I couldn't understand.

Sophie. Agatha. Mum. Dad. The car. A sob tore from my throat.

The twisted emptiness. Agatha's vacant eyes. Mum and Dad—gone. Sophie—screaming.

And all I could think as the chaos swallowed me whole was: What had I done?

My alarm blared. I gasped awake, already falling—back into that night.

My breath caught. Pulse hammering. Mind trapped between sleep and memory. The rain. The arguing. The headlights. The lurch. The crash. I sat up, heart racing. The room spun.

Swish-thud.

Swish-thud.

I could still hear it. The wipers. The last sound before the world ended. Hands trembling, I scrubbed my face. Dragged in ragged breaths.

My therapist says trauma doesn't disappear. It waits. Buried. Ready to claw its way back.

Eleven years. It still comes for me. The rain. The smell of burning rubber. Agatha's empty stare. Sophie's cries. I squeeze my eyes shut. Palms over my face.

I didn't cry at the funeral. I couldn't. I had to keep it together. Sophie was eight. She lost everything that night—just like I did.

But I had a choice. I could've let the system take her. But I knew what happened to kids like us.

So I walked into the courtroom, signed the papers. I became her legal guardian.

At eighteen, I gave up everything. The future I'd fought for.

Across the room, my ballet trophies gleam in the morning light. Golden figures frozen in perfect poses.

I was weeks from Paris. From the dream I bled for. The scholarship I earned. I was supposed to be on stage.

Instead— I worked dead-end jobs. Learned to budget. Cooked for a grieving child. Buried my own grief so she didn't drown in hers.

My dreams ended when the wipers stopped. When the roof peeled back. When Agatha's eyes went still. I stare at my hands. Still shaking.

I made the choice. I don't regret it. But some nights, when everything is quiet, My body still remembers what it felt like— to have a future.

And every morning, when I wake up gasping, I have to remind myself: That future isn't mine anymore.

2

Just a Little Bit of More

Riley

Motion Sickness – Phoebe Bridgers

The morning sunlight slipped through the thin curtains, casting warm streaks of gold across the kitchen floor. It looked peaceful—almost beautiful—but I barely noticed anymore.

Mornings weren't for beauty. Mornings were for surviving the routine.

The scent of coffee lingered in the air, rich and grounding. I poured myself a mug, cradling it for a moment before setting it down to butter the toast that had just popped.

The toaster made a tired wheeze, like it was just as overworked as I was.

My navy blouse clung slightly with the heat of the kitchen, and my black slacks still held the crease I'd ironed into them last night. Of course, there was also a faint coffee stain on my sleeve I hadn't noticed until now.

Naturally.

I glanced at the clock above the stove.

"Six fifty-five," I muttered. "Sophie, you're going to be late!"

A loud thump echoed down the hallway, followed by a muffled, "I'm coming!"

I sighed, grabbed the second piece of toast, and waited.

Sure enough, Sophie appeared moments later with her arms full—backpack half-zipped, textbook clutched to her chest, water bottle dangling from her pinky like an afterthought.

She looked effortlessly polished, as usual. Long chestnut hair down, green blouse perfectly pressed—the one that made her look less like a sleep-deprived nineteen-year-old university student and more like someone with a LinkedIn profile and strong opinions about email etiquette.

I handed her the toast.

"You didn't pack lunch, did you?"

Sophie gave me a sheepish grin. "No time."

"Of course not."

I grabbed the brown paper bag off the counter and held it out to her. "Turkey sandwich. Apple. Eat it this time instead of letting it rot in your backpack like a forgotten science experiment."

"That was one time," she groaned, snatching the bag dramatically. "And I still carry emotional scars from it."

She laughed, but the familiar knot in my chest stayed put.

Because underneath the sarcasm, the worrying never really stopped.

She was smart. Capable. Driven. But sometimes I still saw the little girl clinging to me at the funeral, tear-streaked and shaking, asking where Mum and Dad had gone.

God, she'd grown up fast.

I blinked and suddenly she wasn't eight anymore.

I grabbed my crossbody bag and checked the clock again.

"I've got to go or I'll miss the train. You sure you've got everything?"

"Laptop, notes, phone—I'm good," Sophie said through a mouthful of toast.

I paused at the door.

"Call me if anything comes up, okay?"

She rolled her eyes in that dramatic teenage way she'd somehow carried into adulthood.

"You worry too much."

"I always will," I said with a small smile. "Love you, Soph."

"Love you too."

Outside, the early morning air bit through my coat collar as I hurried down the pavement, flats clicking steadily against the concrete.

The city was already waking up—headlights slicing through grey dawn, bins dragging across footpaths, espresso machines hissing behind café windows I never had time to stop at anymore.

This part of the day always felt strangely anonymous.

One face in a sea of commuters. Everyone wrapped in their own routines. Their own exhaustion.

My feet followed the same path they had for years.

I could've walked it blindfolded.

At the station, I slipped into my usual spot on the platform, clutching the railing as cold wind stung my cheeks. The train arrived with a screech of brakes and a low metallic groan.

I boarded with the crowd, found my usual window seat, and sat down.

The city blurred past in muted streaks of grey—graffiti-covered walls, chain-link fences, laundry lines hanging from apartment balconies.

Every building held a story I'd never know.

Every person passing outside the window had a life completely separate from mine.

And mine?

Mine ran on autopilot.

Wake up. Coffee. Get Sophie out the door. Commute. Work. Commute. Cook. Clean. Budget. Worry. Sleep—when I could. Repeat.

Somewhere along the way, I became the woman who colour-coded bills, unclogged drains, and checked the locks twice before bed.

Somewhere along the way, I stopped being a dancer without ever saying the words out loud.

At eighteen, I hadn't known how to raise a child. But the second they told me Sophie might end up in foster care, I didn't hesitate.

I couldn't.

Mum and Dad had grown up in the system. They never sugar-coated it—the neglect, the cold homes, the foster parents who cared more about the cheque than the child.

I wasn't letting that happen to Sophie.

So I walked away from Paris. From ballet. From the future I'd spent my entire life training for.

The bruised toes. The auditions. The rehearsals. The scholarships.

None of it mattered anymore.

Because Sophie needed me more than I needed a stage.

I still remembered what dancing felt like.

The silence before the music started.

The way the world disappeared when I moved.

How alive I felt.

Now freedom looked different.

A full pantry.

Paid electricity bills.

Sophie laughing with a mouthful of toast.

Was it fair? Maybe not.

But I'd do it again.

Every single time.

The train jolted as it pulled into my stop.

I stood, adjusted my coat, and stepped back into the flow of commuters.

My office building sat wedged between a vape shop and a convenience store—a squat three-storey brick building with all the charm of an overdue tax return.

It wasn't glamorous.

But it was stable.

And stable paid rent.

I pushed through the glass doors, immediately hit with the familiar scent of cheap coffee, printer ink, and industrial carpet.

The fluorescent lights buzzed overhead.

"Morning, Riley," Janine called from reception, already halfway through her second coffee.

"You're early again."

I gave her a quick smile.

"Habit."

And stress. And the fact my brain liked waking up already preloaded with tomorrow's problems.

I slipped into my cubicle, surrounded by neatly stacked folders, colour-coded sticky notes, and the framed beach photo of Sophie and me.

She'd been ten in that picture.

Sunburnt cheeks. Sandy hair. Huge grin.

I'd been twenty-one and permanently exhausted, pretending I knew how to raise a grieving child.

As I powered on my computer, a voice drifted over the cubicle wall.

"You know one of these days you're going to beat the janitor in."

I looked up to find Ethan leaning casually against the divider, coffee in hand.

Dark blue button-up. Sleeves rolled to his elbows. Tie loosened just enough to look effortless while still clearly trying.

He smiled like someone who'd never experienced the unique terror of checking your bank account before grocery shopping.

"Early bird gets the spreadsheet," I replied.

He snorted. "That's tragic."

"Improvised. I'm exhausted."

He stepped into the cubicle and held out the spare coffee.

"I figured."

I blinked at him.

"Oh. Thanks. That's actually really thoughtful."

"You look like you've had a week and it's only Tuesday."

"That's because I have."

I accepted the coffee, warm against my palms.

"Sophie okay?"

"Yeah," I said, opening my emails. "Busy with uni, internship stuff, surviving entirely on caffeine and academic stress."

"She's lucky to have you." His tone softened slightly. "You do everything."

I shrugged awkwardly. Compliments always made me itchy.

Like if people expected too much from me, eventually they'd realise I was just winging adulthood with increasing levels of panic.

"Well," I said lightly, "someone has to keep the ship afloat."

Ethan lingered for a second before glancing back toward the hallway. "If you ever wanted to grab lunch or something that isn't entirely work-related... I'm around."

I froze for half a heartbeat before forcing a polite smile.

"Thanks. I'll keep that in mind."

After he left, I took a sip of the coffee. Hot. Sweet. Exactly how I liked it. It took me a full minute to process the interaction.

Wait. Was that flirting?

I frowned at my computer screen.

No. Probably not. He was just being nice.

Romance wasn't exactly a priority when my weekly excitement peaked at buying dishwasher tablets before running out completely.

I barely had time to shave both legs in one sitting.

"Mum mode," I muttered under my breath. "Forever."

By mid-morning, the office had settled into its usual rhythm—typing, phones ringing, someone swearing quietly at the printer.

But my focus kept slipping.

Because Ethan's words kept replaying in my head.

You do everything.

Like he actually meant it.

Like he saw me as something beyond schedules and responsibilities and survival mode.

I glanced at the framed beach photo again. That weekend trip had nearly financially ruined us. We'd lived off instant noodles afterwards.

Worth it. Completely worth it.

Sophie was my anchor. My reason.

But lately... something restless had started stirring underneath all the routine.

The world outside the office windows felt huge.

Alive.

And I felt stuck in place.

Efficient. Reliable. Exhausted.

I couldn't even remember the last time I'd dated someone.

Not because I didn't want to.

I'd just forgotten how to make space for myself.

I'd traded romance for custody papers. Midnight kisses for school lunches and overdue electricity notices.

And I didn't regret it.

Not once.

But maybe wanting more than survival didn't make me selfish.

Maybe it just made me human.

The thought settled somewhere deep in my chest, unfamiliar and fragile.

A knock against the cubicle wall startled me.

Janine peeked around the corner.

"Conference room in five."

"Right. Thanks."

I stood, smoothing down my blouse and carefully tucking the thought away.

Not gone. Just paused. For now.

3

Because I Chose You

Riley

The Mother – Brandi Carlile

The days slipped by in their usual rhythm.

I woke up early. Worked long hours. Came home exhausted.

Meanwhile, Sophie buried herself in textbooks, uni lectures, and internship prep. We were like two trains running side by side—always moving, always tired, but still checking in on each other along the way.

Our conversations mostly happened through text messages now.

Me reminding her to eat something other than caffeine.

Her replying with dramatic library selfies and captions like:

Tell my future husband I died doing readings on tort reform.

It was chaos. But it was ours.

By Friday night, we were both completely fried.

After dinner, Sophie flopped onto the couch like a starfish and dumped her legs across my lap.

"Okay," she declared, already halfway into bossy mode. "I've decided. Tomorrow we're going to the mall."

I raised an eyebrow. "Oh, are we?"

"For outfits," she said, sitting up suddenly. "I cannot show up to my first day at the firm looking like I rolled out of bed and screamed into a textbook."

I smirked. "But you do roll out of bed and scream into textbooks."

She immediately launched a pillow at my face.

"Not the point! I need to look professional. Polished. Like I belong there."

I pretended to think about it. "Well... we've got a lot of work to do on that front."

"Riley!"

"Fine, fine," I laughed. "We'll go. But if you drag me into that overpriced café you love, you're buying your own ridiculous latte."

"Deal," she said instantly, already scrolling through store listings like she was planning a military operation.

The mall the next morning was absolute chaos. Kids crying. Pop music echoing from every direction. People weaving through crowds like bumper cars with credit cards. The smell of cinnamon pretzels and burnt coffee hit us the second we walked in.

And honestly?

It felt nice. We hadn't done this in ages.

Sophie practically dragged me into the first clothing store, immediately disappearing into the racks like a woman possessed.

"Okay, help me choose," she said, holding up two blazers. "Black or grey?"

I tilted my head thoughtfully.

"The black one says competent and intimidating. The grey one says approachable but still capable of ruining someone's legal career."

She considered that seriously. "I don't want to terrify people on day one."

"Grey it is." She grinned triumphantly.

"See? You're good at this."

"Don't spread that around," I warned. "I have a reputation as a cranky workaholic to maintain."

We wandered through store after store while Sophie bounced between mirrors and changing rooms, modelling blouses and skirts while I provided brutally honest big-sister commentary.

Somewhere between her fifth pair of shoes and my third dramatic sigh, I realised I was actually enjoying myself.

Not surviving. Not managing responsibilities. Actually having fun.

By the end of the shopping spree, Sophie had accumulated enough business casual clothing to intimidate an entire accounting department.

"You're absolutely going to end up barefoot by lunchtime in those heels," I told her as we left one of the stores.

"Probably," she admitted cheerfully. "But I'll look amazing while suffering."

We stopped at a tiny café near the food court with mismatched chairs and suspiciously aggressive espresso.

Sophie cradled her caramel latte like it was a spiritual experience while I demolished a chicken wrap with absolutely no dignity.

"This was a good idea," I admitted, leaning back in my chair. "Feels like we haven't done this in forever."

"Yeah," Sophie said softly. "Just us."

The silence that settled between us wasn't awkward. It felt full. Comfortable.

I watched her sip her drink, completely relaxed for once, and something in my chest tightened unexpectedly.

She looked older lately.

Not in a sad way.

Just... grown. Less kid. More woman.

Still Sophie. Still my Sophie. But becoming someone strong and independent outside of me.

"I'm really proud of you, you know," I said suddenly.

She blinked.

"Wait—what?"

I shrugged awkwardly.

"You've just... come really far. You're smart, focused, and somehow surviving university despite operating almost entirely on caffeine and chaos."

"That's fair."

"And okay," I continued, "you're still a gremlin who loses her keys every second day. But in the ways that matter? You've got your shit together."

Her cheeks flushed pink. "Thanks, Riles."

Then her expression softened. "I'm proud of you too."

I immediately scoffed.

"For what? My incredible ability to complain about foot pain and remind people to eat vegetables?"

"For everything," she said quietly. "For raising me. For giving up so much. For never making me feel like I ruined your life."

The words hit harder than I expected.

I looked away for a second, swallowing against the sudden tightness in my throat.

"You didn't ruin anything," I said softly. "You are my life." Her eyes went suspiciously glassy.

I immediately grabbed a napkin and fanned myself dramatically.

"Absolutely not. No crying in the café. It's illegal."

She laughed through the emotion.

That night, we collapsed onto the couch surrounded by shopping bags, takeaway containers, and melting ice cream.

Some ridiculous comedy played in the background while we passed the tub between us like a sacred offering.

Sophie curled against my side, laughing softly at something happening on-screen.

I looked down at her and smiled before I could stop myself.

She wasn't just my sister.

She was my best friend. My co-pilot. My person.

And sitting there beside her, surrounded by clutter and cheap ice cream and the sound of her laughter, I realised something quietly devastating:

Maybe I hadn't lost everything after all.

4

Where New Chapters Begin

Riley

Older – Sasha Alex Sloan

Monday arrived far too quickly.

The weekend hadn't really felt restful so much as a brief pause before life started sprinting again.

The apartment buzzed with low-level chaos as Sophie darted between her bedroom and the kitchen with one shoe on, blazer wrinkled, muttering about losing something that was almost definitely in her own hand.

I leaned against the counter, sipping coffee while watching her spiral with fond amusement.

"Relax, Soph," I said. "You've got this."

She froze mid-step, clutching her leather portfolio against her chest like a flotation device.

"What if I don't? What if they realise I have absolutely no idea what I'm doing?"

I smirked over the rim of my mug.

"Then you fake confidence until it becomes a personality trait. That's basically what I do at work."

She rolled her eyes, but some of the tension left her shoulders.

"Thanks for the inspirational speech."

"Anytime. Now eat something before you leave. You can't impress lawyers while running entirely on stress and iced coffee."

The train ride to work felt unusually long, even for me—and I wasn't the one starting a new chapter today.

While I sorted emails and settled into my usual routine, I kept my phone close beside the keyboard, half-waiting for updates.

Sure enough, the texts started rolling in.

Me: You're gonna crush it, kid.

Sophie: Bold of you to assume I'm not currently 85% anxiety and 15% caffeine.

Me: Perfect ratio. Just don't vomit on anyone important.

I smiled down at my screen, picturing her somewhere smoothing down her blazer while internally panicking.

The next text arrived mid-morning while I was halfway buried in spreadsheets.

Sophie: Orientation done. Everyone seems nice. Office is HUGE.

Me: Of course it is. Lawyers love reminding people they're important.

Sophie: Accurate. Gotta go meet my supervisor

I stared at the screen for a second after the messages stopped, warmth settling heavily in my chest.

She was doing it.

Actually doing it.

Starting her life.

And while pride swelled inside me, there was something bittersweet tangled up in it too.

Because she didn't need me the way she used to anymore.

Not completely.

The rest of my workday disappeared into the usual chaos.

Printer jams. Last-minute edits. Carla somehow breaking an entire PowerPoint presentation fifteen minutes before a meeting.

I also forgot lunch existed until nearly three o'clock.

Twice.

Every now and then, I'd glance at my phone hoping for another update before forcing myself back to work.

On the way home, I grabbed Sophie's favourite pasta sauce, garlic bread, and a bottle of lemonade before heading back to the apartment.

By the time she walked through the front door, the spaghetti was already boiling.

Her smile was bright immediately.

But there was a slight crease between her brows I noticed straight away.

Tired.

Overwhelmed.

Maybe both.

"How'd it go?" I asked, setting bowls onto the table.

"It was amazing," she said, kicking off her shoes near the couch. "The office is incredible, everyone's ridiculously professional, and my supervisor Greg is actually really nice."

I pulled out her chair as she sat down.

"And?"

She hesitated slightly.

"And some of the cases are... intense."

The excitement in her voice dimmed around the edges.

"I knew they'd deal with violent crimes obviously, but hearing the details firsthand is different. It's heavy."

I nodded slowly as I poured our drinks.

"Yeah. Reading about things and actually sitting in front of them are two very different experiences."

She twirled pasta around her fork absently.

"Greg said they'll ease me into it. But he also said this kind of work can really get to people."

"You think you can handle it?"

She sat quietly for a second before nodding.

"I think so. It's a lot, but... I want to do something that matters."

God.

I loved her so much it physically hurt sometimes.

Pride swelled painfully in my chest alongside the overwhelming urge to wrap her in a blanket and protect her from literally everything forever.

"I know you do," I said gently. "And I think you'll be incredible at it."

I waited until she looked up before continuing.

"But promise me something?"

"What?"

"Set boundaries. Take care of yourself. Don't let the job consume you."

I held her gaze.

"You can do hard things, Soph. Just not at the cost of yourself."

The spark slowly returned to her expression.

"I won't," she promised softly.

The conversation drifted lighter after that.

Funny coworker stories.

A paralegal who spilled coffee on himself mid-meeting.

A secretary apparently running an underground candy empire from her desk drawer.

By the end of dinner, I was laughing so hard my stomach hurt.

Later that night, we curled up on the couch with popcorn and reruns of an old sitcom we'd both memorised years ago.

Sophie rested her head against my shoulder with a content sigh.

"Best first-day dinner ever," she mumbled. "I needed this."

"Only the best for my favourite future lawyer."

As the episodes rolled on, I glanced down at her relaxed expression and felt something settle quietly in my chest.

This.

This was everything.

Every sacrifice. Every sleepless night. Every dream I'd packed away and shoved onto a shelf somewhere.

It had all led here.

To her being safe.

Happy.

Hopeful.

Sometime during the second episode, Sophie drifted asleep against my shoulder.

The television flickered softly across the apartment while the popcorn bowl sat abandoned between us and the blanket slid half onto the floor.

Carefully, I pulled it back over her.

My chest tightened painfully.

Not from sadness exactly.

Just the strange ache that comes from watching someone slowly grow beyond needing you.

She wasn't that frightened eight-year-old girl sneaking into my bed after nightmares anymore.

And I wasn't the girl dreaming about Paris and centre stage either.

We'd both changed.

A lot.

The apartment sat quiet around me as I stared blankly at the muted television.

Because now that Sophie was building something of her own, I could feel the shape of my life shifting too.

Like the universe had finally paused long enough to ask:

Okay, Riley. What now?

And honestly?

That question terrified me.

For so long, my life had been about survival. About keeping us afloat. About making sure Sophie had everything she needed.

I'd never really stopped to ask myself what I wanted.

But now she was finding her footing.

And I was still standing in the same place.

Maybe it was time to move too.

Eventually, I eased Sophie onto a pillow and quietly cleaned up around the apartment.

The kitchen light glowed dimly while I rinsed dishes and stared absently at the fridge covered in takeaway menus, shopping lists, and beach photos.

So much had changed already.

And somehow it still felt like everything was only beginning.

Later, lying in bed staring at the ceiling, one thought kept circling through my brain:

What if it's okay to want something more for myself?

And honestly, at this point "something more" could literally just mean:

- sleeping longer than four hours
- keeping a houseplant alive
- or making toast without the smoke alarm acting like I'd committed arson

Ambition is great and all, but right now I'd settle for my bra straps and blouse not trying to kill each other before 7 a.m.

Maybe personal growth wasn't glamorous.

Maybe sometimes it just looked like quietly hoping for more while standing in your kitchen at midnight wondering how adulthood became this exhausting.

Still...

Maybe that's how new chapters really start.

Not with dramatic life-changing moments.

Just small, stubborn little acts of hope.

5

The Space Between Us

Riley

Let It All Go – Birdy + Rhodes

The clock on my desk blinked 6:47 PM in cold red numbers.

I leaned back in my chair with a groan, rubbing at the knot forming between my shoulders.

The quarterly report was due tomorrow, which naturally meant every last-minute edit had somehow become my responsibility.

Most of the office had emptied out already. The usual noise replaced by silence, fluorescent lights, and the distant sound of the janitor vacuuming somewhere down the hallway.

My phone buzzed across the desk.

Sophie: Hey, just letting you know I'm going for drinks with some people from the internship after work!

Immediately, my stomach did that deeply annoying overprotective older-sister thing. I frowned at the screen before typing back.

Me: Where?

Her response came almost instantly.

Sophie: The Rusty Anchor. Couple stops away. Super chill place. Don't panic.

Too late. I tapped my fingers against the desk, chewing the inside of my cheek. \

I trusted Sophie completely.

The world, however, remained deeply suspicious.

Without even thinking about it, I opened the location tracker on my phone for reassurance. The little blue dot blinked exactly where she said she'd be.

Some tension eased from my chest.

Me: Okay. If you need me to pick you up, call me. Or I'll pay for a cab. Love you. Be safe.

I set the phone down and tried to focus on work again, but my concentration had already disintegrated.

I could picture her sitting in some dimly lit bar laughing with coworkers, trying cocktails with names like Pink Flamingo Disaster or something equally concerning.

And I wanted that for her.

I really did.

But part of my brain still saw her with scraped knees and pigtails asking if monsters were real.

By 8:30 PM, I finally shut my laptop.

The office looked almost abandoned by then, dark except for the flickering overhead lights and the occasional glow of computer monitors left in sleep mode.

As I packed my bag, my phone buzzed again.

A photo this time.

Sophie squeezed between a group of smiling coworkers, cheeks flushed pink, eyes bright.

Happy.

Safe.

Something in my chest loosened immediately.

Me: Wow. Look at you and your fancy little work friends.

Me: I'm heading home. Message me when you get back.

Sophie: Will do <3

That stupid little heart emoji nearly took me out emotionally.

Because she was growing up.

Building her own life.

But somehow still making room for me inside it.

The apartment felt strangely quiet when I got home.

I reheated leftovers, turned on some mindless television, and checked my phone every ten minutes like an emotionally unstable lighthouse keeper.

At 10:15 PM, another text finally came through.

Sophie: Heading home now. Took your advice and got a cab.

Me: Good. Message me when you're inside.

Sophie: Yes mum <3

I rolled my eyes affectionately at the screen.

That should've relaxed me.

It didn't.

I still sat there half-watching TV and listening for the front door because after eleven years of being someone's safety net, your brain doesn't exactly develop an off switch.

The lock finally clicked at 11:18 PM.

Sophie stumbled inside carrying her heels in one hand and her bag in the other, eyeliner slightly smudged but smiling brightly.

"Guess who got invited to karaoke after drinks?"

I raised an eyebrow.

"You? Singing voluntarily? Were you threatened?"

"A free mocktail was involved," she admitted, collapsing dramatically onto the couch beside me.

I laughed softly, feeling the last lingering tension finally leave my body.

"Sounds like you had fun."

"I did," she said quietly.

Then her expression softened.

"But honestly? Having your text there made me feel safer."

God.

My heart actually hurt sometimes.

I reached over and ruffled her hair.

"That's my job, Soph."

She swatted my hand away with a sleepy grin.

"You're such a mum."

"And you're still a gremlin."

We settled into a comfortable silence after that, the kind built from years of surviving life side by side.

I looked at her properly then.

At the confidence growing inside her.

At the way she carried herself differently lately.

She was stepping into her own life now, piece by piece.

And I was proud.

So unbelievably proud.

Even if part of me was still adjusting to the idea that she didn't need me quite as desperately anymore.

But no matter how grown-up she became, I'd always be her person.

The one with spare blankets, emergency snacks, overprotective lectures, and cab money.

And she'd always be mine too.

Eventually Sophie disappeared to bed, leaving the apartment quiet except for the hum of the fridge and the soft glow of the television.

I sat curled into the couch with cold tea in my hands, staring blankly at a sitcom I wasn't actually watching.

She'd had her first real grown-up night out.

Drinks with coworkers.

Karaoke.

Stories to tell.

A future unfolding right in front of her.

And now that the apartment was quiet again, I was left alone with the one thing I couldn't organise or control:

My own thoughts.

Because if Sophie kept growing—and she should, she absolutely should—then what happened to me?

For so long my entire identity had revolved around surviving. Protecting her. Holding everything together.

I didn't know who I was outside of that anymore.

The thought sat heavily in my chest as I stared at the dark television screen after the credits rolled.

Tomorrow would be another workday.

More meetings. More spreadsheets. More routine.

And suddenly the idea of doing this exact same thing forever made something deep inside me ache.

What if I wanted more than survival?

The thought felt dangerous. Selfish, even.

Earlier that week, another email about the company leadership initiative had landed in my inbox.

I'd ignored it immediately.

Told myself I didn't have the time. Or ambition. Or energy.

But maybe the truth was simpler than that.

Maybe I was scared.

Because wanting things for myself still felt unfamiliar after all these years.

I stood slowly, carrying my mug into the kitchen.

The apartment sat dark and quiet around me.

Tomorrow, I decided, I'd reopen the email.

And this time… I'd actually read it.

6

Where I Can't Follow

Riley

My Blood – Twenty One Pilots

The next morning, the apartment was quiet except for the soft clink of my spoon against the cereal bowl and the hum of the kettle heating behind me.

I'd woken earlier than usual after a restless night spent thinking far too much. About work. About the leadership email.

About myself, which frankly felt deeply inconsiderate of my brain before 7 a.m.

Normally I didn't bother with television in the mornings, but the silence felt unusually loud. So I flicked on the news for background noise and settled onto the couch with my cereal balanced on my knees.

The report was halfway through traffic updates when the headline changed.

"Breaking overnight—Harbour City police have confirmed another suspected gang-related murder connected to the ongoing Eastway District investigations."

I froze mid-bite. The screen shifted to flashing police lights and yellow crime scene tape.

Then a mugshot appeared. Mid-thirties. Hard expression. Tattoos climbing his neck.

"Sources confirm the man in custody is Elijah Hayes, alleged enforcer for the Eastside syndicate, currently facing multiple charges including assault, drug trafficking, and suspected homicide—"

A cold knot tightened in my stomach. The reporter continued speaking, throwing around phrases like violent record and known affiliations, but I barely absorbed any of it.

Then Sophie appeared in the hallway. She slowed when she noticed the television.

"Oh," she said casually, adjusting the strap of her bag. "That's one of ours."

I blinked.

"What?"

"Elijah Hayes," she clarified. "He's one of the firm's clients."

I slowly lowered my spoon into the bowl.

"You're joking."

"Nope."

She crossed toward the kitchen like we were discussing weather forecasts instead of an alleged murderer.

"Big case apparently. Greg mentioned him yesterday. We're not directly handling the trial—it's a senior team thing—but interns might get looped into research support."

I stared at her in disbelief. Assault. Homicide. Drug trafficking.

And she was saying it all with the calm professionalism of someone discussing printer maintenance.

Sophie must've noticed my expression because her own softened slightly.

"It's part of the job, Riles."

"Yeah, but Sophie—"

"That man could be dangerous," I finished flatly.

She sighed gently before sitting beside me.

"I'm not going clubbing with him. I'm reviewing case files inside a secure office building."

I didn't laugh.

My pulse had already started climbing.

"These aren't petty theft cases, Soph. These people are dangerous. What if someone at the firm says the wrong thing? What if someone retaliates?"

She tugged absently at the sleeve of her blazer.

"I know it's serious," she said quietly. "But this is why I want to do this kind of work. To understand the system. To help people."

I looked at her properly then. Really looked. She was nervous, sure. But underneath that nervousness was something steady. Certain. She wasn't afraid.

Unfortunately, I was terrified enough for both of us.

I reached over and squeezed her hand.

"Just promise me you'll be careful."

My voice softened. "I know I can't shield you from everything, but Soph... I can't lose you too."

Her expression immediately gentled. "I know."

She leaned her head briefly against my shoulder. "I promise."

I wanted that promise to settle the panic in my chest.

It didn't.

Because while she'd been growing into someone brave and capable, I'd apparently developed the emotional regulation skills of an anxious Victorian mother standing at a train station waving a handkerchief dramatically.

Sophie shifted slightly beside me. "Actually... there's more."

My stomach dropped instantly. "Why do I suddenly hate that sentence?"

She winced. "The Hayes case is the one I'm sitting in on for courtroom observation."

I stared at her. "You're going to be in the courtroom?"

She nodded carefully. "It's part of the internship rotation. Greg said it'd be a valuable learning experience."

A valuable learning experience. Fantastic. Amazing. Love that for us.

I looked back toward the television where the news had already moved onto weather updates, but Elijah Hayes' face still felt burned into my brain.

"I really don't like this," I admitted honestly.

Sophie gave me a sympathetic look. "I figured."

I dragged a hand through my hair, trying to keep myself calm.

Because the instinct to tell her absolutely not was immediate and overwhelming.

But this mattered to her.

And I never wanted to become the reason she shrank herself smaller.

So I swallowed the fear down as best I could.

"I don't like it," I repeated more quietly, "but I know it matters to you. And if this is what you want, then I'll support you."

Relief visibly loosened her shoulders.

"Thanks, Riles."

"Don't expect me not to worry though."

She smirked. "Worrying is basically your superpower."

"And being stubborn is yours."

She laughed softly before standing to leave for work.

But after the apartment door closed behind her and her footsteps disappeared down the hallway, I stayed sitting on the couch for a long moment, staring at the steam curling from my forgotten tea.

Because Sophie was stepping into a world I couldn't protect her from anymore.

And all I could really do now was stand behind her and hope that was enough.

I rubbed a hand over my face tiredly.

Then briefly considered Googling: How to place your adult sister into witness protection without her consent.

Or maybe: Nun convent applications near me.

Honestly, either option felt reasonable at this point.

7

Witness

Sophie

Run – Daughter

The courtroom was colder than I expected. Not just in temperature—though the air conditioning was dialled up to arctic levels—but in atmosphere. Quiet. Restrained. Clinical. Like everyone had agreed to put on masks before walking in.

I sat two rows behind the defence team, my notepad resting on my lap, pen clutched too tightly in my fingers. My name wasn't on any docket, but Greg had made a few calls and cleared it.

"Just observe," he'd told me. "Pay attention to the rhythm. How people speak. What they say—and what they don't."

Elijah Hayes sat at the defence table in a charcoal suit that didn't quite hide the tattoos curling around his neck and knuckles. He didn't look at anyone. His posture slouched, his expression unreadable. Like someone who'd been here a hundred times and knew exactly how it all worked.

Maybe he had. I tried not to stare.

I tried not to think about the news headline or the grainy footage of police shoving him into a van. I was here to learn. To understand. To be better.

Still, my stomach twisted when the prosecutor began laying out the charges.

Assault. Drug trafficking. Gang affiliation. Two counts of attempted murder. One confirmed homicide.

Each word hit like a hammer. Blunt. Heavy. Real.

This wasn't a law textbook or a classroom debate. This was a man on trial for someone's death.

Families torn apart. Lives changed forever. And here I was—nineteen, barely more than a student—scribbling notes, pretending I didn't feel like I'd stepped into something much bigger than me.

The prosecutor moved with surgical calm, peeling back layers of truth with every question.

Greg had said he was one of the city's top litigators—sharp, strategic, relentless.

I believed it.

The defence attorney countered with smooth objections and cool confidence, questioning witnesses like he was pulling strings on a marionette.

His voice never rose. His face never cracked.

It was like watching a chess match played with lives. I was in awe of the skill.

But I couldn't shake the hollow feeling building in my chest.

Because somewhere, buried beneath motions and procedures, there were victims.

Someone who never made it home.

Someone whose family might be sitting just feet away from me.

I shifted in my seat, grounding myself. Be objective. That's what Greg said. Don't absorb the emotion.

Easier said than done.

A witness took the stand. Young.

Probably my age. Shoulders tense. Voice shaking. He didn't look at Hayes. His testimony was quiet but clear.

About the night someone died. About what he saw. I wrote everything down—names, dates, details. But my hand was trembling, and I didn't know if I was supposed to admit that.

At one point, Hayes turned his head—just slightly—his eyes sweeping the gallery.

And for half a second, they locked on mine.

It was probably nothing. A coincidence. A glance.

But my pulse skipped anyway. I wasn't afraid, exactly. But I felt... seen.

And I didn't like it.

When court recessed for lunch, I trailed the defence team toward the elevators, keeping my distance.

Greg met me in the hallway, holding two takeaway coffees and wearing an unreadable expression. "You okay?" he asked, handing me one.

"Yeah," I lied automatically, accepting the cup with stiff fingers.

"Just taking it all in." "You did well," he said, glancing back toward the courtroom.

"It's a lot to absorb—especially your first time. But you held it together."

I took a sip, more grateful for the warmth than the caffeine. "I didn't think it would feel so... personal," I admitted.

Greg nodded. "That means you're human. You'll learn to carry it without letting it carry you."

I wasn't sure I believed that. But I nodded anyway.

We sat on a bench near the window, the city sprawling below us.

People moved on—carrying groceries, walking dogs, catching trams. Completely unaware of the trial happening just a few floors above them.

A world within a world. Part of me wanted to go home. To curl under a blanket with a stupid movie and tell Riley she was right. That maybe this was too much.

But another part of me... felt certain. This mattered. It was messy and uncomfortable and hard. But that was the point.

If I wanted to help change the system, I had to understand it first.

Even when it broke my heart.

The courtroom was tighter in the afternoon. Not loud. Not dramatic. Just... tight. Tension threaded through every row like wire pulled taut.

No one moved, but I could feel it—see it—in clenched jaws, twitching fingers, narrowed eyes. I hadn't written anything in ten minutes.

Everyone was waiting for the moment we'd all seen coming. Elijah Hayes sat motionless at the defence table. Silent. Waiting.

The judge's voice sliced through the stillness like a scalpel. "We, the jury, find the defendant—" We all knew what was coming. "—guilty on all counts."

No gasp. No shouting. Just silence. Complete. Total.

Then Hayes turned his head. I felt it before I saw it—his eyes sweeping the gallery, landing on me. Not a glance. A choice. Like he wanted me to know he'd seen me. That he'd been seeing me.

My stomach dropped. I tried to keep a neutral expression—just like Greg had said. But I couldn't stop my hands from curling into fists. Or the way my pulse hammered in my throat.

His stare was flat. Empty. Calculating. Like he was filing me away. And behind him, in the gallery— A group of men in dark coats. Watching. Unblinking. One of them—tall, heavyset, slick black hair and a broken nose—shifted forward just enough for his eyes to meet mine.

Then he smiled. It wasn't kind. It wasn't curious. It was the kind of smile that made your skin crawl.

After the courtroom cleared, I stuck close to Greg as we moved through the marble lobby.

My heels clicked too loud. My hands were white-knuckled around my notebook.

I was fine. I had to be. Near the elevators, Greg turned to speak with a paralegal. And then— That weight again.

Behind me. A voice, low and oily, slid into my ear. "Boss liked you." I froze. The man from the gallery leaned against a column, looking like he'd stepped out of a crime drama cliché.

Slick. Smug. Terrifying in his calm. He wasn't looking at Greg. He was looking at me. "Eyes like someone who listens," he said. Like it was a compliment.

The breath left my lungs all at once. I stumbled backward, shoes slick against the floor. My heart pounded.

Greg's head snapped around. "Is there a problem?"

The man's grin widened, but he didn't acknowledge him. "Just saying hello."

I couldn't breathe. I couldn't think. I shoved past them both, barely hearing Greg call my name. I jammed the elevator button until the doors slid open, then stumbled inside like the floor was falling away beneath me.

By the time I reached the office, I wasn't composed—I was cracked. I ignored the curious stares and made a beeline for the staff bathroom, locking myself in the last stall.

I sat down hard, fists pressed to my thighs. And I tried to breathe through the panic boiling in my chest.

I had told myself I could do this. That I was strong enough to face the ugliness of the legal system. That I wouldn't flinch.

But Hayes had looked at me like I was a name on a list.

And one of his men had spoken to me. Not a threat. Not technically. But I had never felt so exposed in my life. And I didn't know if I would ever feel safe again.

8

You Didn't Ask

Riley

Tired – Beabadoobee

I heard the front door slam before I even looked up from the stove.

It wasn't Sophie's usual entrance—not the cheerful shuffle of heels, not the exaggerated groan about her long day.

No, this was sharper. Loud. Like the door had done something to deserve it.

I turned the heat down on the stir-fry and leaned out of the kitchen. "Hey, you're home early."

No response.

Sophie kicked off her shoes hard enough that one hit the wall. Her blazer landed in a crumpled heap on the floor, and she stormed straight past me toward her room like I wasn't even there.

Okay then.

I wiped my hands on a towel and followed. "Sophie?"

She reappeared in the hallway, her jaw set, arms crossed. "What?"

"What's going on with you?"

"Nothing," she snapped. "Can I not be tired for once without being interrogated?"

That caught me off guard. "Whoa, alright. I just said hi."

"Well maybe I don't feel like chatting right now." I blinked. "Okay... Are you hungry?"

"No."

"You skipped lunch again, didn't you?"

Sophie rolled her eyes and let out an annoyed breath. "Jesus, Riley, can you stop? I don't need a lecture."

I stared at her, heat rising in my chest.

"I wasn't lecturing. I'm worried about you."

"Yeah? Maybe worry about yourself for once." I flinched.

The silence stretched between us, crackling. She looked like she wanted to take the words back, but her shoulders stayed stiff, her eyes hard. Defiant. Defensive. Something was wrong.

I stepped closer, lowering my voice "Did something happen at work?"

"I said I'm fine." "Sophie—" "I'm fine, Riley."

I watched her for a long moment, her hands curled into fists at her sides, her breathing shallow. Her usual glow—gone. Her confidence—shattered, even if she was trying to fake it. She wasn't okay. Not even close. But whatever had happened, she wasn't ready to let it out yet.

"Okay," I said quietly, backing off. "Fine. You don't want to talk? Don't. But I'm here when you're ready." She didn't answer. Just turned away and walked into her room, slamming the door behind her.

I stood there for a moment longer, staring at the closed door like it might explain what just walked past me.

Then I walked back into the kitchen, turned off the stove, and let the silence settle in again. Something had happened. And I had no idea what. But I knew my sister. She was scared. And eventually... that fear would come out. One way or another.

The apartment was quiet the rest of the evening—too quiet.

Sophie hadn't come back out of her room.

I left a plate of food on the counter for her, but it stayed untouched.

I tried not to take it personally, but it wasn't easy. I'd spent years balancing both of our lives like spinning plates, and she was acting like I was the enemy for asking if she was okay. I told myself she was just tired.

Shaken. Stressed from work.

But by the time I heard her footsteps padding into the kitchen—well past nine—I was already sitting at the table, arms folded, ready for round two.

She opened the fridge, grabbed a bottle of water, and barely looked in my direction.

I waited. She turned, catching my stare, and let out an exasperated sigh. "What now?"

"I don't know," I said flatly. "Maybe an apology for being a complete brat earlier?"

Sophie gave a sharp, humourless laugh. "Right. Because God forbid I have a bad day and not worship the ground you walk on."

My jaw tensed. "That's not what I said."

"You didn't have to."

I stood, trying to keep my voice calm. "You're clearly upset about something. I've asked if you're okay, I've tried giving you space, and you've done nothing but snap at me like I'm the problem." Her eyes flashed.

"Maybe you are the problem." That hit like a slap. I stared at her. "Excuse me?"

She didn't back down. "You act like you've sacrificed everything, like you're this perfect martyr who gave up her entire life for me."

My heart pounded. "And maybe you did," she continued, "but that doesn't mean I owe you every second of mine. I didn't ask you to give it all up, Riley!"

Silence. Stunned. Sharp. Crippling. I felt the breath leave my chest like I'd been punched. And then the anger came.

"No," I said, my voice low and shaking, "you didn't ask. Because you were eight years old, Sophie. You didn't have to ask. Someone had to step up, and I did."

Her face paled a little, but I didn't stop. "You think I wanted to give up ballet? Paris? That dream I worked my ass off for since I was five? You think I don't remember what I lost?"

Tears burned at the edges of my eyes, but I didn't let them fall. "I did it because I love you," I said, each word like a stone dropped into the silence.

"And I don't regret it. But don't you dare stand there and act like I've been holding that over your head."

Sophie didn't say anything at first. Her mouth opened, then closed. And for the first time since she walked in, I saw it. Fear. Not of me. Of something else. Something deeper. Something she wasn't ready to say. I exhaled sharply and turned away, grabbing my keys off the table.

"Where are you going?" she asked, voice smaller. "For air," I snapped.

"Because if I stay here, I'm going to say something I'll really regret." And with that, I left.

The door clicked shut behind me. And the silence I'd tried to hold together for so long shattered.

I didn't even realise I was crying until I tasted salt on my lips. I'd made it to the park three blocks from the apartment before it hit me—before the fight, the silence, the weight of everything I'd buried finally cracked open.

The air was cold. Sharp. Streetlights buzzed above me.

The park was empty except for a bench near the swings, and I collapsed onto it like my knees had stopped knowing how to hold me. And then I just... broke.

My chest shook as the first sob ripped out of me—quiet but violent. I clutched my hands in my lap, like holding them tight would keep the rest of me from unravelling.

But it didn't. I sat in the dark, crying harder than I had in years.

Maybe since the day I signed the custody papers.

Maybe longer. She didn't ask me to give it up.

God. That was the part that hurt the most—not because it wasn't true. It was.

She hadn't asked me to give up my dreams. My body. My identity. But I had. Willingly. Instantly.

Because the thought of her ending up in foster care like our parents had terrified me more than losing ballet ever could.

And maybe... maybe some days I did feel bitter. Not at her. Just at the sheer unfairness of it all. Of losing them. Of watching my dreams wither quietly in the corner while I worked two jobs and cooked every meal and made sure homework was done and nightmares were soothed.

I had never let myself say it before—not even in therapy—but in that moment, I did. "I'm tired," I whispered.

The wind answered with a chill across my face. "I'm so damn tired."

Of holding it together. Of being the strong one. Of being the backup plan. Of always putting myself last.

I loved Sophie. I lived for her. But I didn't know how to be a person outside of being her sister, her guardian, her safety net. And now she was growing up. Becoming her own woman.

And maybe she didn't need me the way she used to.

Which left one terrifying question echoing through my chest: Then who am I now?

I sat there for a long time, until the tears dried, until the shaking stopped, until all that was left was the ache of everything I couldn't say to her earlier.

I wiped my face on my sleeve and looked up at the stars, blinking hard. A gust of wind rattled the leaves above me, and somewhere nearby a possum crashed gracelessly through the branches, sounding like it was auditioning for a nature documentary on public breakdowns.

I let out a shaky, surprised laugh—half-sob, half-snort—wiping my eyes on my sleeve for the hundredth time.

The world hadn't ended. Not tonight. My hands were still shaking, my chest still raw, but for the first time in a long time, the silence inside me didn't feel so suffocating.

Maybe, beneath the hurt, there was space for something new. Maybe even for me.

I stood, stretching stiff legs, and looked up one last time at the stars winking above the park—indifferent, bright, and impossibly far away.

Then I took a deep breath, squared my shoulders, and started the slow walk home. Not fixed. Not healed. But moving. And for tonight, that was enough.

9

Cracked Together

Riley

As It Was – Hozier

I woke up to a migraine that throbbed through my skull, the kind that made even the softest light feel like daggers. Groaning, I pulled the covers over my head, deciding that today would be a sick day.

The thought of facing the office's fluorescent lights and constant chatter made my stomach turn.

So, I spent most of the day in bed, drifting in and out of sleep.

The room darkened to a comforting dimness, and by late afternoon, the pain had dulled to a manageable ache. I ventured into the living room, wrapping myself in a cosy blanket.

The front door creaked open, and Sophie walked in, her face flushed with excitement. She dropped her bag by the door and kicked off her shoes, practically bouncing into the room.

"Hey, Riles! You won't believe the day I had," she exclaimed, her eyes sparkling.

I managed a weak smile. "Tell me about it."

Sophie plopped down on the couch beside me, tucking her legs beneath her.

"So, this morning, this guy walks into the office—tall, dark hair, absolutely gorgeous. Turns out, he's one of our new clients."

I raised an eyebrow. "And what exactly is he being charged with?"

Sophie waved a hand dismissively. "Oh, something minor. But seriously, he was so charming. He even smiled at me when I handed him his paperwork."

My expression hardened. "Sophie, you remember your firm specialises in criminal law, right?"

She blinked, her excitement dimming slightly. "Well, yeah, but—" "So, this 'gorgeous' "The guy you're swooning over is potentially a criminal," I interrupted, my tone sharper than I intended.

Sophie frowned, a defensive edge creeping into her voice. "Innocent until proven guilty, remember? That's kind of the whole point of our legal system."

I sighed, rubbing my temples. "I know, I know. But just… be careful, okay? It's easy to get caught up in appearances and forget the reality of the situation."

Sophie softened, reaching out to squeeze my hand. "I get it. I'll be careful. But you need to trust me to handle myself."

I looked into her earnest eyes and nodded. "I do trust you. Just promise me you'll keep your wits about you."

"Promise," Sophie said with a small smile.

We sat in companionable silence for a moment before Sophie spoke again. "How are you feeling? You look like you've been through the wringer."

I chuckled softly. "Migraine from hell. But it's better now."

"Want me to make you some tea?" Sophie offered, already standing up.

"That would be great," I replied, grateful for her thoughtfulness.

As Sophie busied herself in the kitchen, I leaned back against the couch cushions, closing my eyes. Despite my earlier irritation, I couldn't help but feel a swell of pride for Sophie. She was navigating the complexities of her internship with grace and confidence, even if she occasionally got a little too enthusiastic about certain clients.

Sophie returned with two steaming mugs, handing one to me before settling back down beside me. "Thanks," I said, taking a sip and savouring the warmth.

"Anytime," Sophie replied, curling up with her own mug.

We spent the rest of the evening chatting about lighter topics, the earlier tension forgotten.

My headache continued to fade, replaced by the comforting presence of my sister. No matter the challenges we faced, we always found our way back to each other, our bond unshakeable.

Sophie didn't say anything for a while. She just lay there beside me, our bodies facing the ceiling, the blanket pulled up to our chins like armour we'd borrowed from childhood.

I felt her fingers brush against mine, hesitant at first—then more certain, lacing through mine. "I didn't sleep last night," she said quietly.

I didn't answer. I didn't need to. She kept going. "I kept thinking about what I said. And what you didn't. And then I started thinking about Mum and Dad, and the accident, and how messed up everything was after that. And how you were always... just there.

Like you didn't get to fall apart." I blinked, tears slipping sideways onto the pillow. Silent, steady.

"You didn't even cry at the funeral," she said. "I did," I whispered. "Just not where you could see." Sophie's breath hitched, and I felt her fingers tighten around mine.

"I remember sitting in my room the night after the funeral," I continued. "I had this picture of us—Mum, Dad, you, Agatha, me. I kept staring at it, waiting to feel something. But I just... couldn't. Not until you came in crying, asking me if we were going to be okay." "You told me yes," she said, voice cracking.

"Yeah. I lied."

She let out a trembling laugh, wet with guilt and grief. "I always thought you had it handled. Like you were just built stronger than the rest of us."

"I wasn't," I said. "I just didn't have the luxury of falling apart." The room went quiet again. It was the kind of silence that didn't feel empty. It felt full.

Full of every unspoken word, every sleepless night, every ache and quiet sacrifice. Full of years we never really talked about, because we didn't know how.

"I'm scared, Riles," she said. "The courtroom... it's not like I thought. It's darker. And yesterday, after the verdict, one of them—one of his people—he came up to me."

My chest clenched. I turned my head slowly, searching her face. "What?"

"He said something about Hayes liking me. Watching me."

She sniffed, eyes locked on the ceiling, voice distant. "I've never felt like that before. I wasn't even me in that moment. I was just... something small. Something powerless."

I sat up, ignoring the pain behind my eyes. My pulse surged. "Sophie..."

"It's okay," she said quickly. "I'm safe. Greg was there. He didn't do anything. But it shook me. And instead of telling you, I attacked you." I touched her cheek, guiding her gaze toward mine.

"You don't have to protect me, you know. I'm not the only one who's allowed to be the strong one."

Her eyes brimmed again, the vulnerability raw. "I didn't want you to think I couldn't handle it," she whispered.

"I already knew you could," I replied. "Being scared doesn't make you weak, Soph. It makes you human."

She crumpled against me then, curling into my side, her tears soaking into my shirt. I held her, one arm around her shoulders, the other smoothing back her hair the way I used to when she was eight and her world was shattered. This time, ours had cracked together.

And maybe that was okay. Because this—this pile of tears and grief and truth between us—felt more honest than anything we'd said in weeks.

We lay there until the sun started to set, our breathing slow and in sync. I wasn't okay. She wasn't either. But we were together. And for the first time in a long time... that felt like enough.

10

Retaliation

Riley

Bravado – Lorde

The office was too warm. Or maybe I was just imagining that, considering the way Ethan had been hovering around my desk all morning like a Labrador who'd discovered his new favourite person.

"Two sugars, splash of oat milk," he said proudly, setting a coffee on my desk like it was a peace offering or a declaration of war. I blinked up at him.

"Are you stalking my caffeine habits?" "I prefer the term 'attentive colleague,'" he said, giving me a wink that was probably supposed to be charming.

It might've been, if I weren't trying to juggle three deadlines and a migraine.

Still, I muttered a thank-you and took a sip—perfect. Annoyingly so. Ethan leaned against my desk like he had all the time in the world.

"Any plans for lunch? Thought we could grab something from that place you like down the street."

"I've got that sync with the outreach team at noon," I said, grateful for the excuse.

"Maybe another time?" He nodded with an easy smile, but I caught the flicker of disappointment behind his eyes.

He covered it quickly, of course—Ethan was always smooth like that—but I still felt a little guilty.

I didn't have much time to dwell on it though, because that's when Kai walked in. The consultant. The man who'd somehow weaponized basic office wear. Dark slacks. Rolled sleeves. Collar slightly open like he'd stepped off the set of some criminally under-budgeted soap opera where the men just looked that good all the time.

And then he walked by my desk with a confident stride that practically demanded attention. Naturally, my eyes followed.

It was science. Gravity. Instinct. Nothing I could control. Because god—his ass should've had its own zip code. That was not a regular level of fit. That was sculpted. Intentional. A whole damn situation.

My brain short-circuited halfway through reading a spreadsheet and rerouted directly to objectively distracting gluteal architecture.

I blinked hard, staring at my monitor. Nope. Focus. Not today, Satan. I was still halfway through mentally slapping myself when Kai doubled back to hand me a folder.

"Didn't want this getting lost in your inbox," he said, brushing his fingers against mine with the kind of subtle ease that made my heart skip embarrassingly.

"Thanks," I managed, my voice tighter than intended.

He smiled—slow and knowing—and turned to leave. And I looked. Again. I wasn't proud. Across the room, Ethan watched the entire interaction with his arms folded and an unreadable expression on his face. It was subtle. Easy to miss if I hadn't glanced up at the wrong—or right—moment. And yet... I dismissed it.

Because none of it meant anything, right?

Ethan was just being friendly. Kai was just... stylish. Confident. Probably like that with everyone.

There was no way either of them was actually interested in me.

I was just Riley. Tired, overworked Riley who took care of her sister, forgot to do her own laundry half the time, and still double-checked every sentence in emails to avoid sounding too blunt.

They were just being nice. That was all. Totally professional. Totally.

My cheeks burned as I reopened the folder Kai had given me. I needed to focus. I had reports due. And no time for my brain to be reduced to a puddle over tailored pants and good cologne.

By the time I left work, my brain was fried. Not just from the meetings or the numbers I'd tried to force into making sense, but from trying to untangle whatever strange triangle I'd apparently wandered into with Ethan and Kai.

I told myself it wasn't real. That I was imagining it. That I wasn't someone people flirted with, not really.

I had too much going on. Too much worry. Too much Sophie. God, Sophie.

A familiar heaviness settled in my chest as I boarded the train, finding my usual seat near the back. I pulled my jacket tighter around me and leaned my head against the window, letting the rhythm of the tracks lull me into something close to stillness.

Until I heard the words. "...yeah, some lawyer's office. Firebombed, can you believe it?" I blinked, my head snapping upright.

Two men across the aisle were deep in conversation—one in a charcoal suit, the other still in his gym gear, earbuds dangling around his neck.

The man in the suit shook his head. "I heard it was related to that gang trial. Same case that wrapped this week. Sentencing is tomorrow, I think."

My stomach dropped. No. The gang trial. Sophie's case.

I shifted in my seat, trying not to look like I was eavesdropping—too obviously. "They say it was deliberate," the gym guy added. "Some kind of retaliation. No one was hurt, but the whole front office was scorched. Apparently, it was one of the smaller firms assisting on the prosecution side."

I couldn't breathe. My fingers dug into the strap of my bag. That cold, unmistakable feeling of dread was blooming in my chest again—familiar and unrelenting.

Sophie hadn't mentioned anything about it. Nothing in her texts. Nothing in her voice this morning. Just a quick "have a good day" like she wasn't sitting on top of something dangerous and potentially explosive. Literally.

The rest of the train ride was a blur. My mind was already racing ahead. Was she okay?

Had she seen it?

Had she known anyone who worked there?

Was her firm being targeted, too?

By the time I reached our apartment building, I was moving on autopilot, taking the stairs two at a time. The second I unlocked the door and stepped inside, I called out, "Sophie?" No answer.

The apartment was dark except for the glow of her desk lamp in her room. I dropped my bag, my heart still racing, and made my way toward her door. I knocked once. "Sophie?" After a pause, I heard her shuffle to open it.

She looked exhausted—pale, shadows under her eyes, hair thrown into a messy bun. Her expression faltered when she saw me.

"Hey," she said, too casual. Too guarded.

"You didn't think to mention that someone firebombed a law office involved in your case?" I asked, not bothering to sugarcoat the panic lacing my voice.

She blinked, clearly caught off guard. "How did you—" "People were talking about it on the train. Sophie, are you okay? Was anyone you knew hurt?" "No," she said quickly.

"It wasn't our firm. Just a smaller office we partnered with once or twice. No one was there when it happened."

"But still," I said, stepping inside, "this is serious. These people are dangerous, Soph."

"I know," she snapped, then winced, like the force of her own voice startled her.

"I know," she repeated, softer.

"And I didn't say anything because... because I didn't want to worry you."

"Well, congratulations," I said, voice trembling. "I'm worried anyway."

We stared at each other in silence, both of us vibrating with too many emotions and nowhere to put them.

Sophie's shoulders slumped. "I'm okay. I promise. But yeah... it's starting to feel real now. Like the danger's not just in the courtroom."

I stepped closer, my anger already fading into fear. "Then talk to me. Don't shut me out."

"I'm trying," she whispered, and for the first time, I saw the fear crack through her mask. And mine cracked too.

11

Not like her

Riley

Je te laisserai des mots – Patrick Watson

I woke early the next morning, long before the sun even touched the horizon. My body was drained, sore in that quiet, aching way that doesn't come from physical exertion but from carrying too much emotional weight for too long.

I stared up at the ceiling, covers pulled to my chest, knowing I wasn't going back to sleep. A decision had already settled in my bones. I couldn't do nothing. I couldn't sit in this apartment, pretending everything was fine while Sophie walked into danger every day.

I'd told myself she needed space. Independence. That I had to trust her instincts. But I wasn't stupid. Trust didn't protect people. Action did.

By the time the city started to wake, I was already dressed. I didn't bother with makeup, barely even ran a brush through my hair.

I just grabbed my keys and left, my phone clenched tight in one hand as I walked toward the police station like a woman marching into battle.

The officer at the front desk looked up as I approached, offering me a courteous but tired nod. "Morning, ma'am. How can I help you?"

I swallowed, forcing my voice to stay steady. "My sister's involved in that gang case—the one with the firebombing. She's interning with the firm. She's been getting... strange looks. Comments. And now an entire office is in ashes."

Recognition flickered in his expression, but his tone remained even. "Yes, ma'am. We're aware of the incident. The building was empty at the time, and there were no injuries."

"That's not the point," I snapped before I could stop myself.

"The point is that someone sent a message. And my sister's part of the legal team they're targeting."

He studied me, arms folded over his chest. "We've increased patrols around the area, and we've placed plainclothes officers near the lawyer's premises. We're monitoring the situation carefully." I crossed my arms tightly, willing myself not to break.

"That's not enough. Sophie's been targeted directly. You're telling me that a couple of patrols are all the protection she gets?"

His expression didn't change, but his voice softened slightly. "I understand your concern, Ms. Morgan. I do. But we're handling the situation as best we can. If there's any immediate danger—anything at all—she should call 911. We'll respond."

I clenched my jaw. The logic was sound. The protocol was standard. But protocol didn't stop threats. It didn't catch the tension in Sophie's voice when she tried to pretend she was okay.

It didn't stop me from replaying worst-case scenarios every time I closed my eyes. I left the station feeling only marginally better than when I arrived.

The city bustled on around me—people heading to work, coffee in hand, earbuds in, as if the world wasn't cracked open underneath their feet. Mine was.

On the walk home, I called Sophie. She picked up on the third ring, voice still sleepy. "Riles?"

"I'm picking you up from your internship every day," I said without preamble. T

here was a pause. "What? Why?"

"Because I said so," I said, firmer now. "This isn't up for debate."

“Riles, you don’t have to—” “I do,” I cut in. “You’re my sister, and I’m not taking any chances.”

Another pause. I could hear the shift in her tone when she finally replied.

“Okay,” she said quietly. “Okay.” I hung up, not because I wanted to but because I didn’t trust my voice not to crack.

For the next week, I stuck to my word. I picked Sophie up from the office every evening like clockwork. I’d park across the street, scan the sidewalk, my hands tight on the steering wheel until I spotted her walking toward me.

She hated it. I knew she did. But she didn’t fight me on it—not at first. She started opening up again, little by little. T

alking about work, laughing at her coworkers’ weird habits, even complaining about one of the partners who insisted on scheduling 4 PM meetings. She was smiling again.

But something inside me wouldn’t rest. I kept scanning every alleyway, every parked car. My eyes didn’t stop moving. My gut told me something was off. Even as Sophie seemed to relax, I couldn’t. Then, a week later, she said it.

“Riles,” she said as we drove home, “I think it’s time we go back to normal.” I didn’t look at her. Just kept my eyes on the road.

“What do you mean?” “I mean... I don’t need you to pick me up every day anymore. It’s been a week. Nothing’s happened. I’m fine.”

“No,” I said, sharper than I meant. “You’re not. Not really.”

She turned to look at me. “You can’t keep doing this forever. Hovering. Protecting. I need to feel normal again. I need to take my life back.” “

Normal doesn’t mean safe,” I shot back, my hands white-knuckling the steering wheel.

“I don’t trust this situation, Sophie. I don’t trust those people.”

“I know,” she whispered. “But I can’t live like this. Looking over my shoulder every second. I need you to trust me. Just a little.”

I didn't answer. I couldn't. Because I did trust her. I just didn't trust the world. And deep down, I knew the truth: I couldn't protect her forever. But I wanted to. God, I need to.

For the next few days, I tried to let go. I gave Sophie the space she asked for. Forced myself not to check my phone every ten minutes. I told myself she was fine—that the police were watching, that the danger had passed, that maybe, just maybe, I was being paranoid.

And yet, the unease didn't leave me. It sat low in my chest, gnawed at the edges of my thoughts even when I was distracted by work or making dinner or folding laundry.

I told myself it was just habit. Just a big sister thing. Until Thursday. I got home late—later than usual—after a long meeting that dragged well into the evening.

I didn't stop for groceries like I'd planned. I just wanted to get home, pull on sweatpants, and listen to Sophie ramble about her day while we ate something microwaved.

But the second I walked into the apartment, I knew something was off. It was dark. Silent. No sound of keys clattering onto the counter. No soft music playing from Sophie's room. No half-eaten apple sitting on the coffee table.

My stomach clenched. "Sophie?" I called out, flicking on the hall light. "You home?" Nothing. I walked through the living room, my footsteps suddenly too loud on the hardwood floor.

The kitchen was untouched—no dishes in the sink, no grocery bags, no signs she'd been home at all. The entryway was empty too. Her shoes, her work bag, the worn cardigan she always tossed over the back of a chair—all missing. Panic started to rise.

I pulled out my phone and checked the time: 6:45 p.m. She should've been home by now. Or at least on the train. She always texted if she was running late, even by ten minutes. Always.

I opened our shared location app. And froze. No signal. Her phone was off.

My breath caught in my throat. Sophie never turned her phone off. Not unless the battery had died, and even then, she always told me in advance.

It wasn't just a habit. It was a promise we'd made to each other a long time ago. After the accident. After the loss. Always check in.

I tried calling her anyway, holding my breath. Straight to voicemail. I left a message, voice shaky. "Soph, it's me. Just checking in. Call me when you get this, okay? I'm getting a little worried."

A little worried turned into full-blown panic twenty minutes later when the sun dipped below the skyline and I still hadn't heard from her. I called again. Voicemail. I tried her supervisor's office. No answer.

I called every hospital within a ten-mile radius, my voice trembling with every word: "Hi, I'm looking for my sister—her name is Sophie Morgan. She might've been brought in—no, no, thank you, I'll try somewhere else." Each time the answer was the same. Nothing.

By 8:30, my hands were shaking so badly I could barely hold the phone. I called the police. The woman on the other end had a calm voice, practised and neutral.

"When was the last time you spoke to her?" "This morning. She texted when she got to work." "Has she ever gone out of contact before?"

"No," I snapped, then caught myself. "I mean—no. She always checks in."

The woman paused. "We can take a missing person's report, but it hasn't been twenty-four hours yet. In the meantime, I'd recommend contacting hospitals and friends, just in case she's delayed." I barely managed to thank her before hanging up. And then I was moving without thinking, pacing the room, checking the window, dialling numbers I hadn't called in years—old friends, classmates, anyone who might've seen her.

Nothing. No one had heard from her since she left the office that afternoon. She was just... gone. And all I could do was wait.

By 9:00, I was on the bathroom floor, hands gripping the edge of the sink, trying not to vomit. My stomach twisted, my whole body trembling.

I kept whispering the same words over and over like they might make a difference. "She's okay. She's okay. She's okay."

But I didn't believe it. Because deep down, something told me this wasn't a delay.

This wasn't a dead phone battery. This wasn't Sophie getting drinks after work and forgetting to text. Something had happened. And I hadn't stopped it.

I should've kept picking her up. I should've insisted. I should've listened to my gut. I sat on the floor, clutching my phone in one hand and the hoodie she wore yesterday in the other, tears running silently down my cheeks. Come home, Soph. Please.

But even as they made calls and pulled up files, all I could think about was Sophie. And the way I'd let her go.

The clock on the wall mocked me. 10:02 p.m. Then 10:06. 10:14. Every minute felt like an hour, stretching out endlessly as I paced the living room floor, phone clutched in my hand, heart thundering in my chest. Still no word. No text. No call. No location ping. No Sophie.

I kept checking her phone's last known location, refreshing the app like it would suddenly change and give me the miracle I was begging for.

Nothing.

My breathing had started to come in sharp bursts. I was sweating, trembling. I couldn't sit still. Every creak of the apartment, every gust of wind outside, made me jump. She was gone. And every second she was gone, the images in my head got worse—her on a train platform, cornered in an alley, trapped in a basement somewhere calling out my name, hoping I'd come. And I hadn't. I let her walk away.

My legs gave out beneath me, and I sank to the floor, arms wrapped tightly around myself. A sob ripped from my throat—ugly, broken.

I buried my face in her hoodie, clutching it like a lifeline. It smelled like her. Like the vanilla lotion she always used. Like home. "Please,"

I whispered, rocking slightly. "Please be okay. Please come back." I couldn't wait any longer.

Something snapped inside me. I grabbed my bag, yanked my keys off the hook, and rushed out the door. The cool air hit me like a slap, but I barely noticed. My hands were shaking so badly I dropped my keys once before managing to unlock the car.

The driver's seat felt foreign beneath me—tight and too small, like the air inside the car was thinner than outside. My chest tightened. I hadn't driven at night in years. Not since the accident.

Not since I watched my family's car crumple around us like paper. Not since I woke up to Sophie's cries and Agatha's still body and the smell of smoke and metal and blood.

I hated cars. I hated driving. But I hated the thought of sitting and doing nothing even more. I gripped the steering wheel with white-knuckled fingers, forcing myself to breathe. One. Two. Three. You can do this. You have to do this.

I turned the key, the engine rumbling to life. The headlights illuminated the empty street ahead of me. And I drove. I drove through the city with my jaw clenched and heart pounding, every red light a test of my patience, every honk and brake squeal making me flinch.

The streetlights blurred with the tears in my eyes, and I blinked hard, trying to focus.

By the time I pulled into the parking lot of the police station, my entire body was shaking. I slammed the gear into park, shoved the door open, and all but ran inside.

The front desk officer looked up as I stormed in. "Miss—" "My sister's still missing," I said, voice sharp with panic.

"I filed a report earlier, but nothing's happened. No one's called. Her phone is off, and she hasn't come home, and this isn't like her—something is wrong.

I know something is wrong." I was breathless, half-wild.

The officer stood slowly, concern flickering across his face. "Okay. Take a breath. Let's start from the top."

"I don't have time for the top," I snapped.

"I know her. She wouldn't disappear like this. She wouldn't go this long without checking in."

He tried to guide me toward a chair, but I resisted. I didn't want to sit. I couldn't sit. Sitting meant waiting. Sitting meant helplessness.

"I'm not leaving here until someone finds her," I said, my voice cracking.

"Please. Just—please help me."

And this time, something in my voice must've registered.

Because the officer nodded, motioned for someone in the back. And then finally—finally—things started moving.

And as the officers made their calls, I stared at the door, waiting for a miracle, knowing there was nothing left to do but hope—and hate myself for letting go.

12

She's All I've Got

Riley

All I Want – Kodaline

I sat in the cold, sterile waiting area of the police station, my hands gripping my phone so tightly my knuckles had gone white.

The officers were out searching. They'd put out an alert, they'd promised to call as soon as they knew anything—but the waiting was a new kind of hell. Every minute felt like an hour, every tick of the wall clock another twist in my gut.

I kept trying to breathe, but the air in here was thick and stale and suffocating. Too quiet. Too bright.

I wanted to scream. Every second my mind spun out a new nightmare.

What if Sophie needed me? What if she was scared? What if... No. I squeezed my eyes shut, willed the phone to ring, just to do something.

An officer finally came back—my officer, the one who'd been patient enough to listen to me beg and break.

He sat down beside me. I barely registered his words at first, just the way he didn't crowd me, the way his voice stayed low and steady, like maybe if he stayed calm I'd believe him. "We'll find her," he said.

I shook my head, tears threatening to spill over again. "You don't understand," I whispered, voice ragged.

"She's not just my sister. I raised her. She's—she's all I've got."

He nodded, but the words just bounced off.

Nothing would reach me except Sophie. My world was still a phone screen that refused to light up. Time stretched, snapped, reformed, and stretched again.

I stood up, paced the length of the waiting room, sat down, stood up again—too wired and numb all at once.

I kept checking the door, the phone, the clock, as if one would suddenly give me a miracle.

When the officer returned, his face said everything before his mouth did.

My heart kicked so hard I nearly doubled over.

"Miss Morgan," he started, and I was already on my feet.

"Did you find her?" My voice barely made it out. He hesitated. I saw it—the weight of what he wasn't saying, the news curdling behind his eyes.

"We found your sister. She's at the hospital. She's alive, but her injuries are severe."

My legs buckled. Severe. I nearly missed the next part, clinging to the counter, cold sweat prickling at my scalp.

"She was found in the old industrial district. Targeted by the same gang involved with the threats. But she's alive. She's getting help now."

Alive. But. The room tilted. I heard myself say, "Where is she?" like I was underwater.

"St. Mary's Medical Centre. They're prepping her for surgery." He didn't ask if I wanted to go; I was already moving, barely registering the world around me.

Somehow I ended up in the back of his car, everything outside a blur.

My head pressed against the cold glass, staring at nothing. I was half-hoping this was some fever dream, that I'd wake up and Sophie would be home, bickering over who used the last of the milk.

St. Mary's. The words kept repeating in my head. My mouth tasted like pennies.

When we finally pulled up, I nearly fell out of the car, legs shaking, eyes burning. I had no idea what I'd even grabbed—my purse? My phone? I didn't care.

The officer's hand was gentle but firm as he led me through the bright, too-quiet hospital corridors.

I barely registered the nurses' faces, the click of shoes on linoleum, the smell of antiseptic and burnt coffee.

Room 313. I made it to the door and stopped, suddenly terrified. I wasn't ready for this. Didn't matter. I opened the door. Sophie was there—pale, small, machines hissing and beeping, bandages wrapped tight around her arm, bruises blossoming over her skin.

Her hair—God, even her hair looked out of place, limp and unwashed, strands escaping whatever the nurses had tried to do with it.

For a moment I just stood there, swallowing hard. Then I stumbled to her side, reaching for her hand, desperate to find any sign of the sister I'd raised. She didn't move. Didn't wake.

Her fingers were cold and stiff. "I'm so sorry," I whispered, bowing my head over her hand.

Tears burned my face, and I let them. I should have protected you. I should have been there. I should have done something.

I stayed like that for a long time, clinging to her hand, listening to the machines breathe for her, hating myself for every second she'd been alone.

I was supposed to keep her safe. I was supposed to be the strong one. But all I could do was kneel here and beg for her to stay

13

Too Quiet

Riley

To Build a Home– The Cinematic Orchestra

I sat in the uncomfortable plastic chair by Sophie's bedside, my hand wrapped around hers, fingers tracing the cool skin beneath the IV.

She looked so small under the tangle of tubes and blankets—nothing like the girl who used to steal my hoodies or mock my dance playlists.

The hospital room felt outside of time, lit by the washed-out glow of fluorescent lights. The steady beep of the heart monitor was the only sound, cutting through the hush with brutal regularity.

Each rise and fall on the screen was a lifeline I clung to, counting them in my head like prayers.

Too slow. Too quick. Was that normal? Was she breathing right? Why didn't the nurse come back?

I wiped my eyes on my sleeve, then reached for her hand again.

"Hey," I whispered, even though she was still unconscious, "I'm here. I'm not leaving. You're going to be okay, Soph. You hear me?"

Her chest rose and fell, shallow but steady. The machine beside her pulsed green and gold, numbers flickering like a code I couldn't crack. I tried to focus on those numbers, like if I stared hard enough, I could will them to stay steady.

But I could see how pale her face was, how swollen her knuckles were around the bandages. A nurse swept in, quiet and efficient. She checked the bag of fluids, glanced at the monitors. I wanted to scream at her to do something.

But I just sat there, helpless, clutching Sophie's hand like it was the only thing keeping her tethered here.

The nurse offered a quick, rehearsed smile. "She's stable, for now," she murmured, almost apologetic. "We're watching her closely." I nodded, swallowing back a thousand words I couldn't say.

As soon as she left, the silence came crashing back in. Minutes passed. Or maybe hours. I lost track, caught between memories and the blinking lights of the machines.

I told Sophie stories—half nonsense, half desperate hope—just to fill the air. "Remember the time we got caught in that storm at the beach?" My voice was hoarse.

"You thought we were going to die. But we just ended up at that tiny café, soaked to the bone. You made friends with the barista. Of course you did..."

I squeezed her hand, wishing she'd squeeze back.

The beep of the monitor stuttered. Once. Twice. My head snapped up. No. Just a blip. Just a hiccup.

I waited, breath caught somewhere between hope and terror.

The numbers flickered. The machine hummed. Sophie's chest barely moved beneath the hospital gown.

I found myself counting her breaths—one, two, three—until I lost count and started again.

Outside, someone laughed in the hallway. A woman's voice—soft, distant. Life, just beyond this bubble of agony inside, the monitor pulsed. And then... it skipped.

No, no, no. A cold prickle shot down my spine.

I stared at the screen. The line wobbled, dipped, caught itself. My heart pounded in my ears. Please.

The air was thick with disinfectant and dread. Every sound seemed sharpened: the tick of the clock, the distant squeak of wheels on tile, the fluttering beat of Sophie's fragile heart.

And then— A warning beep. Higher. Faster. Sophie's chest hitched. The numbers on the screen tumbled—too fast for me to follow.

My own heart thundered. I stood up, not knowing what to do, hand pressed to her forehead, her cheek. "Sophie? Sophie—wake up, please—"

The sound didn't stop. That flat, keening note drilled through my skull, drowning out everything else. For a split second, the world itself felt still—frozen in that sterile, fluorescent light.

I staggered, chest heaving, the machines blurring behind a film of tears. "Sophie!" I choked, voice shredded, useless. "Come on, Soph. Please—please!"

But no one heard me. The nurses moved in a controlled frenzy, slamming the bed rails down, forcing me back.

The doctor was already shouting orders—"One milligram of epi, now! Start compression!"—and I watched, helpless, as they pressed down on Sophie's chest with brutal, methodical precision.

I flinched with every push, every click and whirl of the machines.

Someone's hand landed on my shoulder, firm and cold. "Miss, you need to leave—"

"No!" I lunged forward, but hands caught my arms, hauling me away from the bed.

"Let me stay! That's my sister! I need to—" My voice cracked, the sound sharp as broken glass.

"She's all I have, please—"But I was already out in the hallway, the door slamming shut behind me, the glass fogged with fingerprints. T

he wail of the monitor still bled through the walls—a cruel reminder, refusing to let me forget. I collapsed onto the floor, knees buckling, back pressed to the wall.

My body shook so violently it hurt. My head spun, nausea roiling in my gut, the world narrowing down to a pinpoint of pure, animal panic. Inside the room, I could see the blur of motion. White coats, blue scrubs, someone running for the crash cart.

Words floated out—"Come on, pulse check!"—followed by more frantic activity.

I pressed my forehead to the cold tile, squeezing my eyes shut, whispering desperate bargains to the universe. I'll do anything. I'll give anything. Just let her come back. Please. Take anything you want. Just not her.

A minute. Two. An eternity. I didn't know how long I sat there—five seconds or a lifetime. I dug my nails into my palms, trying to anchor myself, the air thick with the stench of antiseptic and terror.

The door finally opened. A nurse stepped out, her face blank and professional, the mask of someone who's done this too many times. "Miss. Morgan—"

I was on my feet instantly, gripping the door frame. "Is she—did she—?" She shook her head, eyes soft with pity.

"They're still working. But you need to prepare yourself." Prepare myself. How do you prepare for the end of your world?

I pressed my forehead against the glass, watching their hands moving over Sophie's body. I saw her face, still and impossibly pale, a tangle of wires and tubes, surrounded by strangers fighting for her life.

Please. Please, Soph. Just one more miracle. Just open your eyes. Just squeeze my hand, like you used to when you were scared of storms.

Another alarm blared.

The doctor's voice rose—one last command—and then, suddenly, the motion slowed.

One by one, the medical staff stepped back, eyes falling, heads bowed. The flat line never stopped.

The universe ended. My knees gave out. I slid to the floor, arms wrapped around my body, rocking gently as the nurse knelt beside me.

She said something—I couldn't hear it over the screaming in my own mind.

My breath came in gasps, raw and torn, each one a desperate grasp for a world that no longer made sense.

The only thing that made it real was the emptiness—the way the world felt suddenly too big, too quiet. Sophie was gone. And I was truly, utterly alone.

14

A Piece Left Behind

Killian

Take Me Home – Jess Glynne

I'd come to visit a friend—a guy who'd caught a bullet in the leg during one of our messier business dealings.

It wasn't life-threatening, just painful enough to keep him off his feet.

He'd be walking in no time, but until then, the hospital was the last place I wanted to be.

Too sterile. Too much death in the air. The smell of antiseptic, the faint buzz of fluorescent lights, the constant beeping of machines—it all got under my skin.

I was leaning against the wall outside his room when the Code Blue came over the intercom.

My body tensed on instinct. I froze, listening to the ripple of movement down the hall.

Then I heard it. Not the code. Not the doctors moving in. A sound that cut right through the hospital noise—a raw, gut-deep sob.

It started low, almost strangled, then rose into something that made the hair on my neck stand on end. It wasn't the kind of crying you could ignore. This was someone breaking.

Goddammit. I waited for someone—anyone—to get to her, to quiet it, to do something. But no one did.

And against my better judgement, my feet started moving toward the sound. I wasn't the type to go chasing after other people's pain.

But something about that voice... something about the way it cracked made it impossible to stay put.

When I rounded the corner, I saw her. A woman, hunched over on the floor, arms wrapped around herself like she was holding her ribs in place.

Her face was a mess of tears and devastation, eyes wide and glassy, her breathing sharp and uneven.

She was broken. Completely shattered. How the hell could they just leave her like this?

She didn't notice me at first, but when she did, there was nothing in her gaze but grief. It hit like a punch—raw, unfiltered, and dangerous in the way it pulled something out of me I didn't like to name.

I wasn't built for this. I didn't do comfort.

But my boots carried me forward anyway. Two long strides, and I was in front of her. I reached down without thinking, pulling her in, her body collapsing against mine like she'd been waiting for someone to catch her.

She shook hard, her sobs tearing out of her in waves.

The sound went straight to my gut.

"You're not alone," I heard myself say, my voice steady despite the weight pressing down on my chest.

My arm locked around her, holding her upright.

She didn't answer. Just buried herself deeper into my chest, the heat of her tears bleeding through my shirt.

I kept my hand on her back, moving in slow, steady circles, trying to keep her from falling apart completely.

Her sobs eventually eased, just enough for her to catch her breath.

I loosened my hold a fraction, giving her space without letting go. I didn't know why I was still here. I didn't even know her name. But I couldn't pull away. Not yet. Her grief was like gravity, and I was already caught in it.

She clutched at me like I was the last tether she had left, and something twisted in my chest. I wasn't supposed to care.

But I did. I pressed her a little closer, my palm warm against her shoulder.

I didn't know if I was doing this right.

Hell, I didn't know how to do this at all.

But I stayed.

Then I heard them—the officers—coming down the hallway, their voices low, their footsteps sharp against the tile.

It was time to go. I pulled back, my hand lingering on her shoulder a beat too long.

She didn't seem to notice, too lost in her own storm. "I'm sorry," I murmured, the words barely making it past my throat.

One last look—her face hidden in her hands, shoulders shaking—and I turned away. Her sobs followed me down the hall. I could still feel the tremor of her body against mine, the salt of her tears seeping into my shirt. I shouldn't have stayed. I shouldn't have given a damn. But I had.

Hands shoved deep into my pockets, I muttered a curse under my breath.

I didn't know her. I wasn't supposed to feel like I'd left something behind.

But I had. And even as I tried to walk away, I knew—I'd be back.

I wasn't done with her. Not yet.

15

After

Riley

Saturn – Sleeping At Last

The ride back to the apartment felt surreal, like I was drifting through fog.

I sat in the back of the police car, a blanket wrapped around my shoulders.

Not just any blanket—the quilt Sophie had been covered with in the hospital.

The nurse had folded it neatly before handing it to me, along with a small condolence package and a sachet of lavender.

The lavender was supposed to soothe me, I guess, but it only made my chest ache.

Sophie loved lavender—her favourite hand lotion, her favourite tea.

Now it was just another cruel reminder of the person who was gone.

The officers walked me up to the front door.

Their presence was quiet and steady, like they were afraid of disturbing the silence that had already settled over the apartment. Inside, everything felt too still. Too quiet. I sank onto the couch, clutching the quilt to my chest like a lifeline.

"Miss Morgan," one of the officers said gently, taking the chair opposite me, his notepad balanced on his knee.

"We need to ask you a few questions about Sophie—about the threats, her movements before tonight, anything that might help." I nodded numbly.

My voice was flat as I answered. Yes, Sophie had been worried. Yes, there had been threats from the gang.

No, she hadn't mentioned anyone following her.

The words came out mechanically, each one pulling me further into the hollow inside me.

It felt like I was watching someone else speak, someone else answer.

I was just a shell, my mind stuck on the only truth that mattered.

Sophie is gone.

When the questions were over, they offered more condolences before leaving quietly.

The click of the latch as the door shut was deafening.

I sat there for a long time, staring at nothing.

The lavender sachet sat untouched on the table.

I wanted to scream.

To throw something.

To rage against the universe for taking Sophie from me. But I didn't.

Instead, I stood and walked to Sophie's room. T

he moment I stepped inside, the ache in my chest became unbearable. Everything was exactly as she'd left it that morning—bed neatly made, a half-empty mug of tea on the nightstand, her favourite hoodie draped over the back of the chair.

It felt wrong. Like the room was still waiting for Sophie to come home.

I dropped onto her bed and buried my face in her pillow. It still smelled like her—lavender and the faintest hint of vanilla. That was all it took for the dam to break.

The sobs ripped through me, deep and violent. I clung to the quilt and cried into the pillow until I could hardly breathe.

This wasn't just grief—it was agony. I cried for Sophie, for the life she should have had, for the years we'd never get to share.

I cried for myself, for the emptiness that now filled the space where my sister had been.

"Sophie," I whispered through my tears, my voice cracking.

"Sophie, I need you. Please... please come back." There was no answer. Just silence.

I curled up tighter, the quilt wrapped around me like armour. The tears kept coming until I was empty, until even breathing hurt.

I didn't care about the world outside.

Not about food. Not about sleep. I just wanted my sister back.

And she was gone. The ache in my chest didn't fade as the night dragged on—it deepened, heavy and constant.

I stayed in Sophie's bed, my sobs eventually fading into quiet, exhausted tears.

When sleep finally came, it was heavy and cold, filled with dreams of the sister I would never hold again.

16

What's Left is Mine

Riley

Control – Halsey

The knock on the door came far too early for someone who hadn't slept properly in days.

I stirred in Sophie's bed, my body stiff, head pounding. I'd cried myself into an exhausted stupor the night before, curled beneath the blanket that still smelled like her—lavender and something sweet.

For a moment, I forgot where I was. Then reality slammed into my chest like a freight train.

The knock came again. Louder this time. I sat up slowly, rubbed at my face, and shuffled to the door, my limbs heavy, my heart a hollow, aching thing.

Two detectives stood there, grim-faced and composed.

They introduced themselves, but I didn't catch their names—just voices in a haze. "Miss Morgan," the taller one said gently.

"We need to ask you a few more questions about Sophie."

I nodded and stepped aside. They sat in the living room, notepads out, pens ready. I took the seat across from them, Sophie's quilt clutched tight in my lap like armour against the world.

They asked about the gang threats. About Sophie's mood in the days before she died. About anything odd she'd said or done.

I answered automatically. My voice was flat, empty. Like I was recounting a stranger's story, not my own. Not hers. When they finished, the shorter one looked up, his expression a practised blend of sympathy and professionalism.

"I'm truly sorry for your loss. We're doing everything we can to build a case and hold the people responsible accountable."

I nodded again, numb, and walked them to the door. When it clicked shut behind them, the silence pressed in like a weight I couldn't shake.

The next few weeks blurred together. Phone calls. Paperwork. Grief. The coroner called to tell me Sophie's body would have to stay with them for up to several weeks because of the investigation. I didn't have words for the pain that caused. Knowing she was alone in some cold, sterile room and I couldn't bring her home—it wrecked me.

So I poured myself into planning her funeral. It was the only thing I could control. The only way I could still take care of her.

I picked her favourite flowers. Chose songs that reminded me of her.

Reached out to friends, colleagues, anyone with a story to share.

I wanted it to be perfect—because she deserved that. She deserved everything.

When the day finally came, two months after she was taken from me, I stood at the front of the chapel, hands trembling around the note cards I'd scribbled and rewritten a hundred times.

The room was full of people, but all I could see was the photo at the altar—Sophie, frozen in time, smiling the way she always did when she caught me watching her with pride.

The service was beautiful. People spoke about her warmth, her intelligence, the way she lit up every room. I got through my speech. Barely. My voice cracked too many times to count.

But I did it. And afterwards, when the hugs came, the condolences, the whispered promises that time would heal... all I felt was emptiness.

Because she was still gone.

Two months later, I sat on the couch staring at an envelope from the Victims of Crime Fund.

I opened it without thinking. Inside was a check—enough to cover the funeral. And then some. A bitter laugh slipped from my mouth. What good is this now?

Money couldn't bring her back. It couldn't erase what I'd lost. It was just another reminder of how easily the world moved on while I remained stuck in place.

I set the check on the coffee table and leaned back, eyes scanning the apartment.

Her books. Her blanket. The hoodie draped over the back of a chair. Everything was still here, exactly where she left it.

Like she might walk through the door any second. But I knew better. And I didn't know how to keep going.

Then the phone rang. I almost didn't answer. "Miss Morgan," the detective said, voice careful, rehearsed. "I'm afraid we've exhausted all leads.

Without additional evidence, we're reclassifying the case as cold." I froze. "So that's it?" I gripped the phone so hard my knuckles turned white.

"You're giving up?" "We're not giving up.

But we lack sufficient evidence to—"

"Right," I cut in, flat and bitter.

"Good to know my sister's life doesn't matter." "Miss—" I hung up.

The phone slipped from my hand before I even realised it.

Then I launched it. It slammed into the wall with a deafening crack, the screen shattering, the battery skidding across the floor. I stared at it for a second, breathing hard—before something inside me snapped like a wire pulled too tight. I lost it.

I wasn't thinking. I wasn't feeling. I was burning.

My hand curled around the edge of the coffee table and flipped it, hard, sending candles, books, and a half-full mug of cold tea flying across the room.

Liquid splattered up the wall, dripping like blood as ceramic shattered across the floor.

For a moment, I was frozen—paralysed by the weight of it all.

Then the numbness cracked.

Rage poured out, black and bitter. I smashed every plate, every cup, every photo that dared to show me happy.

The walls were too close—I wanted to punch through them. I wanted to claw my way out of my own skin.

I screamed until my throat bled. I ripped the couch cushions to shreds, threw a chair at the wall until it splintered.

I grabbed Sophie's favourite mug, stared at the dumb cartoon cat on the side, and hurled it so hard it shattered into a thousand useless pieces.

I wanted to wreck the whole world. I wanted to punish the universe for letting this happen.

And then I collapsed, kneeling in the ruins, glass biting into my skin.

I sobbed until I couldn't breathe, my body wracked with loss so total it was a kind of death. Who was I now? My purpose—gone. My life—pointless.

I had spent every second keeping Sophie safe. Without her, I was nothing but a shell filled with screaming.

But as the blood dripped from my hands and the last echo of my sobs faded, something else took root.

Something sharp and cold and alive. Rage. If I had nothing else, I had this. I could make them pay.

My voice was guttural, savage. "I'm coming for you. I'll burn your world down for what you did.

I'll haunt you until you wish you'd never heard her name." I stood, legs shaking, surrounded by ruin.

No purpose. No hope. Nothing left to lose.

That made me dangerous. That made me free. And for the first time since Sophie died, I felt something close to alive.

17

Thirteen Steps to Ruin

Riley

Dark Side – Bishop Briggs

The first three months were just survival—except survival makes it sound cleaner than it was. There's nothing clean about it.

I didn't eat. I didn't sleep. I existed on black coffee, old adrenaline, and the kind of grief that makes your bones ache.

If there's a twelve-step program for turning into a monster, I skipped straight to step thirteen: set yourself on fire and see what crawls out of the ashes.

I haunted underground fighting pits, chasing oblivion with both fists.

I learned to take a punch, then another, then another—until bruises were just another kind of camouflage.

Until pain was a reminder I wasn't dead yet... even if I kind of wanted to be.

There's something freeing about realising you can be broken a thousand times and still keep getting up.

Spoiler: it means you stop caring what gets broken next.

By month four, I was unrecognisable. Gaunt, bloodshot, hands shaking from withdrawal—of what, I couldn't say. Grief, maybe. Or purpose. Or Sophie.

Sometimes I'd see her in the crowd—soft hair, bright laugh—and then I'd blink and it was just some stranger flinching at the animal I'd become.

That's when Viktor found me.

He was less a man and more a blunt instrument.

"Three days. One knife. No mercy." Like it was nothing.

They dumped me in a warehouse with five men and one knife.

I spent the first night curled in the rafters, listening to them tear each other apart.

By sunrise, I wasn't sure which scared me more: them, or the way I didn't flinch at the sound of bones breaking.

The second night, I slit a man's throat while he slept, and I didn't even feel sick. I felt... efficient.

By the third day, I was the only one left.

Viktor watched me wipe blood from my face and nodded like he'd just confirmed a theory.

"You'll do," he said. If that was approval, I'd hate to see his version of love.

Month six: enter Salazar.

He looked at me like I was something sharp and slightly rabid—and he wasn't wrong.

"Precision," he told me.

"No second chances in this world." He gave me a gun, threw me into a warehouse full of maniacs, and told me to hit the moving target—while being chased, half-blind, bleeding from the mouth.

If I missed, he'd call me "pathetic" in Russian, Spanish, and English, just to make sure I got the message.

By the time I could shoot through a tin can at twenty feet without blinking, he finally stopped rolling his eyes. Progress.

By then, I was starting to get a reputation.

Men twice my size didn't see a woman—they saw a feral thing that didn't care if it walked out alive.

The monster under their beds, except I didn't wait for them to fall asleep.

If I'd ever had a soul, I must've pawned it for ammunition somewhere along the line.

Month ten was Mina's test—no weapons, just words.

She was a manipulator, a sadist with a Harvard degree, and I hated how much I learned from her.

How to break a man with a sentence.

How to get what I wanted by making people think it was their idea.

"You're terrifying," she said once, and for the first time, I believed it.

I looked in the mirror and barely recognised my own eyes—flat, hungry, wild.

I'd stopped waiting for the grief to swallow me. Turns out, it just fed the monster.

By year's end, I'd burned down a stash house with three men inside.

Watched the flames reflect in my eyes and wondered if there was anything human left behind them.

For a moment, I hoped not.

Year two was about refinement.

I didn't react—I calculated. I could torture, interrogate, and vanish like a ghost.

I became a rumour in the underworld: the dead-eyed woman with nothing left to lose, whose laughter sounded like broken glass in the dark.

And then—finally—I came back to the city. The gang who'd killed Sophie didn't recognise me.

But I recognised them. I watched them like prey.

I bled, starved, and trained until all I wanted was the sound of them begging.

Not for mercy—for understanding.

The last night.

The warehouse. The end of it all. Blood on my hands, pain singing through every nerve, a smile on my lips that made even me uneasy.

I killed them one by one, methodical as a butcher.

One tried to crawl away and I pinned him like a butterfly.

"Say her name," I whispered. He choked. "S–Sophie..."

"Good. Remember it while you die." And when he did, I didn't feel a thing.

Afterwards, I stared at the mess I'd made—my hands shaking, every muscle screaming, eyes empty.

If monsters are born, this is how it happens: you lose everything, and you decide you don't want to be found. I laughed, sharp and hollow, and caught my reflection in a broken shard of glass. Wild hair. A face streaked with blood. Eyes that didn't blink.

Look at you now, Riles. You used to collect tea towels. Now you collect bodies. Good job. Maybe next I'll take up cross-stitch. Or arson.

The last step was the warehouse. I'd been saving it. Not for closure—for the sake of knowing I could still finish what I started. Salazar's text lit up my burner: It's ready. So was I.

I flexed my ruined hands, felt every break, every scar, every night I'd spent tearing myself apart so I could build something meaner. Something unstoppable.

I wasn't sure if I'd succeeded, but I was sure as hell going to find out.

Let them tell stories about me—the girl who lost everything and burned the world to keep warm.

Let them lock their doors and pray to any god that still listened.

The boogeyman has a name, and she's wearing my skin.

And if the universe is listening.

All I've got left is rage and a punchline. So I'll burn it all down—and laugh while I watch

18

Elegy in Flame

Riley

Swan Lake – Hidden Citizens

The air inside the warehouse was thick, the bass of the music vibrating the concrete walls. But I had no intention of blending in.

This wasn't about stealth anymore.

This was about fear. Pain. Revenge.

This was about making the Eastside Crew choke on everything they'd ever done.

The thumping bass of their usual playlist pounded like a war drum—predictable, testosterone-fuelled garbage that sounded like someone put a speaker in a blender and hit rage.

But I had different plans.

I reached into my jacket and tapped the small transmitter.

A quick swipe of my finger—and the music cut. Silence. Beautiful, tense silence.

Then—Swan Lake. Soft, delicate, haunting.

The warehouse echoed with violins instead of violence, but the irony?

That was mine.

The men froze, their bravado twitching under their skin.

I could practically hear their tiny brains grinding as they tried to comprehend Tchaikovsky in their bloodstained kingdom.

Then the lights died. Goodnight, boys. Click. Night vision on. Let the show begin.

I climbed up the metal scaffolding along the warehouse walls, gaining a bird's-eye view of the chaos I'd orchestrated.

Below, they flailed—rats in a trap, blind and dumb. I watched, quiet and still, the green glow of my goggles painting the scene in ghostly light.

When the panic reached its peak, I moved.

I leapt down from the high ground, boots crashing into the back of the nearest thug like a meteor strike. He screamed—briefly—before I slammed his face into the floor and shattered his knee with a crunch that echoed through the cavernous space.

"Shhh," I cooed, zip-tying his wrists and ankles in one fluid movement.

"You don't want to miss the grand finale."

The next one turned too slow. I slashed his Achilles with surgical precision, dropping him like a puppet with cut strings.

He howled, trying to crawl. I kicked him over and jammed a shard of glass through his palm, pinning it to the floor.

"Try to run again, and I'll staple your balls to the concrete," I whispered sweetly, zip-tying his other limbs with practised ease.

One by one, I dismantled them. Not quickly. Not painlessly.

The third thug screamed when I shot out his kneecaps and let him writhe.

"You ever feel your bones crumble? It's like popcorn, but bloodier." I bound him with wire and left him sobbing. I moved like a phantom through the dark.

Another flash bang. Another man staggered blindly. I tackled him into a wall, dislocated his shoulder, and used his own belt to hogtie him.

"Hope you like bondage," I sneered, jamming a piece of rebar between his ribs—not fatal, but deep enough to make him beg for mercy.

There were ten of them when I started. Ten cocky bastards who thought they were untouchable. Now they were broken. Bound. Bleeding. And still breathing.

That was the point. I circled them, dragging the leader by the collar into the centre of the room. He sobbed. I could smell the piss. "Say her name," I hissed, crouching beside him. "Sophie." He whimpered it. Pathetic. "Louder."

He screamed it. Too late. I'd already carved it once. But this time, I made sure he'd remember it in hell.

Each letter of her name cut slow and jagged into his chest with a box cutter.

My hand shook briefly—not from fear, but from the unbearable weight of what I was becoming. Was this still justice, or was it something else entirely?

But the thought passed like a shadow. My fingers tightened around the box cutter.

"Consider this a matching set. She has scars too. Courtesy of you."

When they were all laid out—zip-tied, tied with belts, tangled in chains—I planted the charges. Around the walls. Beneath the fuel drums. Next to the fuse box.

I walked the perimeter slowly, checking each line, each placement. I stood in the centre. My gallery of ruin.

"You won't get the mercy of a bullet," I said.

"You'll get heat. Smoke. Fire. Just like Sophie did when you left her to die."

I walked the perimeter slowly, feeling the hum of the charges beneath my feet.

The weight of what was coming was heavier than the sound of the screams behind me.

This wasn't just about fire and death.

It was about erasing everything they had taken from me.

Every last shred of peace.

They moaned, struggled, some cried, but none of them could move.

I walked to the exit.

The music still played—haunting, surreal.

My finger hovered over the detonator.

The wind shifted. The silence was heavy. My pulse slowed. One heartbeat for Sophie. One for every scream she never got to release. Outside, the cameras caught my silhouette as I stepped into the open. I paused, raised my middle finger to the lens, blood glistening on my gloves.

Smile for the camera, boys.

Then I pressed the button.

The explosion was thunderous, a bloom of fire and steel ripping the warehouse apart in a deafening roar.

The sky lit up orange and red, casting long shadows as metal and glass shot into the air like shrapnel from hell. Screams—brief, high-pitched, and final—echoed behind me.

I didn't flinch. They'd died the way they lived—cruel, terrified, and helpless.

I mounted my bike, kicked the engine to life, and vanished into the dark. Justice had a new face. And it was mine.

As I rode off into the night, the sound of the explosion still ringing in my ears, I didn't feel the rush I expected.

No triumph. No release. Just the quiet, empty weight of what I had become.

The world was on fire—and so was I. But there was no turning back now. Not for me. Not for Sophie.

19

The Ghost in the Smoke

Killian

Tantrum – Ashnikko

The four of us—Jaxon, Cole, Lucas, and me—we didn't just build the Steel Vipers.

We forged it from chaos, violence, and grit.

We weren't some back-alley gang. We were precision. Purpose. Power.

Jaxon was the brute force—a battering ram in human form.

Cole? The tactician with a smile sharp enough to cut.

Lucas, our phantom behind the curtain, made machines whisper and cities stutter.

And me?

I was the one they all looked to when the blood started spilling.

The leader. Reluctant, maybe. But undeniable.

Tonight, we sat in our war room, screens flickering as the East Side Crew's warehouse became a bonfire.

Smoke curled like a signal flare, screaming that someone just did the impossible.

Cole swirled his whisky. "That's impossible."

He was right. We'd fought the East Side bastards for years.

Guns, bribes, ambushes.

And someone else burned their empire in a single night.

Jaxon folded his arms. "Whoever did this isn't playing games."

Lucas's fingers flew across his keyboard. "No chatter. No trace. Surgical. Professional."

Then the footage shifted. A figure stepped through the wreckage.

All black. Masked. Methodical.

They checked bodies like a checklist.

Knife. Bullet. Clean kills.

Then they looked directly into the camera.

And flipped us off. The middle finger was slow. Deliberate.

Cole chuckled darkly. "Got balls, I'll give 'em that."

I didn't laugh. "They're not hiding. They're making a statement."

"I've got traffic cams picking up a bike heading east," Lucas said.

"Plates are fake. Riding like they own the road." The footage showed the rider shooting out a camera mid-turn. Precision. Intentional.

"They want us to follow," I muttered. I stood.

"We're not letting this slide. We find out who they are, what they want. Then we respond."

Because you don't spit in a viper's face without expecting to get bit.

Cole

Killian gave the order. I moved. Glass down. Jacket on. Mind racing. I was already calculating: exits, pressure points, weaknesses.

I live for this shit.

My bike purred like a predator outside the compound. Sleek, tuned to perfection, as deadly as its rider.

Lucas emerged, tablet in hand, hoodie half-zipped.

"You didn't think I'd miss the party, did you?"

"You're lucky I like your nerdy ass," I muttered, already mounting.

"Tracking them in real-time. Eastbound, old industrial route.

They're not hiding."

"Good." Throttle twisted. Engines roared.

The city blurred around us. This wasn't about turf. This was war.

Riley

The city wasn't a place anymore—it was a blur of roaring engines, bleeding neon, and the thunder of chaos.

Streetlights pulsed like a heartbeat as I flew past, the wind clawing at my jacket, my bike shrieking like a banshee under me.

Every sense was dialled to eleven. Every instinct screaming: don't stop.

They were still on me. Two of them. Not cops. Not amateurs. Ghosts in leather and steel. Too tight in formation. Too steady on the throttle. Too goddamn determined.

The East Side Crew was gone—reduced to red mist and broken bones. I made sure Sophie's ghost could sleep.

But these two? These weren't survivors.

They were predators. I hit the throttle hard, the bike jerking forward like a kicked horse. Tires screeched as I took a sharp corner, narrowly missing a mailbox that shattered in my side mirror. Glass sprayed behind me.

I didn't look back. Didn't have time.

A glimpse in the mirror—one of them was gaining. Fast.

"Fuck it," I growled, shifting weight.

Downshift. Brake tap. Spin. I slid the bike sideways around a corner, rear wheel fishtailing in a storm of sparks. My knee kissed the asphalt.

My heart tried to punch out of my chest.

I came up behind a delivery truck. Popped left.

The bastard behind me followed, a black shadow with a death wish.

I let him get closer. Closer... Too close. CRACK.

One clean shot. The front tire exploded mid-turn. He didn't even have time to scream. His bike folded in half, the rider launching into the air like a crash-test dummy on fast-forward.

He smashed into the back of a parked SUV, glass shattering in a starburst of violence.

His body bounced—twice—then lay crumpled.

I hissed a breath through my teeth, slowing just a second. And then the fucker moved. Sat up. Gave me a thumbs-up.

What the actual— "Is he made of Kevlar?!"

No time. The second rider was still locked on me like a goddamn missile.

I weaved through traffic, horns blaring, someone screamed.

I ducked under an overpass and flew through a red light, a taxi skidding sideways to avoid me.

Still on my tail. Fine. Let's dance.

I swerved into a narrow alley, trash bins exploding in my wake. I clipped one with my foot peg—pain flared, but I didn't slow. Up ahead—an old construction site.

My eyes locked on the scaffolding ramp. I grinned.

"Hold on, baby," I whispered to the bike.

"Let's get stupid."

I hit the ramp full throttle. The bike lifted. For a breathless second, I was airborne—soaring over chain-link fence and scattered tools. Landed hard.

Shocks screamed. Still moving.

The bastard followed. But he wasn't me. He hit the edge wrong. Wobbled. Clipped a pipe.

Down he went. Metal on metal. Concrete on bone. But I didn't wait to see the fallout.

Instead, I pulled into a side street. Fumbled for my phone.

My voice broke as I dialled. "H-hello? He's chasing me—I—I don't know what to do—" Tears welled in my eyes on cue. A perfect little performance. I guided my path toward flashing lights up ahead—real ones. Blue and red, slicing through the dark like salvation.

He pulled up behind me. Slower now. Calculating. His helmet tilted as he scanned the scene.

A beat. Then he stepped off the bike.

Calm. Composed. Hands out.

I trembled. Sobbed. Eyes wide under my helmet.

The cop approached me first—sympathy etched in every line of his tired face. "You alright, miss?"

"Y-yes. I think so. He was following me..." He turned to the rider.

The bastard shrugged, all innocence and fake concern.

But my gut twisted. I knew. He wasn't East Side. Wasn't just some tag along.

His eyes met mine—calm. Cold. Professional. I pulled away before they could ask more questions, twisting the throttle and disappearing into the night.

He wasn't here to kill me. Not yet. He was testing me.

But I smiled as the city swallowed me again. Because this time? I passed.

Cole

I chased him like a shadow. Tight. Relentless. Didn't blink. Didn't breathe.

Whoever he was, he rode like a ghost. Fast. Clean. Mean. Professional. T

hen he turned. One shot—clean and surgical. Boom.

Lucas's front tire exploded. Bike down. Metal skidded. Lucas launched through the air like a sack of bricks. I braced for the sound of bone snapping. Didn't come. Lucas groaned. Sat up. Gave a damn thumbs-up. Idiot.

Didn't matter. I didn't stop. The target was still ahead, slicing through the city like a blade—cutting corners, gunning alleyways.

Whoever this guy was, he wasn't running scared. He was leading me.

Then the sirens lit up the sky. A cop stepped into the road, hand raised.

The rider pulled over—slow, smooth. Engine purred to silence.

I stayed back, visor down. Observing. Calculating. T

he cop leaned in, talking to the rider. Soft tones. Concerned face. Then he waved me off like I was the problem.

I moved to protest. "You don't understand—he's—"

"She," the cop corrected, barely glancing at me.

"She called us in crying. Said you were following her. Sounded terrified." She.

My brain stuttered. I looked again.. Leather jacket. Visor down. Shaking hands clinging to the bars. Shit. That wasn't a man. That was her.

She'd played the part perfectly—fragile, scared, wide-eyed.

But I'd seen the truth on the road. Heard it in the gunshot. Felt it in the way she moved. This wasn't some girl in over her head. This was a wolf in pretty skin.

Riding like death. Shooting like a sniper. Hiding in plain sight.

And now?

She was gone. Vanished into the night like smoke.

But I knew just one thing: She was dangerous.

And I was going to find her again. No matter what it took.

Jaxon

Smoke still hung in the air, thick and oily.

The scent of burning rubber clawed at my nose as I slowed the bike, boots crunching over shattered glass.

Headlights flickered against a dented sedan—its rear end caved in like a soda can.

And sprawled beside the wreck like a crime scene extra was Lucas's bike.

Or what was left of it.

Bent frame. Broken spokes. One wheel had detached completely and was still spinning a few metres away like it hadn't gotten the memo.

"Jesus fucking Christ," I muttered, cutting the engine and dismounting fast.

"Lucas?!" Movement. A groan. Then, from behind the crumpled hood of the car, he sat up. Sat up. Helmet crooked, faceplate cracked, but grinning like a bastard.

"Sup," he rasped, wincing as he gave me a casual little wave.

I stared at him, slack-jawed. "How are you not dead?"

He shrugged. "Helmet."

"Helmet?" I stepped closer, scanning him.

"Your bike's in more pieces than my last relationship."

"Yeah, but I'm not. So technically, I win."

"Technically," I muttered, yanking his busted visor off.

"You look like you got hit by God's own flyswatter."

He laughed—and immediately winced, clutching his ribs. "Hurts to exist. Pretty sure my spine's arguing with my kidneys."

I was checking his limbs for breaks when a second bike rolled up fast, tires skidding slightly as it stopped. Cole. Of course.

He strolled over like he was late for brunch, popping his helmet off with one hand and sunglasses still on under it—the fucker.

He looked at the wreck. Then at Lucas. Then at me. "Well, this looks bad."

"No shit," I snapped, gesturing at the mangled metal massacre that used to be Lucas's ride.

Cole walked around the wreck slowly, hands in pockets.

"Damn, man. You really let her blow you off your bike like a goddamn bug on a windshield?"

"He shot my tire, Cole."

"She sniped it," Cole corrected.

"It was surgical. That girl's got aim." I raised a brow.

"Girl?"

"Yeah," I said, glancing toward the direction she vanished into.

"Apparently we've been chasing a she the whole time."

Cole let out a low whistle, looking impressed.

"Well, now I'm in love."

"Back of the line," Lucas grunted from the pavement.

I sighed, looking back at the scene. One downed bike. One wounded idiot. One psychopath with a motorbike and a Glock out there somewhere.

This wasn't over. Hell, it was just getting started.

20

Ashes and Wine

Riley

My Mind – Yebba

I opened the door and froze.

Standing there were two very familiar faces—Detective Monroe and Officer Peters, the same duo who'd handled Sophie's case two years ago.

Or more accurately, the ones who'd fumbled Sophie's case and then left me with a file full of "not enough evidence" and sorry for your loss.

My stomach twisted, but I masked it behind a carefully neutral expression. I leaned against the door frame, arms crossing in a show of disinterest I'd perfected by now.

"What do you want?" I asked, voice flat.

"Unless this is about finally solving my sister's murder, I don't have time for this."

Monroe exchanged a glance with Peters, and immediately I knew this wasn't a courtesy call.

Her face was more serious than I remembered—less guarded, more... tense. "Miss Morgan," she said, "we're here to inform you of a significant development."

I raised a brow and tilted my head, letting just a bit of sarcasm slip into my tone. "Oh? What is it? Did someone trip over a clue two years late?"

Peters stepped forward, clearing his throat like he was about to deliver a eulogy. “We thought you’d want to know... the East Side Crew has been completely wiped out.”

For a moment, I went still. Perfectly blank. One heartbeat. Two. Then I let my jaw drop.

“What?” I whispered, injecting just the right amount of trembling into my voice.

“They’re... gone?” Monroe nodded slowly.

“Yes. Their main base was destroyed in a coordinated attack. No survivors. We’re still investigating who was behind it, but it was... surgical. Not random.”

I gripped the door frame, letting my knees buckle slightly as I slid down, hand flying to my mouth like I’d just been punched in the gut. My eyes stung—not with tears, but with effort.

The emotion had to look real. Raw. “Oh my God,” I choked out.

“You mean... the people who killed Sophie... they’re gone?” Peters knelt beside me, his face a strange mix of sympathy and confusion, like he didn’t expect this reaction.

“Yes, Miss Morgan. It’s over. They won’t hurt anyone else.” I nodded slowly, tears sliding down my cheeks like I’d rehearsed them.

And I had—just not for this audience. I’d waited two years to hear those words. Two years of silence. Two years of rage. Two years of preparing, planning, and finally executing. And now?

I got to sit here and perform grief while the world handed me closure like it had fallen from the sky.

“I... I can’t believe it,” I sobbed, my voice cracking on cue.

“After everything they did, they’re just... gone?” Monroe crouched beside me, her voice gentle. “

We know this doesn’t bring Sophie back, but—” I cut her off with a shaking hand, dabbing at my face.

“It means everything,” I said softly. “It means the world to me.” I let the silence sit for a beat, like I was collecting myself. T hen I looked up, wide-eyed and trembling. "Do you... do you know who did it?"

Monroe shook her head. "Not yet. Whoever it was covered their tracks well. This wasn't amateur work. It was personal." I swallowed hard, letting the faintest smile tug at my lips before I killed it. "

Someone who hated them as much as I did," I whispered.

I wrapped my arms around my knees, curling in like I was trying to hold myself together. The tears slowed. The breathing evened out. I let myself look fragile. Because it was easier to believe a woman mourning her sister than suspect one who burned an empire to the ground.

Peters rested a hand on my shoulder. "If we find anything else, we'll let you know. But for now... you can rest easy knowing they're gone." I nodded, biting my lip, giving them the kind of look that said thank you for saving me even though I was the one who'd saved myself.

"Thank you," I whispered. "For telling me."

They both stood. Monroe gave a tight nod. "Take care, Miss Morgan."

The second the door clicked shut behind them, I locked it, leaned against it—and smiled.

Not a soft smile. Not a sad one. A slow, wicked grin that crept across my face like smoke.

I wiped the tears from my cheeks, shook out my hands, and exhaled. "They won't hurt anyone else," I repeated under my breath, voice dripping with satisfaction.

"No, they won't." I glanced at my reflection in the cracked mirror by the door, adjusting my expression back to something sweet. Harmless. Believable.

I had fooled them completely. "Rest easy?" I scoffed softly, brushing a tear from my chin with the back of my hand. "Please. I'll sleep like a fucking baby."

I didn't head to the bedroom right away. I stood in the living room like a ghost, the weight of what had just happened pressing into my chest. The silence was suffocating. The kind that didn't comfort—it judged. Eventually, I turned down the hallway and pushed open the door to my room.

Dust and time greeted me like old friends.

The air was stale, the kind that clung to your skin, heavy with memories. I went straight for the closet. Back corner. Bottom shelf. Behind a box of old boots and a stack of notebooks I never read.

The bottle was still there. Wrapped in a ratty, half-torn brown paper bag, like I'd tried to hide it from myself. I pulled it out slowly, fingers brushing the label. Deep red. Expensive, too—well, expensive for me. I'd bought it the day Sophie got accepted into her program. Told her we'd open it when she graduated.

She'd rolled her eyes and said she wanted something sparkly, not "whatever moody red you're obsessed with."

I'd told her it was grown-up and dramatic. She'd called it "snooty juice."

We'd laughed. I sat on the edge of the bed and stared at the bottle for a moment. My thumb traced the label like it might rewrite time.

I'd kept it all this time. Not because I thought she'd come back. But because some small, bitter part of me couldn't let go of the idea that something might still be worth celebrating.

Well. Here we are. I cracked the seal and twisted off the cork. No ceremony. No glass. Just me and the bottle and the past.

I raised it slightly in the air. "To you, Soph," I said quietly. "My favourite pain in the ass." I took a long drink. It tasted expensive. Bitter. Heavy. Just like everything else in my life.

"They're gone," I muttered, tilting the bottle, staring at the dark red swirl inside.

"Every last one of them. The men who hurt you. The ones who laughed when I cried. They're nothing now. Not even bones."

I leaned back against the headboard, dragging my knees up and holding the bottle against my chest. "I thought it'd feel better." It didn't. It just felt... quiet.

Like the world had finally stopped screaming, but now all I could hear was the echo of her laughter in a room she never got to grow old in.

I looked around at the dust, the forgotten hoodie on the chair, the dreams we shelved that never got unpacked.

"I kept this for when you finished your degree," I whispered, shaking the bottle gently.

"Now I'm drinking it alone in a war zone I built." Another long pull. "I don't know what comes next." I stared at the ceiling, my throat tight.

"I got revenge. I burned everything down for you. But I'm still here. Still broken. Still breathing. What the hell am I supposed to do with that?" No answer. Just silence and the slow, steady burn of red wine in my veins.

For the first time since the warehouse burned, I felt something that wasn't rage. I felt empty. And that scared me more than anything.

21

The Raccoon with Military Training

Jaxon

You Should See Me in a Crown – Billie Eilish

The meeting room buzzed like a beehive with a caffeine addiction.

Screens flickered with photos, maps, surveillance loops—all orbiting around the East Side Crew's flaming exit from the mortal plane.

It wasn't sloppy. It wasn't random. It was the opposite. Clean. Surgical. Intentional.

Someone hadn't just taken them out. Someone had studied them—dissected them—and then lit the match like it was personal.

And dead in the middle of the chaos?

Killian. Arms crossed. Jaw locked. Staring at the screen like someone had just insulted both his suit and his mother.

One by one, faces scrolled past.

Eddie "The Blade" Torres.

Marie Langston.

Darius Cole.

All scum, all scorched. Then... her. Riley Morgan.

The temperature in the room dropped ten degrees.

Killian's stare landed on her photo—and stuck. Too long. Too tense. First clue. Second? The vein twitching in his jaw.

I leaned back in my chair, arms crossed. "You know her, don't you?" He didn't blink. Just flicked those eyes at me like I'd asked whether he flossed daily.

"I've met her," he said. Low. Like maybe it was technically classified.

I raised a brow. "What kind of met? Like bumped into her at a bar? Or like... cried at her sister's funeral?"

His jaw tightened. "The night her sister died. She is just a grieving girl."

"Right." I let that sink in.

"And now that grieving girl might've blown a gang off the face of the earth."

He didn't answer. Just stared at her face like it owed him an apology.

"She had nothing to do with it," he said flatly. Which, of course, meant he wasn't sure at all. I leaned in, staring at the screen.

"You sure? Because she ghosted for two years, then reappears with alibis too clean, arms too toned, and eyes that say I've made peace with murder."

His silence screamed louder than a confession.

"She didn't disappear, man," I continued.

"She trained. Probably joined a gym with punching bags and trauma-bonded with explosives. Hell, she probably has a burner phone just for motivational TED Talks."

Killian snapped then. "Drop it. Find facts. Not ghost stories."

Then he turned and stormed out. Yup. Totally normal reaction. Not suspicious at all. I sat in the hum of machines and suspicion, staring at Riley's photo. She looked like someone who could make you fall in love and stab you with your own fork before breakfast. Hard to tell which came first.

I turned to Lucas, who hadn't lifted his head once. Just fingers and caffeine and key clacks.

"Dig into her," I said.

"Real deep. If she ordered takeout in the last six months, I want names, addresses, and whether she tipped."

Lucas nodded, still typing. "Already on it."

Minutes passed in the click and hum of intel gathering. Then Lucas froze. "Well, that's interesting."

I leaned in. "Talk to me."

"She's been active. Quiet, but consistent. Underground forums.

Anonymous networks. Ties to weapons dealers, demolitions experts, a burner phone trail thicker than a cartel accountant's paranoia."

I blinked. "So, vengeance with a LinkedIn?"

Lucas snorted. "If she didn't pull the trigger, she wrote the goddamn playbook."

I stood, heart hammering a little harder now. Riley Morgan wasn't a name anymore. She was a reckoning. And something told me? She wasn't finished.

Killian

No. No fucking way. I stared at the photo on the screen, heart pounding like I'd just taken a punch to the ribs. Riley Morgan.

Her name, her face—burned into a digital file like any other suspect, but I couldn't breathe.

She wasn't a suspect. She couldn't be. Not her. But the longer I looked, the harder it became to lie to myself.

My mouth was dry. My hands curled into fists at my sides, knuckles aching from the tension.

She was a stranger.

I didn't know her. Not really. But that night— The hospital. Her sisters death.

The chaos. The blood. The fucking stench of antiseptic and unanswered prayers.

I remember walking through the corridor, trying to keep it together, trying to stay cold.

Then I saw her. Sitting there like she'd already died too. Face slack. Eyes hollow. Shaking like her bones were cracking under the weight of silence.

No one was with her. No one even looked at her. I should've kept walking. But something made me stop. She looked up, and something in me paused. Her grief wasn't loud. It was quiet. Caged. Dangerous. I don't know why I sat beside her. I don't do that. I don't comfort. But I did.

I remember the way she clutched my jacket like she didn't even realise she was doing it. How small she felt pressed against me.

How still she was. Like she'd already made a decision. She never said a word. Just cried into my shoulder like I was a wall, not a person. And I let her.

She was a stranger. I left. I forgot. That's what I told myself. But I didn't forget. Not really.

And now... I'm staring at her photo two years later, and the silence in my head is screaming.

Riley Morgan. No prior training. No red flags. Disappeared for two years, and now she's suddenly orbiting the wreckage of a gang that got wiped off the map like a goddamn surgical strike?

I told Jaxon she wasn't involved. Told myself the same. But my gut twists every time I say it. Because deep down, I know better.

She didn't fall apart after her sister died. She became something else. Something sharp. And I'd held her. I'd felt it.

Even back then. No. There's no way she did this. ...But if she did? I'm not sure I want to stop her.

Jaxon

Tailing Riley Morgan was like trying to follow a raccoon that got Navy SEAL training.

She didn't walk—she glided.

Controlled. Intentional. Always just ahead. Twenty minutes in. No phone. No purse. Just black jeans, a hoodie, and what I assumed were murder boots.

I followed in a piece-of-shit sedan from our side lot, cold fries in the passenger seat and a prayer in my back pocket.

"Real subtle, Jax," I muttered as she glanced over her shoulder.

She didn't see me. I hoped.

She slipped into a narrow alley. Of course she did.

This woman had side quests I wasn't briefed on. I parked, got out, and followed on foot.

Sticking to the shadows like I was auditioning for Most Likely to Get Mugged by Mistake.

The alley? Empty.

"She Houdini'd me," I whispered.

Then—footsteps. Above.

I looked up. There she was. Climbing a fire escape like she was strolling up a runway. Not rushed. Not frantic. Just routine.

She paused at the top, pulled a black duffel from behind a loose vent.

Suspicious didn't begin to cover it.

I ducked behind a dumpster that smelled like expired secrets.

Peered out.

She unzipped the bag. Peeked inside. Zipped it again. Slung it over her shoulder like it weighed nothing. Guns? Bombs? A new identity and a plane ticket to somewhere without laws?

Whatever it was, she moved like someone who'd done this before.

More than once.

She dropped back down with a fluidity that made my knees hurt just watching.

And walked away like she hadn't just retrieved a bag of probable felonies.

I followed, careful.

She didn't look back. Maybe she hadn't seen me. Or maybe she wanted me to think that.

She stopped outside an old auto shop. Rusted signage. Closed hours ago. Not a light in sight.

She knocked—three quick taps, one slow. Like a code. Door opened. Grizzled guy. Mechanic-turned-mercenary, if I had to guess.

She stepped inside.

I waited a beat, then snapped a photo of the building.

"If she doesn't come out in fifteen, I call Lucas," I muttered. "Tell him I followed a possibly unhinged avenging angel into a murder den. Again."

"...And if I die, someone better tell Killian he's full of shit."

22

Nightingale

Lucas

Run for Your Life – The Siege

I stayed behind in Central Command after the others had cleared out.

The room was silent now, except for the low, steady hum of the monitors, still glowing with static light and half-finished truths.

Footage of the East Side Crew's funeral pyre flickered on loop—chaos, smoke, fire.

And through it all: a single figure, moving like they were the one who wrote the script.

I sat in the dark, jaw tight, fingers twitching over the keyboard.

Then—rewind. Play. There they were again. The silhouette. The movement. Fluid. Purposeful. Too graceful.

I leaned in, elbow braced on the desk, chin in hand, watching the figure slip through fire and wreckage like smoke.

Dodging. Disarming. Dismantling bodies with an elegance that didn't belong to any merc, soldier, or street fighter I'd ever studied.

It wasn't just trained. It was art.

Ballet.

The thought came uninvited. A whisper in my head I wanted to dismiss but couldn't. I froze the footage mid-motion. Watched the figure spin—avoid a blow—and sweep a man's legs from under him with perfect balance.

The follow-through? Clean. Efficient. Choreographed.

And then it hit me. Hard. Unavoidable. My sister. I could still see her, years ago, centre stage in one of her endless recitals.

Moving like every step was made of muscle memory and divine timing. Controlled. Poised. Disciplined to the bone.

The figure on the screen moved the same way. I rewound again. Watched it twice.

Then three times. This wasn't some vigilante with luck and rage on their side.

This was deliberate. Planned. Rehearsed. And suddenly, only one name made sense.

Riley Morgan. I yanked up her file, heart pounding.

Two years off the grid. Sister dead. Case cold. Motive? Obvious.

But this? This level of skill—where had it come from? I dug deeper. Harder. Buried beneath the noise: Dance background. Twelve years. Classical ballet.

I sat back. Exhaled like I'd been gut-punched. Holy shit.

It was her. Not just the motive. Not just the history. The movement. The discipline. The poise. That wasn't coincidence. It was Riley.

She didn't just want revenge. She trained for it. She turned grief into precision. Heartbreak into a weapon. And no one—none of us—saw it coming.

I grabbed my phone and dialled Killian.

He picked up on the second ring. "Yeah?"

"It's Lucas," I said, keeping my voice steady.

"I think I've found her." Pause.

"Found who?" "Riley Morgan." I swallowed.

"She took out the East Side Crew. And Killian—she's using ballet. That's how she moves. That's how she fights. It's all there."

The silence on the other end was sharp enough to cut steel.

"She's not just some pissed-off victim. She engineered this." Another beat.

Then Killian's voice dropped. "Where is she now?"

"I don't know yet. But I'm digging. She's been hiding in plain sight. And we missed it."

"Find out what she's after," Killian said, cold and clipped.

"If she's working alone. If this ends here... or if it's just the beginning." I nodded, even though he couldn't see me.

"I'll get back to you." The line went dead.

I sat in the glow of her frozen frame, staring into eyes that no longer held grief—they held resolve. This wasn't just a ghost story. This was a reckoning. And I was going to follow it straight into the fire.

As soon as the call ended, I turned back to the screen, heart thudding. I didn't sit—I dropped. Like my bones had given out beneath the weight of what I'd just confirmed. The room around me was all quiet hum and flickering light.

Everyone else had gone home. I hadn't moved in hours. I cracked my neck. Flexed my fingers. "Alright, Morgan," I muttered. "Let's see how deep this rabbit hole really goes."

Started with the basics.

Socials. Public records. Activity logs. Dead. All of it. Like checking a corpse for a pulse. She'd vanished. But not without leaving a trail. Everyone does. So I dropped into the dark. Deeper nets. Encrypted forums. The kind of places where names are fake, ethics are flexible, and silence means you're dangerous. And there—buried under proxies and digital noise—I found something. Nightingale.

Not her name. But it felt like her. Every post. Every breadcrumb.

Nightingale didn't sell hits. Didn't do this for money. Nightingale did projects. Precise. Cold. Personal.

I traced the handle across forums: sabotage discussions, infiltration models, blueprint schematics of places that no longer existed.

Burner accounts. Multi-layered routing.

Dead drops and scramblers.

She was careful. Too careful.

But I was better. And I was angry. And she had no idea how long I could sit in front of a monitor with nothing but cold coffee and obsession to keep me upright.

I broke through one of her traps—barely. She'd coded in a self-wipe trigger. Almost got me. Almost.

"Sloppy," I muttered.

"You getting tired, Morgan?" Then I found it—coordinates. Timestamps. Movement patterns synced with former East Side Crew safe houses.

She scouted them. Timed them. Prepped them. Erased them.

And she did it alone. Jesus. I stared at the map on screen, each red dot a grave she'd dug herself.

And the line they formed?

It wasn't random. It was a path. Leading somewhere. A final ping. Old security cam footage. Three hours ago. Riley Morgan. Hoodie. Backpack. Gloves. Walking with intent. Toward the outskirts.

My phone buzzed.

A message from Killian: Update?

I typed fast. Found her trail. She's headed toward the old rail yard. This wasn't just about revenge. She's not done.

Killian replied instantly: Then we follow her. Don't let her out of your sight.

I nodded. To no one. To the ghost in the machine. Grabbed my gear. Pulled my hoodie up. Time to move.

Because Riley Morgan wasn't just grief personified. She was the storm we should've seen coming. And now? I was either going to stop her— Or be the next thing she buried.

23

Graveyard Games and Tactical Thirst

Riley

Cherry Bomb – The Runaways

I sat cross-legged in front of Sophie's grave, elbows on my knees, chewing a sandwich that barely qualified as food.

Mayo. Again. Disrespectful levels of it.

"Yeah, I know," I muttered, eyeing the headstone.

"You'd roll your eyes at this whole scene. Daisies, basic sandwich, emotional monologue—I've basically become the sad main character in an indie film."

I brushed a few petals off the bouquet I'd left, tapping my fingers against the cool granite.

"I'm not gonna lie... it still sucks. You not being here. It's quiet now, and I thought that'd help. No more East Side scumbags lurking in alleys. No more flashbacks when I close my eyes." I let out a slow breath. "But the quiet? It's loud in a different way."

I picked at the crust of the sandwich and dropped a piece near the grave for the birds. "So... I'm thinking about dancing again."

I waited for the judgement I knew would never come. "I know. Sounds insane. My joints creak, muscles ache in places I forgot existed, and I haven't stretched properly in two years.

But I found a studio down the block. Wood floors, mirrored wall, smells like dust and potential." I smiled faintly. "Might rent it. Try a few moves. Nothing fancy. No spotlight. Just me and maybe a speaker that doesn't suck."

I stared at her name in the stone. "You used to say dancing made me lighter," I whispered.

"But I think you were wrong. It made me real. Not just someone surviving—someone moving." I blinked, gave a lopsided shrug.

"Anyway. We'll see. No promises. I've got a new haircut, clean jeans, and a growing existential crisis. Might as well throw pirouettes into the mix."

I dragged a hand through my hair, gaze drifting across the rows of headstones—and froze.

There was a man standing thirty feet off. Too clean. Too still. Hands in his pockets. Staring at a grave like it owed him something. "...You expecting company, Soph?" I murmured.

He crouched to place a flower. Real, not plastic. But his posture? Too deliberate. His eyes were scanning. Watching. My fingers curled into my jeans.

"I don't recognise him," I muttered. "But that doesn't mean he's not a problem." He hadn't looked my way. Not yet. But every part of him screamed trained. Law-adjacent. Trouble-adjacent.

Then, another figure appeared. This one moved differently. He had a limp—subtle but practised, like he'd had time to adjust. Most people wouldn't notice. But I wasn't most people.

My eyes narrowed. My pulse spiked. No. It couldn't be. Flashback—bike tires screeching, gun in my hand, shot fired, body airborne, helmet smacking asphalt.

I'd yeeted him off his ride like a fly hitting a windshield. He should not be vertical.

"Oh, you've got to be kidding me," I muttered.

"There's no way. You shouldn't be walking without a cane. Or a priest."

But there he was. Limping. Breathing. Talking to Broody No-Name like they were casing the goddamn cemetery.

Cockroach Biker lived. And now he was lurking.

My fingers twitched against the grass. This wasn't a coincidence. They weren't here to mourn. They were here for me.

Grave visit? Cancelled. I leaned back, casual as hell, and waited. Game on.

Jaxon

I heard the uneven steps before I saw him. Lucas hobbled up beside me like the world's angriest ninja, jaw tight, eyes sharp.

He didn't say anything. Just stood next to me like we were here to mourn someone we didn't know.

"Look at you," I murmured, eyes forward.

"Back on your feet and only semi-crippled. She'd be proud." Lucas exhaled slowly.

"She hasn't moved." "She blinked once, I think."

Riley Morgan sat cross-legged by her sister's grave, half a sandwich gone, looking somewhere between in mourning and existentially snacky.

"She's not armed," I noted.

"She's never armed," Lucas muttered.

"Doesn't stop her." Fair.

"She's talking to the grave."

"Pretty sure she's monologuing," I said.

"Real main character energy. If she starts slow clapping, I'm leaving."

Lucas stayed quiet. Watching. "She doesn't know who we are," he said finally.

"No. But she knows we're watching. And she's choosing not to react."

Which was worse. "She's... kind of pretty," I added, because I have no internal filter and poor survival instincts.

Lucas turned his head slowly. "Don't."

"I'm just saying—she looks like she burns buildings by day and journals by candlelight at night."

"She blew my tire out with a pistol going fifty through a construction zone."

"Which is objectively hot." We went quiet again.

Riley stretched her legs, twisted the cap back on her water bottle. Her gaze swept the cemetery, casual but calculated.

"She's checking escape routes," Lucas muttered.

"Yup."

"She's scouting."

"Definitely."

"And eating a sandwich while she does it."

I sighed. "That's what pisses me off. She makes it look easy."

Riley

They thought they were subtle. They were not. I didn't look. Not directly. But I'd clocked them instantly—especially the limping one. That bastard had my bullet to thank for his new gait. I leaned toward Sophie's headstone. "Soph, I think I'm being stalked," I whispered. "By two men who look like Calvin Klein models and probably murder people recreationally." I chewed thoughtfully. "They're tall. One's got the haunted ex-military thing going. The other's limping but still somehow hot. What does that say about me?" I tilted my head. "I'm pretty sure I have a female boner right now."

No lightning struck. Just vibes. "Sophie, you'd be judging me so hard right now. But you'd also call dibs on one and roast me for wanting the limpy one." I sipped water. Checked my peripheral. Still watching. Still thinking I hadn't noticed. "Alright," I muttered, brushing a crumb from the stone. "Let's play." I stood slowly, stretched, slung my bag over one shoulder. "Let's see if they follow," I said under my breath. "And maybe... if they survive."

Riley

They thought they were subtle. They were not. I didn't look. Not directly. But I'd clocked them instantly—especially the limping one. That bastard had my bullet to thank for his new gait. I leaned toward Sophie's headstone. "Soph, I think I'm being stalked," I whispered. "By two men who look like Calvin Klein models and probably murder people recreationally." I chewed thoughtfully. "They're tall. One's got the haunted ex-military thing going. The other's limping but still somehow hot. What does that say about me?" I tilted my head. "I'm pretty sure I have a female boner right now."

No lightning struck. Just vibes. "Sophie, you'd be judging me so hard right now. But you'd also call dibs on one and roast me for wanting the limpy one." I sipped water. Checked my peripheral. Still watching. Still thinking I hadn't noticed. "Alright," I muttered, brushing a crumb from the stone. "Let's play." I stood slowly, stretched, slung my bag over one shoulder. "Let's see if they follow," I said under my breath. "And maybe... if they survive."

Jaxon

"She's moving," I whispered.

Lucas straightened. "Finally."

"She patted the grave. That's sweet."

"Or sinister." "She's walking away," I said.

"She's not speeding up."

"She doesn't have to."

"She's baiting us." "Like a Disney villain. With excellent posture." Lucas sighed.

"She's going to disappear."

"She's already halfway there."

We trailed her from a distance. Too far to be threatening. Close enough to lose dignity if she turned and called us out.

And then?

She was gone. "Are you kidding me?" I hissed.

Lucas swore under his breath. I pulled out my phone. "Observation mission my ass."

Riley

I crouched behind a stone angel like a crypt goblin, watching my stalkers bicker in confused frustration.

They spun. Scanned. Glared at each other. I nearly choked laughing.

They were built like Greek tragedies and post-war trauma, pacing like tactical Roombas that had lost signal.

"God, Sophie," I whispered, wiping a tear.

"They're hot and stupid. I'm doomed."

I lobbed a pebble at a sign. CLANG. They jumped. I wheezed.

"You absolute morons," I whispered.

"I could've killed you ten times by now, but here I am, giving myself a horny asthma attack behind a dumpster."

I followed them all the way to their car.

Exactly what I expected: blacked-out SUV, suspiciously clean, parked like it had diplomatic immunity. Big. Imposing. Overcompensating. Just like them.

I smirked, biting my lip as I circled it once, casually trailing my fingers along the driver's side. Tinted windows. Clean finish. Probably detailed weekly. Boring.

Then I pulled out my lipstick—deep red, borderline criminal shade.

The one I only used when I wanted to ruin someone's life or stain a bed sheet.

I leaned in, lips just brushing the cool glass, and kissed the passenger window like it was a cheek I intended to haunt.

The print came out perfect. Bold. Sensual. War paint in kiss form.

Then, still grinning, I twisted the lipstick and scrawled beneath it in looping cursive:

Nice ass. Both of you. 10/10 would stalk again. –X

I stepped back and admired my work. The kiss mark. The writing. The implied chaos. Chef's kiss. From my pocket, I pulled out a single playing card—the Queen of Hearts.

A little bent at the edge. One of Sophie's old deck, still faintly marked with pink nail polish from our last game together.

I slid it carefully under the windshield wiper. Symbolic. Precise. Feminine and fatal.

Let them wonder. Let them stew. Let them know.

"Perfect," I whispered, spinning on my heel and sauntering away like the sexy little plague I am.

"Tactical thighs and no respect for boundaries? This is what you get."

24

Glitter, Guns, and Psychological Warfare

Jaxon

Love Bites (So Do I) – Halestorm

Something was wrong. I knew it the second we turned the corner and saw the SUV. Lucas stopped beside me like his entire system had just blue-screened.

I squinted. "What the hell is that?"

He limped forward, slow and stiff, eyes narrowing at the thing perched on our windshield like it had every right to exist.

He blinked. "It's a... playing card."

I followed, heart already sinking. There it was. The Queen of Hearts. Bent at the corner. Wedged just-so under the wiper. But it wasn't the card that made my stomach flip. It was the message. Written directly on the passenger window, in bright, unmistakable lipstick—not ink, not Sharpie. Lipstick. Deep, dangerous red.

Nice ass. Both of you. 10/10 would stalk again. –X

Beneath it, a lipstick kiss. Perfect. Deliberate. Like she'd pressed her mouth to the glass just to brand it.

I froze. Lucas made a sound that might've been a laugh. Or a death rattle.

"She kissed the glass," I whispered.

"She kissed. The. Glass."

"She also rated our asses," Lucas replied, deadpan.

"We've been... flirt-fucked."

"Flirt-fucked isn't a thing." "It is now."

I circled the SUV like it might offer a logical explanation.

She'd been here. Stalked us. Watched us long enough to walk up to the vehicle, write a note in lipstick, and then vanish.

Lucas just stood there, dead inside.

"She vandalised my life with a Queen of Hearts."

"She left her actual lips on the window."

"And you're aroused, aren't you?" I said nothing. Which was answer enough.

Lucas

There was lipstick on the glass. Actual lipstick. Red. Bold. Untouched by weather, flawless in pressure and intent. And next to it?

The Queen of Hearts. Tucked like a love letter and a landmine.

The cup holder held the card now. I couldn't bring myself to throw it away.

This wasn't surveillance. This was psychological warfare in heels.

"She turned the tail," I muttered, staring at the print. "Tracked us. Got in close. Left a calling card. And a... declaration."

Jaxon looked like he was still trying to reboot his frontal cortex.

I pulled out my phone and called Killian.

He picked up instantly.

"Talk."

"She got to the SUV," I said.

"Left a lipstick message." A pause.

"What kind of message?

" I read it aloud: Nice ass. Both of you. 10/10 would stalk again. –X

Killian didn't speak.

"She was right here," I added.

"Wrote on the glass. With her face."...Send me a photo."

I did. Jaxon glanced at me. "You good?" "No," I said honestly.

"I feel like I just got emotionally undressed by a war goddess with a vendetta and a lip kit."

Killian came back on the line. "She wanted to be seen."

"No," I said.

"She wanted us to know she's always watching. She's not hiding. She's leading us."

Jaxon muttered, "She got in your head."

"She's renting space," I muttered.

"Wallpapered my frontal lobe with crimson kisses and sarcasm."

Killian sighed. "Track her. She's baiting you." Click.

I stared at the window again. At that perfect kiss mark. T

his wasn't panic. This wasn't recklessness. This was seduction—layered over confidence, strategy, and unapologetic dominance.

"She's dangerous," I said aloud

. Jaxon shrugged. "She's hot."

"...Also that."

But deep down, we both knew. She wasn't just flirting. She was issuing a challenge. And we were already hooked.

Killian

The playing card sat in the middle of the table like it knew it had us all by the balls. No one spoke at first. We just... stared.

"She has a sense of humour," Jaxon said finally, voice dry.

Lucas scoffed. "Oh, she's hilarious. She flipped surveillance, got within arm's reach of our SUV, left us a handwritten ass review—and a playing card. Queen of Hearts. Real subtle."

Cole was practically glowing with joy. "I don't care what anyone says. That's iconic behaviour."

"She stalked us," Lucas hissed.

"She didn't just leave a message—she left merchandise. That is villain-level sass."

"Or fan-level," Cole offered, unfazed.

"Depending on the vibe. I mean, she complimented us."

"On our asses." Cole grinned.

"Which, let's be honest, was overdue."

I pinched the bridge of my nose. "We are not here to flirt with the enemy."

Cole leaned forward. "Are we sure she's the enemy? If she wanted to take us out, she could've. We'd be lying in that parking lot with glitter in our wounds."

"She toys with people," Lucas growled.

"She's dangerous."

"She's talented," Jaxon said, reluctantly.

"Disciplined. Calculated."

"And funny," Cole added cheerfully.

Lucas rubbed his face like he was fighting off an aneurysm. "Can someone sedate him, please?"

I cleared my throat, pulling us back to the point.

"Look, whether you're impressed or turned on—" Cole raised a hand. "Can it be both?" "—we need to decide what we're doing when we find her."

That shut them up. For a beat. Then Jaxon said, "Bring her in."

Lucas nodded. "Agree. She's a liability. Knows too much."

Cole tilted his head. "Knows too much... or knows exactly what she's doing?"

I shot him a look. He just shrugged. "I'm saying, anyone who can run rings around us, flirt mid-mission, and pull off tactical lipstick placement—that's someone I'd rather have on our side."

Jaxon muttered, "If she wants to be on a side."

"Maybe she's tired of playing solo," Cole said.

Lucas leaned back in his chair, arms crossed. "You want to recruit the glitter assassin."

"I'm saying we consider our options before we shoot her in the face," Cole replied.

"She played us," I reminded them.

"That's not something we reward." "But it is something we study," Lucas said grimly. "Because she made fools out of us. We either learn how... or she does it again."

I nodded slowly. That was the part that mattered.

"She's not reckless," I said.

"She's patient. Smart. She waited until we were comfortable.

Then made her move." "So..." Jaxon asked, "what's the call?"

I let the silence hang. Then, quietly: "We bring her in. We see what she wants. And if she's as good as she thinks she is... maybe we use that."

Cole smirked. "So it's settled. We capture the hot glitter-gremlin and see if she wants to be one of us."

Lucas groaned. "I hate everything about this plan."

Jaxon chuckled. "You hate how impressed you are."

"I am not impressed," Lucas snapped.

"You're still covered in glitter." Lucas looked down at his sleeve. "I am going to burn this jacket."

I leaned back and stared at the playing card again.

She'd gotten into our heads. Now we just had to figure out what she wanted—and whether she could be turned. And if not? Well. We'd see how long the lipstick held up under fire.

Riley

I sat cross-legged on a grimy rooftop across from Central Command, earbuds in, tablet on my lap, slurping a suspiciously blue slushie like it was my own private soap opera.

"—she left us a note. A bow. Flirted with us during recon—" I smirked, biting down on my straw. Damn right I did.

The comms tap was still holding strong, piping the whole debrief straight into my ears. Every word.

Every meltdown. Four very capable men unravelling in real-time. Honestly?

Best entertainment I'd had in years.

"They're spiralling, Soph," I whispered, glancing up at the cloudy sky.

"And I haven't even started." I imagined her rolling her eyes. Riley, behave.

"Behave?" I snorted, voice low like I was sharing secrets.

"Have you seen them? They look like they were grown in a military-grade thirst trap lab."

Lucas was already pacing—voice tight, energy spiky. Smart boy. Pretty mouth. Great shoulders.

Jaxon? All calm and competent until someone pressed the wrong button. Then that growl came out, and whew. I made a note to push it soon.

Killian? Jesus. Didn't even raise his voice. Just sat in silence like God was loading a new boss fight. Daddy issues: activated.

And Cole? That man needed to be supervised. Not by HR—by a priest.

I licked slushie off my spoon and sighed. "They're not ready, Soph. They thought I was done. Thought I was grieving in silence like some tragic little flower." I tilted my head back, smiling bitterly. "But you and I both know I don't do quiet. I do fire. Chaos. Glittery vengeance."

Lucas muttered something over the feed—something about me being insane.

"Maybe I am," I whispered. "But I'm motivated."

They had no idea what was coming. This was just the warm-up. Flirty psychological warfare with a splash of unresolved trauma.

"I'm going to drive them absolutely mad," I muttered, tossing my empty slushie cup into the vent shaft.

"One by one. Strip them bare—mentally, emotionally, sexually—then walk away with their pride in my back pocket."

I leaned back, grinning like the little chaos goblin I was.

"This is for you, Soph," I said softly, almost tender.

"You always wanted me to dance again."

Then I opened my tablet, eyes gleaming, and started drafting my next move. Something bold.

Something unnecessary.

Something involving temporary tattoos and a selfie on Cole's motorcycle. God help them. Because I sure as hell wouldn't.

25

BadBitch.exe

Riley

Black Sheep – Metric / Brie Larson version

I'd spent the last week systematically tormenting them.

Not metaphorically.

Literally.

A glitter bomb rigged above their locker room ceiling.

A protein bar labelled For Your Trouble Thighs left on the hood of their SUV.

Hacking into their comms mid-briefing just to blast Careless Whisper and listen to the absolute chaos that followed.

I even slipped a fake lead into their system convincing enough to send Lucas into a caffeine-fuelled coding spiral for eight straight hours.

Subtle chaos.

Targeted psychological warfare.

Honestly? Art.

Watching them slowly unravel had become one of my favourite hobbies.

But today wasn't about taunts.

Or chase scenes.

Or leaving lipstick marks on classified equipment like some deeply unstable phantom menace.

Today was for me.

Today, I danced.

I slipped into the rented studio just after sunrise, before the city fully woke up.

Before my brain had time to remember grief existed.

The room was empty except for mirrored walls, battered speakers, and polished wooden floors scarred with old scratches.

Perfect.

I didn't need music.

My body remembered the rhythm on its own.

Barefoot, dressed in black leggings and a cropped tank, I stood in the centre of the studio staring at my reflection.

There she was.

The girl I used to be.

Controlled.

Sharp.

Still standing despite everything.

I exhaled slowly.

"Morning, Soph," I murmured quietly into the silence. "You're gonna love this one."

And then I moved.

No choreography.

No structure.

Just instinct.

Every spin, every sharp turn, every breath felt like reclaiming something stolen from me years ago.

I wasn't just violence.

I wasn't just revenge.

I was still art too.

Grace wrapped around fury.

And naturally—because apparently my brain couldn't function normally anymore—my thoughts drifted toward them.

Lucas with his nervous energy and sharp mouth.

Jaxon built like human blunt force trauma.

Cole flirting with literally anything that breathed.

And Killian...

Jesus Christ.

Killian looked at people the way storms probably looked at coastal towns before destroying them.

One glance from that man and my self-preservation instincts filed formal complaints.

I spun hard across the floor, laughing breathlessly at myself.

“I swear to God, Soph,” I muttered to my reflection, “if you were here right now, you’d tell me to stop developing crushes on mercenaries and seek professional psychiatric assistance.”

The grin slipped from my face slowly as the movement stopped.

Silence flooded the studio again.

Sweat cooled against my skin.

And underneath all the chaos and flirting and revenge...

I felt good. Actually good.

Which honestly felt suspicious at this point.

Because part of me—the deeply unwell part—wanted to walk directly into their headquarters, steal another hoodie, and see which one snapped first.

Possibly all four.

The thought alone nearly made me laugh again.

Instead, I crossed the room and picked up the small black box waiting in the corner.

Inside sat a single black glove still dusted faintly with glitter from last week’s locker room incident.

Beneath it rested a sealed envelope.

On top, I placed a note written carefully in red lipstick.

Let’s dance. – X

I tied the ribbon neatly and smiled to myself.

They thought the game was ending.

Cute.

This was barely the opening act.

Killian

The package appeared in the middle of our operations room without triggering a single alarm.

No camera footage. No entry logs. Nothing.

Just a matte black box sitting neatly on the conference table like it had materialised out of thin air.

Which, knowing her, honestly wasn't impossible.

We all stared at it in silence.

Cole leaned forward first.

"Okay," he said carefully. "Question. Is this a threat or foreplay?"

Lucas didn't even glance up from his tablet.

"It's a security breach," he snapped. "There are no motion detections. No camera interference. No digital trace whatsoever."

Jaxon folded his arms.

"She's taunting us."

"She's enjoying herself," I corrected quietly.

Because she was.

The ribbon alone practically radiated smugness.

A sticky note sat tucked beneath the bow.

Let's dance. – X

I exhaled slowly.

"Scan it."

"Already done," Lucas replied tightly. "No explosives. Just fabric."

Cole opened the box with dramatic caution anyway, peeling back the lid like he expected it to explode in his face.

Inside sat one black glove dusted with glitter.

Jaxon stared at it flatly.

"Is she declaring war through arts and crafts?"

"She's mocking us," I muttered.

"Or distracting us," Lucas cut in sharply.

His entire posture stiffened suddenly as red warning lights flashed across his tablet screen.

"Unauthorized internal movement."

Every instinct in my body sharpened instantly. My gun was already drawn before he finished speaking.

We moved through the corridors fast, weapons ready, pulse steady.

And then we stopped dead. Because she was already inside. Sprawled across our lounge couch like she owned the building. One leg hanging lazily over the armrest.

Black leggings. Loose shirt.

And— Jaxon blinked slowly.

“Is that my hoodie?”

Cole looked genuinely offended.

“She stole my whisky.” Riley raised the glass toward us casually.

“Hi, boys.”

I kept my weapon trained on her. She didn’t even flinch.

“Your security system was adorable,” she said smoothly. “Very beginner hacker chic.”

Lucas looked moments away from cardiac arrest.

“You broke into a black site.”

“Correction,” Riley replied. “I wandered into a black site. Huge difference.”

Jaxon remained silent, studying her carefully. Cole, meanwhile, looked one inconvenience away from proposing marriage. I stepped closer slowly.

“Why are you here?”

For the first time since we entered the room, her expression shifted slightly.

Still amused.

But sharper now.

More serious underneath it.

“Because I think we want the same thing,” she said quietly.

Then she stood. Slowly. Deliberately. The tension in the room tightened immediately.

“And,” she added with a crooked smile, “because I wanted to see who’d crack first.”

She stopped directly in front of me. Close enough that I could smell smoke and whisky clinging faintly to her skin.

"You did well," she murmured.

I didn't move. Didn't trust myself to. Because Riley Morgan was dangerous in a way bullets never were.

Beautiful. Chaotic. Completely unpredictable.

And worst of all?

She knew exactly what she was doing to us.

Riley

The whisky burned pleasantly going down. Or maybe that was just satisfaction.

Either way, I made direct eye contact with all four of them while I drank it because subtlety had never really been my thing.

Cole looked fully prepared to ruin his own life voluntarily.

Lucas still seemed personally offended by my existence.

Jaxon watched me with the exhausted expression of a man realising his favourite hoodie was never coming home.

And Killian...

Killian watched me like he was trying to decide whether to handcuff me or kiss me.

Honestly?

Both had potential.

"I've been thinking," I said casually, setting the glass down. "You boys aren't terrible at your jobs."

Cole pressed a hand dramatically to his chest.

"She compliments us at last."

"Don't get emotional," I warned. "It's embarrassing for everyone involved."

I leaned back against the table.

"You've got resources. Training. Connections." I tilted my head slightly.

"But you've also got blind spots."

Killian's gaze sharpened instantly. "What are you proposing?"

"Maybe we stop trying to outmanipulate each other for five minutes and work together instead."

Lucas narrowed his eyes suspiciously. "And why would we trust you?"

I smiled sweetly. "You absolutely shouldn't."

That earned four very different reactions.

Perfect. I tugged Jaxon's hoodie sleeves down further over my hands.

Still smelled like him. Still unfairly comforting.

Then I grabbed the whisky bottle by the neck and headed for the exit.

"Think about it, boys," I called over my shoulder. "You know where to find me."

A pause. "Well. No you don't. But I'll find you."

By the time they reached the windows, I was already outside swinging onto my motorbike. Black paint glittered beneath the streetlights like liquid midnight. I revved the engine once purely for dramatic effect before saluting them with the whisky bottle and tearing out into the street.

If they were smart, they'd accept my offer.

If they weren't?

At least I still had the hoodie.

Killian

Recognition hit me slowly. First the eyes. Then the posture.

Then the memory slammed into place hard enough to knock the breath from my lungs.

Holy shit. It was her. Not someone I truly knew.

Just a stranger I'd stood beside once during the worst night of her life.

The hospital smelled like antiseptic and grief that night.

She'd sat beside Sophie's bed gripping her sister's hand tightly enough to hurt herself, staring blankly ahead like if she looked away for even a second, Sophie might disappear completely.

But Sophie had died anyway.

I remembered the tremor in Riley's hands afterward. The hollow look in her eyes. The way she'd gone completely silent. I remembered staying because leaving her alone somehow felt wrong. Neither of us spoke.

I never expected to see her again.

And now she was here wearing Jaxon's hoodie, stealing our alcohol, breaking into black sites, and turning our entire operation upside down like some kind of glitter-covered apocalypse.

Jaxon muttered darkly beside me. "That was my favourite hoodie."

By the time we reached the window, she was already disappearing into traffic on a black motorbike that scattered streetlight reflections like shattered stars.

I watched until she vanished completely.

Because Riley Morgan had done something almost impossible.

She'd dismantled the organisation responsible for Sophie's death entirely on her own.

Which meant one thing very clearly: If Riley ever decided we were enemies instead of allies...

We wouldn't survive it.

26

Permission Denied, Bitch

Riley

You Don't Own Me – Grace ft. G-Eazy

The second I kicked the door shut behind me, I tossed the half-empty whisky bottle onto the counter, spun my laptop around, and dropped into my chair like the feral gremlin I was.

"Showtime," I whispered.

A few keystrokes later, the live feed from the Vipers' internal system blinked onto my screen.

Beautiful.

The payload I'd buried in their network was still running perfectly—stable, elegant, and deeply disrespectful.

Like me.

The lounge camera loaded first.

Killian stood motionless, looking one inconvenience away from homicide.

Lucas was typing like the keyboard owed him money.

Jaxon looked ready to punch God directly in the face.

And Cole?

Cole was actively losing his mind laughing.

Then Lucas opened his laptop. POP. Pink glitter exploded directly into his face.

I hit the floor wheezing.

"Oh my God," I gasped between breaths. "Lucas, you fragile little Victorian orphan. You're moulting."

I replayed the footage three times. Then took screenshots.

Then made a gif. Then briefly considered framing it.

When Jaxon opened the drawer and found the glitter-covered fake severed finger I'd left for Cole, I nearly ascended spiritually.

"Yes," I hissed, clutching a pillow dramatically. "He appreciated the craftsmanship."

Cole's delighted reaction absolutely made my day.

"That man radiates I want to be emotionally ruined by a woman energy."

I lifted my whisky glass toward the screen.

"Honestly? Same."

On-screen, Lucas was spiralling hard.

"She signed the sabotage," he snapped. "She named the virus. She's chaos."

"I am!" I shouted proudly at the laptop. "I'm the chaos fairy summoned by men underestimating women in STEM."

The hacked camera loop replayed Lucas getting glitter-bombed every few seconds.

Art. Pure art. This wasn't revenge anymore. This was self-care.

A glitter-covered healing journey.

The world's most unhinged recovery process.

The camera cut briefly back to Killian.

Still calm. Still watching. Still not shutting the system down. Interesting.

I tilted my head slowly. "Oh," I murmured, smiling to myself.

"He's in."

Lucas

My eye twitched violently. Again.

The monitor flashed bright pink for the fifteenth time in ten minutes.

Every time I isolated one breach, another appeared somewhere else like digital whack-a-mole designed by Satan and Lisa Frank collaboratively.

Miss me yet? :)

"I'm going to combust," I muttered, dragging both hands down my face. "This is psychological warfare coded by a glitter demon."

Cole leaned against the table beside me, completely unhelpful.

"Did she seriously leave heart emojis in the code comments?"

"Yes," I snapped.

"Glitter emojis too. Do you understand what that does to a man spiritually?"

"Improves him?"

I turned toward him so slowly I deserved an award for restraint.

"She rewrote the base voice commands," I hissed.

Cole's grin widened instantly.

"Oh no."

"Yes," I growled. "Every time someone says Killian's name, the system responds with—"

"Daddy mode activated," the speakers announced cheerfully.

Cole folded in half laughing. Even Jaxon cracked a smile. I nearly blacked out from rage.

"I'm ripping the motherboard out with my teeth."

Killian, infuriatingly calm, remained silent near the back of the room.

Watching. Thinking. Probably thriving, honestly.

"She's still inside the system," I continued. "Every time I clear one breach, another pops up. She's mocking me in five programming languages."

I reopened the logs. A fresh line of code blinked onto the screen with a timestamp from less than three minutes ago. Three. Minutes. Meaning she was actively watching us.

Another message appeared. You're cute when you're angry, Lucas. Hydrate before you stroke out. I slammed the laptop shut hard enough for it to whimper.

"She's in the walls."

"She changed the fridge settings too," Jaxon added flatly.

I stared at him.

"What?"

"It says Try Again, Sweetheart every time I open it."

Cole was fully crying laughing now.

"I want to marry her and also never be alone with her."

Killian finally spoke. "She's making a point."

"No," I snapped immediately. "She's declaring war using sparkles."

"She could've destroyed the system," Killian said calmly. "She didn't."

"She renamed my files tryme.bitch."

"She's warning us."

"She renamed your office Command Daddy's Dungeon."

Killian paused. Very briefly. "...Noted."

I dropped back into my chair with a groan. Because the worst part? I should've hated her. Instead, I was impressed. Deeply annoyed. But impressed.

"I want to beat her," I admitted reluctantly.

Cole pointed at me instantly. "That right there is how enemies-to-lovers starts."

"I'm going to rewire your jaw."

"You're blushing."

"I'm having a rage aneurysm."

"And it's adorable."

Killian ignored both of us, eyes fixed on the glowing message still sitting on-screen. Let's see if you can keep up.

"We need to decide what we're doing about her," Jaxon said.

"I vote panic," I muttered.

Killian's expression remained unreadable.

"No," he said finally.

"We keep going."

I stared at him.

"She's not stopping unless she wants to."

His voice turned cold and sharp as steel. "Then we give her a reason to stay."

I looked back toward the screen again. The glitter. The insults. The absolute confidence dripping from every line of code.

God help me. I was already rebuilding the firewall. And renaming the protocol. Operation: Glitterbane.

Killian

The cursor blinked steadily on-screen. Taunting. Rhythmic. Almost playful. Let's see if you can keep up.

I couldn't stop staring at it.

I'd dealt with mercenaries, warlords, traitors, and men stupid enough to mistake cruelty for power.

I built the Vipers on precision. Control. Discipline.

And then Riley Morgan kicked the door in armed with glitter, sarcasm, and psychological warfare.

And somehow?

She was winning.

"You're quiet," Jaxon observed beside me.

"I'm thinking."

Lucas groaned somewhere behind us, probably discovering another pink disaster hidden in the code.

Cole still had his boots on the table like our headquarters wasn't actively being haunted.

But I barely heard them. Because Riley hadn't attacked us like an enemy. She'd challenged us.

There was a difference.

She didn't want destruction. She wanted engagement. A reaction. A game worth playing.

"She rewrites the rules," I said finally.

Lucas looked up from his monitor with dead eyes.

"She's rewriting me."

Jaxon folded his arms. "So what's the move?"

"We don't corner her." Cole blinked.

"So we just let the glitter cryptid keep roaming free?"

"No."

I kept my eyes on the blinking cursor. "We let her make the next move."

Lucas looked horrified.

"She renamed your tactical folder Missionary Position: Try Again."

"And she still left our systems intact."

That mattered. A lot. Because Riley wasn't trying to destroy us. She was testing us.

Measuring us.

Seeing whether we'd try to cage her... or understand her.

"She's dangerous," Jaxon said carefully.

"She's strategic," I corrected.

"And she knows exactly what she's doing."

Cole studied me for a long second before grinning slowly "You're in deep."

I didn't answer.

Because unfortunately?

He was right.

Riley Morgan walked into our lives like a lit match tossed into gasoline.

Chaotic. Brilliant. Completely uncontrollable.

And instead of putting the fire out... Part of me wanted to watch it burn.

27

Glitter, Gasoline, and God Complexes

Riley

Toxic - 2WEI

I gave them a week. Seven full days of silence. No break-ins. No glitter. No viruses. No cryptic messages. Nothing. It drove them insane.

I watched the entire thing unfold remotely, obviously, because Lucas still hadn't managed to remove me from their systems. Watching him try was honestly adorable. Like watching a stressed-out housecat attempt to fistfight the moon.

Killian brooded. Jaxon paced. Cole spiralled into such catastrophic levels of thirst I almost mailed him a spray bottle.

But eventually, I decided they'd suffered enough. So I came back.

No dramatic entrance. No alarms. Just a cloned keycard swipe and a casual stroll through the Vipers' compound like I paid taxes there.

I walked straight into Killian's office. Sat in his chair. Swivelled once. Slowly. Then propped my boots on his desk like I owned the damn company. Honestly?

The chair suited me. Expensive. Dangerous. Slightly emotionally unavailable. Very Killian.

I waited. And eventually, I heard them coming. Fast footsteps. Raised voices. The office door opened hard enough to rattle the walls. Killian stopped dead in the doorway.

I smiled lazily. "Hi, boss."

His gaze swept across the room before settling on me. "You're in my chair."

"And you've been in my business," I replied sweetly. "Seems fair."

The others filed in behind him. Jaxon first, expression unreadable. Lucas immediately looked like his nervous system began buffering. And Cole? Cole looked genuinely delighted to see me alive.

"You're alive," Lucas blurted.

"Aww," I said mockingly. "You missed me."

"You vanished for a week," Killian said carefully. "Why?" I shrugged.

"Wanted to see how you handled separation anxiety."

Cole snorted. Lucas looked personally victimised.

"Oh, it was rough," I continued thoughtfully. "Lucas had at least four existential crises. Jaxon nearly beat someone unconscious during sparring. Killian stared at my file like it offended him spiritually."

I pointed toward Cole. "And you googled signs she likes you even if she threatens arson."

Lucas made a choking noise. "Wait—how do you know that?"

I blinked slowly. "You think I ever actually left?"

Silence. Then: "You were WATCHING us?" Lucas sounded horrified.

"Oh honey," I said, leaning forward slightly. "I was watching everything."

The room tension immediately tripled. Delicious. I pushed myself out of Killian's chair and circled slowly around the desk toward him.

"I came back because I made a decision."

"You want in," Killian guessed.

"No," I corrected softly.

"I want control."

His gaze sharpened. "You think you can run with us?"

I smiled. "No. I think you've been trying to keep up with me."

Behind him, Cole muttered a deeply respectful: "Goddamn."

Lucas whispered: "She's going to kill us all."

Jaxon stayed silent, but even he looked impressed. I stepped closer to Killian until only inches separated us.

“So,” I murmured near his ear, “what’s it gonna be, boss? You gonna hand me the keys... or keep chasing the engine that already left you behind?”

Then I walked past all of them like they were furniture. Naturally, they followed. The training hall was empty when I entered. Sunlight spilled through the skylights overhead, dust floating lazily through the air.

The others filed in behind me. Killian first. Always first.

Jaxon stayed quiet, watching everything carefully.

Lucas clutched his tablet like emotional support equipment.

Cole leaned against the wall looking entirely too entertained.

I crossed my arms. “Here’s the deal. If I work with you, it’s on my terms.”

Killian tilted his head slightly. "Go on.”

“One: no leash. No trackers. No babysitting.” Lucas already looked offended.

“Two: I don’t take orders. If anyone calls me sweetheart unironically, I break fingers.”

Cole grinned. “What if it’s ironic?”

“I’ll break yours first.” He somehow looked even happier about that.

“Three: you don’t question how I get results. I finish jobs my way.”

“And what do we get in return?” Killian asked evenly.

I stepped forward slightly. “You get access to someone your enemies won’t see coming.”

A beat of silence followed. Then: “Deal,” Killian said. Just like that.

Lucas nearly dropped his tablet. “WAIT—seriously?”

“We need her,” Killian replied simply.

I raised an eyebrow. “Well. That was alarmingly easy.”

Killian handed me a thick black file marked CLASSIFIED. “We have a mission.”

Interesting. I took the file. "I'll read it. But if it's boring, I'm ghosting you again." Cole snorted.

I paused at the doorway before glancing back over my shoulder. "Oh, and if this turns out to be a trap?"

I smiled sweetly. "I'll burn your entire operation to the ground. Glitter included."

Lucas looked like he might faint.

Cole whispered reverently: "God, she's perfect."

And Killian? Killian smiled. Barely. But it was there.

Jaxon

I didn't wait for small talk. The second everyone stepped into the briefing room, I dimmed the lights and dropped the file onto the table with a heavy thud.

"Prostitution ring," I said, clicking the remote.

The main screen lit up instantly with grainy surveillance stills, profiles, shipping manifests, redacted intel, and crime scene photos.

"But it's not just escorting or drug-running." I clicked to the next slide.

"They're using it as a front for trafficking. Women. Teenagers. The real kind of scum."

Cole's smirk disappeared immediately. Lucas sat up straighter. Killian didn't move, but his jaw tightened. He already knew.

And then there was Riley. Leaning against the wall like she wasn't remotely interested—until I clicked to the next image.

WAREHOUSE LOCATION — SOUTH PORT / PIER 16

She shifted. Barely. But I caught it. Her arms uncrossed. Her eyes sharpened. And a dangerous little smile touched the corner of her mouth. Bingo.

"This ring's protected," I continued. "Dirty cops. Politicians. Imports moving through fake manifests. And from what we've gathered, there's a shipment arriving tonight."

I looked around the room. "If we wait too long, we lose everything."

The atmosphere shifted instantly. Mission mode.

"We hit hard," I said. "We hit fast. In and out. Gather intel, secure victims, shut the operation down."

"And burn it?" Riley asked casually.

Killian answered before I could. "Not the assignment."

Riley tilted her head thoughtfully. "But if the building happened to collapse in a tragic gas leak accident..."

Lucas blinked at her. "We do not need a gas leak."

"We always need a gas leak," she replied sweetly.

I ignored both of them and zoomed in on the dock blueprints. "Primary entry point here. Security's light, but not blind. We'll need a distraction to keep port security occupied while we move in."

"I can handle that," Riley said immediately.

Everyone looked at her. She lifted her hands innocently. "What? I'm excellent at distractions."

Cole muttered under his breath, "You're also excellent at giving me anxiety."

"Thanks," she chirped. She dropped into a chair backwards, arms folded over the backrest while she spun lazily toward the screen again. Too eager. I didn't like it.

Killian glanced toward her. "You've been there before?"

"Once," Riley replied. Her voice flattened slightly. "Didn't end well."

"Why?" I asked.

Her expression didn't change, but something colder slid into her eyes.

"Because one of the girls looked like my sister."

Silence. Heavy. Nobody spoke for several seconds.

Then Riley added casually: "Don't worry. I got her out."

She didn't elaborate. Didn't need to.

Killian nodded once.

Small. Controlled. "Then we're agreed."

I closed the file.

"We move tonight. Gear up."

Everyone stood. Except Riley. She stayed exactly where she was, spinning slowly in the chair, fingers tapping together like a cat waiting patiently beside a mouse hole.

And even though she didn't say another word— I could feel it. She was already figuring out how to make this personal.

Riley

The warehouse loomed over the docks like a rusted corpse, all corrugated steel and rotting secrets.

I parked my bike three blocks away and killed the engine, listening to the distant crash of waves against pylons. Salt hung thick in the air. So did the smell of oil, blood, and bad decisions. Home sweet home.

The boys were still en route in their matching tactical SUVs, probably discussing entry points and communication protocols like responsible professionals.

Couldn't relate. I tugged my hoodie tighter around myself and started walking toward the warehouse alone.

Because honestly?

Sometimes the best distraction was a woman who looked vulnerable.

I slowed near the front gate, letting my shoulders slump. Letting my breathing hitch just enough. One of the guards spotted me almost immediately. Hook. Line. Idiot. He frowned and stepped forward. "You lost?"

I looked up through my lashes, forcing my voice soft and shaky. "I—I was told to come back here."

His entire posture changed. Predatory. Disgusting.

"You alone?" he asked. I nodded once.

The second his hand grabbed my arm, I snapped his nose sideways with my elbow. Crunch. He screamed. I grabbed the back of his jacket, spun, and launched him clean off the dock. Splash. I stared down into the water. "One."

Another guard came sprinting from around the crates, gun halfway raised. "Oh good," I sighed dramatically. "More volunteers."

He barely got the weapon level before I kicked his wrist sideways, drove my knee into his stomach, then headbutted him hard enough to send him reeling backward.

I shoved him off the dock too. Splash. "Two."

Honestly? This was becoming therapeutic.

A third guy appeared from the shadows looking deeply concerned about his life choices. Smart man. I smiled brightly. "Hi."

He hesitated. Then made the catastrophic mistake of rushing me. Ten seconds later he joined his coworkers in the harbour. Splash. I cracked my neck lazily. "Free swimming lessons tonight, gentlemen."

That was when headlights swept across the dock behind me. The Vipers' SUVs rolled to a stop.

Doors opened fast. Killian stepped out first, naturally. Jaxon right behind him. Lucas looked one inconvenience away from a stroke. Cole stopped dead the second he saw me standing there beside the water.

And behind me? Another body hit the harbour.

Splash. Cole blinked slowly. "Is she... singing?" I realised I was. Oops.

Lucas looked horrified. "She's throwing people into the ocean."

"I think I'm in love," Cole whispered reverently. Jaxon pinched the bridge of his nose. Killian just stared at me. Silent. Assessing. Always assessing.

I spread my arms dramatically. "You boys took your sweet-ass time."

Lucas finally snapped. "WHAT THE HELL ARE YOU DOING?"

"Recon," I answered smoothly. "Distraction. Emotional enrichment. Multitasking."

"You were supposed to wait for backup," Jaxon growled. "I did." I pointed toward the unconscious guards floating nearby. "They were just disappointingly bad at it."

Killian stepped closer, gaze flicking briefly toward the water before returning to me.

"You went in alone."

"Technically," I corrected, "I walked in alone. The drowning was more of a spontaneous creative decision."

Cole looked genuinely delighted. Lucas looked moments away from cardiac arrest.

Killian's eyes narrowed slightly. "Are there more inside?"

The humour dropped from me instantly. "Yeah," I said quietly. "A lot more." The dock suddenly felt colder.

"And some of them won't go down as easily as the welcoming committee."

For one brief second, nobody spoke. Then Killian nodded once. "We move now."

Finally. I pulled my hoodie over my head, revealing the tactical gear underneath.

Jaxon blinked. Caught off guard for exactly half a second. I winked at him. Then cracked my knuckles.

"Alright, boys," I said with a grin sharp enough to cut glass. "Let's ruin some lives."

The inside of the warehouse smelled like mould, sweat, cheap cologne, and human misery.

Dim red lights flickered overhead, throwing shadows across stacked crates and rusted shipping containers. Somewhere deeper inside, music thumped through old speakers—something bass-heavy and grimy enough to make the entire place feel infected. I hated it instantly. Which honestly just made me meaner.

The first guy barely had time to register me before I slammed a crowbar across his face.

Crack. "Oh, good," I muttered as he dropped. "It still works."

Gunfire exploded behind me as the Vipers stormed in through the loading bay.

Chaos bloomed instantly.

Lucas shouted something in my earpiece about server access.

Cole laughed like a maniac while unloading rounds into two guards behind a crate.

Killian moved through the room like controlled violence wrapped in a suit jacket.

And Jaxon—Jaxon fought like a tank somebody taught martial arts. Efficient. Brutal. Terrifying.

Honestly?

Little bit hot.

A guard lunged for me from the left. I ducked beneath his swing, drove my knife into his thigh, then shoved him headfirst into a stack of cargo boxes.

"Maybe try yoga," I suggested as he collapsed wheezing.

Someone opened fire from the upper walkway. Bullets sparked off metal beams overhead.

"Sniper!" Lucas yelled.

"I see him!" I vaulted onto a crate, sprinted across the top, and launched myself toward the railing.

The guy's eyes widened. Fair. I hit him hard enough to send both of us crashing into the catwalk. Metal screamed beneath us. He reached for his gun.

I stabbed the railing beside his head. "Wrong answer." Then kicked him clean over the side. The drop ended with a very satisfying crunch.

Below me, Cole looked up slowly. "...Jesus Christ."

I bowed dramatically. "Thank you, thank you. I perform nightly."

Another scream echoed deeper inside the warehouse.

Not a guard. A girl. Everything inside me went cold. I landed hard beside Killian.

"There," I snapped, already moving toward the corridor. Two guards blocked the doorway. I didn't slow down. The first one got my elbow to the throat.

The second caught a stun grenade directly to the chest. "WHO WANTS TO PLAY TAG?" I shouted as the blast detonated.

White light exploded through the hallway.

Somewhere behind me, Lucas yelled, "FOR THE LOVE OF GOD STOP ENJOYING THIS."

"No promises!"

The corridor opened into a larger holding area. Cages. Actual fucking cages. Rage hit so fast it tasted metallic.

Three men turned toward me from the back room. One smiled. Big mistake.

I grabbed the nearest metal chair and launched it directly into his face. Bone cracked. He dropped instantly. The second came at me with a knife. I disarmed him in two seconds flat and introduced his forehead to the concrete.

The third ran.

Coward. I shot him in the knee before he made it three steps. He screamed. Good.

The girls pressed themselves against the back walls of the cages, terrified. One of them couldn't have been older than sixteen. I swallowed hard. Then softened my voice immediately.

"Hey," I said gently, kneeling beside the nearest cage door. "You're okay. We're getting you out."

Nobody moved. Understandable. Behind me, boots thundered into the room.

Killian stopped dead beside me as his gaze swept across the cages.

Something dangerous shifted behind his eyes.

Jaxon looked like he wanted to kill every breathing thing in the building. Cole went unusually quiet. Lucas swore softly under his breath.

I ripped the keys off the unconscious guard beside me and unlocked the first cage.

"You're safe now," I told the girls carefully. One of them started crying. That nearly broke me more than the bloodshed did.

Killian crouched beside me. "Riley."

I looked at him. His voice stayed low. "We clear the building first."

I knew what he meant. Procedure. Safety. Protocol.

But all I could hear was Sophie's voice in my head.

What if nobody comes in time?

I stood slowly. Then looked deeper into the warehouse. Toward the remaining doors. Toward the men still breathing. Something inside me smiled. "Cool," I said quietly, spinning the knife once in my hand.

"Then let's finish the fucking job."

Jaxon

I'd seen Riley fight before.

Seen the chaos. Seen the glitter bombs, the arrogance, the reckless confidence. This was different. This wasn't Riley playing with her food. This was Riley hunting.

The second she disappeared deeper into the warehouse, the entire atmosphere shifted around her like the building itself recognised a predator had entered it. Gunfire echoed from the eastern corridor. A scream followed. Then silence. "...Should we maybe be concerned?" Lucas asked tightly over comms.

"No," Killian answered calmly while reloading his weapon. A beat. "Concerned for who is the real question." Honestly? Fair.

I moved through the warehouse beside Killian, clearing rooms one by one. Most of the guards were already down by the time we reached them. Some unconscious. Some bleeding. One zip-tied naked to a forklift with "BAD TOUCH = BAD DAY" written across his chest in permanent marker.

Lucas stared. "...Where is she getting the markers?"

"No one ask questions you don't want answered," Cole muttered.

Another explosion rattled somewhere deeper inside the building. Lucas physically flinched.

"That better not be a gas leak."

"Statistically?" Cole said thoughtfully. "Probably a gas leak."

We rounded another corner and found Riley standing in the middle of absolute carnage. Three men unconscious. One hanging halfway through a table.

And Riley? Calmly reloading a stolen handgun while humming under her breath. She glanced up as we approached. "Oh good," she said brightly. "Backup."

Killian's gaze swept the room. "What happened here?"

She pointed casually toward one of the unconscious men. "He called me sweetheart."

Lucas whispered, "Dear God." Riley holstered the gun and stepped over a body like it was mildly inconvenient furniture.

"There are more rooms downstairs," she said. "Locked. Reinforced. Probably where they're holding the rest."

Killian nodded once. "Then we move."

But before any of us could step forward— A gunshot cracked through the corridor. Too close. Riley moved instantly. One second she was beside me.

The next she slammed directly into my chest hard enough to throw both of us sideways as bullets tore through the wall behind us. Concrete exploded across the hallway.

I hit the floor with Riley sprawled on top of me, knife already in her hand before we'd even stopped moving. "RUDE," she yelled toward the shooter.

Then she launched herself back up like gravity personally offended her. The guard barely got another shot off before Riley vaulted the railing, grabbed him by the throat, and drove both of them over the staircase.

Cole leaned over the railing. "...Is she okay?"

A loud crash echoed upward. Then Riley's voice floated back casually: "He's not!"

Killian closed his eyes briefly. Not frustration. Resignation. Like he was slowly accepting the universe had assigned him a personal disaster. Lucas looked pale.

"She jumped down an entire flight of stairs."

"Yeah," Cole replied. "Did you miss the crate incident?"

Riley reappeared thirty seconds later dragging the unconscious shooter behind her by one ankle. Hair a mess. Blood splattered across her cheek. Smiling. "Problem solved." I stared at her for a long moment.

Then finally said the thing I'd been thinking since the docks. "You enjoy this way too much."

Riley tilted her head. "You say that like it's a character flaw."

Honestly? Couldn't even argue with that.

28

Damage Report

Cole

I'm not sorry – Eric Bellinger

"All things considered," I announced, collapsing dramatically onto Killian's office couch, "that could've gone way worse."

I cracked open a beer and took a long sip. "Nobody died. Jaxon didn't punch me. Lucas only had three near-death panic attacks. I call that a huge success."

"Speak for yourself," Lucas snapped, pacing like an overclocked squirrel. "I nearly had a stroke watching her go full Mortal Kombat in real time."

"She did save Jaxon's ass," I pointed out.

"I had it handled," Jaxon growled immediately.

Lucas spun toward him. "You had it handled? She launched herself off a crate like a glitter-covered missile and flattened three armed men before you could blink."

Jaxon folded his arms tighter. "She's reckless."

"She's efficient," I corrected.

Killian still hadn't said anything. He sat motionless behind his desk staring at the muted television like it personally offended him.

Then the headline changed.

BREAKING: EXPLOSION AT PORT WAREHOUSE — HUMAN TRAFFICKING RING DESTROYED, DOZENS RESCUED

The room went dead silent. Footage rolled across the screen—flames swallowing the warehouse, emergency lights flashing across smoke and twisted steel.

The news anchor continued talking. "Witnesses report a woman on a motorcycle fleeing the scene moments before the explosion—"

The grainy CCTV image appeared. Motorcycle. Leather jacket. Smirk. Unmistakably Riley.

Lucas nearly inhaled his own water. "She waited until we left and THEN blew it up?!"

"She got the girls out first," Jaxon said slowly. "And called the cops."

I blinked thoughtfully. "Okay, but respectfully... is it weird that I find that incredibly attractive?"

The office door swung open before anyone could answer. And there she was. Riley walked in like she hadn't just committed several federal crimes before dinner. Leather jacket. Wind-tangled hair. Boots still stained with blood. A bag of chips in one hand. Sunglasses still on indoors because apparently she'd committed fully to becoming a menace. "Sup, boys."

She crunched a chip casually before glancing at the TV. "Oh hey. Is that me?"

Lucas made a noise that physically should not have come from a human body. "YOU BLEW UP A WAREHOUSE."

"Yeah," Riley replied simply. "Obviously."

She tossed her sunglasses onto Killian's desk and dropped into his chair like it belonged to her. Honestly? At this point it probably did.

"She committed MULTIPLE felonies," Lucas continued.

"Only five," Riley corrected. "Maybe six if the Coast Guard gets dramatic."

Jaxon looked like he wanted to punch concrete. Killian looked like the concrete.

Meanwhile, I was dangerously close to proposing. "She's terrifying," I said admiringly. "And I am deeply into it."

"She could've told us," Jaxon muttered.

Riley popped another chip into her mouth. "Where's the fun in that?"

Killian finally leaned forward, fingers steepled. "You just declared war."

Her smile sharpened instantly. "I always declare war."

A beat. "I just happen to win mine."

Silence settled over the room after that. Eventually everyone started filtering out.

I lingered behind for one last glance at Riley sitting smugly in Killian's chair like she'd conquered the building by sheer force of personality.

And honestly?

Maybe she had. Because somewhere between the explosions, glitter terrorism, and psychological warfare… I realised something terrifying. We didn't need Riley on our team. We needed to survive being on hers.

29

Kill List

Riley

Bottom of the River – Delta Rae

He was the last one left alive. Bleeding. Wheezing. Dragging himself across the dock like a dying insect trying desperately to escape the inevitable. Unfortunately for him?

I'd always enjoyed inevitability. I stalked after him slowly, boots creaking against damp timber as the harbour churned beneath us.

The water slapped hungrily against the pylons below. Waiting. "Hey, sweet cheeks," I called lightly. "You got a minute?"

He whimpered and tried crawling faster. Didn't help. His leg bent wrong from where I'd launched a crate at him earlier hard enough to fold him like cheap furniture.

Strike.

"Come on," I sighed dramatically. "Don't be rude. We haven't even had our little heart-to-heart yet."

I stepped onto the middle of his back, pinning him hard against the dock. He screamed. Squirmed. Clawed uselessly at the wood. Pathetic. I crouched beside him slowly, lazily spinning the bloodied knife between my fingers.

"You know what I hate?" I asked conversationally.

"Cowards." I tilted my head slightly.

"Men who let girls scream while they laugh behind cameras." The knife traced lightly across his cheek, just enough to split skin.

"Did you enjoy that?"

"Please," he sobbed. "Please, I didn't—"

"Wrong answer." I grabbed his collar and dragged him bodily toward the edge of the dock. He screamed louder this time, nails scraping uselessly against the timber while dark water churned below us.

I held him suspended over the edge. Let him panic. Let him feel it.

"I know your name," I whispered softly.

"I memorised your voice from the video."

His crying turned hysterical. "I listened to her scream for six weeks because of you."

I leaned closer. "She had a brother." His breathing hitched.

"He killed himself last month." Silence. Then quietly: "Your fun destroyed an entire family." And then I let go.

Cole

"Sup," Riley said casually, like she hadn't just executed a man and fed him to the harbour.

I genuinely forgot how breathing worked for a second.

She turned away from me with a cherry lollipop hanging from her lips and wandered toward the nearest corpse like she was starting household chores.

Then she started singing softly. "When I was just a little girl..."

Sweet. Off-key. Wrong enough to make every hair on my neck stand up. She crouched beside the first body, hooked her hands beneath his arms, and started dragging him backward across the dock.

Blood streaked behind him in long red smears. "I asked my mother, what will I be..."

The corpse's head thunked once against the wood. Riley barely noticed.

"Will I be pretty? Will I be rich?"

"Not anymore," she muttered.

Then she shoved the body into the water. Splash. "One," she whispered softly.

Not counting bodies. Counting sins. She moved to the second corpse. "Que sera, sera..."

This one was heavier. Covered in stab wounds. She grunted slightly while dragging him, boots slipping through blood and seawater. And somehow that made it worse. Because none of this felt dramatic to her. It felt routine. "Whatever will be, will be..."

I stood frozen watching her work. Watching moonlight catch blood on her hands. Watching her hum lullabies while dumping monsters into the harbour like unwanted trash. Another body hit the water. Splash. "Two."

By the third corpse, I finally found my voice. "Riley..."

She glanced back at me over her shoulder while hauling dead weight across the dock. "Don't worry," she said lightly. "I disinfected the crowbar."

Then she dumped the third body into the water too. Three. The last one—the crawler—was already gone beneath the surface. Only ripples remained.

Riley stood at the dock edge humming softly beneath her breath while harbour water swallowed the evidence.

Then she turned toward me smiling. Satisfied. Beautiful. Terrifying. "Whatever will be, will be..."

And standing there beneath moonlight and blood and black water... She didn't look human. She looked like vengeance wearing lipstick.

And God help me— I was already falling straight toward the centre of it. We sat side by side at the edge of the dock afterward. Legs dangling over dark water like she hadn't just fed four bodies to the ocean.

The harbour had gone quiet again. Peaceful. "...How?" I finally asked.

She looked sideways at me. "How what?"

"How do you do this?" I gestured vaguely toward the blood. "The hacking. The tracking. Walking into places alone. Killing men without flinching."

Riley stayed quiet for a moment. Then: "I did hesitate once." I looked at her carefully. "Yeah?"

She nodded slightly. "Before the first one."

The water moved quietly below us. "I looked at him and thought maybe he wasn't involved."

A pause. "Then I remembered her face." Her voice flattened.

"The bruises. The video. Her brother's suicide note." She looked back toward the water.

"That hesitation lasted about two seconds."

"You could've called us."

"And let Lucas spend another month building a perfect case while they disappeared?"

"That's not fair."

"No," she agreed quietly.

"It isn't."

I swallowed hard. "This wasn't justice, Riley."

Her gaze shifted toward me again. Cold now. Sharp.

"No," she said softly.

"It was execution." Silence settled heavily between us.

Then finally: "You want to know what it cost me?"

I nodded slowly. Her eyes stayed fixed on the dark water below. "It cost me the part of myself that still believed justice was coming."

Killian

My phone buzzed. Cole. "Did you find her?"

A long silence answered first. Then: "She sang to them, Killian."

I frowned. "...What?"

"She sang while dragging the bodies into the harbour."

Jaxon looked up from cleaning blood off his gear. "Is he drunk?" I held up a hand for silence.

Cole kept talking quietly. "All four men from Lucas's case."

Lucas froze instantly. "What?"

"She hunted them herself," Cole said.

"Planned it for weeks." Jaxon leaned back slowly.

"...Holy shit." Cole exhaled shakily through the phone.

"It wasn't messy. It was controlled. Like watching ballet choreographed by a serial killer." Lucas swore softly.

"She was humming Que Sera, Sera while dumping bodies."

A pause. Then Jaxon muttered: "That's... weirdly hot." Lucas didn't even argue.

I dragged a hand down my face slowly. Because I wasn't thinking about the bodies. I was thinking about the calmness Cole described. The absence of hesitation. That kind of calm came with a price. "She okay?" I asked finally.

Cole went quiet for a second. "Physically? Fine." Another pause. "But mentally... she's calm in a way that doesn't feel normal." "She earned that calm," Jaxon said quietly. Nobody disagreed. Least of all me.

30

Still Dancing

Riley

Bones – MS MR

It had been a month since I turned a warehouse into a very aggressive public service announcement about human trafficking.

A month of jobs. Recon. Intel drops. The same cycle over and over until the adrenaline started tasting dull.

So I danced.

The studio pulsed with heavy bass, low enough to rattle through my ribs. I moved harder than usual. Not graceful. Not delicate. Violent.

My pointe shoes cracked against the floor like gunshots. Spin. Drop. Snap upright.

Every movement felt like a fight against gravity itself. Against memory. Against grief.

Sweat slid down my spine while the mirrors reflected someone sharp enough to cut herself open on the edges.

No Vipers. No missions. No ghosts. Just me. I collapsed onto the studio floor breathing hard, chest burning.

"Still dancing, Soph," I whispered toward the ceiling.

"Just... differently now." Then the door creaked open.

Cole

I hadn't meant to interrupt what looked suspiciously like a spiritual awakening.

Killian sent me to check on Riley because apparently I'd become designated chaos wrangler.

Instead, I walked directly into the most devastating thing I'd ever seen.

Riley stood in the centre of the studio wearing a black leotard and pointe shoes like violence had decided to become art.

She moved like gravity personally offended her. Not dancing. Destroying. Rebuilding. Surviving. The floor creaked beneath me accidentally. She froze instantly. The mirror caught her gaze snapping toward mine.

Caught. "...Hey," I managed intelligently.

God. I should've brought flowers. Or a sonnet. Or emotional support.

For a second neither of us moved.

Then Riley quietly crossed the room and sat near her bag, fingers moving to untie the ribbons around her pointe shoes.

The soft sound of fabric sliding through her hands somehow felt more intimate than nudity.

One shoe came off. Then the other. Bare feet pressed against the cold floor. She pulled warm-up pants over her legs next. Then a shirt. Layer after layer going back on like armour sealing shut.

Like I'd accidentally seen something I wasn't supposed to.

"You dance," I said finally, because apparently my brain had dissolved completely.

She arched one eyebrow. "Incredible observation skills."

"I just..." I rubbed the back of my neck awkwardly. "Didn't picture you owning anything without tactical pockets."

"And I didn't picture you knowing how to knock."

"You didn't lock the door."

"I didn't expect company."

Fair. I leaned against the doorway watching her carefully.

"If you're gonna move like that," I said slowly, "you should probably start locking it."

Her eyes flicked toward me.

"You're staring."

"You're barefoot in a ballet studio wearing a skirt and emotionally ruining me, Riley. I feel like staring is understandable."

A smirk tugged briefly at her mouth.

"And yet you're still standing there."

God help me. "I came to check on you," I admitted.

It came out sounding way too honest.

"Check on me," she repeated mockingly.

"Cute."

"You've been quiet lately."

"Maybe I've been behaving."

I snorted. "Define behaving."

"I haven't blown anything up in several weeks."

A beat.

"That's growth." Then she stood and walked toward me slowly.

And just like that, the softer version of her disappeared again beneath the smirk and swagger.

Dangerous.

Untouchable.

"So," she asked lightly, "did you get what you came for, Cole?"

Riley

I made it halfway down the alley before I heard him jogging after me.

Boots hitting pavement.

Slightly out of breath.

Entirely too flustered.

"You're seriously leaving like that?" Cole called after me.

I glanced over my shoulder.

"What? You don't like the barefoot-supervillain aesthetic?"

"You're wearing a skirt and carrying combat boots like this is some kind of psychological operation."

I grinned.

"Cover shoot for Bad Decisions Quarterly."

Cole groaned dramatically.

"You have got to stop doing this."

"Doing what?"

"Flirting. Disappearing. Saying wildly illegal things and then riding off like a Bond villain."

I stepped closer until he stopped talking.

"You want me to stop?"

His mouth opened slightly.

"I—"

"Because I won't."

For a second he just stared at me like a man actively losing a fight against his own nervous system.

"I don't do strings," I said quietly.

"No emotional support playlists. No complicated mornings. I get what I want and I leave."

His jaw flexed. "That's it?"

"Mostly." I leaned closer, lowering my voice just enough to wreck him properly.

"You are very high on the list of people I'd let bend me over this bike though."

Silence. Absolute silence.

Then I winked, slid my helmet on, and swung onto the bike in one smooth motion. The vulnerable version of me from the studio vanished instantly beneath leather, steel, and sarcasm.

"Have a nice day, Officer Thirst Trap." Then I revved the engine and disappeared into traffic.

Cole

She vanished down the street like a fever dream on two wheels.

And I just stood there.

Staring.

Like a complete idiot.

The image of her dancing still burned behind my eyes.

Not the skirt.

Not the flirting.

The vulnerability.

That brief moment where she'd forgotten to hide.

And now that I'd seen it?

I couldn't unsee it.

"...Shit," I whispered.

That was genuinely all my brain could produce.

Behind me, boots crunched against gravel.

Jaxon.

"You look like you need a cigarette and immediate medical attention."

I groaned loudly.

"She's going to kill me."

"Eventually," Jaxon agreed calmly.

"But first she's gonna emotionally torture you for sport."

I dragged both hands over my face.

"She said—"

"Yup."

"And then I just stood there—"

"Like a kicked puppy."

A pause.

"A horny kicked puppy."

I pointed at him accusingly.

"You're not helping."

"No," he agreed. "But it is funny."

I exhaled slowly and leaned back against the wall.

Because Riley Morgan was a problem in every possible sense of the word.

A wildfire wrapped in silk and combat boots.

And somehow, against all common sense... I was already addicted.

31

Lines in the sand

Jaxon

Glory and Gore– Lorde

We'd run with Riley long enough to know she wasn't just a wildcard anymore. Six missions in, we knew her tells — the tilt of her head before she bolted off-plan, the roll of her shoulders before she broke cover, the sharp glint in her eyes right before she made someone regret their life choices.

And she knew us.

Knew exactly how far she could push before we snapped, and exactly how to get away with it. Tonight, though, something shifted. She cut down a side alley before I'd finished scanning.

"Left," she called over comms, already moving. I should've pulled her back to the plan. Instead, I followed without thinking — because Riley's detours always worked, and some part of me liked being where she was.

She vaulted a barricade, landed light, and looked back, grinning.

"You coming, slowpoke?" I should've been watching the street ahead. Instead, I caught myself watching the way her braid swung over her shoulder, the way she looked more alive here than anywhere else.

"Eyes forward," I muttered when I caught up, hiding the curve in my mouth. She shoved my shoulder in passing, laughing, and kept moving. She thought it was just a joke.

Lucas

The hallway split ahead. Two bad angles. "Left or right?" I asked.

"Both," she said, slipping right without hesitation.

We'd done this enough times now that I didn't even question it. She trusted I'd handle my side. I trusted she'd survive hers. Somewhere between the first mission and now, that stopped feeling reckless and started feeling natural.

When we regrouped, she was leaning against the wall, cheeks flushed, eyes bright beneath the dim emergency lights. "What took you so long?" she teased.

I should've snapped back. Instead, I caught myself memorising the exact curve of her smirk like it mattered. Which was deeply concerning.

Cole

She'd learned exactly how to get under my skin. Case in point: the rooftop. Wind tore across the building hard enough to rattle debris over the gravel while Riley stood at the ledge pointing out the sniper nest like she was hosting a sightseeing tour.

"You know," I said, stepping beside her, "this would be romantic if people weren't actively shooting at us."

She smirked without looking at me.

"Don't flatter yourself."

Didn't stop her from staying close while I lined up the shot she'd scouted for me. Didn't stop me from noticing the way her hair whipped across my arm every time the wind shifted. And it definitely didn't stop me thinking about it afterward.

Killian

She was chaos. But she'd learned how to move with us. When Jaxon shifted positions, Riley was already covering him. When Lucas breached a room, she filled the blind spot before he asked. Cole needed a rooftop angle, and she was already calling targets.

None of it was rehearsed. It was instinct. That was when I realised she wasn't orbiting us anymore. We were all turning around her without noticing.

When we piled back into the van afterward, Riley dropped onto the bench seat laughing breathlessly, adrenaline still bright in her eyes.

"Tell me that wasn't fun," she said.

None of us answered. Because for her, maybe it was just another good night.

For us?

It was the moment we realised we were already attached.

Riley

They were staring again. "What?" I asked, peeling my gloves off.

"Nothing," Jaxon answered way too quickly.

I smirked. "If I didn't know better, I'd think you boys were getting soft on me."

Cole snorted. "Not a chance."

"Good," I said, kicking my boots up onto the bench.

"I'd hate to break your hearts." The van jolted forward. Just another Tuesday.

Killian

The safehouse smelled like rain, gunpowder, damp gear, and exhaustion. Cole dumped his rifle onto the table without clearing it properly. Lucas immediately started complaining about it while stripping down his sidearm for maintenance. Jaxon had claimed the couch like he'd personally fought a war against the cushions.

And Riley?

Riley was barefoot in the kitchen raiding the fridge like she owned the building.

"You know," she said around a mouthful of cold pizza, "you boys are dangerously boring after a win. Where's the champagne? The fireworks? The naked victory laps?"

"Go light something on fire yourself," Jaxon grumbled. "Preferably outside."

Her grin flashed sharp and quick. "Oh, big man's grumpy. Someone didn't get enough cardio?"

I leaned against the doorway quietly, watching them trade insults back and forth. Watching her here felt different than watching her in the field.

Out there, she was all sharp timing and dangerous instincts. Here, she was lighter. Unarmoured in ways she probably didn't even realise.

Lucas's ears turned pink when she teased him about sprinting. Cole passed her a beer automatically without even asking if she wanted one. None of them would admit it yet, but we'd all started orbiting her without noticing.

And she still had no idea. Riley dusted her hands together.

"Alright. I'm gonna shower, eat something that isn't half-fermented cheese, and sleep for twelve hours."

She pointed vaguely toward us. "You boys can decide whether you want to mope or actually come up with something fun."

She brushed past me toward the hallway, rainwater and gunpowder still clinging faintly to her skin.

I straightened slightly as she passed before I could stop myself. The bathroom door shut.

Jaxon exhaled slowly.

"She's never going to make this easy, is she?"

"Nope," Cole said, sounding almost proud of it.

Lucas glanced toward the hallway. "Wouldn't want her to."

I stayed silent. Still staring at the empty doorway. Because I knew exactly what they were all thinking. And none of us were ready to say it out loud yet. She was already becoming ours. She just didn't know it.

Riley

The rain had dropped to a light mist by the time I grabbed my helmet. "Heading out already?" Cole asked from the couch.

"Yeah," I replied, tightening the strap beneath my chin. "Trying to beat the late-night drunk drivers home."

On my way through the lounge, I spotted the heavy dark-grey hoodie hanging over the back of Killian's chair. The fabric looked soft. Warm. Broken in. I was still damp from the rain and riding the leftover high from the mission, so I grabbed it without thinking and stuffed it into my bag.

It smelled faintly like smoke, clean laundry, and Killian's aftershave — the kind that lingered in a room long after he left it. Not that I cared. It was just comfortable.

"Night, boys," I called, pulling the door open.

"Don't do anything stupid," Jaxon said automatically.

I snorted. "Then what would you lot have to talk about?"

The rain misted cold against my skin as I stepped outside. My bike waited beneath the streetlight — black paint flecked with glitter that caught the light like scattered stars.

I swung a leg over it, the engine rumbling to life beneath me. Then I rolled out into the empty street without looking back. The hoodie sat warm against my side inside the bag. Just a little comfort for the ride home.

32

And Lo, The Thighs Did Tremble

Jaxon

Daddy Issues – The Neighbourhood

We'd been trying to reach her all morning.

Message sent? Ignored.

Call placed? Ignored.

Lucas even tried a voice note like we were teenagers in 2011.

Still nothing. We had a job lined up — time-sensitive, dangerous, big payout. And Riley?

She ghosted us like spam finally discovering the block button.

I was not dealing with that kind of radio silence. Not from her.

We were circling the city when Lucas suddenly sat up straighter in the front seat, pointing through the windshield like he'd just spotted a UFO.

"There," he said. "Tell me that's not her."

I followed his line of sight, fully prepared to argue. Then I saw her. And my brain promptly blue-screened.

It was Riley. Except… it wasn't. Not the Riley we knew in hoodies, boots, and tactical jeans.

No.

This Riley was a damn fever dream. A black satin gown clung to her body like it had been sewn directly onto her skin. A thigh-high slit flashed toned legs every time she moved, and the heels she wore looked less like footwear and more like a workplace safety violation.

Her hair was pinned up elegantly, loose curls framing her face beneath city lights. Dark lipstick. Smoky eyes. Diamond earrings catching gold beneath the streetlamps.

She looked like sin wrapped in silk and set to jazz music.

Cole choked on his water bottle. Lucas whispered something that sounded suspiciously like a prayer.

And me?

I just stared. Because that wasn't Riley Morgan. That was Lady Vengeance.

And she was currently laughing with some handsome asshole in a suit like she hadn't ditched our tactical operation to live out her Bond Girl fantasy.

Then she hugged him. Soft. Familiar. I tightened my grip on the steering wheel instantly.

"Oh, I hate this," I muttered.

Cole looked personally betrayed by reality. "I'm sorry," he said slowly, "what timeline are we in?"

Lucas leaned forward, horrified. "She has earrings. Earrings, Jaxon. She accessorised for him."

That somehow made it worse. I pulled the SUV toward the curb like a man making several poor emotional decisions simultaneously.

Riley turned at the sound. Saw us. And the look she gave us?

Cold. Dismissive. Like she'd just discovered mould growing in her penthouse.

I leaned halfway out the window "Come on, princess. You've got work to do."

Her head tilted. Eyes narrowing just enough to become legally threatening.

Oh. She hated that. Noted.

Then Cole — who had clearly accepted death as an inevitability — leaned across me and grinned. "Come yonder, Your Royal Highness of Tactical Hotness. The peasants require your stabby assistance."

I braced for violence. Instead, Riley smiled. Slow. Sweet. Terrifying. She murmured something to her date, kissed his cheek — which absolutely did not bother me psychologically at all — and turned toward us.

Every step she took toward the SUV should've been illegal.

Heels clicking. Dress swaying. That slit flashing just enough thigh to make my brain briefly leave my body.

She leaned down through the open window, voice soft as silk over sharpened steel. "You call me princess again," she said calmly, "and I'll dislocate your jaw and staple it to your kneecap." Then she opened the back door and climbed inside like she hadn't just emotionally destabilised every man within a two-block radius.

Cole twisted around in his seat. "So still a no on 'Queen of Thighs,' or—?"

She kicked the back of his seat hard enough to rattle him.

"Drive before I decide to accessorise with your spleen." I stared straight ahead, jaw tight against a smile.

Riley Morgan had abandoned a mission, committed a fashion felony by looking that good, and somehow left me feeling like a stunned Victorian man seeing ankle for the first time.

I was confused. I was irritated. And I was pretty sure I had a crush.

Riley

Of course they picked tonight. Not a stakeout. Not a warehouse. Not a shootout. No. Tonight I was at an actual black-tie charity gala. Fairy lights. String quartets. Expensive champagne.

Tiny food served on spoons for no reason.

And Evan — bless his therapist-trained, emotionally available, non-criminal heart — had just bought me a drink and made me laugh for the first time in months.

Then an SUV screeched to the curb outside like the Kool-Aid Man had joined organised crime. The window rolled down. Jaxon leaned out looking like a mobster with unresolved emotional repression and barked:

"Come on, princess. You've got work to do." I saw red. Then black. Then probably murder charges.

Now we were back at the warehouse. And I was furious. I stormed across the floor while the four idiots followed behind me like emotionally compromised ducklings. I yanked open the hidden compartment behind my locker and grabbed my tactical gear.

Then I reached behind myself and ripped the zipper down my back hard enough to qualify as emotional violence. The gown slid to the floor in a whisper of ruined elegance. Gone was silk. Gone was glamour. Gone was my good mood. I peeled off my earrings first.

Then paused halfway through changing and spun around sharply.

"You four," I snapped, pointing aggressively, "are the human equivalent of stepping on LEGO barefoot."

Jaxon blinked like he'd sustained a head injury Lucas turned around so fast he nearly sprained something. Cole looked delighted. Actually delighted. Killian just stood there with his jaw clenched like self-control was becoming a full-time job.

"I had shrimp canapés," I informed them furiously.

"And a white wine buzz." I jabbed a finger toward them.

"And you dragged me back here to chase drug dealers like I'm starring in a low-budget Bond knockoff nobody asked for."

Killian

She tore the zipper down like she was shedding an entire identity. The gown pooled at her feet in black silk.

And suddenly Riley stood there looking less like a woman and more like temptation weaponised.

Bare shoulders. Velvet skin. Scars cutting across elegance like reminders she'd survived every ugly thing the world threw at her.

She planted her hands on her hips without even a flicker of embarrassment. Not shy. Not hesitant. Daring us to look away. Nobody did. Because Riley didn't just enter rooms. She took ownership of them.

"This better be fucking good," she snapped.

Silence. Complete silence. Jaxon looked like somebody had unplugged his brain. Cole had the glazed expression of a man discovering religion in real time. Lucas appeared approximately three seconds away from spontaneous combustion.

And me? I was still trying to remember how breathing worked.

Then Riley stormed down the hallway toward the briefing room, fury rolling off her in visible waves. I cleared my throat roughly. "I'll make it up to her," I muttered. Unfortunately for me, Riley heard that.

She spun instantly, eyes blazing. "Oh, you bet your fucking life you will."

Then she disappeared into the briefing room like vengeance in combat boots. I forced myself to breathe normally and followed after her, posture controlled despite the deeply inconvenient fact my nervous system had fully betrayed me.

Cole leaned closer while we walked. "Glad you're suffering with the rest of us."

"I will end you," I said flatly.

Lucas sighed heavily behind us. "We're doomed."

The worst part? Nobody disagreed.

Riley

I slammed the briefing room door hard enough to shake the glass. If I couldn't kill them, I could at least make them nervous. "You know what pisses me off the most?" I demanded, pacing furiously.

"I could be getting laid right now." Silence. Beautiful, stunned silence.

I pointed directly at Jaxon. "Evan was nice. Funny. Emotionally functional."

I pointed at the rest of them. "And instead I'm here with the Tactical Himbo Association."

Cole snorted. Wrong move. I wheeled toward him instantly.

"No, laugh harder. I dare you." He physically sat up straighter.

"I was this close to a peaceful evening," I continued dramatically, throwing my hands up. "But no. You muscle-brained idiots dragged me into another crime scene because apparently none of you know how calendars work."

I kept pacing. Boots thudding against concrete.

"And the WORST part? Nobody even let me finish dessert."

Lucas muttered quietly, "You were flirting."

I spun so fast he visibly regretted speaking. "Yes, Lucas. That's generally how dates work."

His ears turned bright red. Good. I folded my arms tightly.

"So congratulations. I hope this mission is worth the psychological damage and interrupted orgasms."

Cole whispered reverently. "She gets hotter when she's threatening violence."

"Cole," Killian warned. "What? I'm right."

I groaned loudly and dropped into the nearest chair. "You all have the emotional intelligence of folding chairs."

Then I pointed at them one last time.

"This better be worth it. Or I swear to God I'll disappear again and none of you will ever find me." The room stayed quiet. Mostly because they were smart enough not to test me.

Cole

Every set of eyes eventually landed on me. Riley's included. Which was mildly terrifying considering she currently looked ready to commit homicide recreationally. I cleared my throat and clicked to the next slide.

"This isn't just another drug operation," I said quietly.

The screen lit up with case files, missing persons reports, crime scene photos. "Human trafficking. Child trafficking. Organ harvesting."

The room changed instantly. All humour disappeared.

"This guy's been targeting foster homes, shelters, vulnerable kids." I pointed toward the evidence board. "Children disappear and never come back."

Riley went completely still. Not angry anymore. Worse. Quiet.

"There's also a new drug moving through the city," I continued. "Fast-acting. Fatal. We linked it to multiple overdoses already."

I clicked to the next photo. Teenage boy. Fourteen, maybe fifteen. Dead. Lucas swore softly under his breath.

Jaxon's jaw tightened hard enough to crack teeth. And Riley?

Riley looked like the calm centre of a nuclear explosion. Cold. Focused. Lethal.

"This operation ends tonight," I finished quietly. "All of it."

Silence settled heavily across the room. Then Riley leaned back slowly in her chair. And smiled. Not the playful smile. Not the teasing one. The dangerous one. The one that usually happened right before buildings exploded.

"Oh," she said softly.

"Now I understand why you interrupted my date."

And God help every bastard involved in this operation. Because Riley Morgan had officially decided to make it personal.

Lucas

I knew I was screwed the second Riley stepped out of that gala. Not tactical Riley. Not sarcastic Riley.

Not hoodie-and-combat-boots Riley. This was silk-and-smoke Riley. The kind of beautiful that physically interrupted thought processes.

Then we dragged her away from the first peaceful night she'd probably had in months. And she exploded exactly the way we deserved.

But the second Cole explained the mission?

Everything changed. Her anger sharpened into something colder. Focused. Like a blade being drawn slowly from a sheath. And I couldn't stop watching her.

Every glare. Every threat. Every flicker of violence behind her eyes. I should've been focused on the operation.

Instead I was sitting there realising, with absolute horror, that I was completely gone for her.

Not just attracted. Gone. Because Riley Morgan wasn't a crush anymore. She was becoming gravity. And the worst part?

I didn't even want to escape it.

33

Define fine

Riley

My Name is Dark – Grimes

Larry purred beneath me, smooth and deadly as I threaded through traffic like a goddamn professional.

“Outta my way, assholes,” I muttered, leaning hard into a turn that sliced me between two cars with barely an inch to spare.

Horns blared behind me. Someone yelled something aggressively creative out a window. I didn’t care. By the time I rolled up to the warehouse, the boys were still miles behind.

“Boys,” I murmured, killing the engine and swinging off the bike, helmet tucked beneath my arm. “Catch up.”

I popped a cherry lollipop into my mouth and cracked my neck slowly. Time to work

. The first guard never saw me coming. Amateur. I slipped behind him silently, drove the knife between his ribs, and caught his body before it hit the ground.

“Night-night,” I whispered, dragging him into the shadows.

My comm crackled instantly. “Riley.” Killian. Low. Furious.

I grinned around the lollipop. “Miss me already?”

“Where the fuck are you?”

“Taking out the trash,” I replied casually, ducking behind a stack of crates.

"Riley, we agreed—"

"Did we, though?"

"Yes," Killian growled. "We very specifically did."

I spotted another guard leaning against the fence scrolling through his phone. Hmm. Distracted. My favourite kind.

Lucas cut into the comms. "You said that last time."

"And it was fine."

"You ended up in the ER."

"Details."

I moved behind the guard soundlessly. "Texting your girlfriend?" I murmured. He turned just in time for my blade to slice across his throat. Blood sprayed warm across my hand.

"Oops," I whispered as he collapsed. "Guess you'll have to reschedule."

"Riley," Killian snapped again.

"Still here," I sing-songed.

"Define 'fine.'"

"Breathing."

"For now," Lucas muttered darkly.

I grinned.

"Wow. Such faith."

"We don't trust you," Killian said flatly.

"Smart."

With the perimeter cleared, I slipped beneath the rusted loading dock and into the warehouse proper.

The cameras were insultingly easy. One flick of my wrist and the security feed died instantly.

"Cameras are down."

"Good," Lucas replied immediately. "Now get back outside and wait for us."

"Yeah, about that..." I was already planting C4.

"Riley." Killian's warning tone deepened.

"Relax, big guy," I said lightly as the first charge armed with a soft beep. "Just doing a little redecorating."

I moved deeper into the building.

Then froze. Children. Huddled together in the corner behind rusted cages. Pale. Hollow-eyed. Terrified.

And across the room— A teenage boy, limp and bloodless, being dragged across the floor like discarded garbage while red smeared behind him in streaks.

Something inside me snapped clean in half. The lollipop cracked between my teeth.

"Fuck going quiet," I muttered.

I crouched beside the children slowly. "Hey," I whispered softly.

Blank stares met mine. "It's okay. I'm here to get you out."

Nothing. Jesus Christ. I forced a crooked smile.

"Okay, listen carefully. I need you all to close your eyes and cover your ears."

Still frozen.

"Pretend I'm Santa Claus," I said patiently. "And if you don't listen, Christmas is cancelled forever."

A few hesitant nods. Progress.

"Good. Stay here. Don't move."

"Riley, status," Killian barked.

"Alive. Angry. Armed." I shoved a grape lollipop into my mouth this time and rose to my feet.

"Do not engage until we get there," Killian ordered.

"Oops." Too late. I moved fast. Knife to the throat. Bullet through an eye socket. Another body hit the floor before the screaming even started.

Then— BANG. Fire exploded through my side. White-hot pain ripped the air from my lungs.

"Fuck." I stumbled behind a crate, slamming a hand against my side.

Warm. Wet.

Too much blood.

"Riley?" Killian again. Sharp now. Worried.

"Still here," I rasped.

"What happened?"

"Nothing." My voice tightened.

"Testing the durability of my jacket."

"Riley—"

"Relax. Just a scratch."

"Define scratch."

"Not dead."

"Yet," Lucas muttered.

I forced myself upright, pain detonating through my ribs. "Walk it off," I hissed to myself.

"Riley, stay the fuck down," Killian ordered.

"Yeah, yeah." I staggered deeper into the warehouse, pressing harder against the wound.

"Just finishing up."

"Finishing WHAT?" Killian snapped.

"The boom's about to go off."

"Riley—"

"Relax, big guy." The edges of my vision blurred.

"I'm fine."

"You don't sound fine."

"Define fine." A long silence crackled through the comms.

Then quieter: "Just hold on until we get there."

Because when they arrived?

These bastards were going to learn exactly why you never cornered something already willing to die angry.

And unfortunately for everyone involved— I was officially out of lollipops.

Jaxon

We barely had the SUVs parked before I was already moving. Boots slammed against gravel as I sprinted toward the warehouse.

"Where the fuck is she?" Adrenaline pounded through me hard enough to hurt.

Because Riley had gone in alone. Again. And judging by the bodies scattered across the perimeter? She'd already turned this place into a goddamn massacre.

"Jaxon, left flank," Killian ordered through comms. "On it."

Blood soaked the gravel beneath my boots as I moved. Guards. Traffickers. Bodies everywhere. Jesus Christ.

Gunfire erupted from inside the warehouse.

"She's inside," Lucas said sharply.

"How bad?" A pause. Then: "Bad."

That cold feeling in my stomach turned lethal. "Move," I barked.

The second I entered the building, I knew Riley had been here. Because everything was on fucking fire.

Smoke rolled across the ceiling. Bullet casings littered the floor.

Bodies lay crumpled across the concrete like Riley had personally declared war against human anatomy.

Cole stared around slowly. "It looks like Tarantino directed a hate crime."

"Stay focused," Killian snapped.

"Riley," he barked through comms. "Where are you?" Nothing. "Riley." Still nothing.

My chest tightened painfully.

Then finally— "I'm fine."

Bullshit. Her voice sounded weak. Strained.

Way too quiet. "Define fine," I growled, moving deeper into the smoke.

"I mean..." she rasped. "Breathing? Conscious? Bleeding a little. So technically? Fine."

"How bad?" Killian demanded.

"Nothing I can't—fuck!"

Gunfire exploded over comms. Every muscle in my body locked.

"Riley, where the fuck are you?!" Killian shouted.

"Behind a crate," she snapped back breathlessly. "Southwest corner. Also I've made some new friends."

I rounded a stack of crates and saw her. And my blood went cold.

Riley crouched behind splintered crate with blood pouring through her fingers where she clutched her side.

Too pale. Too still. Too much fucking blood.

"Riley's hit," I bit out.

I dropped beside her immediately. "Jesus Christ."

She looked up at me with a weak grin and the world's worst timing.

"Hey, Jaxon." There was still a grape lollipop hanging from her mouth. My brain nearly shut down.

"You've been shot," I snapped.

"Grape," she corrected weakly, pulling the lollipop out. "Want a taste?"

I stared at her in disbelief. "You're joking right now?"

"Deflection, baby." Jesus fucking Christ.

"Can you move?"

"Define move?" Nope. Absolutely not. I grabbed her chin carefully, forcing her eyes onto mine.

"Do not pass out on me."

"Wasn't planning to." Her eyelids fluttered anyway.

"Killian," I barked into comms. "We need extraction NOW."

Gunfire erupted again. Four men moved through the smoke toward us. I stepped out from cover immediately.

Pop- Pop-pop.

Three bodies dropped before they fully registered I was there. The fourth tried to flank left. Wrong choice.

I put him down too.

"Nice," Riley murmured weakly behind me.

"Stay down," I snapped. She leaned back against the crate.

"Relax. I'm not going anywhere."

"Damn right you're not." I pressed harder against her wound to slow the bleeding.

"Hold on, Princess."

Even bleeding out, she smirked.

"Aw. You getting soft on me, Jax?" Christ.

"Shut up, Riley." Boots thundered across the warehouse floor seconds later. Killian. Cole. Lucas.

"Clear!" Killian barked before his eyes landed on Riley. Everything in his face changed instantly.

"Shit."

"Yeah," I muttered tightly.

Killian dropped beside us immediately.

"Riley."

"Hey, Kill."

"Don't," he said sharply. "Don't you fucking do this."

She coughed weakly. "Relax, big guy. I'm fine."

"You are not fine." Lucas slid beside us with the med kit already open.

"Riley, you're bleeding out."

"Patch me up." Lucas blinked.

"What?"

"I said patch me up." Her eyes lifted toward Killian.

"The kids." That stopped all of us cold.

Because suddenly the mission wasn't about her anymore. It was about them.

And Riley would crawl through broken glass before she abandoned those children. Lucas swore quietly and started bandaging the wound.

"If you pass out—"

"I won't."

"If you pass out—"

"I literally do not have time for this conversation, Lucas."

Riley

Everything hurt. Like... spiritually. The second Lucas finished bandaging me, I pushed myself upright.

Huge mistake.

My vision tilted violently sideways and suddenly all four idiots were yelling at once.

"Riley—"

"Sit the fuck down!"

"You're gonna pass out!"

"I'm FINE." Lie. Massive lie.

But there were still kids curled in the corner staring at us like frightened animals and I didn't have time to collapse dramatically.

I staggered toward them anyway. The second I crouched down beside them, their terrified little faces turned toward me. And something inside my chest cracked open. They were so small.

Too small.

"Hey," I whispered gently. Their tiny hands tightened around each other.

I forced a smile. "Guess what?"

Silence. "We won."

One of the older boys blinked slowly. "Really?"

"Uh-huh." I lowered my voice conspiratorially.

"But there's one final level."

That got their attention. "I need everybody to hold hands and close their eyes REALLY tight. No peeking."

"Why?" a little girl whispered. I brushed hair carefully away from her face.

"Because fireworks are about to go off." Her eyes widened.

"And they're really bright." Understanding flickered slowly across their faces.

"Good," I whispered.

Then I scooped the smallest child into my arms. Ow. Bad choice. Horrible choice.

"Okay," I breathed through the pain. "When I say go... we run."

"Run where?"

"Out of here."

I grinned despite the blood soaking through my bandages. "Before the fireworks go boom."

Jaxon

I genuinely don't know how she was still standing. One minute she was bleeding out behind a crate.

The next? She was carrying a toddler while comforting terrified kids like some kind of feral Disney princess with a body count.

"Holy shit," I muttered.

Killian looked murderous. "We move now."

Riley straightened slowly.

"Alright, guys," she whispered to the children. "Eyes closed. Hold hands."

The building rumbled beneath us. Shit.

"Go!" Riley shouted. Then we were running. Chaos exploded behind us.

Gunfire. Smoke. Sirens in the distance. Cole had one kid slung over his shoulder complaining loudly about cardio.

I grabbed two others under my arms. Killian stayed locked beside Riley the entire time like he physically couldn't let her out of his sight. We barely cleared the perimeter before Riley screamed: "GET DOWN!"

The explosion hit a second later. The warehouse erupted behind us in a wall of fire and steel. Heat slammed across my back hard enough to knock me sideways.

And Riley?

Riley started laughing. Actually laughing.

"What the FUCK?!" I shouted over the ringing in my ears.

She grinned weakly. "Surprise?"

"You planted explosives while bleeding out?!"

"Multitasking."

"Jesus Christ," Killian muttered. The kids huddled around us crying and shaking while Riley adjusted the toddler in her arms carefully.

"You okay, sweetheart?" she asked softly. The little girl nodded. "Good girl."

Then Riley's knees nearly buckled. I moved instantly. Killian caught her first. For one terrifying second, Riley sagged against him like her body had finally decided enough was enough.

Still smiling. Still stubborn. Still Riley. "Alright, kiddos," she rasped weakly. "Who wants ice cream?"

A tiny chorus of exhausted voices answered immediately. And behind me?

I think Lucas whispered: "What the actual fuck."

34

Tarts, Trauma, and Tactical Smut

Riley

Don't Come Down – The Maine

By the time I stumbled into my apartment, I was dead on my feet. Literally.

If I wasn't bleeding out from a hole in my side, I'd have done a little victory dance right there in the doorway.

But nope. All I managed was a half-stagger, half-collapse onto the couch, where I flopped face-first and groaned so loud the neighbours probably thought I was auditioning for a ghost movie. Fucking hell.

But honestly?

Worth it. Because before we'd left that damn park... I had somehow conned Killian into paying for ice cream.

"Thirty-seven ice creams, please."

The poor ice cream vendor had stared at us like we were crazy, but I was too busy basking in the glory of Killian swiping his card and looking like he was having an out-of-body experience as the total flashed across the screen.

"One hundred and seventy-eight dollars for ice cream, Killian."

The look on his face was priceless. I mean, I was bleeding out and still managed to convince him to fork over enough cash to buy ice cream for every one of those kids — plus a few extras for me.

Priorities. And the best part?

"We've called the cops. They'll be here in five."

That little anonymous tip I'd left?

Flawless. Kids safe. Traffickers dead.

Warehouse?

Boom.

And now?

I was alive — barely — and eating raspberry tarts like a fucking queen.

"Riley, you need to go to the hospital."

Killian's voice was all serious alpha male as he stood near the door, arms crossed, glaring at me like I was a naughty child. I didn't even bother to lift my head.

"Go fuck yourself," I mumbled into the pillow, grabbing the half-eaten tart off the coffee table and shoving it into my mouth.

"Riley."

"I know a guy," I mumbled around the tart, waving them off with my free hand. "Grant will be here soon. Relax."

"Grant?" Lucas asked, brows shooting up.

"Who the fuck is Grant?" Jaxon muttered, pacing near the window.

"He's a doctor," I murmured, licking raspberry filling off my thumb. "An actual doctor. Not one of those 'ask too many questions' types."

Killian's glare could've melted steel.

"Riley—"

"I said I know a guy."

"A guy," Killian repeated dryly.

"Yes, a guy," I grumbled, finally peeling my face off the couch to glare at all of them.

"And now you can leave." None of them moved. Not one.

They just stood there like fucking statues. "Seriously?" I groaned. "What part of 'get the fuck out' was unclear?"

"We're not leaving," Killian said flatly.

"What if you bleed out?" Lucas added.

"Bleed out? Me?" I snorted. "Please. I've survived worse."

"Riley."

Oh, great. Now Jaxon was using his concerned big brother voice.

"I swear to God..." I muttered, throwing my head back dramatically. "You're all like a fucking herd of confused sheep."

And that's how I ended up stuck with four oversized man-children crammed into my tiny-ass apartment.

Jaxon paced. Killian stood near the door looking like he was one inconvenience away from homicide. Lucas hovered by the window pretending not to track things on his tablet.

And Cole? Fucking Cole. Perched on my counter eating my chips.

"Seriously?" I muttered. "You're eating my snacks?"

"You left them out."

For a few blessed minutes, there was silence.

Then— "Riley, why do you have blueprints for the city's electrical grid?"

Lucas. My head snapped toward him instantly.

"For reasons." "What kind of reasons?" "My reasons."

"And why do you have a box of burner phones in your closet?" Jaxon asked.

"Insurance."

"For what?"

"Life."

Jaxon blinked. "You have an escape plan?"

"Doesn't everyone?"

Apparently not, judging by their faces. Then Killian's voice cut through the room.

"Riley, what the fuck is this?"

I cracked one eye open. He was holding Loretta. My medieval flail.

"Emergency situations," I muttered weakly. "Leave Loretta alone."

"You named it?"

"Of course I named it. Everything gets a name."

And just when I thought I might actually get some peace— Grant walked in.

The second he stepped through the door, he froze. His eyes swept over the absolute disaster in front of him.

Me half-conscious on the couch. Four massive armed men loitering around my apartment like they were planning a coup.

And blood. So much blood.

"What the fuck is this?"

"Grant!" I grinned weakly. "My hero."

His eyes narrowed immediately. "Riley."

"Before you yell at me—"

"Don't."

He dropped his bag on the coffee table and strode toward me already radiating pissed-off doctor energy.

Grant crouched beside me, eyes scanning my side.

"Jesus Christ, Riley."

"Nice to see you too, Doc."

"This is worse than the last time."

"Define worse."

"You're half a pint away from passing out."

"Eh." I waved lazily. "I've had worse." Then he noticed them.

Grant slowly looked over at the four idiots hovering nearby.

"Who the fuck are they?"

"The Four Musketeers," I mumbled. Grant blinked once. Twice. Then stood up.

And growled— "Why the fuck are you all still here?"

Silence. Pure fucking silence.

Killian, Jaxon, Lucas, and Cole all exchanged looks. Not one of them answered.

"Well?" Grant snapped.

"We're... keeping an eye on her," Lucas muttered.

"Making sure she doesn't bleed out," Cole added around a mouthful of chips.

"She has me for that."

I couldn't help grinning.

"Aww," I slurred. "They care." Grant's jaw tightened.

"You're lucky you're cute."

"I know." Grant worked quickly, stitching me up while muttering curses under his breath.

When he finished, he pointed directly at my face.

"Rest."

"Yes, sir."

"And you four—" Every single one of them straightened automatically.

"Keep her from doing anything fucking stupid."

"Got it," Cole said immediately.

Grant sighed heavily. "I'm too old for this shit." Then he left.

And finally, exhaustion dragged me under. "Night, boys," I murmured sleepily.

As I drifted off, I heard Cole mutter— "I'm taking the recliner." "Like hell you are," Killian growled. And then darkness swallowed me whole.

Riley

I woke to soft murmuring. Voices. Familiar voices. Still here. Of course they were.

I kept my eyes closed, breathing slow and even while my brain catalogued every sound in the room.

Jaxon was sprawled across my floor like a sleeping prince.

Cole lounged on the arm of the couch.

And Lucas— Wait. Lucas was sitting in my chair. Reading.

My sluggish brain slowly caught up.

Then my eyes focused on the bright purple cover in his hands.

Alpha's Four: Claimed by the Pack.

Oh. My. Fucking. God.

Lucas was reading my smut.

I was going to kill him.

Slowly. Painfully. Possibly with the knitting needles on the coffee table.

But not yet. Because Lucas had no idea.

He sat there completely focused, lips moving faintly while he read like he was studying classified tactical intel.

I stayed perfectly still. Patient. Silent. Because this?

This was going to be worth it.

At first his expression stayed neutral.

Focused.

Then— A slight furrow. A pause. Another page turn.

"Oh..." Barely a whisper. But I heard it.

His entire body went rigid. He blinked. Went back a page.

Read it again. "Ohhhhh..." Boom. I had to bite the inside of my cheek to stop laughing.

Because his face? Priceless. "What the..." he whispered faintly. "Strategic positioning...?"

Oh, sweetheart. Not that kind of positioning. Then came the moment. Eyes widening. Jaw dropping.

Pure existential horror. "Oh, fuck."

I was dying. Absolutely fucking dying.

"Lucas?" Cole asked slowly.

No response.

Lucas was too busy having a religious crisis. Jaxon sat up groggily. "What's he reading?" Cole leaned forward.

Then grinned. "Holy shit."

Jaxon squinted at the cover. Then immediately lost his fucking mind. "No way." "Whatcha reading, buddy?" Cole asked sweetly.

Lucas jerked like he'd been electrocuted. "It's— I thought it was about pack dynamics—"

Jaxon collapsed wheezing onto the floor.

"PACK DYNAMICS?"

Cole was openly crying laughing now. "That's not pack dynamics, Lucas."

Lucas slammed the book shut like it was cursed. "I need to leave."

"Oh no," Jaxon wheezed. "You're not escaping this."

"Gonna do some... research?" Cole asked innocently.

"Fuck all of you." Lucas shot upright, face bright red, grabbing his jacket.

"I'm leaving." Not yet, sweetheart.

"Hey, Lucas..." He froze at the door. "There's a sequel." His soul visibly left his body.

"Nope." Door slam. Immediate chaos. Jaxon wheezing.

Cole crying. Killian barely holding it together. I finally cracked one eye open.

"You're all fucking idiots." Every head snapped toward me.

Cole grinned immediately. "Oh, you're awake?" "Did you enjoy the show?"

"Immensely." Best. Day. Ever.

Cole

She moved. A groan. A shift. And suddenly the entire room lost its collective shit.

Jaxon launched upright. Killian nearly tackled the coffee table trying to get to her. And me?

I stayed exactly where I was. Smirking. Because of course I did.

"Sit. The fuck. Down." The way she growled it?

Music. Absolute fucking music.

Jaxon froze instantly. Killian stopped moving like she'd physically restrained him.

And me?

Still smirking. Because she looked half-dead and still somehow managed to boss all of us around like she owned the world.

God, I loved her. "I said I'm fine."

Lie. Massive fucking lie.

She looked like a corpse someone hit with jumper cables. Pale. Sweaty.

Held together entirely by painkillers and spite. But she pushed herself upright anyway.

Because Riley doesn't rest. She survives out of pure stubborn rage.

I watched every tiny movement.

The shaking hands. The shallow breathing. The way she clenched her teeth every time she moved.

"Riley—"

"Don't." Jaxon shut up immediately.

Smart man. She limped toward the kitchen.

Lucas leaned against the doorway calmly. "You need a hospital."

"You need to fuck off."

God. I could kiss her.

She grabbed pills from the cabinet and swallowed them dry with water. Then leaned heavily against the counter pretending everything was fine.

"Why the fuck are you still here?"

"You're hurt."

"Genius."

"You almost bled out, sweetheart."

"We're not leaving you alone."

"I'm not gonna die."

"Barely," Killian muttered darkly.

"You shouldn't even be standing."

"I've been through worse," she lied.

Again. Pride and prescription drugs. That was Riley in a nutshell.

Killian stepped forward like he was about to argue. I beat him to it.

"And we'll be here next time you decide to be a stubborn ass about it."

She threw her arms up dramatically. Mistake.

Her entire body flinched hard enough to make my stomach drop.

Fucking Lucas. Weaponising my own smut against me. I was going to kill him. Immediately after changing my underwear.

"Nope." I shoved more clothes violently into the bag. Nope. Absolutely fucking not. Three months with these assholes?

Fine. But they weren't getting a sweet cooperative Riley. They were getting chaos. Pure fucking chaos.

"Alright, sweetheart, let's go."

Jaxon. Of course.

"You need help, sugar?"

"You're all concussed."

"Because we don't want you bleeding out alone?"

"No. Because you've all suddenly decided to use every nickname in existence."

"What's wrong with princess?" Cole called.

"Or sweetheart?" Jaxon added.

"What about sugar?"

I wanted violence. "Riley," I ground out. "My name is Riley."

"Sure thing, baby girl," Lucas said innocently.

Fucker. "Lucas." Dangerously calm now.

"Say it again."

"Baby girl?" Absolute menace.

"We're just getting started, baby girl."

35

Four Idiots and a Bed of Satin Lies

Riley

Bottom of the Deep Blue Sea – MISSIO

I woke up to soft twinkling lights blinking overhead like smug little stars judging me. My eyelids fluttered open. I blinked once. Twice. Nope. Still there.

The ceiling was painted a delicate pastel lavender, fairy lights strung up like constellations. Gossamer fabric draped from the corners of the room, tied back with satin ribbons around the enormous canopy bed I was currently sinking into like a goddamn marshmallow.

A literal canopy. Over a bed. With heart-shaped pillows.

I sat up slowly, every muscle screaming in protest — and not just from the gunshot wound. No.

This pain was existential. Traumatic. Because I was in a fucking princess room.

"What in the name of sparkly hell..."

The comforter was soft violet satin, plush and obnoxiously luxurious. Glitter shimmered across decorative pillows. A tiara — an actual fucking tiara — sat on the bedside table beside a delicate glass slipper figurine.

If this was someone's idea of a joke, I was going to find them and break their kneecaps.

My shoulder and ribs ached beneath the bandages. My pride hurt worse.

I swung my legs over the side of the bed, one boot half-on, dangling loosely from my foot.

Didn't even bother tying it. What was the point? There was no escaping this level of pastel horror.

Then voices drifted through the door. Great.

The assholes were awake. I stood slowly, taking in the full nightmare with fresh eyes.

Lavender curtains. A bookshelf filled with romance novels. A vanity. A fucking vanity.

Complete with pearl-handled brushes and blush pink makeup trays I would rather die than touch.

It looked like the Barbie aisle and a royal palace had a baby. And somehow I was its hostage.

I dragged a hand through my hair, already regretting every life decision that led me here.

I should've stitched myself up. Should've faked being fine. Should've kicked Cole in the face while I still had the chance.

But no. I passed out. And apparently that counted as consent to imprison me in a glitter-coated fever dream.

I glared at the door. If one of them knocked, I was launching a sequin pillow directly at their face.

Right on cue— Knock. I froze mid-step.

Eyes narrowing. "Riley." Killian.

Of course. His voice was calm. Too calm.

Like he hadn't trapped me inside a unicorn's dying hallucination. "Go away."

"No."

Naturally. I debated yelling something threatening involving blunt-force trauma and tiaras, but instead I stomped toward the door and yanked it open.

Killian stood there, broad arms crossed over his chest like some brooding gargoyle carved from stubbornness and emotional repression.

Behind him? The usual suspects. Cole. Lucas. Jaxon. All looking far too pleased with themselves.

“What,” I asked flatly, “do you want now?”

Killian didn’t blink. “You’ve been asleep fourteen hours. Time to check in.”

“You mean time for the four of you to hover like stressed-out nannies with military-grade trauma.”

Cole grinned immediately. “You missed us.” I flipped him off slowly. With feeling.

Lucas smirked. “Nice room?”

I gestured wildly behind me. “Oh, I love it. Truly. I feel like a Disney princess who does her own assassinations.”

Jaxon snorted.

“Hey, we could’ve put you in the weapons locker.”

“I would’ve preferred the weapons locker.” K

illian still hadn’t moved. “We need to talk.” I raised a brow.

“What now? You extending my stay in Sparkle Palace indefinitely? Should I start naming the pillows?”

“No,” he said evenly. “But you’re not going anywhere until we’re sure the threat’s contained.”

I bristled instantly. “So I’m a prisoner.”

“You’re recovering.”

“I’m recovering fine.”

“You passed out,” Lucas reminded me.

“I was tired.”

“You were bleeding.”

“It was aesthetic bleeding,” I snapped. “For dramatic effect.” Cole choked on a laugh.

“Yeah? Ten out of ten. Very theatrical.” I turned away dramatically, hands on my hips.

"What next? You all gonna braid my hair and talk about your feelings? Should we start a glitter scrapbook?"

Killian's gaze flicked over me slowly. And for half a second, something in his expression shifted. Worry. Maybe guilt. Hard to tell with him.

"You need rest," he said quietly. "We're not leaving."

The fight drained out of me in one long exhale. Because my ribs hurt. Because standing felt increasingly optional. Because apparently blood loss was a real thing and not just an inconvenience. "Fine," I muttered, stepping aside. "But if any of you touches that tiara, I will end you."

Cole immediately grabbed it and shoved it onto his head. "How do I look?"

"Like a dead man."

Lucas walked in next, tablet already in hand. Killian entered last. Quiet. Watchful.

Jaxon dropped into an armchair shaped like a fucking unicorn.

Because apparently God had abandoned me entirely. I sank back onto the mattress with a wince while fairy lights mocked me from above.

"Great," I sighed. "Now we're all trapped in a Lisa Frank fever dream together."

Killian crossed his arms. "You'll thank us later."

"I'll stab you later."

The four of them spread throughout the room like they owned it. Lucas settled against the bookshelf, eyes flicking to me every few seconds like he was deciding whether sedation was necessary. Jaxon sprawled across the unicorn chair like a king claiming territory. Cole stretched out across the foot of the bed wearing the tiara like he'd been born for it.

And Killian remained closest to the door. Guarding. Always guarding. I pointed accusingly at the ceiling. "Whose fucked-up idea was this room?"

Lucas didn't even glance up. "Define fucked-up."

Cole proudly raised his hand. "That would be me."

"I knew it." I glared. "You gave me princess curtains and a bed so soft I nearly drowned in it."

"You're welcome."

"I was unconscious, you psychopath."

"Exactly why you didn't get a say," Jaxon added.

"I hate all of you."

"Sure you do," Cole said smugly, fluffing a heart-shaped pillow behind his head. "But deep down? Under all the sarcasm and blood loss? You love us." I checked my bandages dramatically.

"Nope. Still bleeding. No love here. Just vengeance."

Killian finally spoke again. "You're still running a fever."

"Because I'm surrounded by idiots," I shot back. "And fairy lights. Why are there fairy lights?"

"To create a soothing healing environment," Lucas deadpanned.

I launched a pillow at him. He caught it one-handed without even looking up. Show-off.

A wave of dizziness hit suddenly. Sharp enough to make the room tilt sideways. I blinked hard. Fine. I was fine. Probably. Killian noticed immediately. Of course he fucking did. "Lucas."

Lucas stood instantly. "Painkillers?" I didn't argue. Mostly because arguing suddenly sounded exhausting.

He slipped from the room quietly, leaving me alone with the other three disasters.

Cole started humming obnoxiously. Jaxon drummed his fingers against the armrest like he was composing the soundtrack to my suffering.

And Killian kept watching me like I might explode. I dragged the blanket higher over my legs.

"You're not actually staying here all night, right?"

Jaxon grinned. "We brought snacks."

"I call floor duty beside the unicorn nightlight," Cole announced proudly. I stared at them in horror.

"I swear to God, if any of you snore, I'm setting this bed on fire."

"Guess we're all dying together then," Cole said cheerfully.

Killian didn't smile. But something in his eyes softened. Just slightly. And somehow that was worse.

Because I could handle the teasing. The banter. The chaos. But care?

That was dangerous. That was how people got under your skin. Lucas returned carrying water and painkillers, silently handing them over. I took them. Swallowed them. Didn't say thank you.

Instead I flopped backward into the mountain of obnoxiously soft pillows and sighed dramatically. "If I wake up tomorrow and there's a pink robe waiting for me, I'm smothering someone with it."

"I'm personally rooting for lilac," Jaxon said.

"Not helping."

Killian finally moved closer, sitting carefully on the edge of the bed. Close enough to feel his warmth. Not touching. Never touching unless I let him.

"Get some rest," he said quietly. "We'll be here." I didn't answer.

Just closed my eyes while exhaustion dragged me under again. Because the painkillers were kicking in.

Because maybe I was tired of pretending I didn't need anyone.

Because maybe — just for tonight — I didn't mind if they stayed. Even in this ridiculous, sparkling, overstuffed fairy-tale prison.

36

Sleeping Beauty and the Dumbass Who Tried It

Cole

Kiss With a Fist – Florence + The Machine

The laughter in the living room had started to dull, plates scraped clean and the air thick with post-mission exhaustion. But me? I was restless.

Riley hadn't made a single peep since she stomped off to her princess prison hours ago, and that wasn't like her.

Usually she'd storm through the house flipping us off before dinner was even cold. I glanced toward the hallway.

"She still hasn't come out," I muttered, standing and brushing crumbs off my shirt.

Jaxon snorted from the couch. "She probably booby-trapped the door. Good luck."

I grinned. "If I die, I want Went Out Being Hot and Curious on my tombstone."

That earned a laugh from the room, but the second I stepped into the hallway, something shifted. The air got quieter. Heavier. Like the whole damn house was holding its breath.

I stopped outside her door and knocked once. Soft. "Riley?" Nothing. I frowned.

Then slowly pushed the door open. And stopped dead. She was asleep. Actually asleep.

Sprawled across that ridiculous fairy-tale bed like some exhausted little war criminal princess wrapped in violet satin and heart-shaped pillows.

The fairy lights overhead cast a soft glow across her skin, turning all the sharp edges of her into something gentler. Quieter.

That constant tension she carried in her jaw? Gone. The fight behind her eyes? Resting. For once, Riley Morgan looked peaceful. And Christ.

That did something dangerous to my chest. My grin faded slowly. Shit. She looked beautiful. Not that I'd ever say it out loud. Especially not in front of Killian. He'd murder me and hide the body himself.

But then— Because apparently I'm a complete fucking idiot with no self-preservation instincts whatsoever—

I pulled out my phone. Click. Click.

The second picture caught the fairy lights perfectly behind her like some unholy romance novel cover.

Oh yeah. Absolutely going in the group chat. But standing there watching her breathe slowly beneath all those blankets... Something else crawled up my spine. Something reckless. Just one kiss. Harmless. Funny. Maybe even cute. If I didn't know Riley so well.

If she'd ever let anyone close enough while awake. "Wake up, Sleeping Beauty," I whispered softly.

Then leaned down. Barely brushing my lips against hers. Soft. Warm. For half a second my brain completely fucking short-circuited.

Then— BOOM. Her eyes snapped open. Wild. Sharp. Murderous. Oh fuck. Time slowed.

Her fist launched upward before my brain could fully process incoming death. CRACK.

White-hot pain exploded across my face. "JESUS FUCKING CHRIST!"

I stumbled backward clutching my nose while blood immediately poured through my fingers. Hot. Wet. Immediate.

Riley shot upright breathing hard, eyes blazing like she was two seconds away from committing homicide.

"WHAT THE HELL IS WRONG WITH YOU?!"

"I thought—" My voice came out weirdly stuffed and nasal. "—it'd be funny!"

"FUNNY?!" She looked genuinely ready to kill me. "You kissed me while I was asleep, you absolute pervert!"

Okay. Yeah. Fair. Still worth it. "I took a picture too—" Why the fuck did I say that? Her entire face flushed red instantly. "YOU WHAT?!"

Before she could launch herself at me again—

The door exploded open. Killian. Lucas. Jaxon. Fantastic. Full audience.

"She punched me!" I yelled through blood-covered hands.

"He kissed me without my consent!" Riley screamed back, pointing at me like she was preparing an execution.

Killian's expression immediately dropped into full someone's dying tonight mode. Lucas looked like his brain had temporarily disconnected from reality. And Jaxon?

Jaxon was folded in half laughing so hard he could barely fucking breathe.

Killian's voice went low. Cold. Final. "Cole. Get your nose looked at. Now." "But—" "Now."

I shuffled toward the door like a wounded soldier returning from battle, blood still dripping everywhere while Jaxon wheezed beside the wall.

"Dude," he gasped. "You're gonna need more than stitches."

"Shut up," I muttered, jamming tissues against my nose.

Behind me Riley was still yelling threats involving bodily harm and possible castration.

Honestly? Valid.

But as I limped down the hallway grinning like a complete asshole anyway, there was only one thought running through my head. Totally worth it.

"I HEARD THAT!" Riley screeched from inside the room.

The door slammed hard enough to rattle the walls. Jaxon lost his shit all over again.

And me?

Yeah. Maybe I deserved the broken nose. Maybe I was a fucking idiot. But the memory of those soft sleepy seconds before she decked me?

Still worth it.

37

Things I Pretend Not to Feel

Riley

Fire on Fire – Sam Smith

The warehouse had settled into one of those rare quiet lulls. The kind where even the air seemed hesitant to stir.

Jaxon was sprawled beside me on the couch, feet kicked up on the coffee table while some mindless action movie played across the TV.

I wasn't really watching it. Wasn't really here. My body was — curled into the corner of the couch, hoodie sleeves pulled over my hands — but my mind was somewhere darker.

Every thought tangled into another. Static. Noise. A storm I couldn't switch off.

Then— A soft clink of glass against wood.

I blinked slowly. A glass of water. A small plate of snacks.

My gaze tracked upward. Lucas. He didn't say anything at first. Just stood there with his hands tucked into his pockets, watching me carefully.

Not pity. Never pity. Just something steady. Quiet. Intentional.

I hesitated before reaching for the water, fingers brushing condensation.

Cold. Grounding.

"Thanks," I muttered softly.

Lucas nodded once. "You barely ate yesterday."

A tiny smile tugged at my mouth. Barely there.

"Smart move," I murmured before taking a sip.

"Even you need fuel," he replied simply.

Beside me, Jaxon snorted.

"Careful, Lucas. Keep acting like this and she's gonna start thinking she's special."

I flipped him off without looking. "Shut up, Jax."

Lucas chuckled quietly before retreating toward the kitchen. Gone in seconds. But the warmth lingered anyway.

I picked at the food slowly while the TV hummed softly in the background. The noise dulled the sharp edges in my head. And before I realised it, my eyes drifted shut. Sleep pulled me under fast.

I didn't know how long I'd been asleep before voices dragged me back toward consciousness. "Don't."

Jaxon. "You're no fun," Cole complained.

I didn't even need to open my eyes to know he was hovering too close.

"You smother her, she punches you," Jaxon muttered.

"It's basic survival."

"That's what makes it fun."

I heard Cole shuffle away dramatically.

Then— The air shifted. Heavy. Controlled. Killian. I stayed still. Breathing slow. Measured. Like if I pretended hard enough, maybe he'd leave. Or maybe stay.

The couch dipped beside me. Then strong arms slid beneath me carefully. One under my shoulders. One beneath my knees. Gentle. Deliberate.

I stirred faintly but didn't fight him. Didn't have the energy to. Or maybe I just didn't want to. My head rested against his chest as he carried me down the hallway.

Warm. Steady. Safe. Dangerously safe. And for one terrifying heartbeat... I let myself enjoy it.

The second we stepped into my room, I knew exactly what he was seeing. Everything neat. Organised. Portable.

Like I could disappear in five minutes flat. Because I could. Because I always had.

Killian lowered me onto the bed carefully, one hand behind my back easing me down against the mattress.

I stayed still. Barely breathing. Then his hand brushed my hair back gently, tucking a strand behind my ear.

Soft. Careful. Too careful. Something in my chest cracked painfully beneath it.

He lingered for a second longer. Then warmth brushed against my forehead.

A kiss. Barely there. Gone almost instantly. I didn't open my eyes.

Couldn't. Because my throat ached. Because feeling this much this fast felt dangerous.

The door clicked shut softly behind him.

And somehow... That hurt worse.

Killian

I should've walked away. But I didn't.

I stood outside her room for far too long staring at the closed door like it held answers I didn't deserve.

Then, naturally— Cole appeared. Leaning against the opposite wall with the smuggest expression I'd ever wanted to punch off someone's face.

"Didn't take you for the sentimental type," he drawled.

My fists clenched automatically. "Walk away."

He ignored that immediately. "Just saying," he continued with a grin, "you kiss anyone like that again and we're gonna need an emotional support animal."

I stepped toward him. He wisely shut the fuck up. For about three seconds.

Then his expression shifted slightly. Softer. Real. "Just... be careful, yeah?"

That caught me off guard more than the joke did. Because he meant it. And somehow that made everything worse. I turned away before I said something I'd regret.

Back in my room, I didn't pace. Didn't break anything. Didn't punch walls.

I planned. Because apologies weren't enough. Not for Riley. Not after what we'd done. So I did what I do best.

I started moving pieces.

Lucas

We owed her.That thought had been clawing at me for days. No matter how many tactical reasons we'd had for dragging Riley out of that gala...Emotionally?

We'd butchered it. And she felt it.

I looked up from my coffee as Killian leaned against the kitchen counter, unreadable as always.

"She's not talking to any of us," he said.

"Correction," Jaxon replied while flipping pancakes, "she called me 'the least irritating of the four dumbasses who ruined her night.' So technically I'm her favourite."

Cole snorted. "She flipped me off with both hands and a toe. That's basically affection."

I didn't laugh. Because I'd already crossed lines none of them knew about.

"I hacked her laptop," I admitted quietly.

Silence. Jaxon blinked. Cole looked delighted. Killian just sighed like this was somehow expected.

"I saw her search history," I continued. "She bookmarked an exhibit downtown. Feminine Fury. All-female artists. Modern rebellion themes. She added it to her calendar."

Jaxon paused mid-pancake flip. "The what?"

Cole frowned thoughtfully.

"That sounds like a vibrator."

"It's an art exhibit," I snapped.

"It mattered to her."

"You hacked her laptop again?" Killian asked flatly.

I didn't answer. Didn't need to. Cole grinned slowly.

"You absolute creep." "I'm weirdly proud of you."

"She deserves something good," I said quietly. "After everything."

The room went silent again. "He's right," Killian finally said. "We take her."

Jaxon blinked. "Like... voluntarily?"

"Yes," Killian deadpanned.

"No chains. No manipulation. No bullshit. We ask."

Cole scoffed. "Do any of us actually know how to do that?"

"No," Jaxon admitted. "But I'm willing to fake emotional maturity for Riley."

I stared down at my coffee. Thinking about the look on her face at the gala. Not just anger. Betrayal.

Like we'd made another choice for her instead of with her.

"I'll book tickets," I murmured. "VIP access. Private showing if possible."

Killian nodded once. "Do it." And for the first time in days... None of us argued.

Jaxon

So. We were grovelling. Good. We fucking should.

But while Lucas researched galleries and Cole argued with his own reflection about whether open-toe stilettos were "too slutty for contrition," I kept thinking about that dress. The black satin one. The one Riley wore to the gala. The one that made all four of us short-circuit like idiots. And we ruined it. Dragged her away from feeling beautiful just because we panicked.

"I've got an idea," I said suddenly.

"Clothes." Cole blinked.

"You wanna buy her forgiveness?"

"No," I rolled my eyes. "I wanna replace the thing we wrecked." Silence settled briefly.

"That dress mattered to her," I continued more quietly.

"You could tell."

"The way she walked in it? That wasn't vanity. That was confidence."

Killian stared at the counter for a long moment. Then nodded once. "Alright."

"Clothes. Gallery. What else?"

"Choice," I answered immediately. "No pressure. No forcing her into anything. We let her pick."

Cole snorted. "Bold of you to assume she won't stab us on sight."

"She probably will," I admitted. "But she might appreciate the effort first."

Lucas was already typing furiously beside me. And honestly? For the first time since the warehouse... This felt like the right direction.

Killian

While they planned— I moved. Phone already in my hand as I stepped outside. Not angry. Not frustrated. Focused.

Because Riley Morgan wasn't someone you won over with words. You earned her. And we hadn't earned a damn thing yet.

First call: Eli.

"I need a private gallery showing," I said immediately.

"Feminine Fury exhibit. Quiet. Minimal staff. No press."

A pause. "For her?"

"Yes."

Another pause. "Done."

Second call: Dima.

"I need dresses."

"What kind?"

"Black satin. Velvet. Silk. Something elegant."

I hesitated briefly before adding— "Something that makes her feel unstoppable."

Dima hummed thoughtfully. "Accessories?"

"Heels," I replied.

"Practical enough to run in if she bolts." She laughed softly.

"Combat glamour. Understood."

When the call ended, I stood there for a while letting the cold air settle into my lungs.

Because beneath all the planning... There was still fear. Because we'd already broken her trust once.

And if this failed?

That would be on me. When I finally turned back toward the house, Lucas stood waiting on the porch.

"She'll know," he said quietly.

"I'm counting on it," I answered.

Because Riley Morgan noticed everything. And maybe— Just maybe— It was finally time we proved we were paying attention too.

38

Stormbreaker

Riley

Good As Hell – Lizzo

I was horny. Pissed. Emotionally compromised. And one stupid comment away from setting this whole place on fire with nothing but a tampon, a lighter, and righteous female rage.

I'd fought two men, kissed one, made deeply questionable eye contact with another, and possibly scarred Jaxon for life during an emergency pharmacy run when he'd dared to ask:

"Do all tampons have wings, or is that optional?"

I'd nearly stabbed him with a mascara wand. And now I was trapped in a house full of testosterone and tactical weapons while the group chat argued about whether pineapple belonged on pizza like we weren't currently living through the prologue to my villain origin story.

No. Absolutely not.

I hadn't had one second alone to scream, cry, rage, or get off without somebody hovering nearby like a hormonal security detail.

So I did what any exhausted, overstimulated woman would do.

I marched into my room, ripped open my drawer like a raccoon breaking into a trash can, and retrieved my trusty pouch of silicone salvation.

Stormbreaker. The matte black wand of righteous fury herself.

"Honey," I whispered reverently, "it's time to earn your damn Oscar."

I bolted into the bathroom, locked the door, and stripped with the speed of a woman fleeing emotional repression.

Killian and his brooding. Lucas and his stupidly observant eyes. Jaxon and his smug commentary. Cole and his mouth. God, that man needed a muzzle.

I collapsed dramatically onto the bath mat and held Stormbreaker aloft like Excalibur. "Alright, bitch," I muttered. "Save me."

Twenty minutes later, I emerged from the bathroom looking spiritually reset and mildly electrocuted. My legs were weak. My soul was centred. My rage had been temporarily sedated.

Stormbreaker had done her duty with honour. And now? Now it was time for skincare.

I stared at my reflection in the mirror. Mascara smudged. Hair feral.

One eyebrow doing something deeply offensive.

"Well," I sighed, "we can't fix the trauma, but we can unclog some pores."

I opened the bathroom cabinet. Immediately regretted it.

Inside sat the most horrifying collection of male hygiene products I'd ever witnessed.

Half-empty bottles. Dented spray cans. One neon green bottle labelled simply:

BLAST. No explanation. No branding. Just BLAST.

I unscrewed the cap cautiously and sniffed it. Regret. Jet fuel. Divorce.

Another bottle promised "24-hour protection," which felt wildly optimistic considering the state of the bathroom.

And someone — probably Cole — owned something called Ocean Thunder. It had leaked down the cabinet shelf and fused with the grout like toxic waste.

"What the fuck even is Ocean Thunder?" I whispered.

Meanwhile Lucas's side of the cabinet looked clinically sterilised. Cleanser. Toner. Moisturiser. Sunscreen.

Everything lined up with terrifying precision.

Of course the man who hacked government servers also had a ten-step skincare routine.

I picked up one tiny glass bottle suspiciously.

"Okay, Lucas," I muttered. "Didn't have you pegged as a glycolic acid bitch, but honestly? Slay."

I shoved aside a crusty can of shaving foam and unearthed my own toiletry bag like an archaeologist reclaiming civilisation. Tonight wasn't about cute self-care. This was war. The rage-exfoliating kind.

I tied my hair into a messy bun, slapped on a charcoal face mask like battle paint, and attacked my eyebrows with tweezers.

"Didn't ask to exist?" Yank.

"Thinking about texting my ex?" Yank.

"Still emotionally haunted by something from 2007?" YANK.

Then came the lotion. The expensive one. The one reserved for emotional emergencies and acts of psychological warfare.

Honey. Vanilla. Mild violence.

I rubbed it into my skin while glaring at the mirror and actively ignoring the grey sponge decomposing beside the sink.

It wasn't even sponge-coloured anymore. It was biohazard-coloured.

I slapped expired under-eye patches onto my face anyway because rules no longer applied to me. Then I filed my nails with the focus of a woman choosing growth instead of homicide.

Self-care wasn't relaxing. It was maintenance. It was survival. And I was thriving.

Thirty minutes later, I emerged from the bathroom transformed. Fuzzy socks. Oversized hoodie. Skin moisturised enough to blind a man. Aura spiritually unstable but significantly improved.

I felt reborn. Smoother. Angrier. More powerful. Exfoliated Riley had entered the chat. And God help the next man who called me emotional.

39

Operation: Buzz and Betrayal

Riley

Look What You Made Me Do – Taylor Swift

It had been a month since I got shot.A month of painkillers, half-assed apologies, lingering stares, and the kind of recovery that made me want to rip my own stitches out just to feel something productive.

My ribs and shoulder still ached if I moved too fast. I was still sleeping in sports bras like somebody's exhausted grandmother. And apparently none of that mattered to the four idiots who thought barging into my room uninvited was acceptable human behaviour.

I was warm. Comfortable. Possibly drooling. Curled under my blanket dreaming about a world where people respected the sanctity of sleep.

Then the door slammed open. "RISE AND SHINE, PRINCESS!" Cole bellowed like a deranged Disney villain.

I bolted upright, brain rebooting like a Windows 98 computer while I grabbed the nearest object and launched it.

"WHAT THE FU—"

The pillow narrowly missed Jaxon's head. "She was snoring!" he shouted, already wheezing with laughter. "I knew it!"

Killian entered behind them carrying garment bags and shoe boxes like he was about to forcibly re-brand my existence.

"You're late," he said flatly. "Get up."

"I WILL KILL YOU." My voice sounded like gravel and murder.

Lucas — the only one with a functioning survival instinct — sat carefully on the edge of the bed, eyes immediately scanning my shoulder. "You okay?"

"I was," I groaned dramatically, collapsing backward. "Until the idiot brigade staged a home invasion."

"You're welcome," Cole said proudly, tossing a shopping bag onto the bed.

"If there's anything pink or frilly in there," I warned, "I will commit war crimes."

Jaxon mimed zipping his mouth shut. Which meant absolutely nothing.

Lucas reached for the hem of my shirt before I could stop him. "You're gonna pull your stitches again."

"It's fine," I hissed, jerking away. He didn't stop.

"It's not fine," Killian said calmly while unloading the rest of the bags. "You don't get to ignore this."

I gritted my teeth while Lucas peeled back the bandage with annoyingly competent hands. "I'm still alive, aren't I?"

"Barely," Lucas muttered. "This isn't healing properly."

"Damn, princess," Cole said, leaning over for a better look. "That's ugly."

I turned slowly toward him. "Say that again and your face will match."

Killian handed Lucas fresh bandages. "Hold still."

"I hate all of you," I informed the universe.

"You love us," Jaxon replied smugly from the dresser. I stared at him with the full intention of spiritual violence.

Lucas finished wrapping my ribs and shoulder before leaning back slightly.

"No unnecessary movement. Let it heal."

"Define unnecessary."

"Anything involving you acting like a reckless dumbass," Killian answered immediately.

"So breathing?"

Cole clapped enthusiastically. "Now that the princess is patched up — makeover time!"

"I swear to God," I groaned. "If this is ridiculous rich-people nonsense—"

"You'll wear it anyway," Killian said.

"I never once said, 'Please come dress me like a Barbie at sunrise.'" Cole wiggled his eyebrows.

"Eh. Close enough."

I was mid-eye roll when I saw Lucas move toward my bedside drawer. My soul left my body.

No.

No, no, no.

Before I could physically launch myself across the bed, he opened it. The colour drained from his face instantly.

Oh my God.

He slammed the drawer shut like it had bitten him.

Jaxon narrowed his eyes. "What's in the drawer?"

"Nothing," Lucas said way too quickly.

"Definitely not nothing," Cole declared, already reaching for it.

"DON'T—" Too late.

He pulled out my bright purple vibrator like he'd just discovered buried treasure.

"Oh, this is GOLD," Jaxon wheezed.

I died. Actually died. Spirit ascended. Funeral pending.

"EXPELLIARMUS!" Cole shouted before turning it on. The thing buzzed violently in his hand like an angry chainsaw.

Jaxon collapsed onto the floor laughing.

Killian physically facepalmed.

Lucas looked ready to walk into traffic.

"Give it BACK!" I launched myself at Cole, tackling him straight onto the floor. We wrestled for several deeply humiliating seconds before I finally ripped it from his grip and shoved it under the mattress like cursed evidence.

"You are all dead to me!"

Lucas

It should've ended there. Really, it should've ended the moment Riley tackled Cole like a woman possessed by rage, humiliation, and sleep deprivation.

But no. This was us. Cole was still sprawled on the floor cackling like a rabid hyena.

"If I die," he wheezed, "bury me with it."

"You ARE going to die," Riley snapped. "And I'm gonna beat you to death with that thing on the lowest vibration setting for maximum psychological damage."

I looked at Killian. "So... what's the return policy on trauma?"

"There isn't one," he replied without hesitation. "We repress it and move on."

"Cool," I muttered. "Love that for us."

"GROUP THERAPY," Jaxon announced dramatically from the floor. "Starting now. First topic: what the actual hell just happened?"

Riley hurled another pillow directly into his face. "This never happened," she hissed. "If any of you tell anyone, I will cut off your dicks and feed them to raccoons."

Silence. Then, because God had abandoned us entirely, Cole sat upright and grinned.

"So that's a yes to dinner later?" That should've been the end of it.

Instead, Killian made the catastrophic mistake of speaking. "Interesting choice of weaponry," he said dryly, folding his arms.

Riley's eyes narrowed dangerously. "Don't start."

"I mean," he continued calmly, "I've seen you beat someone unconscious with a frozen burrito and a stiletto heel. But this? This is new."

"Killian."

"I'd rate it six out of ten for intimidation," he added thoughtfully. "Ten out of ten for WiFi interference."

And that was the exact moment Riley snapped.

"Oh no," I breathed immediately. "No, no, no—"

She marched toward the closet and yanked open a drawer none of us had ever seen before. Then she dragged out a heavy locked box. The second it opened, I knew we were doomed.

"I present to you," Riley said with terrifying calm, "THE REAL ARMOURY."

Then she started throwing them. A hot pink rabbit vibrator smacked Jaxon directly in the chest.

He screamed. "OH MY GOD — IT'S GOT EARS!"

Cole ducked as a glitter-covered monstrosity flew past his head. "SHE'S GOT MODELS!" he shouted. "THIS IS A COLLECTION!"

Riley stood in the middle of the room like a wrathful war goddess hurling vibrators with frightening precision. "YOU WANNA MOCK ME?" she yelled. "HERE'S FORTY REASONS TO SHUT THE HELL UP."

One landed beside my foot and immediately started vibrating aggressively against the hardwood. "I THINK THIS ONE'S SENTIENT," I shouted.

"IS THAT ONE SHAPED LIKE A DRAGON?" Jaxon yelled in horror.

"YES," Riley bellowed proudly. "AND IT HAS SCALES."

Killian slowly backed toward the door.

"I came in here to check her stitches," he muttered. "Instead I'm being attacked with prehistoric penis monsters."

Cole dove behind the bed while silicone artillery rained from above.

"It's like Toy Story: After Dark!"

And then — because my brain had completely stopped functioning — I made the mistake of speaking.

"...Is that the one with wings?"

Riley froze. Then smiled. Not a good smile.

"That," she said sweetly while holding up a horrifying winged monstrosity with LED lights, "is the Double Dragon Deluxe."

Jaxon backed away slowly. "Oh my God."

"Anyone else got comments?" Riley asked, gripping it like Thor's hammer.

Absolute silence.

Even Cole stayed hidden.

"Good." She tossed it back into the box and slammed the lid shut with enough force to rattle the room.

"Now if you'll excuse me," she snapped, "I'm going to shower and pretend none of you exist."

Then she stormed off triumphantly.

The room fell silent. Vibrators littered the floor like fallen soldiers.

Killian rubbed his face. "Next time someone suggests a wake-up call," he said quietly, "remind me to fake my own death."

"Agreed," I said solemnly, staring at the glowing teal vibrator by my shoe. "And for the record — this never happened."

"NEVER," Jaxon agreed immediately. "...I am gonna have nightmares about the dragon one though," Cole admitted from behind the bed.

"Deserved," I said.

Riley

I slammed the bathroom door behind me and locked it with the force of someone trying to shove a demon back into hell.

Then I just stood there. Silent. Alone.

Surrounded by pastel tiles, lavender soap, and the distant echoes of Buzz Lightyear's angry cousins still vibrating somewhere out in the hallway.

I stared at myself in the mirror. Hair feral. Face flushed. Eyes wide like I'd just committed several war crimes. Which, to be fair, I kind of had. With vibrators. Plural. God help me — I'd launched an artillery strike made entirely of orgasms.

Slowly, I dropped onto the closed toilet lid and buried my face in my hands.

What the actual fuck just happened?

One minute I'd been asleep. Peaceful. Minding my own damn business.

The next? Broadway Cole was screaming "RISE AND SHINE, PRINCESS!" like a cracked-out Disney villain and somehow we'd spiralled into a live-action version of Riley's Secret Drawer: Exposed and Weaponized.

I groaned loudly into my palms. I tackled Cole. In my sleep shirt. My boobs were probably out.

Honestly? I couldn't even remember anymore. My brain was buffering somewhere between public humiliation and aggravated assault.

And then... Then I'd snapped. And opened the box. The box.

The carefully hidden, deeply private, absolutely nobody's-business collection that had peacefully existed for years without hurting a single person. A collection meant for stress relief. Emotional support. Nights where I wanted to feel literally anything besides adrenaline and unresolved trauma.

But no. No, apparently the four idiots I lived with had decided today was the day we publicly unpacked Riley Morgan's Battery-Powered Shame.

And then Killian — God bless his emotionally constipated soul — had the audacity to rate my bedside vibrator like he was leaving a Yelp review.

So yes. I snapped. Opened Pandora's Box of Pleasure™ and declared psychological warfare through precision-guided dick missiles.

I was never recovering from this. Never. They'd seen the dragon one. The suction wand. The glittery monstrosity with the confetti chamber that I bought ironically and then unfortunately loved.

Lucas had asked about the wings.

Jaxon screamed when the pink rabbit hit him in the chest like a horny Pokémon.

And Cole?

Cole looked genuinely delighted by the entire experience, which somehow made everything worse.

My face burned hotter the longer I thought about it. There was no coming back from this. I had become the stuff of group chats. A cautionary tale. A living HR violation.

They were never going to take me seriously again.

I was the General of the Battery-Powered Battalion. The Commander of Cursed Comforts. The Duchess of Dildonics.

A knock sounded against the bathroom door. I froze instantly.

"Riley?" Lucas's voice came carefully through the wood. Hesitant. Like he was trying to negotiate with a hostage situation.

I narrowed my eyes at the door. "If you're here to ask about settings or aerodynamic performance," I warned darkly, "I swear to God—"

"Nope!" he said immediately. "Definitely not." A pause. Then, quieter: "Just... wanted to say we deserved that."

Damn right they did. Another beat of silence passed before he added awkwardly: "...And the dragon one was kinda cool."

I grabbed the nearest towel and hurled it at the door with enough force to express the full depth of my disappointment in humanity.

Silence followed. Then the sound of very smart tactical retreating.

I sighed heavily, dragging both hands down my face.

I needed a shower. A reset. A complete timeline wipe. But deep down, I already knew the truth. No matter how clean I got... No matter how aggressively I scrubbed my skin... I would always be the woman who assaulted her team with a fleet of vibrators. And honestly? I wasn't even sorry.

40

Buzz. Bruised. Still Beautiful

Killian

Take Me Back To Eden - Sleep Token

Her voice came muffled through the door. "Go away."

"Not Cole," I said, leaning against the frame, voice calm enough to soothe and smug enough to irritate her. "I come in peace."

"That's what you said before the vibrator airstrike."

My mouth twitched. "Yeah... fair."

A beat passed. "What do you want, Killian?"

"I brought a peace offering."

I nudged the door open just enough to slide the bag through — black, sleek, designer. An apology disguised as temptation. "Leave the bribe and get out."

"I'm not coming in. Not after yesterday."

Through the narrow opening, I caught a glimpse of her sprawled across the bed, towel wrapped lazily around her body, damp hair falling over bare shoulders and endless legs.

It had been a little over a month since she'd been shot, and my mind still replayed the image of her bleeding out on concrete whenever I closed my eyes.

But the woman in front of me now didn't look fragile. She looked dangerous. Warm. Alive.

My body reacted instantly — tight heat coiling low in my stomach, familiar and relentless. It had been weeks of this. Weeks of wanting her and pretending I didn't. Weeks of cold showers, clenched fists, and sleepless nights trying to force myself back under control.

But control got harder every time I looked at her.

"Though, for the record," I said lightly, forcing my voice steady, "I'm still finding glitter in my shoes."

"Serves you right for opening your mouth."

"Again... fair."

I nodded toward the bag. "It's not just a dress. There's shoes. Accessories. A full apology package." A pause. "And maybe one thing in there I'm legally not allowed to comment on."

"Killian."

"I'm kidding." Another pause. "...Mostly."

Her groan was low, tired, unguarded. A dangerous sound. I dragged my focus back where it belonged before my thoughts spiralled somewhere reckless.

"What do you want?" she asked again. "We're taking you out today."

She blinked slowly. "Out?"

"Somewhere normal. No missions. No tactical briefings. No gunfire. Just food, air, and people who hopefully aren't trying to kill us."

"You're letting me leave the house?" The accusation in her voice landed harder than I expected.

"After weeks of 'you're too injured to go anywhere'?" she continued. "Even though I'm clearly healed enough to kill all of you with a shoe?"

"We were trying to protect you, Riley."

From the world. From ourselves. From how close we'd come to losing you.

"From what?" she muttered. "Bad vibes and daylight?"

"You got shot," I said quietly. "You nearly died."

Her jaw tightened instantly. She hated weakness. Hated vulnerability even more.

And maybe the most dangerous thing about her was that she never realised how badly people wanted to protect the parts of her she tried hardest to hide.

I exhaled slowly. "Just... check the bag, okay?" I said. "Come downstairs when you're ready. Try not to commit any felonies before coffee."

I started to walk away, then paused. "Oh — and I think you emotionally destroyed Lucas."

Her head snapped up. "What?"

"He had the saddest expression I've ever seen after the dragon incident."

A horrified sound escaped her throat. "He opened my drawer!"

"I'm not saying you were wrong," I replied smoothly. "Just saying maybe showing up downstairs looking particularly hot and pretending none of it happened might help his recovery."

"You manipulative bastard."

I let the grin slip into my voice. "Only with you, sweetheart."

Then I pulled the door shut behind me. But I stayed there longer than I should have, forcing myself to breathe through the ache sitting heavy beneath my ribs.

Wanting her was becoming dangerous. Not because she tempted me. Because she mattered. And that was infinitely worse.

The kitchen was quieter than usual. Cole sat at the counter spinning a banana like a revolver. Jaxon was upside down on the couch for reasons no one questioned anymore. Lucas stared into his coffee like it had personally betrayed him.

I dropped a folder onto the table. "All right. Listen up."

Lucas looked over immediately. "This about Riley?"

"Yes."

Jaxon pointed accusingly. "If this is another 'don't provoke her' speech, I'd like the record to show she threw a dragon-shaped vibrator at my head."

Cole grinned. "And it was majestic."

I ignored both of them. "We need to stop treating her like an asset we're trying to contain."

That got their attention. "She's already halfway out the door emotionally," I continued. "Every time we make decisions for her, we push her further away."

Lucas frowned slightly. "So what's the plan?"

I leaned back against the counter. "We earn back trust."

Cole blinked dramatically. "Oh God. Feelings."

"I'm serious." Silence settled for a second before I continued.

"She doesn't need control taken away from her. She needs choice. Space. Something good for once that doesn't end in bloodshed."

Jaxon slowly sat upright. "So... we grovel?"

"Yes."

Cole looked deeply offended. "I don't grovel. I charm aggressively."

"You harass professionally," Lucas corrected.

"Fair." I folded my arms. "We take her out. We let her decide where we go, what she wants, how long we stay. No pressure. No manipulation. Just... show her we can be decent."

Lucas nodded slowly. "She deserves that." More than that. Far more than anything we'd given her so far.

Jaxon tilted his head. "And the dresses?"

I glanced toward the hallway leading upstairs. "She deserves to feel like herself again."

Cole smirked faintly. "She's gonna look terrifyingly hot, isn't she?"

"Yes," I said honestly.

The room fell quiet again for a moment. Because we all knew the truth now. This wasn't casual anymore.

Riley wasn't temporary. And whether any of us were ready for it or not, she'd already become the centre of everything.

41

This Is Not a Date

Riley

Power – Little Mix

My heels clicked like gunshots against the warehouse floor as I stalked toward the SUV. Each sharp sound echoed too loud in the cavernous space, like it was daring someone to make a comment.

Behind me, I could feel them following. Not hovering, not breathing down my neck—just close enough to be annoying. Close enough that I could feel their eyes crawling over me.

I didn't look back. I already knew what I'd see: smirks. Admiration. Way too much smugness.

When I reached the SUV, Lucas of all people jogged ahead and opened the door like he was my damn chauffeur.

He even bowed a little. Bowed. "Milady," he said, voice annoyingly smooth.

I stopped. Stared at him. Stared at the open door. Then back at him. "What the hell was that?"

"Just being polite," he said, with the faintest twitch of his lips. Behind me, Jaxon chuckled low.

"Go on, Princess. Your carriage awaits." Cole—because of course it was Cole—nudged Killian with his elbow.

"Think she's gonna slap him or just shove him into traffic?"

Honestly? I considered it. Hard. Instead, I clicked my tongue, shot them all a glare sharp enough to draw blood, and slid into the car.

"You're all acting weird," I muttered as I settled in. Killian, the last one in, shut the door behind him.

"Not at all."

Liar. I crossed my arms and stared them down as the engine rumbled to life. This was not normal behaviour. Not for them. Normally they were chaos incarnate—sarcastic, combative, mildly feral. Cole existed solely to annoy me. Killian barely tolerated my existence. Lucas was unreadable. And Jaxon? He was a golden retriever with a death wish.

But now? Now they were being... nice. Too nice. Which meant they were up to something.

So I didn't push. Not yet. I sat back, put on a lazy smirk, and decided to play along.

"Fine," I said, dragging out the word. "Let's see where this goes." Jaxon raised a brow from the driver's seat.

"Now that is dangerous."

Cole whistled low. "God help us."

Lucas said nothing. Just gave me a look—like he already knew I'd figured them out.

Killian stayed quiet, like always, but I caught the subtle clench of his jaw. It was almost nothing. Almost. But there was something in his eyes—hot, sharp, almost predatory.

He looked like a man weighing the difference between protecting something and keeping it locked away. Yep. They were planning something. And I was going to find out what.

When we pulled up outside a building far too clean and well-lit for our usual missions, I stepped out of the SUV and immediately heard the click of my heels on stone.

I hated that I liked it. I hated how good the emerald dress looked, how it moved like water around my legs, how the damn heels hugged my feet just right.

I wasn't used to feeling... nice. Polished. Pretty. Definitely not used to the way they looked at me.

Lucas helped me out of the car, hand lingering just a second too long. Jaxon looked at me like I'd hung the damn moon. Killian's gaze was the worst of all—heavy and unblinking, like he could strip the dress away just by staring.

There was no smirk. No casual charm. Just something dark and assessing, something that made my pulse stutter. I told myself it was nothing. Just him being his usual intense, bossy self. But for a second, I could've sworn I saw hunger there. The kind that didn't ask.

And Cole? That menace was grinning like the cat who'd swallowed a goddamn canary. "Damn, Princess," he drawled, giving me a slow once-over. "You clean up real nice."

I crossed my arms. "I always look nice."

"Sure, sure," he said, still smirking. "But now it's confirmed."

Jaxon snorted. "You're gonna push your luck and get decked."

"I love pushing my luck," Cole said, then winked at me.

"Maybe now that you're fancy, you'll start acting like a proper lady." I tilted my head. Stepped in close. Dropped my voice to a lazy drawl. "You want me to act like a lady, Cole?"

He held still. Didn't flinch. But his smirk flickered—just for a second.

Then I stomped on his foot. He yelped.

Jaxon howled with laughter.

"Lady enough for you?" I said, smiling sweetly.

Lucas chuckled. Killian didn't even blink, but I caught the faintest curl at the corner of his mouth—something private, almost approving.

And damn it… I was having fun. If they were gonna be weird, I'd be weirder.

If they wanted to flirt, I could play that game too. Lucas stepped up beside me and gestured toward the grand glass doors of the building we'd stopped in front of.

That's when I realised where we were. My breath caught. I blinked, looking between the building and the men.

"Wait… are we—?" Lucas smiled and rested a hand lightly on mine. "Welcome to the art gallery."

I stared. They'd listened.

My heart stumbled in my chest as I looked at the doors, then back at them. "You actually brought me here."

Lucas shrugged. "We might drive you crazy, but we pay attention."

I swallowed hard. Something twisted in my chest—tight and warm and terrifying.

"Thank you," I said softly. Meant it.

"Come on, Princess," Cole called from up ahead. "Your royal gallery awaits." Rolling my eyes, I walked toward the doors—but I couldn't stop smiling.

Killian

It had been just over a month since she was shot, but the sight of her in that dress still hit me like a blade between the ribs. Emerald silk. Bare shoulders. Legs for days.

My body reacted instantly—hard, hot, heavy—the kind of need that made it difficult to keep my breathing even.

I forced my jaw tight, hands buried in my pockets so no one saw the tension in my knuckles.

She had no idea.

No clue that every step she took away from us made my chest tighten, that the predator in me wanted to close the distance, to take her throat in my hand and make sure she understood she wasn't going anywhere.

The others were quiet too, eyes fixed on her like she was a rare weapon on display.

"Jesus," Cole muttered under his breath.

Jaxon gave the faintest grin. "Yeah. We can't fuck this up."

Lucas's voice was lower still. "No mistakes. Not today."

I didn't look at them.

Couldn't. My gaze stayed on her, tracking the sway of her hips, the way her hand brushed her hair back as she reached for the glass door.

"Play it soft," Lucas murmured.

Cole huffed a quiet laugh. "Soft's not exactly our strong suit."

My voice came out rougher than I meant. "We manage. She's worth it."

She glanced back at us then—just for a heartbeat—and something in my chest went feral.

Every instinct I had screamed to go to her, to touch, to claim, to drag her into a corner and make her forget her own name.

My body ached with it, and I had to shift my stance before it became obvious. Instead, I moved forward, calm on the surface, violence and want just under the skin.

We couldn't fuck this up. But God help me, I was already thinking about how I might.

42

The Art of Falling

Riley

I Am Not a Robot – Marina (and the Diamonds)

I'd been to this gallery before. Usually it was packed—school groups with their matching hats, tourists with loud cameras, art snobs hovering over canvases like they could will them into giving up secrets. Noise, chatter, footsteps on marble floors. A constant buzz of life.

But now?

Now it was silent.

Not the kind of peaceful quiet I liked, like curling up with a book or sneaking into a library after dark. This was the wrong kind of quiet. Eerie. Empty. Heavy.

I turned slowly, the click of my heels echoing in the cavernous space as I took in the exhibit. Paintings lined the walls. Sculptures stood proud and untouched. But there were no people. No voices. No distractions.

It should've felt indulgent. Instead, it felt like I'd just stepped onto the stage of someone else's fantasy—and I hadn't agreed to the role.

I turned back to them—Lucas, Killian, Jaxon, and Cole—suspicion already tightening in my chest.

"Where is everyone?"

Lucas gave me that maddeningly calm look of his.

"It's just us."

Just us?

I blinked. "What do you mean, just us?"

Jaxon grinned like this was the punchline to his favorite joke.

"We rented it out."

My stomach dropped.

"You what?"

Killian, arms crossed and expression unreadable, met my gaze dead-on.

"We rented it out. For the day."

I stared at him, then at the rest of them like they'd just told me they'd bought a yacht and named it Princess Riley.

"You rented out an entire goddamn art gallery... in the middle of the day?"

Lucas—of course—added smoothly,

"For you."

My brain short-circuited. For me.

My gaze flicked to the open space, to the pristine quiet that should've cost someone their soul to achieve. This wasn't something people did. Not for me. Not for... anyone.

Something tightened in my chest, fierce and unfamiliar. I swallowed it down fast. Nope. Not going there. Not now.

So I defaulted to what I knew: sarcasm. "Goddamn," I muttered, arms crossing. "You guys are ridiculous."

Cole laughed. "You keep saying that like it's an insult."

Jaxon nudged him. "She's short-circuiting."

"I am not—" I snapped automatically, then stopped myself and pinched the bridge of my nose. "Wait. Hold up. How much did this cost?"

Killian didn't blink. "Does it matter?"

"Of course it fucking matters!" I whirled to face him fully. "This is a private gallery, Killian. You don't just drop your Amex and say 'Clear the peasants!' This kind of money could buy a whole damn house!"

Lucas raised a brow. "Several."

I choked on air. "Several?!"

Jaxon looked like he was having the time of his life. "You said you wanted to see the exhibit without crowds."

Oh my god.

"You guys—" I started, then stopped again. Because... fuck. They were right.

I had said that. Offhand. Probably while shoving my way past some group of TikTok teens taking selfies with a Monet. It had been a throwaway complaint. A moment of frustration.

But they remembered. And they listened. And now... here we were. And it was perfect. Which was exactly the problem.

I swallowed hard and crossed my arms tighter, like that could hold me together. "I don't even know what to say to that."

"'Thank you' usually works," Lucas said, totally unbothered.

But thank you felt dangerous. Vulnerable. Like I was giving them permission to keep doing things like this. And I didn't want to need them. I didn't want to start expecting this kind of softness. Because the second I let my guard down, it'd all turn to ash. That's how this worked.

So I inhaled deep, lifted my chin, and put on my best smirk. "You know what? If you're going to be extra, I'm gonna enjoy the hell out of it."

Jaxon chuckled. "That's our girl."

Lucas gestured toward the first exhibit. "Shall we?"

I turned toward the art, letting myself breathe for the first time since walking in.

Because even if this scared the shit out of me—even if it meant more than I was ready to admit—it was mine. Just for today. And maybe, just maybe, that was enough.

Cole

God, she was trying so hard not to melt. Every step she took across the gallery floor was a performance—chin high, arms locked like armor, pretending we hadn't just cracked her open and set the whole place inside her chest.

She thought she was hiding it. She wasn't.

I saw the flick of her fingers when Lucas said it was for her. The panic in her eyes when she realized what we'd done. The way her breathing changed as she stepped ahead of us, like distance would keep us from noticing.

It didn't.

She walked like she didn't feel the heat of our eyes on her back. I wanted to close the gap, to let my hand graze the small of her spine, to see if she'd shiver. To see if she'd stay.

"Smiling like an idiot," Jaxon muttered beside me.

"Shut up," I said, though my grin only widened.

Lucas was his usual statue—unreadable, except for the faint hum of satisfaction rolling off him.

But Killian... Killian didn't move. Didn't blink. Just stared after her like he was trying to decide whether to write her name in gold or carve it into her skin.

The man was all sharp edges and quiet storms—and right now, every drop of it was aimed at her.

We followed her deeper into the gallery. Lucas took up position like a bodyguard. Jaxon kept making faces at the sculptures when she wasn't looking.

Me? I was watching her lose that battle with herself.

No sass. No walls. Just Riley, slowing in front of a painting, her fingers almost lifting as if she'd touch the canvas.

That softness hit harder than any skimpy dress could. By the time she turned back toward us—eyes brighter, steps slower—I knew she'd felt it too. She just didn't want to admit it.

Then she saw the table.

Her whole system seemed to glitch. No flinch, no words—just that full stop, like she'd stepped on a live wire.

Killian's gaze never left her, but I swear something darker flickered there. Not just pride. Not just heat. Something closer to claiming.

When she spun toward us, demanding answers, I only grinned. "What? Can't a girl enjoy a fancy meal after a little art appreciation?"

She called us insane. I called it better than boring. But the truth was simpler—I liked watching her sit down at a table that had been built for her, whether she admitted it or not. She thought she was in control of the game. She wasn't. Not anymore.

Killian

She didn't know what she looked like to us. To me. Emerald silk brushing her thighs. Bare shoulders catching the light. The curve of her neck when she tilted her head at Lucas.

Every step she took, I pictured closing the distance. Fisting a hand in her hair. Making her tilt that chin for me instead.

Possessive? Sure. I'd been called worse.

The others joked, filled the space with noise. I stayed silent. Watched. Tracked.

The way her dress swayed made my fingers twitch. The subtle dip of her spine when she leaned toward a painting. The way her breath hitched when she saw the table—our table—laid out in perfect symmetry for her.

I felt my jaw tighten. My pulse low and heavy. A month ago, she'd been bleeding out on a floor.

Now she looked like a queen. Our queen. She just didn't know it yet.

Jaxon leaned toward me at one point, his voice low. "We can't fuck this up."

I didn't answer. My eyes never left her. He was right. We couldn't.

She had to want us—need us—so completely that she'd never think of walking away. And if that meant letting her believe this was all her idea? Fine. I'd play patient. For now.

But the dark part of me? The one I kept behind clenched teeth and polite distance?

It wanted to ruin her first. Strip her down to the bone. Then rebuild her so every piece knew who she belonged to.

I let my arm brush hers when we passed in the narrow walkway between exhibits. Accidental, maybe. But the jolt in my gut told me exactly what I wanted to do with that reaction. She kept walking, pretending it hadn't happened. I kept watching, already planning the next one.

Riley

It was too much. All of it The gallery, the lunch, the way they looked at me like I was something worth building a kingdom around—it was getting under my skin in ways I didn't like.

Or maybe I liked it too much. Every time I moved, I felt one of them at my back. Cole's grin burning against my shoulder blades. Lucas's eyes, steady and unreadable, like he could see every thought I didn't want him to.

Jaxon's easy charm curling at the edges, softer than I'd ever seen it. And Killian... God, Killian.

Every time I caught him watching me, it was like being marked. Not a look. A claim.

When we passed each other in the narrow walkway between two exhibits, his arm brushed mine—just skin on skin for the briefest second—and my whole body reacted like he'd grabbed me. Heat flashed through me, sharp and disorienting, pooling low in a way I hated myself for.

He didn't even apologize. Just kept walking, gaze locked on me like he'd done it on purpose.

Maybe he had. I stabbed a bite of food at lunch to distract myself, chewing too fast, pretending I didn't feel the weight of them around me. Pretending my pulse wasn't skipping every time one of them leaned a little too close or their knee bumped mine under the table.

It had been just over a month since I'd been shot. A month since I'd been bleeding, broken, and barely hanging on. And now they had me in silk and heels, sitting at a table that looked like it had been stolen from a royal wedding, treating me like... I didn't even know.

Like I was theirs. The problem was, part of me wanted to believe it. The other part knew better.

I excused myself with some bullshit about needing the bathroom, and none of them stopped me. But as I walked away, I could feel it—their eyes following me. Possessive. Hungry. Like they were letting me go, but only because they knew I'd come back.

I didn't go to the bathroom. The gallery swallowed me up in quiet—too quiet—the sound of my heels bouncing off the marble like a pulse I couldn't slow down.

I turned into a small side exhibit, one of those tucked-away corners no one bothers with unless they're lost or hiding. Which, I guess, I was.

The light was soft here, almost dim, spilling over a single painting in the center. I couldn't even name it. Didn't care. My arms folded across my chest, trying to hold in the restless heat still licking through my body.

Because I could still feel them.

The echo of Killian's arm brushing mine. The memory of Lucas's gaze, heavy and assessing. The faint ghost of Cole's knee bumping mine beneath the table. Jaxon's grin when he thought I wasn't looking.

They were in my skin. Every look. Every accidental touch that didn't feel accidental at all.

It was like they'd marked me in invisible ink, and the farther I walked, the more it burned.

My pulse was still wrong—too fast, too aware. Every nerve felt tuned for them, for their closeness, for the way they'd been circling me all day like wolves taking turns keeping me in sight.

I hated that my body responded before my brain could shut it down.

The heat wasn't fading. If anything, it was worse here, alone, because there was no one to distract me from it. I didn't hear Jaxon until he was close enough to touch. And when his voice came—low, careful—it startled me more than it should have. "Thought I'd find you here."

I didn't turn. "What gave it away?"

"The pretending-you're-fine stormed off a little too quietly this time." I risked a glance over my shoulder.

He wasn't smiling now. His hands were shoved in his pockets, and there was a softness in his eyes I wasn't prepared for. That warmth slid under my ribs, too intimate, too steady.

"I'm not doing this for attention," I muttered, sharper than I meant.

"I know." He stepped up beside me—close enough to share the air I was breathing, close enough that the side of his arm almost brushed mine, but not quite.

That restraint made me more aware of him than if he'd actually touched me. And under it all, I could still feel the others.

I knew they were out there somewhere, maybe still talking, maybe not—but part of me swore I could feel Killian's gaze like a phantom hand on the back of my neck.

Silence stretched between us, slow and warm, the kind of quiet that wanted to seep in and make itself comfortable.

I kept my eyes on the painting, but my awareness wasn't on the art. It was on him.

On the way Jaxon's presence filled the space without crowding me. On the heat that seemed to roll off him in measured waves, like he knew if he got too close, I'd run.

And underneath that... there was something else. Something I almost didn't catch if I wasn't paying attention.

Possession.

Not loud, not obvious. Not the kind that snarls and bites. This was quieter, softer—a thread barely there, humming in the way he stayed between me and the door, in how his gaze never once flicked away, in the subtle way his body angled toward mine as though even the air between us was his to claim.

It wasn't just Jaxon, though.

Because when his shoulder brushed mine—a light, unthinking touch—my chest tightened, not from him alone, but from the way my mind instantly conjured the weight of their eyes.

Killian's, cool and calculating. Lucas's, patient and sharp. Cole's, heated and unrepentant.

They weren't here. I knew that. But they didn't need to be for me to feel them.

Jaxon's voice dropped low, quiet enough that it felt like it belonged only to me. "You don't have to have all the answers right now, Riley. Just... let yourself feel it."

That should've sounded safe. It didn't. It felt like standing on the edge of something and knowing, if I stepped forward, there'd be hands waiting to catch me—whether I wanted them there or not.

His words hung there, low and steady, sinking deeper than I wanted them to. They slipped under my skin the way heat does—slow at first, then suddenly everywhere.

I should've moved. Should've stepped away before it got too close. But I didn't. Because some traitorous part of me... liked it.

Not just the comfort in his tone, but the weight of it—the way it slid into my chest like it belonged there. The way it felt less like an offer and more like a promise. A promise he didn't need to speak twice because he already decided.

His shoulder brushed mine again, whether on purpose or by accident, I couldn't tell. The contact was brief—gone in a second—but it left my skin humming. Not just from him, but from the echo of them.

Killian's unblinking watchfulness. Lucas's quiet calculations. Cole's unashamed hunger. They weren't here, yet it felt like they were. Like Jaxon's closeness wasn't his alone, but theirs too—a shared, unspoken claim threaded between them, one I wasn't sure I'd agreed to... and wasn't sure I wanted to refuse.

I swallowed hard, staring at the painting without really seeing it. It was easier than acknowledging the way my body leaned into that warmth, just enough to notice, not enough to give myself away.

"You don't have to know what you want yet," Jaxon said, softer now, almost coaxing. "Just..."

A pause, heavy with something unnamed. "Let yourself feel it."

That word—let—felt like a key turning in a lock I hadn't realised was closed. Like he was giving me permission I hadn't asked for but might secretly need.

And maybe, just maybe, I'd already given them more of me than I thought.

"You don't have to know what you want yet," Jaxon said, his voice quiet enough that it felt like it belonged only to me. "Just... let yourself feel it."

That word—let—slid in under my guard before I could block it. It was gentle, almost harmless, the way you'd talk to someone holding their breath too long.

I hated that it made me want to exhale.

He turned toward me, gaze steady, watching me like I was something rare he wasn't quite ready to touch but already intended to keep.

"Not everything has to hurt, Riley."

My throat tightened. "Things don't stay," I muttered. Something flickered in his eyes—not pity, not denial. Something slower. More deliberate.

"Maybe not," he said. "But sometimes people do." It wasn't a promise. It wasn't a confession. It was just enough to make my pulse skip, just enough to make me wonder.

And maybe that was the point.

He stepped past me, close enough that his arm brushed mine—the smallest, stupidest touch, but it left heat trailing up my skin like a fuse had been lit.

His head dipped, breath ghosting warm against my ear, his voice barely there. "You'd be worth staying for." Before I could react—before

I could read too much into it—he was gone, melting back into the gallery like nothing had happened.

And me?

I was left staring at the painting, pretending my thoughts weren't tangled around that single, quiet line.

43

Battlelines & Lace

Cole

Wicked Game – Ursine Vulpine

The SUV rumbled beneath us, and I swear to God, the tension in the air had a flavour. Like... citrus and repressed feelings.

Riley sat in the backseat beside me, arms crossed, sunglasses on, hair twisted up in some messy clip that made her look like a hit woman disguised as a Vogue cover model. She hadn't said much since the gallery. But she didn't have to.

She existed like an event. A mood. A dangerous season. So naturally, I poked the bear.

"Are you excited to shop till you drop, Princess?" I asked with my most annoying grin. Her eyes flicked toward me.

"If by drop you mean dropkick you through a Sephora display, then yes." God, I loved her.

Jaxon let out a low whistle from the driver's seat. "Damn, she's still spicy."

"She's always spicy," I muttered, watching her pretend not to smirk.

Lucas, riding shotgun like the world's sexiest GPS, just said, "Don't push her. She hasn't had caffeine yet."

Riley hummed ominously. "And I could snap." I made a mental note to steer clear of any store with glass shelves and no security cameras.

Jaxon

Look, I wasn't usually a mall guy. Malls were crowded, overpriced, and filled with people who couldn't park properly. But Riley? Riley in a mall was combat readiness disguised as fashion chaos.

And I was so here for it. She'd been quiet since the gallery. Not cold. Just... buffering. Like her brain was still catching up to the fact that we actually cared.

So yeah, I'd do ten laps of Zara if it meant she'd keep smiling like that.

I turned the music up just a touch—something chill, groovy, nothing too sappy. Riley tapped her fingers against her thigh like she was pretending not to like the song.

But I saw the corner of her mouth twitch. Victory.

Cole leaned forward between the seats.

"What do you think she'll buy first? Shoes? Lingerie? Something black and full of knives?"

Riley tilted her head. "A taser. For you." "Hot," Cole said, not missing a beat.

Killian exhaled audibly like he was this close to ejecting us all.

Lucas

I was watching her in the rearview mirror. Not like a creep—like a guy who knew how to read battlefield tension. And Riley was a war zone in lipstick.

She was pretending not to care about this trip. Pretending this wasn't a big deal.

But it was. Her shoulders were still stiff. Her jaw was clenched. She sat like she didn't believe she was allowed to relax—even after the gallery, even after the softest damn moment I'd seen from her in weeks.

She didn't know how to receive things. That was the problem. She knew how to fight, not how to have.

That's why this trip mattered. And judging by the way Killian had been staring at her hand for the past two minutes, I knew he was about to make a move.

Killian

She thought I didn't notice the way she kept glancing at the mall signs like they were foreign territory. Like this wasn't her trip. Like she hadn't earned this a thousand times over.

I waited until the SUV came to a stop. Everyone else was already halfway to feral excitement—Cole bouncing, Jaxon stretching, Lucas checking his phone like a dad plotting routes.

But Riley? She hadn't moved. So I pulled out my wallet. "Here." She turned to me slowly, brows furrowed. "What?"

I held out the card between two fingers. Black. Matte. Limitless. "Buy what you want," I said simply. Her lips parted. "I—Killian—"

"No conditions," I cut in. "No arguments. No budget. If you even think about saying no, I'll take you to the damn bank myself and start wiring funds into your account."

She blinked, stunned. "Why?"

"Because," I said, voice low, "you deserve it." She stared at the card like it might bite her.

"And because," I added, "if I hear you say one more time that you don't need anything, I'm going to drag you into that mall and personally dress you head to toe in pink rhinestones."

Her nose wrinkled. "You wouldn't."

"I would." She looked at the card. Then at me. "You're an emotionally repressed sugar daddy."

"Correct." She snatched the card.

"Fine. But I'm buying Crocs." I shrugged. "Your funeral."

Cole leaned in from behind. "Ooooh, can we match?"

"Out of the car," I ordered. Riley climbed out last, laughing softly.

And if it was because of me... I'd take the hit. Hell, I'd hand her my entire damn bank account if it meant she'd keep laughing like that.

Riley

Oh, they wanted to play?

Fine. I'd win.

The second Killian dropped the casually dangerous Get whatever you want, I narrowed my eyes. Suspicious didn't even cover it.

This wasn't how they operated. Private gallery tour? A meal? Heated glances across a white tablecloth? And now they were offering to fund a shopping spree like I was some high-end brat with a black Amex and no shame?

Sugar baby energy. That's what it was.

But if they wanted to throw money at me like I was their dirty little indulgence, I was going to make them suffer for it.

So I played nice. Dragged them store to store. Picked out clothes I didn't need, accessories I'd probably never wear, even tossed in some makeup just to watch Lucas pretend not to care.

Every single time I held something up, I made sure to ask their opinions.

Oh, I was collecting reactions like fucking trophies.

Jaxon, smug bastard, gave style critiques like he was Milan's most unhinged stylist. Lucas was quieter—watchful—but his eyes always lingered a second too long when the fabric got tight.

Cole was loving every minute, the little shit. Egging me on. Whispering things in my ear just to see if he could make me squirm.

(He couldn't. But he tried.)

And then there was Killian. Killian didn't say a word. But I could feel him watching me. He didn't need to react—his jaw did it for him.

Clench. Release.

Every time I got too close. Every time I brushed past him or held up something lacy.

So naturally, I weaponized it. The moment we passed the lingerie section, I beelined like a woman possessed.

I plucked a floral lace bra and panty set off the rack and turned to face them, tipping my head with a faux-innocent smile.

"Ohhh, I don't know," I said sweetly, holding the barely-there fabric up to my body. "What do you guys think?"

Killian

I'd been holding the line all damn day. Watching her play, watching her smirk, brushing past me like she didn't know exactly what she was doing.

But then she held that lace against her skin. It hit me like a loaded gun going off in a locked room.

My pulse spiked, heat punched through my chest, and something low in my body went hard and heavy all at once.

The lace was pale, delicate, threaded with tiny flowers that barely covered what needed covering. And against her skin—Christ—my mind went somewhere dark. Somewhere possessive.

I didn't just want her wearing it.

I wanted to buy every single piece in this shop and lock it away so only I'd ever see her in it.

Her fingers brushed the fabric against her ribs, and I tracked that movement like a predator scenting blood. My hands ached to follow, to feel the warmth of her through that teasing scrap of lace.

The others were talking—someone made a joke—but their voices blurred into static.

All I could see was her. Something in me snapped.

I was moving before I'd even decided to. Slow, deliberate steps until I was in her space. My voice came out low, dark, certain. "Try it on."

I'd been leaning against the wall outside the changing room, trying to act like I was just another guy waiting his turn, but the truth was, I was seconds from tearing the damn curtain off its hooks.

Cole was making some half-assed joke, Jaxon was pretending to be on his phone, and Lucas was giving me that look—the one that said he could read every thought I wasn't saying.

I didn't care. My focus was on the thin strip of fabric separating me from her. Then I heard it. The faint, sharp snap of a bra strap being adjusted. It went through me like a live wire.

My grip on my control slipped. My body reacted before my brain caught up—heartbeat hammering, possessive need clawing through my chest.

Lucas started to say something, but I was already moving. I gripped the curtain, pulled it aside, and stepped in. The world narrowed to a single point.

Riley stood in front of the mirror, soft light wrapping around her like she'd been painted into the room. The black lace traced her body in delicate lines, teasing more than it revealed.

Her reflection caught mine in the mirror. And for one long, dangerous second, neither of us moved.

Then her eyes snapped up to meet mine. Sharp. Unafraid. Knowing. That was it. The last thread of restraint snapped clean in half. She turned slowly, deliberately, giving me the full view, and I swear I stopped breathing.

My hand reached past her and dragged the curtain shut, sealing us inside.

The room felt smaller instantly. Warmer. Private.

I stepped closer, my body brushing hers, fingertips grazing the lace at her hip. Every inch of me burned for her. Not just to touch. Not just to take. To keep.

"You don't know what you're doing to me," I said, voice rough, eyes locked on hers in the mirror.

But I knew she did.

Riley

The second Killian stepped in and dragged the curtain closed, the air changed.

He was too close. All heat and gravity and quiet danger, the kind that made every nerve in my body sit up and pay attention. His hand brushed my hip through the lace, fingers trailing like he had all the time in the world—but his eyes?

His eyes were fire and ruin. So, naturally, I taunted him. "You like what you see, Killian?" I tipped my chin, watching him in the mirror, letting my voice curl into something sharp and sweet.

"Or are you just going to stand there breathing heavy like a creep?"

It was the last thread holding him together. And I cut it on purpose.

His jaw flexed once. Then his hand fisted lightly in the lace at my hip and he shoved me back against the mirror—not hard, but with absolute, unshakable intent.

The kiss hit like a detonation. Heat. Pressure. Teeth. His mouth crashed against mine with enough force to steal the breath from my lungs, and my hands shot into his hair on instinct, yanking him closer.

He groaned against my mouth, low and rough, the sound vibrating straight through me. It wasn't soft. Wasn't sweet. It was hunger barely held together. Like he'd been restraining himself for weeks and finally snapped.

The mirror pressed cool against my spine while every inch of him burned hot against me, and my body reacted before my brain could even catch up.

We only broke apart when breathing became necessary. Forehead against mine, breath ragged, he stayed there for one stolen second too long.

Then he stepped back. Just... stepped back. Turned. Left. The curtain swayed shut behind him like none of it had happened.

Outside, I heard his voice—calm, composed, terrifyingly normal. "Bag every piece she tried on."

I stood there trembling in black lace, lips swollen, skin buzzing like I'd been struck by lightning from the inside out.

Then my knees gave up and I sank onto the plush carpet, staring at myself in the mirror.

"Holy fuck," I whispered. What the hell was that?

Killian

When the curtain fell shut behind me, it stopped being just a kiss. It became a line in the sand. Riley wasn't going anywhere. Not now. Not ever. I walked straight to the counter, card already in hand. "Everything she tried on," I told the saleswoman.

She smiled politely. "Of course, sir—" "And everything else she touched," I added. "Every set in her size." Her eyes widened slightly, but she nodded quickly and started signalling to another clerk, who immediately began pulling racks apart. Lace. Silk. Mesh.

All of it disappearing into glossy black bags. "And if there's anything in back stock that matches," I continued evenly, "bring it out."

Out of the corner of my eye, I noticed a darker alcove tucked near the back wall. Sleek shelves. Dim lighting. Velvet-lined boxes. Toys. Restraints. Accessories. Cole let out a low whistle. "Holy shit."

Jaxon rubbed a hand down his face. "This is either gonna end in marriage or a homicide investigation."

"She'll probably want all of those too," I said calmly.

That made Lucas go still beside me. Not curious. Not amused. Just... still.

His eyes locked on a pair of restraints for one long second before he looked away again, jaw tight.

Cole, thankfully, bulldozed straight through the tension. "This is better than Christmas."

Jaxon snorted. "You're buying the whole damn store, aren't you?"

"Yes," I said without hesitation.

"I don't care what it costs."

The sales staff moved faster after that, arms filling with boxes and tissue paper and black ribbon. I never once looked at the total. Didn't need to.

Because when Riley finally stepped back out of the fitting room—cheeks flushed, lips kiss-swollen, hair slightly wrecked from my hands—the entire store seemed to go quiet around her.

My gaze dragged over her slowly. Deliberately. From those bruised lips to the faint pink marks at her collarbone. She noticed. Her colour deepened instantly. And she looked away first. Good.

44

Bound and Broken

Riley

Tears of Gold — Faouzia

The bed was a lingerie apocalypse—lace and silk everywhere, like Victoria's Secret had exploded in my room. Some of it was tempting. Most of it looked like a medieval torture device in disguise.

The pearl thong? Crimes against humanity.

I found crotchless panties, slid them over my wrist like a bracelet, and grinned. "What the fuck is this? Empowerment? Or a yeast infection waiting to happen?"

The door creaked. Lucas. He froze mid-step, eyes locking on the lace around my wrist like I was holding a loaded gun. And that's when the little devil in me stirred.

He was always so composed. So unflappable. The calm one in every storm. I wanted to see what happened when the calm cracked. So I leaned into it.

"Need a second to breathe, soldier?" I teased, voice light.

His gaze flicked up, unreadable. "I'm fine," he said, setting the med kit down hard enough to rattle the table. Perfect. I lifted my wrist so the lace dangled between us.

"Think it'd suit me?" He took it from me without a word, tossed it onto the bed, and grabbed my arm again to work on the bandage. His touch was steady, but not quite as steady as usual. I leaned closer, thigh brushing his. "You're really good with your hands," I murmured, nails scraping down his forearm. "So careful. So precise."

His fingers stilled. His jaw flexed. "Careful, Riley," he said, voice darker now. "You don't know what you're asking for."

Oh, but I did. Or at least, I thought I did. I wanted to push him over the edge. Just to see. Just for the thrill of it.

"What do you want to do to me?" I asked, breath catching slightly.

He didn't answer. Just reached across the bed and pulled something from the lingerie bag.

Not the scarf. The cuffs. Shiny. Padded. Cold in the way that said final. Something in my stomach flipped.

"You sure?" he asked. "Yes." The word slipped out too fast.

He moved like a predator who'd finally spotted the opening — sudden, certain.

In a blink, I was against the headboard, one cuff snapping closed around my wrist, then the other. Not rough — but there was nothing hesitant in the way he locked me down.

And then he stepped back to take me in. Like he was framing the moment in his mind. Like this image would keep him fed through every hunger.

"Killian made his move," he said, voice smooth and low. "Now I'm making mine."

Lucas

She thought she was teasing me. Thought she could play her little game and walk away untouched.

The second the cuffs locked around her wrists, that illusion was gone. I closed in, my shadow spilling over hers, skirt bunched in my fist. I shoved it up — slow enough to make her heart pound, rough enough to remind her who was in charge.

The lace beneath barely covered her, black against warm skin, and it was gone with one sharp rip.

Her gasp hit me like a shot of adrenaline. I dropped to my knees and pressed my mouth to her without hesitation — not kissing, not tasting politely — but feasting. I sealed my lips over her clit, tongue dragging up through her folds with deliberate, hungry strokes.

Her flavour coated my tongue, rich and addictive, the exact taste I'd imagined reading the stolen books from her apartment — the ones that spelled out her fantasies in black and white.

I'd memorised every one. My left hand spread her wider, thumb holding her open for me, while my right hand slid between us, two fingers pushing into her heat slow, deep, curling up until I felt the sweet spot that made her breath break.

I didn't move fast — not yet. I pumped slow and deliberate, tongue circling her clit with maddening precision.

Every reaction went straight into the mental catalogue: Sharp inhale when I slide my fingers in. Breathless whimper when my tongue flicks just right.

The way her hips lift when I curl my fingers and suck at the same time. She tried to move — to rock into me for more — and I pinned her down with my free hand on her thigh.

"No," I growled against her, before sucking her clit into my mouth again, harder this time, fingers stroking in perfect sync.

Her cuffs clinked against the headboard. She pulled, twisted, desperate to close her legs around me, to grind against my face for more friction. I denied her every inch.

I alternated between slow, deep strokes of my fingers and rapid, teasing flicks of my tongue over her clit, keeping her right on the razor edge. Every time she thought she could fall, I eased off just enough to keep her there — trembling, panting, straining.

When she finally broke and begged, I gave her what she wanted — and more. I sucked hard, tongue pressed flat, fingers pumping faster, deeper, curling again and again until her entire body locked around me.

Her orgasm ripped through her in a shuddering wave, her thighs trembling violently, her cry fractured and raw. I didn't stop. I milked every last spasm, my mouth and fingers working her until she was overstimulated, shying away, the pleasure turning sharp.

Only then did I ease up, pulling my fingers free and licking them clean while I watched her chest heave. I crawled up over her, mouth dragging over her stomach, her ribs, the swell of her breasts.

I kissed her hard, forcing her to taste herself on my tongue while my hands framed her face.

She was dazed, ruined — perfect. I undid the cuffs slowly, kissing the red marks on each wrist, committing them to memory. Her skirt fell back down as I stood, looking at her flushed and wrecked, still catching her breath.

I bent to press a kiss to her forehead — not gentle, not sweet. Final. Claiming.

Then I left her there, legs still trembling, mind reeling. She'd lie in shock, thinking holy fuck, what just happened?

What happened was simple. She'd just been claimed.

Riley

I couldn't fucking move. Not because of the cuffs—he'd already undone those, kissed the angry red marks like a brand before walking out—but because my body had mutinied.

My thighs were still twitching, little aftershocks running through me. My chest heaved, ribs aching with every breath. My lips burned from his kiss, still smeared with the taste of me he'd shoved back into my mouth like he wanted to choke me with it.

Holy fuck. Holy fuck.

I was sprawled out like a crime scene—skirt shoved up, panties ripped and hanging off one ankle, the sheets beneath me damp with spit and slick. My skin prickled everywhere he'd touched, everywhere his mouth had marked.

And I could still feel him—tongue circling my clit until I screamed, fingers curling deep inside until I clenched so hard it hurt.

He hadn't just made me come. He'd torn it out of me. Held me there, tortured me with it, wrung me dry while I sobbed for more.

And I'd begged. God, I'd begged for it like a slut. What the fuck was wrong with me?

This wasn't supposed to happen. I wasn't supposed to let any of them in—and now Lucas had my taste on his tongue, my come on his chin, his fingerprints carved under my skin.

The worst part? He'd walked away. Just left me wrecked and shaking, spread wide and dripping on my own sheets, while he carried his smug composure right out the door.

Like I was the one left in ruins.

I could still feel the ache in my cunt, raw from his tongue, slippery with the mess he'd pulled out of me.

My clit throbbed, swollen, too sensitive, every brush of air making me shiver. My wrists tingled where the cuffs had bit. My thighs were sticky with spit and slick.

And all I could think about was him on his knees between my legs, moaning into me like he couldn't stop himself. His tongue, his fingers, Jesus Christ.

I should have showered. Should have wiped him off me, scrubbed the sheets, reminded myself this was temporary. Instead, I lay there, ruined and wet, wishing he'd come back and do it again.

Lucas

I could still taste her. My mouth was raw, jaw aching, tongue sore, and all I could fucking taste was Riley.Slick, salt, heat — sweet and obscene, like sin made liquid. It coated my lips, stuck to my chin, sat heavy in the back of my throat.

I swallowed and it was still there, clinging like it wanted to live in me forever.

I'd eaten her like a starving man, and Christ, I still wasn't full.

My cock was a fucking disaster. Jeans soaked, boxers plastered to me, the hot wet mess of my own release sticking against my skin.

Virgin shame in full stereo. I'd come in my pants like a teenager, like some untouched choirboy who'd never seen a bare thigh before tonight.

Except I had seen it. I'd spread it, torn it, buried my mouth in it until she screamed. Pathetic? Yeah. Exhilarating? More than I could fucking breathe through.

I leaned against the door after I shut it behind me, heart jackhammering, cock twitching even though I was already spent.

My thighs still trembled from grinding into the floor, from holding back the need to shove myself inside her and end it properly. But I hadn't. I couldn't. So I settled for memorising every fucking detail.

The way her cuffs rattled when she thrashed.

The way her clit swelled under my tongue, slick and throbbing.

The way her cunt clenched around my fingers so tight it nearly milked me through denim.

The way she screamed when I broke her open and rode her orgasm until she begged me to stop.

And the taste. Jesus. Her taste. I'd read about it in her books, studied every filthy page like doctrine, but nothing prepared me for the real thing.

Hot, wet, tangy, intoxicating — the flavour of Riley coming undone on my tongue. I licked my lips again, desperate, chasing what lingered.

My cock twitched against the mess in my jeans. Humiliation burned through me, but fuck if it didn't feel like triumph too.

Because no matter how many smut books she'd hidden under her pillows, no matter how many fantasies she thought she'd memorised... I'd given her something better. And she'd never forget the taste either.

45

Just Me and the Dead

Riley

The Way I Do – Bishop Briggs

The morning after is always the worst part. Because it's quiet. No distraction. No adrenaline. No noise loud enough to drown out what's happening inside my head.

The sun barely slipped through the gaps in the warehouse blinds. Soft. Harmless.

I wanted to rip them down anyway.

My breath felt shallow. My skin too hot and too cold at once.

I could still feel him—Lucas. His mouth. His hands. His voice. The way he said my name like it meant something. Like I meant something.

That was the problem. Not the sex — I could handle sex. Not the heat — that part was easy.

The problem was after. The way he looked at me like I wasn't broken. The way his touch was gentle where I was used to sharp edges. The way I let him see more than I ever meant to.

I didn't just give him my body. I gave him too much. And I had no idea how to take it back.

I sat on the edge of my bed, hoodie thrown over my shoulders like a shield. My hands wouldn't stop shaking.

You're slipping. You swore you'd never do this again.

Sophie's face slammed into my head before I could block it—her hand in mine, the monitor flatlining, knowing I couldn't save her.

I clenched my fists until my nails bit into my palms. I can't care. If I let them in, if I lose them too— I won't survive it.

And the worst part?

I already cared. Lucas touched me like I was fragile.
Killian saw every crack.

Jaxon hovered like he was ready to catch me.
Cole already knew I was falling.

My throat tightened. I wasn't built for this. Not for love. Not for softness. I was built for war. Safer that way.

The bed still smelled like him—skin, heat, something I couldn't name. I yanked the sheets off and shoved them in the corner like that would help.

It didn't. Don't be stupid, Riley. Don't be weak.

His voice still echoed. You're safe with me.

He'd whispered it last night like it was the easiest truth in the world. And I'd believed him. I don't know how long I sat there. The light shifted. Shadows crawled across the floor like quiet witnesses. The ache stayed rooted under my skin.

The worst part? I didn't want to run. For the first time in years, I wanted to stay. Wanted to believe him. Believe them. But my body didn't trust what my heart was trying to do.

People leave. People die. People promise forever and then vanish.

Sophie. Her name hit like a freight train. Her hand in mine. The monitors screaming. The sharp tone that said there was nothing left to save.

And me, frozen. Helpless. Never again.

My pulse pounded in my throat. My skin felt wrong. Tight. Suffocating. Like I was drowning in a current I couldn't fight. The worst kind of panic isn't loud.

It's quiet. That sick, gnawing tension where you know exactly what you're running from — but you're too scared to stop. I shoved off the bed and started pacing, boots thudding against concrete like I could stomp out the noise in my skull.

You let them in. They'll break you. I should've packed my shit and left. That was the rule. But I hadn't.

Because I wanted to stay. Because I wanted them. Because I was already halfway ruined.

I caught my reflection. Hated what I saw. Flushed cheeks. Soft eyes. Bruises blooming across my throat, hips, wrists—reminders of his hands.

I slammed my fist into the wall. Pain. Sharp. Brief. Not enough.

Tears burned hot, but I refused to let them fall. I needed air.

If I stayed another minute, I'd lose the war entirely. My feet carried me out of the warehouse before my brain caught up. Cold bit into my skin like punishment. Gravel crunched beneath my boots.

The quiet felt like a funeral. I can't do this. I don't know how. But my body kept moving.

The graveyard waited like an old friend.

Sophie Morgan

Beloved Sister. Loyal Friend.

2001 – 2020

My knees hit the wet earth. I rested my shaking hands on the stone.

"I don't know what I'm doing anymore." My voice cracked.

"I let him in, Soph. I let them in. And it feels good and horrible at the same time and I—" My breath hitched.

"I can't stop it." Tears spilled hot down my frozen face.

"I don't want to lose anyone else."

I gripped the stone harder.

"Because if I do, I won't come back." The grief twisted with something worse. Hope.

"I want to believe him. I want to believe all of them."

Wind sliced across my skin.

"I'm so fucking tired of being scared." My voice broke.

"But I don't know how to stop." I pressed my forehead to her name and let myself shatter. Alone.

By the time I walked back, I was barely holding together.

The cold clung to my skin, boots soaked through. I eased the warehouse door shut like I could sneak past. But they were already there.

Killian by the doorway, arms crossed, eyes unreadable.

Lucas leaning forward, gaze locking on me the second I stepped inside.

Jaxon hovering, chewing his lip like he was holding himself back.

Cole at the counter, loose stance, no humour in his eyes.

The silence pulsed. I opened my mouth. Closed it again.

Killian spoke first, low. "Where were you?"

"I just needed air."

Lucas: "Four hours of air?"

I stared at the floor. "I'm fine."

Cole's voice cut in, unusually quiet. "You don't get to lie to us, Riley. Not anymore."

"I'm handling it."

Jaxon stepped closer, careful. "Handling what? Needing us?"

I flinched. "You don't understand."

Lucas stood. "Try us."

"I'm terrified." The word scraped out of me.

Killian's voice softened. "Of what?"

"Everything. Of needing you. Of losing you. Of hoping for something I'm not supposed to have."

They stayed silent. Let me speak. "My sister was all I had. When she died, part of me broke. Permanently. I told myself I'd never let anyone in again. Because if I did, and they left too—"

My voice cracked. "I don't know if I could survive it twice."

The sob tore loose. I wrapped my arms around myself, shaking. Killian moved first — slow, careful — and pulled me into him. I let him.

The second his arms closed, everything caved.

Lucas's hand on my back.

Jaxon's forehead against mine.

Cole wrapping me from behind like a safety net.

They didn't speak. Didn't try to stop the crying. They just stayed. And they kept staying.

Every time I tried to rebuild distance, they closed it.

Lucas memorised my tea preferences — which mugs, which corner of the couch, which days I needed chamomile or Earl Grey. His hands wrapped mine around the mug like he was daring me to let go first.

I never did.

Jaxon cooked without asking. Simple pasta. Or spiced lamb and roasted vegetables — Sophie's recipe. My fork shook the whole time. He never said a word.

Cole became a shadow I didn't know I needed. His jacket always around my shoulders before I realised I was cold. When I rubbed the scar on my wrist, he'd trap my hand and brush it with his thumb, like reminding me it was healed.

Killian was constant heat. A hand at my back. At my hip. His gaze when he thought I wasn't looking. He stayed in sight until I fell asleep. Guarding me. Claiming me. Both.

Every touch. Every look. Every act of care pried loose another stone from my walls.

They knew it. And I let them. That was the danger. The sex would've been easy. But this — the slow siege — was making me want more. And if I wanted more, it meant I was already theirs. And if I was already theirs, they had the power to destroy me completely.

46

The Taste of Ruin

Riley

Haunted - Beyoncé

The sunlight was supposed to be warm. It wasn't. It just pinned me down, harsh and exposing, while the cold inside gnawed deeper.

My chest ached. My thoughts spun in circles, chewing me up and spitting me out.

I'd been staring at the same spot on the floor for so long the shadows seemed to crawl.

"Princess." Jaxon's voice cut through the static. My shoulders locked. I didn't look up. The couch dipped. Heat bled into my side.

"You look like you're planning your own funeral," he drawled.

"Go away." My voice cracked.

"Not happening." He leaned close, his breath brushing my temple.

"You're drowning. And I'm not letting you."

"Then stop watching."

His chuckle was low, infuriating. "Not until you tell me what you actually want."

I turned, snapping at him — only to find his eyes locked on mine. Dark. Glittering. Hungry. My pulse jumped. "Don't," I whispered. But I didn't move.

His gaze sharpened. "If you don't want this, say it. Out loud."

I swallowed. Silence. "One word," he murmured, fingers brushing mine. "And I stop. Always. Do you understand?"

I nodded. "Not enough." His mouth ghosted my ear. "Say it."

"I... understand."

His grin cut sharp. "Good girl." And then he moved. I was Airborne.

"Jaxon—what the fuck!" I gasped as he scooped me up. He didn't flinch. Just sat back and dropped me into his lap like I'd always belonged there. His cock pressed thick and hard against me, blunt and demanding.

"Relax," he breathed, lips grazing my ear. "You were digging yourself a grave. I'm giving you something better to focus on. If you want it."

Goddamn him. My body melted. My brain screamed. Neither mattered."You don't have to—" I whispered.

"I know." His voice was low, steady. "But I want to. The question is — do you?"

Something cracked inside me. Or maybe I just gave in. "Yes," I breathed.

His lips brushed my temple. "Then you're mine."

The kiss was hard, hungry, unrelenting. His hand shoved my shorts aside, stripping me bare. I was wet before shame even had a chance to surface. His fingers slid through my slick.

He laughed dark in my ear. "Already dripping? Christ, you're easy."

Heat scorched my face. My body clenched. I hated that it turned me on — hated more that it did.

Two fingers drove into me, curling. His palm ground my clit with every thrust. Sparks detonated up my spine.

"Look at you," he snarled, cock grinding against me as he fucked me with his hand.

"Grinding like a bitch in heat. You like it. Don't lie." My moan betrayed me, high and wrecked.

"Say stop and I'm gone," he rasped, voice rough in my ear.

"But you won't, will you? You're too far gone. You want to give in. You want me to take it from you." The word caught in my throat.

I didn't say it.

He smirked. "Thought so." His thumb circled mercilessly. "My filthy little whore."

The orgasm ripped through me, core spasming, scream clawing raw from my chest. His arm cinched around my waist, his mouth hot on my neck — and then I felt it.

The thick head of his cock sliding through my folds. Not in. Not yet. Just rubbing slow, deliberate, every drag catching my clit.

"Feel that?" he groaned. "Me stroking your clit with my cock. Teasing you. Making you soak me." My hips rocked helplessly.

"Please—""Please what?""Fuck me."

He stilled. "You sure?""Yes,"

I gasped, shame choking me. "Just—yes."

"Good girl." He lined up, thumb circling my clit. "You begged. Now take it."

And then he pushed. Slow. Deep. Stretching me until I whimpered, until I shook in his lap.

"That's it," he rasped. "Feel me splitting you open. You're mine, Princess. My perfect little slut."

And God help me, I loved it. I loved surrendering to him.

Jaxon

Fuck, she was perfect. Pinned to my chest, pussy clutching my cock like it had been waiting for me. Every thrust slammed her down, my thumb grinding her clit until she screamed.

"My good little slut," I groaned. "Made to milk my cock."

She sobbed, hips jerking, begging without words.

And then I saw him. Cole. Standing in the doorway. Watching. I didn't slow. If anything, I thrust harder, hauling her higher, hooking her thighs wide, bouncing her in my lap. On display.

"Look at her," I growled. "Look at how she takes me."

Her moans tore through the air. Cole's jaw flexed, eyes dark. I smirked against her throat, biting hard.

"Yeah. Watch. She's mine first."

Cole

Christ. She was split wide on Jaxon, tits bouncing, throat marked, pussy obscene — stretched, dripping, perfect. And I wanted in. Jaxon met my stare, smirking as he bounced her harder. "She's mine." Not for long.

I stepped closer, heat roaring.

"Yeah. But she can take more."His grin sharpened. We both knew. Double.

I crouched beside her, hand smoothing her trembling stomach, feeling Jaxon drive deep. Her glassy eyes fluttered open, whimper catching.

"Princess," I murmured, brushing the mess around his cock.

"If you don't want me, say it now." Her breath hitched. No word. Just a shudder.

"Good." I slicked my fingers with her wet, lining up behind.

"Hold her open." Jaxon obeyed. And when I pressed in, her moan broke — horror and need tangled.

Riley

Jaxon's cock already had me split wide, pounding into me, when Cole's fingers circled my ass, slick and deliberate.

My brain short-circuited. Oh. Oh no.

"Wait—what—" A wet sound cracked the air. He spat. Spread it with his thumb. And suddenly it wasn't a suggestion anymore. My whole body jolted.

"Cole—oh my God—"

A thick finger pressed in. Not unfamiliar. I'd done this before. I knew the stretch, the sting, the obscene fullness. But this?

With Jaxon already buried deep inside me?

It was insane. Out of all the things he could've done — eat me out, shove his fingers in my mouth, literally anything — they went with this? Straight to the filthiest option on the menu?

"Ohhh fuck—" I gasped as Jaxon slammed up into me again, Cole pushing deeper behind.

My brain scrambled for footing. What the hell. What the fuck. This is too much.

But my body didn't care. Every time Cole stretched me wider, my cunt clamped tighter on Jaxon.

Every thrust from one made me crave the other. "This is wrong," I panted, nails digging into Jaxon's chest. "This is—fuck—"

Cole's voice was velvet filth in my ear. "Shhh. You've done this before. You know how good it gets. You're opening for us like you've been waiting your whole life to be split like this."

And he wasn't wrong. The burn twisted into pressure, pressure into heat, and heat into the kind of pleasure that stole my breath.

Still, the thought tore through me, wild and half-hysterical: Could've been oral. Could've been simple. But no. Of course not. With these bastards, it was never soft. Never sane. And maybe that's why I let them. Because I didn't want soft anymore. I wanted to be broken open.

And God help me—my body fucking loved it.

When his cock finally slid in where his fingers had been, I lost the last of myself. Split in half, Jaxon filling my cunt, Cole stretching me from behind, my body spasmed helplessly, clamping around them both as if I could reject and crave it all at once.

"Ohhh fuck, fuck—" I sobbed, convulsing. Jaxon growled into my neck, thrusting harder.

"That's it, Princess. Take us. Take all of it."

Cole's thumb stroked my clit, slow and cruel.

"Greedy little slut. You wanted this. You surrendered to us." And the worst, filthiest part? They were right.

Lucas

I opened the door, soup in hand — and froze. She wasn't curled on the window seat.

She was split open between them.

Jaxon buried in her cunt.

Cole's cock driving into her ass.

Riley convulsing, screaming, perfect. The sounds hit me — wet, obscene, raw.

My chest locked. My cock went hard so fast I staggered.

Shame burned, but I couldn't look away. Because it wasn't just sex.

They owned her. And she loved it.

She gave herself to them. Jealousy hollowed me out. Because when it was my turn, I wouldn't share her.

Riley

I was gone — wrecked between them, orgasms tearing me apart. And then I saw him. Lucas. Soup trembling in his hand.

"Soup," he muttered, setting it down before fleeing.

Cole chuckled low. Jaxon's mouth crushed against mine, hard and bruising, before softening — just enough to anchor me.

They eased me down between them, shifting me off their cocks, lowering me onto the couch cushions like I might break.

My thighs trembled uncontrollably, my whole body slick with sweat.

Cole stroked a hand over my back, smoothing damp hair from my face. "Breathe, Princess. That's it. Easy now."

Jaxon's grip stayed iron around my waist, but his thumb traced slow circles against my hip, grounding.

"You're shaking," he muttered, voice hoarse.

"Look at me. You're okay." I nodded weakly, though I wasn't sure I believed it.

My lungs burned, my body convulsed in aftershocks, but their hands didn't leave me.

Cole's lips brushed my shoulder — soft, reverent — the same mouth that had just spoken filth into my ear. Jaxon kissed my temple, fierce and steady.

"You gave in," Jaxon rasped.

"That's my good girl." Cole added, quieter: "You let us take you. And you took it all."

My eyes stung. My chest ached. I curled into them because I couldn't do anything else — because I'd fought so hard to hold myself together, and they'd broken me apart, and I'd let them. And somehow, surrendering to them was the only thing keeping me whole.

Their murmurs blurred into the haze, rough voices softening, touch steadying.

I let myself sink. I didn't notice the tiny black lens in the corner.

Didn't know Lucas had set it up. Didn't know he was already planning to keep the feed. To keep me.

47

Lust. Rage. Repeat

Riley

Cherry – Fletcher

The lounge door clicked behind me, shutting Cole and Jaxon in with the wreckage. I'd yanked my hoodie over damp skin, tugged shorts up trembling thighs, like clothes could erase the fact that twenty minutes ago I'd been split open, filled, devoured, undone. My body still hummed with them, like every nerve had been rewired to remember.

I'd only technically fucked two of them. Just two. And Lucas had been on his knees before that, quiet and relentless, eating me until I was sobbing. Jaxon too — his mouth brutal, hungry, determined to wring me dry.

That made it all four. Two cocks. Two tongues. One ruined Riley.

What the actual fuck.

How did they know how to do this shit? Normal men didn't fuck like that. Normal men didn't edge you until your soul left your body and then give you water and soft words like aftercare was a religion. Normal men didn't touch you like they'd been trained in some underground academy for advanced clit warfare.

Did they make a deal with the devil? Was there a secret school I'd missed? A black-ops sex seminar where they taught you how to fold a girl open and play her like a goddamn instrument? Because that was not normal.

That was witchcraft. And thank fuck for my IUD, because otherwise I'd be 10/10 pregnant already. Probably quadruplets. Maybe sextuplets. Just from the look Killian was giving me across the room.

I walked out anyway, steady on the outside, chaos chewing me raw on the inside.

Two pairs of footsteps followed — Jaxon and Cole, smug and unhurried. Wolves who didn't need to chase.

The warehouse opened into the living space — couches, TV, kitchen counters under pale light. And waiting there were Killian and Lucas. Killian in the armchair, still as stone, eyes sharp enough to flay.

Lucas at the counter, coffee cold, headphones loose, his stare slicing me open without touching.

They'd heard everything. And now they saw me.

I forced my arms tight across my chest, words like barbed wire leaving my mouth.

"Whatever happened in there? It stays there. I'm not your claim. I'm not your project. Three months. That's all I've got here. And in those three months, I'll fuck who I like, when I like. If it's you, fine. If not? Tough shit."

Silence hit heavy.

Jaxon whistled low. "Sharp tongue for someone who was choking on mine not half an hour ago."

Cole smirked, wolfish. "She really thought she could fuck us into silence. Bless."

"I wasn't trying to silence you," I snapped, too brittle to sound convincing. "I was trying to feel nothing. And it worked."

Lucas's voice cut through the room, cool and merciless. "Keep saying that, Riley. Maybe one day you'll even believe it."

My chest squeezed. "Easier for me if I do."

Killian rose slowly, deliberately, his shadow swallowing me whole. "So you let us ruin you. Let us soothe you. Let us mark you." His voice was velvet drawn over blades. "And then you pretend none of it mattered?"

"That's the plan," I bit out.

Lucas's mouth twitched. "Then you picked the wrong men to test that on."

Cole leaned forward, elbows on his knees, grin sharp. "Three months, huh? That's cute. Like a time limit means anything when you already belong to us."

Jaxon's voice slid hot against my ear. "You keep telling yourself you can walk away, Princess. But we'll be here proving you wrong."

My laugh cracked, paper-thin. "Game on."

Killian's smile spread slow and predatory. "Game's already over. You just haven't realised you've lost."

Heat surged up my throat. I raised my mug in a mock toast, the only shield I had left.

"Three months. No more."

Lucas's voice followed, calm as a sentence handed down. "Three months is all we'll need."

I didn't look back. But even I could feel it — the match had been struck. And they were the fire.

Killian

Three months. She thought that made her safe.

But the clock had started the night she was shot. The night we carried her bleeding into this warehouse. The night she opened her eyes and found all four of us still there.

Waiting. Watching. Staying.

Less than three months now.

Less than three months to wear down every wall she built around herself. To make her stop pretending this was temporary. To make her admit she wanted us as much as we wanted her.

Because Riley already belonged with us. Not in the soft, romantic way she was terrified of. Something rougher than that. Sharper. Built from sleepless nights, bruised knuckles, shared blood, and the way she melted every time one of us touched her like she mattered.

Cole chuckled low. "She really thinks she can walk away."

"She's scared," Jaxon said quietly. "That's different."

Lucas stayed silent, eyes fixed on the hallway she'd disappeared down. Then, finally: "She keeps treating this like a countdown," he murmured. "Like if she says three months enough times, it won't become real."

My mouth curved slowly. "But it already is."

The warehouse settled into silence around us.

Down the hall, a door shut. And for the first time in a long time, I felt something dangerous settle deep in my chest. Not lust. Not possession. Something worse. Hope.

48

Half-Zipped

Riley

Fire – Bishop Briggs

My duffel was half-zipped when the floorboard creaked. "If this is Killian," I said without looking up, "I'm not in the mood for your broody alpha-male monologue about control."

"It's not Killian." Lucas's voice — smooth, steady, quiet enough to make my pulse trip over itself.

He leaned against the doorframe, hands in his pockets, watching me with that maddening calm that felt like being dissected. Lucas didn't loom like the others. He waited.

"You leaving?"

"Thinking about it."

"Thinking," he repeated, like he was cataloguing the word. "Not deciding?"

I yanked at the zipper. "I don't owe you a decision."

"You don't owe me anything," he said, stepping into the room with the slow care of someone approaching a spooked animal. "But you owe yourself the truth. And I don't think you've given yourself that yet."

"Don't start psychoanalyzing me."

"I'm not. I'm asking a question." He stopped close enough that I'd have to brush past him to reach the door. Not blocking. Just there.

"If you really wanted to leave, Riley, that bag would already be closed. You'd already be gone. But you're not. You're packing like you want someone to stop you." The words hit harder than I wanted them to. My fingers froze on the zipper.

"You're angry," he went on, eyes flicking to my still hands. "Not because of what happened. Because of how you feel about what happened. And you think running will kill the feeling before it grows."

"That's called logic."

He shook his head once "That's called fear."

My throat locked. "You think you've got me all figured out, don't you?"

"I think," he said, quiet enough that I leaned in without meaning to, "you're braver than you believe. But you keep mistaking distance for safety. They're not the same."

Something inside me twisted. Too tight. Too raw.

"You can walk out right now, and I won't stop you." His voice stayed maddeningly steady. "But if you stay — not for them, not for me, for you — you might find there's more here to gain than to lose."

I swallowed hard. "You always this convincing?"

The barest flicker of a smile. "Only when it matters."

For a long moment neither of us moved. The duffel sat open between us, and the idea of zipping it up suddenly felt like cowardice. Lucas finally stepped aside, leaving the doorway clear. No command. Just choice. I didn't move.

He noticed — I saw it in the flicker of his eyes — before he left without another word. The silence pressed down. The bag sat there, half-zipped. My stomach was in knots. My chest hurt. Fuck.

I grabbed my phone like a lifeline and hit Magda's number. She answered on the third ring, cigarette smoke already in her voice.

"If you're calling before lunch, korítsi mou, you've either killed someone, fucked someone, or want my help doing both. Which is it?"

"Hi, Magda."

"Oh, it's bad. You only get that voice when your underwear is cheering but your brain's filing restraining orders. Out with it." So I did. The four of them. The tension. The fact that last night happened and I hadn't stopped it. How Lucas had just talked me out of leaving without raising his voice or breaking a sweat. She didn't interrupt except to light another cigarette — I heard the scratch of the match, the drag, the exhale.

When I finished, she cackled. "Oh, my girl. My beautiful disaster. You're living in an orgy waiting to happen."

"This is serious."

"Yes. Serious fun. You're not pregnant, no one's bleeding—"

"Magda—"

"—and you've got four men under one roof. Four! Do you know what I'd give for those odds? Half my stockpile and my good knee."

"You're ridiculous."

"I'm realistic. Let me guess. The quiet one's the problem?"

"...Yeah."

"Quiet ones are always the filthiest. They wait, they plan, and when they strike—"

"Stop."

"—you walk funny for two days and reconsider every life choice you've ever made."

I groaned, pressing my forehead to my knee. "You're supposed to tell me to get out."

"Do you want to get out?"

"Yes. No. I don't know."

"Then you don't. If you really did, you wouldn't be calling me. You'd be halfway to a motel, eating stale pretzels and hating yourself. Instead, you called me, which means you want permission to stay."

"I just... needed someone who isn't them."

"And here I am. Your sweet, innocent auntie who smuggles Berettas in boxes marked button samples. Now, listen. Do you want me to tell you to run, or do you want me to tell you to unpack that bag and make them sweat?"

"Neither?"

"Liar. Unpack. Make them work for it. And if they don't, I'll send a boy to break their knees. Family discount."

Despite myself, I laughed. "You're insane."

"And you love me. Now eat something. And if it turns into an actual orgy, call me. Not because I'm nosy, but because I like to know when my girl is winning."

She hung up, her filthy laugh still ringing in my ears, tangled with Lucas's calm precision. Neither of them had told me to go. That was the worst part. I stared at the half-zipped duffel. My hand hovered on the zipper. Then I let go.

Tea. I needed tea. Something normal. Halfway to the kitchen, Cole stepped out of the lounge like he'd been waiting.

"Following me now?" I asked, not slowing.

"Just wanted to talk."

"That's what people say right before they ruin my night." I moved past him, but he fell into step.

"You're still pissed," he guessed.

"Mm." I filled the kettle. "I just got off the phone with Magda. She says I should shoot you, but she's old-fashioned like that."

He blinked. "Who the hell is Magda?"

"She runs a haberdashery. Also sells semi-automatics out the back. Seventies. Filthy-minded. Better aim than you."

"And she told you to shoot me?"

"She told me to unpack my bag and make you sweat. Said a man like you isn't worth prison time."

Cole chuckled, leaning against the counter. "Charming woman."

"The best. And she's never wrong."

"So... you're staying?"

I didn't give him the satisfaction of an answer. "I'm making tea."

His grin widened. "You know they're all gonna take that as proof they're winning, right?"

My hand paused on the kettle. "Then maybe I'll let them think that," I said, catching his gaze just long enough for him to see the spark there. "It'll make it more fun when I'm the one who makes them fall."

The kettle clicked. Steam curled upward. I poured my tea and left him in the kitchen. Let them think they'd claimed me.

Cole

The door clicked behind her, and I just stood there. Grinning like an idiot. She was staying. Didn't matter what she'd said about tea or shooting me in the face. The bag was still upstairs. She was still here. And my chest felt like it might explode.

Hell, if I owned a diary, I'd be scribbling Dear Journal, she's staying! in glitter pen.

I shoved my hands in my pockets, trying not to literally skip down the hall. Failed. Fine — maybe it was a skip. A manly one. A power skip. Halfway to the lounge, I started rehearsing my announcement.

Understated? She's not leaving. Or dramatic?

You get a Riley! You get a Riley!

By the time I rounded the corner, I was buzzing like a kid at Christmas.

"She's staying," I blurted.

Killian didn't look up from his laptop. "No."

"What do you mean, no?" I demanded.

"Whatever it is. No. I'm working."

Lucas didn't even flinch, sipping his coffee like he already knew. Which, knowing him, he did.

"Fine," I muttered. "Keep your secrets. I'll keep my news."

Jaxon stretched out on the couch, lazy grin spreading. "What news?"

"She's staying."

That got Killian's attention. Lucas's mug paused midair.

Jaxon just laughed. "Yeah, no shit."

Cole blinked. "What do you mean 'no shit'? She told me herself—"

"She told you she was making tea," Jaxon cut in. "She didn't say she's staying."

"She didn't leave with her bag, did she?"

I opened my mouth. Closed it. Exactly.

"You're welcome," Lucas murmured, too smug by half.

Cole narrowed his eyes. "You—wait. Did you—"

"Doesn't matter how," Jaxon said. "What matters is you look like you just got crowned prom king."

"I'm just happy, alright?" Cole muttered, dropping into a chair. "She was this close to bailing. Now she's not."

Killian finally looked up, eyes flat and sharp. "If she's staying, she's already ours. Don't screw it up."

Cole threw his hands out. "Me? Screw it up? When have I ever—"

"Yesterday," Lucas and Jaxon said in unison.

Cole groaned. "You people are exhausting."

"Good," Jaxon said, stretching. "She might as well know what she's in for."

Killian

That kiss in the lingerie store still stalked me. Lace cutting across her skin, her mouth bruising mine, her taste sharp and sweet like sin dressed in silk. I'd swallowed her down and it hadn't come close to satisfying me. It only carved the hunger deeper.

I wanted more.

Not just her lips, but her trust. Her laughter. The parts of herself she guarded like weapons. Every inch of her, until there was nothing left untouched, nothing left hidden.

And when I finally took her completely, it wouldn't be reckless. It wouldn't be careless. It would be deliberate. Patient. Precise.

I would unravel her slowly. Kiss her until she forgot what loneliness felt like. Hold her steady while every wall she thought she needed cracked beneath careful hands. She would learn that strength wasn't distance. Strength was letting someone stay after they'd seen the worst parts of you.

Because Riley thought she could keep herself safe with rules.

Three months only. No feelings. No forever.

Cute. But she was already bending. Already slipping. And when she finally stopped fighting it, it wouldn't just be into my hands.

It would be into ours. Because she wasn't mine alone.

She was Cole's grin.

Jaxon's fire.

Lucas's quiet precision.

My restraint.

Together, we were the only thing dangerous enough to match her.

And one day soon, Riley would stop running long enough to realise it.

49

Caught

Riley

Blood in the Cut – K.Flay

My body had only just stopped bleeding me dry. A week of cramps like knives, nights curled up wishing for unconsciousness, the kind of exhaustion that made me want to claw my skin off.

The period from hell. This morning had felt like a reprieve. Like a mercy.

I'd woken with Jaxon's mouth between my thighs, coaxing me out of pain and into something sweeter.

His tongue slow, reverent, relentless until I was shaking, breathless, ruined in the best way.

He kissed my hips, whispered good girl into tender skin, held me like I was something precious instead of a battlefield.

And Cole... even he'd been soft. Fingers tracing lazy lines over my skin, lips brushing my temple. For one second — one fragile, traitorous second — I'd let myself believe it.

That maybe they weren't just using me. That maybe I wasn't just surviving here. Then I heard him.

"...she'll be fine, man. Riley always blows up, cries a little, then gets over it. That's what she does."

The words sliced straight through me. Cries a little. Gets over it. Like I was a tantrum. A performance.

Like everything I'd clawed through — every scar, every broken bone, every scream swallowed down — was just noise to wait out until I burned myself quiet again.

I froze, blood roaring in my ears. My chest went tight, sharp, like I'd been stabbed and couldn't breathe around it. Is this what they really think of me?

That I'm weak. Hysterical. Temporary.

The betrayal stung deeper than I wanted to admit. It turned Jaxon's mouth, Cole's tenderness, every second of care into a lie. My stomach twisted. My throat burned. Fury rose sharp and choking, because if I didn't wrap myself in it, I'd shatter where I stood. "You want to say that again?"

Cole looked up, guilt flickering before his smirk snapped into place. "It was a joke—"

"Wrong answer." "You are dramatic," he said, careless, cutting. "

Everything's the end of the world with you. You light up, burn out, and then you're fine again. That's just... you."

The words gutted me. I felt myself break under them, even as I laughed sharp, bitter, to cover it.

"Sorry if surviving actually looks messy. Sorry if my life doesn't fit into your neat little box of too much." "Jesus, Riley—"

"Don't." My voice shook, brittle glass ready to cut.

"Don't you dare Jesus Riley me like I'm some hysterical mess you have to manage. I'm not your mood swing. I'm not your fucking joke. And I'm not yours."

My chest ached, hot and hollow. If I stayed one more second, I'd bleed the hurt where he could see it. So I turned, fire in my steps, fury sealing the cracks before they split wide.

"Where are you going?" he called.

"Home." I didn't look back. Couldn't.

"Fuck the contract. I'm done." The door slammed behind me, and only then did I let myself taste the salt on my lips — fury's shadow, or maybe heartbreak's.

Cole

The door slammed like a gunshot. She was gone. No fight left, no storm waiting — just silence.

Fuck. I bolted after her, boots hammering gravel, lungs tearing. She was already halfway to the gates, her shoulders rigid, every line of her body screaming done.

"Riley!" She didn't stop. Didn't even twitch. Panic clawed me raw. If she crossed that line, I'd never get her back. I ran harder. Caught her wrist. Yanked her around.

"Don't touch me!" she snarled.

"Then stop running!" I slammed her into the warehouse wall. Brick rattled, breath knocked from both of us. She glared like she'd set me on fire if she could.

"You piss me off more than anyone I've ever met," I growled, pinning her wrists high.

"Good!" She ripped one free and slashed me across the throat. Heat spilled down my chest, copper sharp in the air.

I groaned. Fuck, I groaned. Her feral little smirk said it all: I could kill you if I wanted.

"Bleed me," I rasped, grinding my cock against her through denim, pinning her harder.

"Mark me. I'll wear it like a crown."

Her hips jerked against mine, traitorous, furious. "You don't get to love me."

"Too late." My hand shoved down her waistband, fingers finding her slick and hot, coating instantly.

Her gasp was sharp enough to cut. "Christ, Riley," I groaned, rutting against her thigh, thumb circling her clit. "You're dripping for me even when you hate me."

She clawed my neck again, deeper this time, blood and fire mixing. I didn't care. I pressed two fingers inside her, curling until she bucked against me.

"Please—" she gasped, head thrown back against the bricks. "Please what?" I taunted, grinding my palm against her clit as I thrust my fingers deeper.

"Please stop? Please more? You don't even know, do you?" Her hips answered for her, grinding hard into my hand. I dragged my mouth down her throat, sucking bruises into her skin, tasting sweat and blood.

"You're ours, Riley. You can run, you can fight, but you'll never escape. You're mine, Jaxon's, Killian's, Lucas's. Ours. You hear me? Ours."

Her nails dug into my shoulders, tearing fabric, breaking skin. Her fury burned, but her body clenched around me, betraying her with every spasm. I pulled my hand free, shoved my jeans down just enough, and stroked myself against her slick folds. She felt the metal first — the slide of my ladder piercings along her swollen clit. She gasped, shocked, trembling.

"Fuck," she panted, eyes wide. I smirked against her ear.

"Yeah, wild thing. You think my mouth ruined you? Wait 'til you feel this."

I dragged the piercings up through her folds, slow, deliberate, until she was squirming, rubbing against me like she hated herself for it.

"Beg," I demanded, voice a wreck. "Beg me to fuck you."

Her head snapped forward, teeth catching my lip hard enough to draw blood.

"Please," she hissed, furious and desperate all at once.

That was all I needed. I lined up and pushed in — slow, brutal inches, the piercings scraping perfectly as I filled her. Her scream tore the night open, nails ripping my neck raw, but her walls clenched so tight around me I nearly came instantly.

"Fuck, Riley," I groaned, forehead pressed to hers, grinding deep until she was pinned between cock and wall.

"I love you. Hate me, cut me, break me—I'll still love you."

Her hips met mine with a vicious slam, her body taking me deeper, punishing and worshipping at the same time. And I gave her everything

— the blood, the bruises, the piercings dragging her core raw with every thrust. Because if this was the only way she'd let me love her, then I'd burn for it.

Riley

The bricks dug into my back, every slam of his hips driving me harder into the wall, rattling the breath from my lungs. I should've shoved him off. I should've walked away. Instead, I clawed down his throat, opened him up, and he fucking groaned for it.

The stretch of him split me raw, brutal, merciless. The piercings dragged inside me with every thrust, a heavy, searing pull against places I didn't even know I could feel. I gasped, nails breaking skin, because the sensation was too much—alien and intoxicating at once.

"Bleed me," he rasped, forehead pressed to mine, voice thick with possession. "Mark me. I'll wear it like a crown." My hips betrayed me, slamming forward, hungry, furious. Because I could've ended it. I didn't. I didn't want to.

Then his hand slipped lower. Fingers circling my clit with obscene precision, working me in time with every brutal drive of his cock. My head snapped back, colliding with the wall, a cry ripping from my throat.

"Fuck—Cole—" "Yeah, storm," he groaned, blood dripping down his chest, sweat hot on his skin.

"Take it. Take all of me." Every thrust pushed the piercings deeper, his fingers rubbing harder, and I was gone—body bucking, grinding into his hand like I hated myself for needing it. I could've killed him.

Could've walked. Instead I surrendered with every clench of my core around him.

My orgasm tore through me like violence. Harsh. Messy. Unstoppable. I screamed into his mouth, nails raking his neck again, blood hot on my hands as my body milked him. He shuddered, groaning my name like a prayer, spilling deep, filling me until the aftershocks tipped into torture.

His fingers never left my clit, circling lazily, keeping me trapped in the storm until I was sobbing, overstimulated and furious and still clinging to him.

And then—his voice. Wrecked. Shattered. "I love you."

His mouth pressed to my temple, tender where minutes ago he'd been savage.

"Even when you hate me. Even when you cut me open. I fucking love you." I froze, chest cracking open against my will.

I should've laughed, spat in his face, pushed him off. Instead, I trembled in his arms, the piercings still pulsing inside me, his blood on my hands.

Because I knew the truth: if I wanted to, I could've ended this.

I didn't. And that terrified me more than his love ever could.

Cole

I pressed my mouth to her temple, then her jaw, then every place she'd let me reach. Kissing apologies into her skin like they could erase the cuts she'd left in mine.

"I'm sorry," I whispered between each one, voice ragged.

"I didn't mean it. I'll never mean it. I just—" My lips brushed her ear, desperate.

"I need you, Riley. You're mine. Ours. No matter how far you run. No matter how hard you fight."

She shuddered again, nails still curled against my throat like claws that hadn't decided whether to hold or tear.

I cupped her face, tilting her gaze back to me. My thumb stroked her cheekbone, catching on the damp heat there. "You hear me? You're it. My girl. My storm. My valley. You'll never be just another body. Never just a fuck. You're the one. You'll always be the one."

Her lip trembled, the fight still burning in her eyes even as her body betrayed her with how tightly she clung. I kissed her again, slower this time — no rage, no bite, just devotion.

My blood was still dripping from the lines she'd carved into me, but I didn't care. I'd let her carve me hollow if it meant keeping her.

"I love you," I said again, because once wasn't enough, because it would never be enough. "You're mine, Riley. Mine. And I'll spend the rest of my life proving it if I have to."

Riley

My chest burned, fury bleeding into something worse. Something softer. His mouth caught mine again — not a battle this time, not teeth and rage — but slow. Careful.

Like he wanted me to believe him. And for a terrifying second, I almost did.

The anger that had been roaring hot in my veins dulled to embers, leaving me hollow, confused, caught between wanting to shove him away and wanting to sink into him until nothing hurt.

My lips trembled against his as he breathed it again, wrecked and unguarded: "I love you."

And then I saw it. Over his shoulder, above the doorframe — the faint, steady blink of a red light.

My stomach dropped like a stone.

"...Oh, fuck." Cole froze against me. "What?"

I jerked my chin toward it, heart lurching. "Camera."

His body went rigid, then he turned his head. Saw it. Blink. Blink. Watching. Recording.

"Oh, fuck," he echoed, too fast.

"Don't panic. I'll wipe it. No one will see."

But my fury came back all at once, white-hot. Because it didn't matter if he wiped it. The fact that it was there at all — that there was a camera, pointed right at us, catching every second of this — felt like another betrayal. Another reminder that nothing in this place was safe. Not even this.

Lucas

I was already tracking Riley the second she stormed toward the gates. Standard op. Cameras live. GPS pinging. Always eyes on her, even when she didn't want them there. Especially then.

What wasn't standard was Cole catching her outside the south wall — chasing her like she was the only thing on the map that mattered.

She fought him like a cornered wolf, shoving, clawing, spitting fire... until the fight bled into something else. Something raw. Something neither of them could stop.

Killian came up behind me. Jaxon, too. None of us spoke. None of us looked away. The three of us stood in the control room glow, watching the feed flicker in real time —her body slamming into the brick, his mouth devouring her fury, her nails dragging blood from his throat.

I should've killed the feed. Should've given them back their privacy. Instead, I adjusted the audio, dialling in every gasp, every groan, every hissed word.

By the time Cole had her pinned, hips driving like he needed her to breathe, I knew I wasn't stopping it. None of us were.

We saved it. Locked the file where only we could reach it. Not for leverage. Not to break her. But because it was ours. Proof of what we already knew: she belonged here. With us. To us.

Minutes later, Cole swaggered back in, sweat still drying on his skin, Riley trailing after him. Flushed. Hair mussed. Eyes sharp and furious, but alive. Claimed.

The silence in the room was heavy. Throbbing. Killian's voice cut through it like a blade.

"She's not walking out of our lives." Cole smirked, still high off the fight.

"Never was." Jaxon leaned forward, voice low, certain.

"You think she'll choose?"

"She won't have to," Killian said. No hesitation. No doubt. Just steel.

All of us, then. No vote. No debate. Just the heavy click of something inevitable falling into place.

A trap closing. A cage locking. Not hers to escape. Ours to keep.

50

Winner Takes All

Jaxon

You're Gonna Go Far, Kid– The Offspring

It'd been a week since Cole shoved Riley against a wall and fucked her like the world was ending — and a week since Lucas and I had sat in the security room, watching it happen on the feed we absolutely should've deleted. Except we didn't.

Because Riley Morgan wasn't just passing through. She was ours. Or she should've been. I'd told myself to stop thinking about her. About the way her hair had clung to the back of her neck when she walked past us after, eyes sharp, chin tilted like nothing could touch her. Like nothing ever could.

Then she stepped into the gym. "Wanna spar?" Casual voice. Not a casual stance. Hip cocked. Gloves over one shoulder. Eyes already measuring me up like she was deciding where she wanted to hit first. "You're still supposed to be resting," I said. I kept my tone flat.

My pulse didn't get the memo. Not with the memory of her slumped in my arms, limp and pale, bleeding out from a bullet wound.

She smirked. It landed square in my chest. "You scared I'll win?" I should've told her to sit her ass down. Instead— "Winner gets a prize?" Her eyes gleamed. "Anything they want." We squared off. Riley fought like she lived — all in, no hesitation, daring you to keep up.

She was fast, but I caught the subtle shift in her stance that meant she was guarding her left side. The wound. She shouldn't have been in here. And the selfish part of me? The one that wanted her under me again, fighting for control with her mouth and not her fists? That part was thrilled.

Sweat slicked her hair to her face. Her shirt clung to her skin. She darted in; I sidestepped, caught her ankle, and swept her down. She rolled, popped up swinging, grin sharp enough to cut. "You're enjoying this," she panted. "You have no idea." She flurried — fists, feet, fire — and I let her drive me back just to see that light in her eyes.

Then I moved. Feinted left, caught her wrist, spun her into my chest, and used her momentum to take us down. I pinned her — knees bracketing her hips, wrists locked above her head. She bucked hard beneath me, and the heat that shot through me had nothing to do with the fight. "That's game," I said, my voice low. Her glare was pure challenge. "And your prize?"

I leaned in until our mouths almost touched. "This." The kiss was a collision — heat, teeth, adrenaline. My grip loosened so I could feel her fist twist in my shirt, yanking me closer until there was no air left between us.

"You're insufferable," she breathed. "And you're mine," I said before I could stop myself. Her smirk was razor sharp. "Keep dreaming." But she didn't stop me when I kissed her again.

Riley

The second his mouth hit mine, it was all heat and pressure and the taste of a fight I didn't plan on losing. Two can play at this game. I kissed him back harder, bit his lip until he groaned, slid a hand into his hair and yanked until his growl rumbled through my chest. He pressed his hips down; I arched like I was giving in, then hooked my knee high against his ribs and rolled us. Now I was on top, straddling him. "Better than not bad," I said.

His smirk said I'd just poked the bear. In a blink, I was flat on my back again, wrists caught, his mouth taking mine like he was reclaiming territory. We were still locked in that push-pull rhythm when— "Are you two done?" Killian's voice. Low. Amused. "Or should I give you five more minutes?"

Killian

I should've walked out. Instead, I stood there, watching Jaxon kiss her like he'd earned the right. She kissed him back — fierce, unapologetic. It hit me low in the gut, sharp and hungry. When Jaxon finally let her go, she spotted me. Smirked like she knew exactly what I was thinking.

"Your turn?" she teased. I stepped onto the mat. "Not unless you're ready to lose." We circled. She feinted; I blocked. She kicked; I caught it and came at her harder. Blow for blow, the heat between us climbed until I caught her arm mid-strike and pulled her flush against me. "Good girl," I murmured. Her breath stuttered. She covered it with an elbow to my ribs — I caught that too, twisted her down, and pinned her.

"You owe me," I said. "For what?" "The wager." Her eyes flickered. "What was the bet again?" "A kiss." The second she tilted her chin, I knew I'd won. Her mouth was soft but unyielding, fighting me for control even as my grip held her in place. The taste of her. The sound of her breath. The subtle shift of her hips beneath mine — it was all a problem. I stood, forcing space. Because next time? I wasn't sure I'd stop.

Riley

The second my feet hit the locker room tile, the adrenaline started to fade, and the ache from sparring both Jaxon and Killian settled in like a smug houseguest. My muscles were singing. My ribs—less so. I grabbed my towel, but before I could even wipe my face, Jaxon was there, blocking the bench like it belonged to him. "Sit." "Excuse me?" "You heard me, sweetheart. Sit."

He didn't wait for compliance—just pressed a cold bottle of water into my hand and dropped a protein bar beside me like I was some UFC champion he was managing. Before I could make a sarcastic comment, Killian appeared, crouching at my feet with the first-aid kit. "You're not seriously—" He was. Calloused hands caught my ankle, checking for swelling I didn't even feel. "You've been limping since that sweep," he muttered, voice low, like this wasn't an argument but a diagnosis. "I have not—"

He looked up, dark eyes cutting through my protest. "Good girls don't lie." Yeah, okay, *that* was a whole problem. And because the universe enjoys messing with me, Cole sauntered in with a smug grin and a takeaway bag.

"Lunch. For our champ." "You guys know I didn't win, right?" I said. Cole didn't answer. Just unpacked enough food for a small army, setting it up on the bench beside me like some kind of offering to the goddess of chaos. Jaxon smirked, leaning against the wall. "Don't fight it, Riley. You're getting the full princess treatment." "I am not a princess." Killian's hands were still on my ankle. "No," he said, voice smooth as sin, "but you're ours to take care of." The air shifted—thicker now, pulling tight around the four of us. They thought they had me cornered. Cute.

I let my eyes drop—slowly—down Killian's chest, lingering just long enough for his thumb to still against my skin, then glanced at Cole's hand flexing at his side like he was trying not to reach for me. "You boys look like you're about to do something stupid," I said, deliberately letting my voice drop half a tone, "and the thing is... I might let you."

Cole's eyes went dark, his smirk sharpening into something predatory. Jaxon's shoulders tensed like he was two seconds from joining in. Killian's grip on my ankle tightened. Gotcha. I shifted my weight, brushing my back against Cole's chest for just a heartbeat before pivoting to face him. "Although," I added lightly, "you'd have to try harder than a protein bar and a foot rub."

Killian's breath hitched. Jaxon's jaw flexed. Cole's gaze dragged over my face like he was recalculating his entire battle plan. Good. Let them be off-balance for once. "Thanks for lunch, boys," I said, stepping sideways through the narrowest gap in their little formation. "But if this is your A-game, I'm not impressed." None of them moved to stop me. They just stood there—three lethal, dangerous men—watching me walk out like I'd stolen something important. Which, to be fair... I had.

51

The Monk Breaks

Riley

FMlYLM by Hozier

Oh, fuck. This wasn't supposed to go like this.

I'd been screwing with him for weeks. Teasing, pushing, baiting. Changing his alarms to fake moans, stealing his towel, crowding him in the hall with a smirk like I wanted to see him sweat. And yeah — I wanted to piss him off. I wanted him to snap. But not like this.

What I really wanted? For him to put his mouth back on me.

Because once — just once — he had. And it had been the best head of my fucking life. Better than Cole's cocky tongue, better than Jaxon's filthy games. Lucas had ruined me with nothing but his mouth, slow and reverent and relentless, and then? Nothing. Weeks of monk-silence. Like he'd decided I didn't exist.

So I pushed. Harder. Hoping maybe if I lit the fuse enough times, the bomb would finally go off. Hoping maybe he'd give in and put me out of my misery. But this? This was not head. This was war. The belt bit into my wrists where he'd strapped me to the headboard. My shirt was in shreds. His face wasn't calm anymore. It was wolf — dark, hungry, and finally unleashed.

My throat went dry. Oh, fuck. I poked the bear.

The knife skimmed down my collarbone, slow and deliberate. Cold steel traced between my breasts, over my stomach, lower, lower, until I flinched. He didn't cut. Not yet. Just teased. Threatened. Reminded me how helpless I was.

"Lucas—" My voice cracked.

"You think I'm quiet because I'm safe?" His breath scorched my ear. His voice shook — not with nerves, but with restraint. "You've been taunting me, Riley. You wanted me to break? You wanted the wolf?"

My heart slammed. My stomach dropped. Yes. But not like this.

And then the cold press of steel between my thighs. The hilt. Blunt, unyielding. He ground it against my clit, slow, merciless.

"Already wet," he rasped. "Grinding like a little slut for steel."

I gasped, a sound I couldn't choke down, shame tangled with need. I'd wanted his mouth again. Instead, he shoved the hilt inside me, hard and merciless, and my scream split the dark.

Each thrust dragged fire through me. My back arched, my wrists yanked raw against the belt, and still my body betrayed me, clenching around the handle like it had been waiting for it.

"Oh fuck—fuck—" The words tore out of me, broken.

And Lucas just watched. Calm. Cataloguing. Calculating every sob, every thrash, like he'd been studying for this exact exam and I was giving all the right answers.

He pulled it out slick and shining, rubbed it slow over my clit until I writhed, then shoved it back in, deeper, harder, until I shattered again, sobbing and ruined.

I'd poked the bear, alright. And now the bear wasn't just biting back — he was feeding.

Lucas

Christ. She was perfect like this. Bound. Writhing. Every thrust of the hilt dragged sobs from her throat, every clench of her cunt squeezing around the steel like it had been made for her. And all I could do was watch. Cataloguing. Memorising. Like I had in the shadows a hundred times — except now, I wasn't watching a recording. Now it was mine.

Her eyes squeezed shut, head thrown back, the belt creaking under the strain of her thrashing. Sweat slicked her chest. Every cry tore through me until I was shaking with the need to replace the knife with myself. But not yet. Not until she was branded.

I pulled the hilt free, dripping, and set the flat edge to her thigh. She gasped, high and panicked, as I pressed. Not hard enough to cut deep — but enough. Slow. Deliberate. A single letter carved into her flesh.

L.

Her scream rattled the walls.

"You'll wear me," I whispered, voice shredded as I licked the blood off the steel. "Every day. Every breath. Mine."

Riley

The pain seared hot, sharp, claiming. My thigh burned, blood running slick, and rage swallowed me whole.

"You bastard," I spat, chest heaving, voice cracking. "You carved yourself into me."

But then — he did something worse. He lifted the knife again. And turned it. On himself.

My breath snagged. "Lucas—don't you fucking—"

His eyes were wolf-dark, unwavering, as he dragged the blade across his chest. Shallow, controlled, but deep enough. Blood welled instantly. A letter. My letter.

R. Carved above his heart. My whole body shook, fury tangled with something I refused to name.

He dropped the knife, blood running down his ribs, and bent low, lips brushing my ear. “Now you’re in me too,” he rasped. “No escape, Riley. You’ll carry me, and I’ll carry you.”

And then his mouth crushed mine, blood and salt and heat and desperation.

Lucas

She was wrecked. Bound. Marked with me. And I was wrecked too, bleeding with her initial carved into my chest, shaking with everything I’d held back for too long. I untied the belt, pulling her wrists free — but before she could move, I dragged her down, pressed her knees wide, and forced her to straddle my face.

Her gasp tore straight into my lungs. “Lucas—”

“Ride me,” I ordered, gripping her thighs hard enough to bruise. “I’ve studied you. Every twitch. Every whimper. Now I want it real. All of it. On my tongue.”

She hesitated, trembling. Afraid. So I licked once. Long, slow, from slick folds to throbbing clit. Her whole body convulsed. And then she tried to pull away. Not happening.

I yanked her back down, locked her hips tight against my mouth, tongue pressing relentless circles over her clit. Her thighs quivered, her sob cracked open, and still I wouldn't let her go.

"Lucas—oh my god—I'm gonna—"

I shook my head against her, lips curling into a smirk even as I devoured her. Every time she edged close, I slowed, teased, backed off just enough to keep her writhing. Edging her. Tormenting her. Making her grind herself raw against my mouth until she sobbed, half-pleading, half-cursing me.

Her fingers clawed at my hair, her hips bucking, and still I wouldn't stop. Not until she was undone. Not until she broke for me.

Riley

I thought the knife was bad. I thought the branding was worse. I was wrong.

Because this — riding his face, his mouth relentless and merciless, his hands bruising my thighs every time I tried to pull away — this was torture. Sweet, brutal, unbearable torture.

He wouldn't let me come. Every time I got close, he slowed. Smirked against me. Drew it out until I was thrashing, begging, shame spilling out in desperate sobs.

"Please—oh god, Lucas, please—"

He just groaned against my clit, the vibration sending me spiraling.

I couldn't hold it anymore. Couldn't breathe, couldn't think. My body seized, thighs clamping around his head, and I shattered. Hard. Violent. Screaming his name like a prayer.

And still he held me there, lapping me through it, drinking every last tremor until I collapsed, quivering and boneless, sprawled across his chest with my blood and his smeared between us.

Lucas

Christ.

She was perfect like this. Bound. Writhing. Every thrust of the hilt dragged sobs from her throat, every clench of her cunt squeezing around the steel like it had been made for her. And all I could do was watch. Cataloguing. Memorising. Like I had in the shadows a hundred times — except now, I wasn't watching a recording. Now it was mine.

Her eyes squeezed shut, head thrown back, the belt creaking under the strain of her thrashing. Sweat slicked her chest. Every cry tore through me until I was shaking with the need to replace the knife with myself. But not yet. Not until she was branded.

I pulled the hilt free, dripping, and set the flat edge to her thigh. She gasped, high and panicked, as I pressed. Not hard enough to cut deep — but enough. Slow. Deliberate. A single letter carved into her flesh.

L.

Her scream rattled the walls.

"You'll wear me," I whispered, voice shredded as I licked the blood off the steel. "Every day. Every breath. Mine."

Riley

The pain seared hot, sharp, claiming. My thigh burned, blood running slick, and rage swallowed me whole.

"You bastard," I spat, chest heaving, voice cracking. "You carved yourself into me."

But then — he did something worse.

He lifted the knife again. And turned it. On himself.

My breath snagged. "Lucas—don't you fucking—"

His eyes were wolf-dark, unwavering, as he dragged the blade across his chest. Shallow, controlled, but deep enough. Blood welled instantly. A letter. My letter.

R. Carved above his heart.

My whole body shook, fury tangled with something I refused to name.

He dropped the knife, blood running down his ribs, and bent low, lips brushing my ear. “Now you’re in me too,” he rasped. “No escape, Riley. You’ll carry me, and I’ll carry you.”

And then his mouth crushed mine, blood and salt and heat and desperation.

Lucas

She was wrecked. Bound. Marked with me. And I was wrecked too, bleeding with her initial carved into my chest, shaking with everything I’d held back for too long. I untied the belt, pulling her wrists free — but before she could move, I dragged her down, pressed her knees wide, and forced her to straddle my face.

Her gasp tore straight into my lungs. “Lucas—”

“Ride me,” I ordered, gripping her thighs hard enough to bruise. “I’ve studied you. Every twitch. Every whimper. Now I want it real. All of it. On my tongue.”

She hesitated, trembling. Afraid.

So I licked once. Long, slow, from slick folds to throbbing clit. Her whole body convulsed.

And then she tried to pull away.

Not happening.

I yanked her back down, locked her hips tight against my mouth, tongue pressing relentless circles over her clit. Her thighs quivered, her sob cracked open, and still I wouldn't let her go.

"Lucas—oh my god—I'm gonna—"

I shook my head against her, lips curling into a smirk even as I devoured her. Every time she edged close, I slowed, teased, backed off just enough to keep her writhing. Edging her. Tormenting her. Making her grind herself raw against my mouth until she sobbed, half-pleading, half-cursing me.

Her fingers clawed at my hair, her hips bucking, and still I wouldn't stop. Not until she was undone. Not until she broke for me.

Riley

I thought the knife was bad. I thought the branding was worse. I was wrong.

Because this — riding his face, his mouth relentless and merciless, his hands bruising my thighs every time I tried to pull away — this was torture. Sweet, brutal, unbearable torture.

He wouldn't let me come. Every time I got close, he slowed. Smirked against me. Drew it out until I was thrashing, begging, shame spilling out in desperate sobs.

"Please—oh god, Lucas, please—"

He just groaned against my clit, the vibration sending me spiraling.

I couldn't hold it anymore. Couldn't breathe, couldn't think. My body seized, thighs clamping around his head, and I shattered. Hard. Violent. Screaming his name like a prayer.

And still he held me there, lapping me through it, drinking every last tremor until I collapsed, quivering and boneless, sprawled across his chest with my blood and his smeared between us.

Lucas

Her thighs shook around my head, slick flooding my tongue, her screams muffled against the ceiling. She broke on me, over and over, until she was nothing but sobs and spasms. I didn't stop. Couldn't. Weeks of restraint snapped like brittle bone, and all I could think was mine.

When she collapsed forward, trembling, I slowed — finally showing mercy. I kissed her thighs reverently, her stomach, the scarlet brand I'd carved into her. My mark. My name.

But I wasn't finished.

I pulled her down, spread her across the sheets, and tied her wrists again. This time looser, just enough to remind her she was mine, even as I shifted over her and pressed my cock against her folds.

Her eyes widened, raw and wrecked. "Lucas—"

"Not safe," I whispered, forehead pressed to hers. "Never safe. But always yours."

And then I slid in.

Riley

The stretch was brutal. Holy. My body split around him, raw, full in a way no hilt, no tongue, no finger could ever reach. Lucas. Inside me. Finally.

I sobbed his name, the sound ripping out without thought. My wrists pulled at the belt, my legs shook, and he held me steady, every inch of him pressing deeper, deeper, until I couldn't tell where he ended and I began.

He kissed me as he fucked me. Not cruel, not mocking — worship. His tongue tangled with mine, his groan vibrating through my chest as if every thrust was a vow.

"You were made for me," he rasped against my lips.

And God help me, I believed him.

Lucas

I flipped her, spread her knees wide, and watched my cock disappear inside her, slick and obscene. My blood smeared across her skin, her blood across mine, the mix proof of what we'd done, who we were.

I fucked her slow. Deliberate. Reverent. Every thrust dragging me deeper until she was crying, begging, clenching so tight it nearly undid me.

I shifted her up, onto my lap, bound wrists locked behind her, riding me with tears streaking her cheeks. Her head fell back, her chest arched, and I kissed the curve of her throat, the place I'd one day mark permanent.

"Look at you," I groaned, grinding her down. "Taking me. Taking all of me. My girl. My storm. My salvation."

Her sob cracked open into a scream, her body convulsing around me, orgasm tearing through her like lightning. But I wasn't done.

Riley

He carried me — literally carried me — across the room and slammed me against the wall. My legs wrapped tight around his waist, his cock driving into me so hard the plaster cracked behind us.

I screamed into his shoulder, bit down, left my own mark on him as he fucked me mercilessly. Each thrust was brutal, claiming, and I couldn't stop shaking. Couldn't stop coming. Every time I thought I was empty, he pulled another orgasm from me like he was harvesting them on purpose.

Then he dropped me onto the mattress again, rolled me onto my stomach, and pushed in from behind. His weight crushed me down, his pace relentless, one bloody hand pressing between my shoulder blades to keep me caged while the other worked my clit.

"Mine," he growled into my hair, snapping his hips harder. "Every scream, every tear, every mark — mine."

I shattered again. Wrecked. Gone.

Lucas

Her body was fire. Her screams were scripture. And I was worshiping like a man on his knees before a goddess.

I dragged her back into my lap, her ass grinding against me as I thrust up into her. Her bound wrists clawed at nothing, her chest bouncing, her eyes rolling back as I bit into her shoulder.

"You think Cole owns you? That Jaxon broke you? No. I did." My voice tore raw as I slammed deeper. "You'll never forget this. You'll never forget me. You're mine, Riley. My girl. My storm. My everything."

Her sob turned into a ragged laugh, delirious, broken, perfect. She came again, clamping around me so hard I lost it.

I growled her name like a prayer as I spilled inside her, grinding deep, grinding until she was shaking and screaming and milking me dry.

And when it was over, when I finally collapsed onto her, chest to chest, blood to blood, all I could do was whisper the truth I'd never meant to say out loud.

"I love you."

She lay wrecked beneath me — trembling, raw, but still breathing, still fighting. Her wrists were rubbed raw from the belt, her thigh was smeared with blood where my letter branded her, and yet she looked...divine.

I cleaned her carefully, reverently, cloth warmed between my hands before I touched her. I wiped the slick from her thighs, the blood from her skin, pressed soft kisses into every welt and bruise. She flinched, but she didn't push me away. Her fingers twitched weakly against the sheets, like she didn't know whether to claw me or hold me.

I kissed her temple, slow and steady, and whispered against her damp hair, "You're mine. Always."

Her breathing evened out under my touch. Her trembling softened. For the first time in weeks, I thought maybe she'd let herself rest. Maybe she'd let me carry the weight. And then she opened her mouth.

Riley

Holy. Fucking. Shit.

I didn't just have sex. I had...whatever the hell that was. That wasn't sex, that was a biblical plague with orgasms.

I stared at the ceiling, still quivering, Lucas tenderly dabbing at my skin like some Florence Nightingale with blood running down his chest, and my brain just—snapped.

"Holy fuck," I croaked. "I just fucked you." I paused. "Correction: you fucked me. With a knife. With. A. Knife."

Lucas stilled, cloth hovering over my thigh. "...Riley."

"No, no, don't you 'Riley' me," I rambled, delirious and feral. "I got branded. Like a cow. You carved your name into me. I am now officially USDA-certified Grade A Slut."

He groaned, pinched the bridge of his nose, like he was already regretting life choices. Too bad. I was spiraling.

"I have," I announced, holding up one trembling finger like a professor delivering a lecture, "officially earned my Slutty Girl Scout Badges. Do you know how many I've racked up tonight? Face-sitting merit badge. Knife-fucking patch. Wall-banging certificate of achievement. Blood-bond honor sash. And oh! Oh, the advanced-level 'I let a virgin carve his initial into my thigh and somehow came so hard I nearly blacked out' award. That one's rare. Limited edition."

Lucas buried his face in my shoulder, muttering something that sounded a lot like prayer.

But I wasn't done. Oh no. The gremlin energy had arrived.

"I swear to God, they're gonna need a whole new sash for me. I've basically completed the entire Kama Sutra in one night. Gold medal slutty Olympics. First place. Fuck it, world record. Call Guinness."

"Riley—" he rasped, half-growl, half-plea.

I turned my head, smirked even as I trembled from aftershocks. "Face it, Monk. You didn't just break me. You inducted me. Full Girl Scout honors. Next meeting, I'm bringing cookies."

Lucas groaned louder, muffled against my neck, and I laughed — broken, exhausted, delirious.

Because holy fuck. I just fucked Lucas. With a knife. And got a Girl Scout badge for it.

And part of me? Part of me wanted to sew the patch on right now.

52

Don't Leave Me Behind

Killian

Do I Wanna Know? – Arctic Monkeys

It started like a whisper. A soft thud. A moan. Not imagined — hers. Riley. I tried to ignore it. To keep my eyes on the recon feed, to breathe steady, to remind myself I was above this. But then Lucas's voice followed, low and guttural, saying her name like it was both a prayer and a curse.

And that was it. The thread of control I'd been holding snapped. The chair scraped back hard. The laptop blurred from my vision. My fists clenched, shaking, and still I couldn't stop listening. Couldn't stop hearing her break apart for someone else.

I locked the door. My belt hit the floor. My hand wrapped rough around my cock. Punishment. Fury. Worship. Her moans spilled through thin walls, tearing me open. Lucas groaned her name again and I stroked harder, angrier, until my muscles screamed. I wanted to be the one inside her. The one pulling those sounds from her throat. The one breaking her open, not him.

The orgasm hit like violence — sharp, bitter, ruined. I bent over the desk, breathless, spilling across my fist. Ash. Empty. Because it wasn't enough. It wasn't her.

I cleaned up fast, movements clipped, mechanical, but my pulse wouldn't steady. My cock was still half-hard, my chest still raw. I'd lied to myself for weeks, pretending patience was strength, that waiting would make it sweeter. But patience wasn't strength. It was starvation. And I was starving.

I left the room. The warehouse smelled like bacon, eggs, coffee — normal. Too fucking normal. Until I saw her. Riley. She was sprawled across the couch like she owned it, legs bare, hair a mess, his shirt sliding off her shoulder. His teeth marks fresh on her throat.

My fists curled. My jaw locked. She tugged the hem lower, but I'd already seen enough. My mind filled in the rest — her writhing, his mouth at her neck, her cries muffled against his chest. The same cries I'd heard through the wall while I fucked my own fist like some desperate voyeur.

Lucas turned at the stove, too calm. "You want eggs?" I didn't answer. My throat was fire and iron. Riley didn't look at me. She stretched further into the cushions, smug, glowing, marked in ways that weren't mine. Maybe she thought she was untouchable like that. Maybe she thought she was safe.

But she wasn't. Not from me. Because this wasn't just about sex. That was too small a word for what I wanted. I didn't want her body. I wanted her soul. To take it apart, to stitch it into mine, to own it until she couldn't draw breath without knowing it belonged to me.

She'd already given it, piece by piece. In every laugh, every scream, every time she looked at me like she hated herself for wanting me. She'd given it, and I wasn't ever letting it go.

Lucas caught my stare. Tried to measure it. Maybe warn me. It didn't matter. Cole had already fallen. Jaxon would follow. Lucas thought he was clever. But I wasn't playing clever. I was playing forever.

Finally, she looked up. Met my eyes. Dared me. And I smiled. Slow. Dangerous. Reverent. The kind of smile that promised ruin and worship in the same breath. She thought she'd survived the storm. She hadn't even seen it yet. Because she was already mine. Not later. Not someday. Now. And if she ever tried to walk? I'd chain her to the bed myself.

53

Enough

Riley

Enough - Morgan Clae

The high didn't last. Not really.

For a few glorious hours, I'd floated in a haze of skin and sweat and cocky grins and fuck me harder.

But then Cole fell asleep—arms wrapped around me, his chest warm against my back—and my brain? My brain woke the hell up.

I lay there staring at the ceiling, limbs aching, skin tingling, guilt gnawing its way into the edges of my soul.

Cole. Lucas. Same day. Same goddamn bed.

I'd joked about mental breakdowns. Hell, I'd laughed. But now it didn't feel so funny. It felt... reckless. Chaotic.

Wrong? No. Not wrong. Just... too much. Too fast. Too exposed. Too real.

I slipped out of the bed quietly, grabbing a hoodie—probably Jaxon's based on the smell—and padded barefoot through the hallway, down the stairs. I didn't know where I was going. I just needed out of that room before my brain chewed through the last of my self-worth.

I found Jaxon in the garage.

He was crouched beside one of the bikes, smudges of grease on his fingers, earbuds in, softly singing along to some godawful early 2000s emo track. Normally I would've mocked him. But I just stood there. Quiet. Small. Bleeding silently from the inside out.

He looked up. Paused. Took one good look at me—and pulled his earbuds out. "You okay?"

It wasn't loaded. Wasn't suspicious. Wasn't judging. Just... a question. I shrugged, crawling onto the workbench beside him.

"Define okay." Jaxon studied me for a beat, then dug into his jacket pocket.

"I was gonna wait," he muttered, "but you look like you need it now."

He handed me a small box. Matte black. Velvet. I blinked. "Did you just propose?"

"Don't be a dick," he said gently. "Open it."

Inside was a thin, delicate chain. Silver. Almost too simple. But hanging from it—dead centre—was a small, hammered pendant.

At first glance, it was nothing. But when I held it up to the light, I saw the engraving. One word. Barely there. Enough. My throat tightened.

"I saw it at that market last week," Jaxon said, scratching his neck. "Thought of you. Figured... I dunno. Might be good to have something to remind you when your brain starts being a little bitch."

I stared at it. The word blurred. And suddenly, I couldn't speak.

He didn't push. Didn't move. Just stayed near. "You don't have to say anything," he said softly. "I know today's been... a lot."

I laughed. Choked. "You heard?"

"Babe, we all heard. The safe house walls are thin, and you scream like you're being exorcised."

I groaned, dropping my face into my hands. "I am going to murder myself."

"Please don't," he said drily. "That would really fuck up the team dynamic."

I let out a breath. "I just—I don't know what I'm doing, Jax."

"I do."

I looked at him.

He shrugged. "You're surviving. In the most Riley Morgan way possible—loud, chaotic, slightly concerning. But you're here."

My fingers tightened around the necklace. "I don't deserve nice things," I whispered.

"Yeah," he said, nudging my knee with his. "That's exactly why you do."

The tears burned hot. But I didn't cry. Not here. Not yet. Instead, I looped the necklace around my throat and fastened the clasp.

"Looks good on you," Jaxon said, smiling softly.

I swallowed. "Thanks."

"You don't have to be okay yet," he added. "But just... try not to forget who you are under all the noise. You're not just what happened today. Or who you slept with. Or what the others think."

I nodded. Just once. Eyes stinging.

Then I leaned over and bumped my head lightly into his shoulder. He bumped me back. And for the first time all day, I didn't feel like I was drowning.

Jaxon

She didn't look back. Of course she didn't. That wasn't her style. Riley Morgan didn't do second glances. She didn't linger. She didn't wait around to see who she'd wrecked.

She just walked away—and damn if it didn't feel like being gutted with something beautiful.

I stood there, breath caught somewhere between a curse and a prayer, watching her fade into the distance like she hadn't just taken a fucking piece of me with her.

Hood up. Hands in pockets. Those combat boots stomping across the driveway like she was storming a battlefield instead of the world outside.

I should've said something. I should've stopped her.

But how do you hold back a wildfire? How do you chain lightning without getting burned?

She was fury and ache and cigarette smoke in my lungs, and I loved her with a desperation I couldn't say out loud—not when I knew she'd laugh, or worse, look at me with pity.

So I said nothing. Just watched. Watched her hips sway in those ripped jeans, watched the messy bun bouncing on top of her head, watched her fist curl tighter when her phone lit up and she didn't answer.

I knew her tells. The way her shoulders tensed when she was trying not to cry. The twitch in her jaw when she was holding something in.

I knew her rhythms, her rituals, the way she looked at the sky like it owed her an apology. And I loved every fucking piece of it.

She haunted me. In my dreams. In my quiet moments. In the songs I couldn't listen to anymore.

I saw her in the grease on my hands, in the hoodie hanging on the hook, in every goddamn creak of the garage when I was alone.

I built her a bench and never said why. I bought her snacks I knew she liked and pretended they were mine.

I watched her fall into the arms of my best friends and smiled like it didn't kill me—because it wasn't about owning her. It was about having her. Seeing her alive. Here. Breathing. Safe. And if that meant worshipping her from the sidelines, then so be it.

But if she ever looked back— If she ever asked— I'd be there. No hesitation. I'd drop to my knees in front of her and mean it. Let her carve her name into my ribs and smile through the pain. Because Riley wasn't just someone I loved. She was the axis my world spun around.

And no matter how far she walked, how far she ran—I'd never stop following. Even if it ruined me. Especially if it ruined me.

Riley

The house creaked softly beneath my feet—too quiet, too still. I moved like a ghost, hoodie sleeves swallowed past my knuckles, bare toes sinking into the carpet.

The hall lights were off. I didn't need them. I knew this place by feel now. By instinct.

And that... that was part of the problem. I wasn't supposed to know this house like that. Wasn't supposed to feel at home here. Wasn't supposed to slip into this life like it was mine to have.

I passed Lucas's room. The door was cracked. I didn't look inside. Couldn't. I'd already borrowed enough from them all. Their patience. Their strength. Their warmth. Their bodies.

Jesus, Riley. I pressed my palm against the wall, grounding myself. Let the cool paint bite into my skin.

How had I gone from locked-down and emotionally divorced to... this?

To almost-a-bingo levels of vulnerability with four different men? Cole. Lucas. Jaxon. And Killian just pacing the perimeter of my sanity like a panther in a cage.

I hadn't meant for any of it. I hadn't meant to stay. And yet—I was still here.

Still waking up in beds that weren't mine. Still drinking coffee I didn't make. Still laughing at stupid inside jokes and letting myself be pulled into board games like I wasn't a time bomb with legs.

Still letting them touch me like I wasn't made of razor blades and history.

Still... feeling.

That was the worst part. The part I couldn't walk off or fuck away. I felt happy. Real, terrifying, close-to-the-bone happy.

The kind that made your stomach twist because you knew, deep down, it couldn't last. That something—someone—was going to come along and rip it from your hands.

Because I didn't get this. I didn't get good things. I got fire. And fallout. And blood under my nails. Not Connect Four and quiet understanding and silver chains with kind words carved into them.

But here I was. Heart still aching from the way Jaxon looked at me like I was worth saving. Like I hadn't already set myself on fire a hundred times just to keep other people warm.

I swallowed hard, backing into the wall and sliding down until I hit the floor. My hands shook. Not from fear. From softness.

Because this was what scared me more than any mission. More than bullets or threats or past lives crashing down around me.

This was real. They were real. And for the first time in what felt like years—maybe ever—I wasn't just surviving.

I was living. God help me, I was starting to want it. And that?

That was the scariest part of all.

This was real. They were real. And for the first time in what felt like years—maybe ever—I wasn't just surviving. I was living. God help me, I was starting to want it. And that? That was the scariest part of all.

54

The Art of Not Begging

Riley

Gasoline – Audioslave

For the first time in weeks, my ribs didn't feel like they were carrying a bomb. The others had dragged me out — not a mission, not a fight, not a fucking disaster waiting to happen. Just... out. Burgers. Arcade games. Jaxon cheating at skee-ball, Cole trash-talking ten-year-olds, Lucas pretending not to laugh when I beat his high score.

For a couple of hours, I wasn't Riley Morgan, chaos incarnate. I was just a woman eating fries, laughing too loud, letting herself be stupid.

And God, I'd needed that.

By the time we got back, my stomach hurt from laughing and my fingers still smelled faintly of greasy salt. I could almost forget the weight of scars, the clock ticking down on my three months, the way this house wanted to pull me apart and keep the pieces.

Almost.

Because Killian was in the gym, and Killian didn't do "fun."

I found him shirtless, hammering the heavy bag like it had slept with his ex. Tattoos shifted with every strike, black ink over muscle that looked forged out of violence. His hair stuck damp to his forehead, his eyes locked on the target like nothing else existed.

"You always beat the shit out of something defenseless, or is that just your idea of a hobby?" I leaned on the doorframe, a grin tugging at my mouth.

He didn't stop. "Better the bag than one of you."

"Touching," I said, stepping in. "Real motivational-poster energy."

Finally, he glanced over. The tiniest curl touched his mouth. That almost-smile that made me want to slap it off and kiss it at the same time.

"You're in a good mood," he said.

"Yeah, well." I shrugged. "Some of us enjoy being human occasionally."

He snorted, catching the bag. "Human. That what you call skee-ball?"

I blinked. "Wait. You were watching?"

"Cameras," he said simply.

Creep.

"Guess you missed Cole crying after losing to a seven-year-old."

"I saw." His tone was dry, but his eyes flickered — like maybe he envied what I'd had tonight. That easy fun. That laughter. The thing he never let himself touch.

"Well," I said, cocking my hip, "some of us don't need to punish leather to feel alive."

"Some of us don't need babysitting to remember how."

My smirk sharpened. "That jealousy I hear?"

He stepped toward me, slow, deliberate.

"Jealous? No. I don't need games. Or laughter. Or fries." His voice dropped, gravel-dark. "I need control."

The air thickened. He was close enough now that I had to tilt my head back.

"Control," I repeated. "Cute word. Sounds like code for 'I'm lonely.'"

His hand shot out, catching my belt loop. Tugged me closer without quite pulling.

"You know what it means, Riley?" His voice dropped lower, rougher. "It means not losing control when it comes to you."

I swallowed. Hard. God help me, part of me wanted it. But fuck him.

"Go fuck yourself," I hissed, shoving at his chest.

He didn't move. Just caged me harder against the wall, arm braced above my head, voice low enough to drag over my skin like a blade.

"One day, Riley. You'll break. You'll scream my name. And when you do, you'll finally know what it feels like to stop fighting."

My pulse stuttered, treacherous. My thighs tightened. But my mouth? My mouth still worked. "And maybe," I spat, eyes blazing into his, "when that day comes, I'll still say no."

For a moment, it was pure fire between us. No oxygen. Just burn.

Then he stepped back like he'd been scorched, chest rising hard. Without another word, he turned, stalked back to the bag, fists slamming into leather like it was safer than me.

I stayed against the wall, shaking so hard I couldn't tell where the anger ended and the desire began.

Fuck him.

He thought he could break me down like one of his punching bags? Grind me into submission until I forgot who I was?

No chance.

If Killian wanted a war, I'd give him one bloody enough to remember. And before this was over, he'd be the one losing control.

Killian

The bag rattled on its chain, swinging wild from the force of my last hit. My knuckles ached. Good. Pain kept me sharp.

But it didn't silence the image in my head: Riley's mouth curved around that vicious little smirk, the spark in her eyes when she told me no like it was a weapon.

I hit the bag again, hard enough that the leather groaned.

"You're gonna knock the stuffing clean out of that thing." Lucas's voice. Dry. Calm. Way too entertained.

I didn't turn. Just reset my stance, shoulders tight. "Don't you have wires to play with?"

"Already done." His footsteps padded across the mat until he was leaning against the far wall, arms crossed, watching me like I was an experiment he'd already predicted the outcome of. "Figured I'd check in on you. You're... louder than usual."

I drove another punch into the bag. "I'm fine."

Lucas snorted. Actually snorted. "You're spiraling."

That pulled my head around fast, glare sharp. "The fuck I am."

He didn't blink. Just lifted one brow.

"Killian, you've got that look. Same one Cole gets when Riley storms out on him. Same one Jaxon gets when she actually manages to shut him up." His smirk cut in, small and dangerous. "Only difference is..."

He let the silence stretch. "...you're the last man standing."

My jaw locked. "What's that supposed to mean?"

"It means," he said, pushing off the wall and sauntering closer, "Cole's had her. Jaxon's had her. I've had her." His eyes gleamed. "And you haven't."

The words hit harder than any punch I'd thrown. I felt them in my gut, hot and ugly.

Lucas leaned in just enough for the grin to sting.

"Starting to get under your skin, isn't it? Knowing you're the only one left."

I forced myself not to react, fists clenching instead. "She'll come to me."

"Mm," he hummed, amused. "Or maybe you'll break first."

The bag swung between us, creaking. Lucas didn't press further. He didn't need to. The bastard had already seen it. Seen me.

And he wasn't wrong.

55

Kneel. Bite. Burn.

Riley

One time - Chinchilla

Killian Moretti's office was exactly what you'd expect from a man who looked like sin in a suit and acted like God's personal executioner — neat. Immaculate. Terrifyingly precise.

I'd come here hunting for leverage. Dirt. Blackmail. Anything I could use next time he thought he could corner me with that voice of his, low and commanding, like gravity had decided to wear a man's skin.

What did I want to find? Hell, I'd have settled for a porn stash tucked in the bottom drawer. Some bad poetry about sunsets and unrequited love. A shoebox of unpaid parking fines. Even one overdue library book would've done the job. Something human. Something messy.

But no. The bastard was clean. No receipts out of place. No skeletons in the drawers. Not even a paperclip bent out of shape. Every document lined up like soldiers. Every file locked down. The man was a ghost with a perfect audit trail.

I cursed under my breath, jimmying open another drawer with a bobby pin. Nothing but security briefings, meticulous notes in that brutal handwriting of his, and folders stamped with clearance levels that made me itch to pry deeper.

And that's when I heard it. The click of the door handle. Shit.

Voices drifted in — Killian's low rumble, Jaxon's amused drawl, and another man I didn't recognise. Panic shot through me like lightning. I shoved the drawer shut and dove under the desk, wedging myself into the shadows like a burglar caught mid-job.

And then Killian sat down.

Boots planted. Chair groaned. His thighs spread wide in front of me, fabric stretched tight over the kind of tension that made my pulse jump against my will.

Oh, fuck.

I should've panicked. Should've gone still, prayed they left fast. But something hot and reckless sparked in me instead. If Killian thought he was untouchable, if he thought that kiss meant he'd broken me — I'd prove him wrong. Right here. Right under his own goddamn desk.

And when my hand ghosted up the inside of his thigh, felt that rigid control of his twitch under my touch, I almost laughed.

And then Killian sat down. Boots planted. Chair groaned. His thighs spread wide in front of me, fabric stretched tight over the kind of bulge that made my mouth water against my will.

Oh, fuck.

I should've panicked. Should've gone still, prayed they left fast. But something hot and cruel sparked in me instead. If Killian thought he was untouchable, if he thought that kiss meant he'd broken me — I'd prove him wrong. Right here. Right under his own goddamn desk.

And when my hand ghosted up the inside of his thigh, felt that rigid control of his twitch under my touch, I almost laughed.

Maybe I hadn't found dirt in his files. But I'd just found it in him. This wasn't just fun anymore. This was surgical.

I ran my nails slowly up his thigh and smirked. The reaction was immediate. One sharp inhale, the muscle under my fingertips tightening — and then the unmistakable tent in his slacks.

Well.

That answered a few questions.

"Hmm," I murmured, dragging my hand higher with deliberate slowness. "What if it isn't me you're hiding under here, big guy?"

His jaw tightened above me. Dangerous. Controlled. Barely.

"Maybe," I mused softly, fingers hooking his belt buckle, "the boys' little bromance runs a bit deeper than I thought."

The metal clicked open.

Killian's hand landed flat on the desk hard enough to rattle the papers, but he still didn't stop me.

Interesting.

I slowly undid the fly of his slacks, then the final button, feeling the tension roll through him like a live wire stretched too tight.

I eased the fabric open slowly and then immediately had to stop myself from making a noise loud enough to expose us both.

Because wow. For one solid second my brain just short-circuited. Completely offline. Smoke coming out the ears. Emergency shutdown.

"Oh, you have got to be kidding me," I whispered under my breath.

Above me, Killian went unnaturally still. Good. Let him suffer.

I stared downward in genuine offence. "No. Absolutely not. That is such bullshit."

The client kept droning on about projections and shipping routes while I sat under the desk having a full emotional breakdown over the fact that Killian Moretti apparently looked unfairly good everywhere.

"This feels narcissistic somehow," I muttered quietly to myself. "Like you woke up one day and said, 'Actually, I think I'll win every argument for the rest of my life.'"

His thigh flexed sharply beside my shoulder.

Oh my God, he could hear every word. I nearly grinned. "Men are supposed to be humbled by nature," I whispered bitterly. "That's the social contract. Weird elbows. Strange proportions. Something. But nooo. Of course Mr Tall-Dark-and-Traumatised had to be handcrafted by horny witches."

Killian cleared his throat above me. Hard. The client paused. "Everything alright?"

"Perfect," Killian said smoothly.

Liar. I bit down on my lip to stop myself laughing and let my fingertips brush the shaft lightly upward, just enough to feel him tense beneath my hand.

The reaction was immediate. His breathing changed. Tiny shift. Barely noticeable unless you were directly underneath him conducting psychological warfare.

"Oh, he's sensitive too," I whispered in delight. "This is devastating information."

Killian's hand tightened against the chair armrest hard enough that the leather creaked softly.

I tilted my head, studying him like a scientist discovering a dangerous new species.

"Look at you up there pretending to be in control," I murmured under my breath. "Meanwhile one woman under your desk and suddenly your whole nervous system's buffering."

God, this was fun. Because Killian Moretti always acted like he was the storm. The untouchable one. The man nobody could shake.

And all I could think, sitting beneath his desk with his composure slowly cracking above me, was: Yeah, sweetheart. You're absolutely going to be the one begging.

Jaxon

At first, I genuinely thought Killian was about to murder this client. The guy had been talking for twenty straight minutes about freight routes and numbers and whatever the hell else rich businessmen pretend matters while Killian sat behind the desk looking like a man one inconvenience away from burying a body.

Too stiff. Too quiet. Too controlled.

His jaw kept flexing. His shoulders were locked so tight they looked carved from concrete. One hand gripped the chair arm hard enough the leather creaked every few seconds like it was filing for workers compensation.

And then I noticed the breathing. Oh no.

Sharp inhale. Pause. Controlled exhale. Not angry breathing. Familiar breathing.

My eyes narrowed slowly. Because I knew that face. I had unfortunately seen that face before.

That was Killian's I am trying not to completely lose my shit right now face. Only there was one deeply concerning difference. He looked turned on.

Not obviously. Killian would rather die than make it obvious. But there was heat sitting under all that control like a bomb with expensive tailoring wrapped around it.

Then his thigh jerked sharply beneath the desk.

And suddenly every single puzzle piece slammed together in my brain so fast I nearly blacked out.

Oh. Oh, fuck. Riley.

That tiny little psychopath was under the desk. I looked at Killian instantly. Worst mistake of my life. Because the second our eyes met, Killian knew that I knew.

And dear God.

The look on his face nearly killed me. Pure murder. Pure humiliation. Pure fury.

And underneath all of it?

Absolute sexual devastation.

I physically had to bite my fist to stop myself laughing out loud.

Because there he sat—Killian Moretti, terrifying criminal mastermind, human embodiment of "touch her and die"—being edged under his own desk during a business meeting while trying to maintain eye contact like a functioning member of society.

And Riley? Oh, she knew I'd figured it out. I couldn't see her, but I felt the exact moment she realised.

Because Killian's whole body suddenly went rigid. Like dangerously rigid.

The kind of rigid where a man either achieves enlightenment or commits tax fraud.

The client frowned mid-sentence. "Mr Moretti?"

Killian didn't blink. Didn't move. "...continue." His voice cracked.

Cracked. I almost passed away on the spot.

Killian Moretti was getting psychologically tortured beneath a mahogany desk while a man named Greg explained shipping manifests.

And now we were making eye contact through it.

The worst part?

Killian couldn't even react properly because reacting meant admitting what was happening.

So instead he just sat there glaring at me with the concentrated fury of a man trying not to come apart in front of quarterly projections.

I watched a bead of sweat slide slowly down his temple and nearly folded in half.

Holy shit. Holy actual shit.

Riley Morgan was under there edging the most emotionally constipated man alive into cardiac arrest for fun.

And judging by the murderous twitch in Killian's jaw every time our eyes met?

She was absolutely winning.

Riley

I was crouched under Killian's desk, his cock heavy in my hand, flushed and already slick, and he was across from a client trying to look like the cool, unflappable bastard he always pretended to be.

The guy was droning on about contracts, timelines, whatever. I wasn't listening. My whole focus was on Killian's body — the way his thighs trembled, the way his jaw ticked, the way his voice kept dipping lower to cover the cracks.

I stroked him once, slow and deliberate. He didn't flinch outwardly. But his voice wavered — just a fraction — as he said, "We can... meet those numbers."

Oh, I was going to ruin him. I flattened my tongue against the underside, dragged it up his shaft in one unhurried lick. He shifted in his chair, covering it with a casual lean back. To the client, he looked relaxed. To me, he was a live wire.

I wrapped my lips around the head. Just pressure. Not a stroke. Not enough. His hand twitched on the armrest. He cleared his throat and said, "Continue."

God, I nearly laughed. Continue. Like he wasn't throbbing in my mouth, one second from losing his shit.

I pulled back. Stopped touching him completely. His cock twitched in the air, leaking, begging.

He gritted his teeth so hard I heard it. The client shuffled papers, oblivious, while Killian was fighting for his life not to thrust into nothing.

I leaned in close enough for my breath to ghost over him. Didn't touch. Just waited. His thighs tensed, his knee bounced, his knuckles drummed once on the desk before he caught himself.

And then I did it again — one slow stroke, one deep suck, and then nothing. Over and over. Edging him like I was the devil whispering in his ear.

By the time I took him deep, his voice actually broke.

A raw edge slipped through his words, mid-sentence: "Yes, the—ah—terms are... acceptable."

The client blinked, confused, but Killian covered it with a cough. I nearly came from laughter alone.

I eased off, spit dripping down his shaft, my hand spreading it slow, slick, obscene. His cock was steel-hard, his thighs trembling now.

His composure? Shattered glass.

The client leaned forward, rambling about delivery schedules, not noticing that the man he was pitching to was gripping his pen so hard it snapped.

Killian shot me a look down the edge of the desk — dark, dangerous, promising murder.

It only made me wetter. I smirked around his cock, deliberately gagged myself on him just enough to make his hips jerk. His breath hissed between his teeth.

The client glanced up at the sound. Killian just smiled coldly and said, "Ignore that. New flooring upstairs."

The bastard was still trying to win. Still trying to hold power. Which was exactly why I wasn't going to let him come. Not yet.

Thirty minutes. That's how long I made him suffer. Half an hour of me kneeling under Killian Moretti's desk while he tried to keep his legendary composure intact in front of some stiff-collared client droning on about logistics.

Thirty minutes of edging him, tormenting him, controlling every twitch of his cock while his voice stayed clipped and dangerous up top — but down here? His body betrayed him.

His thighs trembled. His hips jerked every time my breath ghosted over the flushed head of his cock.

His knuckles dug into the armrest so deep I half expected the leather to tear.

And I? I was enjoying the show.

I dragged my tongue over him slow, deliberate. Took him halfway into my mouth, sucked hard — then pulled off with a wet pop, leaving him twitching, dripping.

I smeared it across my lips, smirked at the angry pulse in his shaft, and sat back on my heels.

Denying him. Again.

He cleared his throat upstairs. "As... projected," he rasped, voice strained.

I bit back a laugh. Poor man was hanging by dental floss.

The worst part for him? I wasn't just torturing him. I was torturing myself.

One hand stroked him lazy, cruel. The other slipped into my shorts. Just a brush at first, slick fingers circling my clit while I sucked his cock-head, shallow, shallow, shallow.

He couldn't see it. But he felt it — every muffled whimper, every vibration of my moan around him when I pushed two fingers inside my-self.

His leg jerked. His breath caught mid-sentence. God, he hated it. But, he also loved it.

I edged him the way I edged myself. Worked us both up until we were shivering, soaked, desperate — then stopped. Made him watch me shudder through another orgasm while I denied him any release at all.

His cock swelled harder, darker, leaking down my wrist, and still I refused to finish him.

By the forty five-minute mark, his chest was heaving.

Sweat trickled down his temple. His tone had gone lethal-calm, each word bitten off like he could chew through steel. By the fifty-minute mark? He was wrecked.

I had him trembling on the edge, my lips slick with spit, his cock wet and angry against my tongue.

My own thighs shook from holding myself back, my clit throbbing under my fingers, but I wouldn't let go again. Not yet. Not until I broke him.

He slammed his palm against the desk, voice cutting through the room like a gunshot. "Meeting's over."

The client flinched, startled. Tried to stammer something. Killian stood, cock still hanging heavy, his body vibrating with fury.

"We're done," he growled, thrusting out a hand. The poor bastard shook it like he'd just been offered his own death warrant.

He slammed his palm against the desk, voice cracking through the room like a gunshot.

"Meeting's over."

The client physically jumped. Papers rattled. Somewhere above me Jaxon made a sound that was suspiciously close to a strangled laugh.

Killian stood so abruptly the chair shot backward across the floor.

And oh. Oh, he looked furious.

Not cold-furious either. Not his usual controlled assassin thing. No. This was raw. Shaking. Vein-popping fury layered directly over being painfully, visibly wrecked.

His shirt sleeves were rolled halfway up now, tie loosened, chest rising hard enough I could see it from beneath the desk. And between us?

Still hard. Still twitching. Still very much my fault.

The poor client stared at him like he'd accidentally wandered into a hostage situation. Which—to be fair—felt spiritually accurate.

"We're done," Killian growled, thrusting out a hand.

The guy shook it immediately with the terrified energy of someone trying to escape a bear encounter alive.

And then the office door opened.

And Killian?

Killian just stood there breathing hard through his nose while his cock twitched angrily inches from my face like it personally wanted revenge.

The door finally shut behind them. Silence dropped hard into the room.

Then Killian's hand tangled violently into my hair and yanked my head back until I had no choice but to look up at him.

Jesus Christ. He looked gone.

Sweat sliding slowly down his throat. Chest heaving. Eyes dark enough to swallow whole cities.

And underneath all that fury?

Need. Pure, catastrophic need.

His cock jerked once against my cheek, flushed and leaking and still painfully hard after everything I'd done to him.

"You," he said hoarsely, staring down at me like he was reconsidering every life choice that led him here, "are an absolute fucking menace."

"You touched yourself while you did this?" His voice was gravel, dark and cracked open.

I licked my spit-slick lips, defiant. "Yeah. And I came."

"Sweetheart... you've got no idea what you've just done." He looked like a god about to fall.

Cock flushed, angry, still glistening with my spit. Chest heaving, jaw wired tight, every vein standing out on his forearms as he gripped the edge of the desk like it was the only thing keeping him sane.

And me? I just smiled. Slow. Wicked. A little cruel.

"Beg."

His pupils blew wide, a dark flash of hunger so raw it nearly scorched me where I knelt. He didn't answer — not with words.

He sat back in his chair, spreading his thighs wider, cock twitching hard, swollen and leaking down his shaft.

He was furious. Furious that I'd edged him through a whole meeting. Furious that I'd touched myself while I did it. Furious that I'd denied him what he'd been seconds from taking.

And it only made him harder.

His hands flexed once on the armrests. His voice, when it finally came, was gravity-deep. "You think I beg?"

I tilted my head, still stroking him with just my fingertips, cruel and feather-light, watching every twitch, every shallow breath. "You already are, Moretti. Your body's begging for you."

His nostrils flared. A sharp exhale. His cock kicked hard in my hand, precum spilling, proof of just how close he was to losing that legendary control.

I leaned in, lips brushing the slick tip, but not taking him in — not yet.

My tongue flicked once, deliberately teasing.

Then I sat back on my heels again, licking my own fingers slow, like I hadn't just been soaked from edging myself raw under his desk.

"Beg," I whispered, the word soft but sharp enough to cut.

His head jerked like I'd slapped him. He sat forward suddenly, his chair groaning under the weight shift, eyes blazing with unholy fire. The kind that promised no mercy.

And his cock? Angry. Heavy. Swollen so thick I could see every pulse of blood beneath the skin. He wasn't just aroused — he was wrecked. Furious. Hungry. Mine.

Killian

She thought she was clever. Thought she could play sadist with me and walk away whole.

My fist tangled in her hair before she even finished licking her fingers.

I yanked her head back, forced her mouth open, and shoved my cock past her lips. No warning. No patience. Just punishment.

Her muffled cry shot straight through me. Good. She needed to feel what she'd been doing to me.

My hips snapped, thrust after brutal thrust, burying myself down her throat until she gagged, drool spilling, her nails clawing at my thighs.

Christ, she was still looking at me. Those wild eyes locked on mine, watering, furious and unbroken. Like she dared me to ruin her more. And I did.

I fucked her mouth like it was the only way to survive, hair wound tight in my hand, groans tearing out of me as heat coiled low and vicious.

Her throat convulsed around me, and I lost it — hips jerking, spilling down her throat with a growl that shook the walls.

I should've let go. Should've pulled away, zipped up, pretended it never happened.

Instead, I dragged her up by the jaw, thumb smearing the mess from her lip.

I bent low, caught her mouth in a kiss that was more claim than apology, tasting myself on her tongue.

"Riley," I rasped, forehead pressed to hers,

"you have no idea how close you are to breaking."

She smirked, lips swollen and wet. "Maybe I want to break you first."

That grin—fucking lethal.

I growled, lifted her by the waist, and dropped her ass on the desk so hard papers scattered like confetti.

My hands shoved her thighs wide, her little shorts useless against my grip.

I dropped to my knees, teeth grazing the inside of her thigh, spreading her further until she gasped.

Her cunt glistened, still soaked from when she'd been touching herself under my nose, and I groaned like a man starved.

"Holy fuck..." I leaned in, tongue dragging slow and reverent up her slit, before sucking her clit into my mouth hard enough to make her jolt.

My hands locked on her hips, anchoring her against my face, devouring like she was oxygen.

She fisted her hands in my hair, tugging hard.

Not pushing me away—pulling me where she wanted me.

Grinding against my mouth, taking control even now.

"You think I'll be submissive for you?" she gasped, her laugh broken by moans.

"You're the one on your knees, Moretti." Fuck. She was right. And God help me, I loved it.

Riley

Holy. Fuck.

Killian Moretti — storm-wrapped, ice-veined, untouchable Killian — was on his knees between my thighs like I was his altar.

His mouth was hot and relentless, tongue flicking, lips sucking, teeth grazing just enough to make me cry out. My fingers gripped his hair, tugging hard, grinding down against his face.

He groaned into me. The vibration sent me spiralling, another wave building sharp and fast.

My laugh came out ragged, desperate. "Look at you," I gasped, hips rolling, smearing my slick across his mouth. "You're supposed to break me? You're the one worshipping."

His eyes flicked up, dark and furious, and fuck if it didn't make me wetter. That hunger. That fury. That devotion. He didn't stop. Didn't slow. He devoured me harder, dragging me higher until my whole body locked tight.

I shattered. Loud. Violent. Shaking on his face, nails scraping his scalp as I came apart in his mouth. My thighs trembled, my chest heaved, and still he licked me through it, swallowing every last drop like I was something holy.

I collapsed back onto my elbows, panting, smug as hell even through the haze.

"On your knees, Moretti," I panted, my voice wrecked but defiant.

"Guess we know who's really in charge."

That did it. His mouth pulled away, slow, wet, deliberate. His chin glistened. His breath came harsh. And then his hand wrapped around his cock, pumping once, twice, veins straining.

My smirk faltered when I realised what was coming. "Say it again," he rasped, voice like gravel.

I opened my mouth, but before I could taunt him again, he surged up, grabbed me by the hips, and slammed into me in one hard thrust that stole my breath.

I screamed. Not in pain. In shock. In need. In the way a body recognises its undoing before the brain can catch up.

But this wasn't like before. No savage rhythm from when he was fucking my face. No reckless speed. He set a pace that was slow, deep, merciless. Each thrust dragged me full, stretched me wide, ground into every place that made me whimper. He was tormenting me with patience. With reverence.

Killian's forehead pressed to mine, his hand cupping my jaw as his hips rolled. "Not fucking," he growled, every word a low rumble against my lips. "Not breaking. Loving you."

My laugh broke into a sob. "You don't love—"

"Shut up," he snarled, kissing me hard, tongue thrusting into my mouth with the same rhythm as his cock. "Feel it. Every inch. Every second. Mine."

His thumb found my clit, circling slow, cruel, perfectly in time with his thrusts.

My walls clenched, traitorous, desperate for more. Tears stung my eyes. From the overstimulation. From the weight of it. From the way his voice cracked when he whispered against my ear:

"A few weeks," he rasped against my mouth, voice rough enough to splinter. "That's all I've got to make you stay." His thumb dragged slowly along my jaw, like he was memorising me already. "And I'll spend every single one loving you until walking away feels impossible."

My body betrayed me, clenching tighter, another orgasm building sharp and unbearable. I hated him. I needed him. And I couldn't stop. I came again, sobbing into his mouth, and his pace never faltered. Slow. Deep. Worship disguised as torment.

And for the first time, I was scared.

Because this wasn't just sex. It was war. And Killian Moretti had just declared it.

I thought it was over. Killian groaned against my throat, hips jerking deep one last time as heat spilled inside me, thick and scorching.

His breath was ragged, his grip punishing at my hips, and I slumped back against the desk, trembling, wrecked. Done.

Or so I thought. Because instead of softening, instead of slowing, he shifted. His weight pressed me flat to the desk, the air knocked from my chest as he pulled out only to slam right back in. Harder. Rougher. Savage.

"Killian—" My voice broke into a half-sob, half-moan.

"You—fuck—you just—"

"Not enough." His voice was a growl, all gravel and hunger. His cock was still iron-hard, splitting me open again and again, the slick drag of his release only making each thrust dirtier.

"Never enough."

The desk rattled under us, papers scattering, a glass toppling and shattering somewhere on the floor. His pace was brutal, each snap of his hips driving me higher even though my body begged for mercy.

My nails clawed uselessly at the wood, my back arching as he pounded me like he wanted to fuse us together.

"How—" I gasped, shaking, overwhelmed.

"How the fuck are you still—"

He cut me off with another vicious thrust, grinding so deep I saw stars.

"Because you're mine," he snarled, teeth catching my shoulder. "Because I'm not stopping until you understand what that means."

And then—oh, fuck. His hand left my hip, yanked open a desk drawer, and came back with something small, sleek, humming.

My eyes widened. "You've got a vibrator in your office?"

His grin was sharp, merciless. "Of course I do."

He flicked it on, the buzz low but deadly, and pressed it straight to my clit as he kept fucking me.

I screamed—raw, helpless—my body convulsing instantly at the double assault.

His cock brutal and relentless, the vibrator merciless on that raw bundle of nerves.

"Killian—oh, fuck, oh fuck—" My voice dissolved into sound, into noise, into nothing but sensation.

My thighs shook, my vision blurred, my body betrayed me completely.

"That's it," he rasped, pinning me flat with his weight, pounding into me with every ounce of feral strength. "Come for me. Come until you can't move. Until you can't even think of anyone but me."

And I did. God, I did. Again. And again.

My body seized, shuddered, came apart so hard I thought I'd break. He didn't stop. Didn't let me down. He fucked me through it, fucked me past it, fucked me until there was nothing left but wreckage and his name ripped from my throat.

By the time he finally stilled, chest heaving against my back, the vibrator still humming lazily against me, I was gone. Ruined. My body a trembling mess, my mind a haze of heat and possession and Killian.

He leaned down, teeth grazing my ear, his voice low and reverent as sin. "Now you understand."

I was gone. Spent. Shaking. My forehead pressed to the desk, breath tearing ragged from my throat while his release still dripped down my thighs and the vibrator hummed against a clit that felt raw, blistered, overused.

I wanted to scream stop. I wanted to beg for mercy. I wanted to sleep.

But Killian wasn't done. The toy snapped off. Relief lasted two seconds before he hauled me upright by the hips and spun me into his lap.

His chair creaked under the force as he dropped into it, dragging me with him until I was straddling him, bare and wrecked, cock still hard and waiting beneath me.

I whimpered. "Killian—I can't—"

"Yes, you can." His voice was gravel, iron, absolute. One arm locked around my waist, the other guiding his cock back to my entrance. "You will."

"I can't," I tried again, my head falling forward onto his shoulder. He caught my jaw, forced my eyes up to his. His stare was endless, devouring, all hunger and command.

"You're going to ride me until I'm satisfied. Until we're satisfied. Do you understand?" My thighs trembled. My nails dug into his shoulders. I shook my head.

"You'll break me." A cruel smile ghosted his lips. "That's the point."

He shifted his hips, and I slid down onto him, inch by brutal inch, until he was buried inside me again, stretching me wide, filling me so deep I sobbed against his throat.

"That's it," he rasped, gripping my hips hard enough to bruise.

"Take it. Take all of me."

I shook, body convulsing, torn between pain and pleasure, but he didn't give me the chance to stall.

His hands forced my hips up, then slammed them back down onto his cock, grinding me into him, wringing another broken cry from my chest.

"Ride," he ordered, low and sharp.

"Ride me, Riley. Show me you can."

My body obeyed before my brain could argue, lifting and dropping, messy and uneven, every slam of his cock inside me both agony and salvation.

My legs burned, my lungs burned, my soul burned. And he just sat there, steady as stone beneath me, jaw clenched, eyes locked on mine like he was burning my ruin into memory.

"You're mine," he growled, dragging me down harder, deeper.

"Not theirs. Not anyone else's. Mine."

I cried out, broken, raw, overwhelmed. He caught my sob with his mouth, devouring it, swallowing it whole, and his hips surged up into mine, brutal thrusts from below that turned my rhythm into chaos.

I thought I had nothing left to give. But on Killian's lap, with his voice like gravity and his cock like steel, I learned I was wrong. Hopelessly, devastatingly wrong.

Killian

She was limp against me, trembling still, boneless and ruined. My cock was still buried in her when the last shudder took her, but I held her through it, whispering against her temple,

"Mine. Ours. No choice, Riley." Her lips quivered, a ghost of defiance even through exhaustion.

"Still made you beg," she rasped.

I laughed — low, rough, dangerous. Christ, she didn't even know what she'd just given me.

I kissed her, slow and reverent, swallowing that bratty spark, then eased her against my chest.

She sagged into me, too spent to fight, still vibrating from the aftershocks.

I stood, lifting her in my arms like she weighed nothing.

Her thighs fell open weakly, her cheek pressed to my shoulder, her breath damp and hot against my throat. My hand splayed wide across her back, the other gripping under her knees, holding her like she was both fragile and already mine to break.

The warehouse was quiet, the kind of quiet that felt watched.

My boots echoed on the concrete as I carried her past the gym, the kitchen, the lounge. If any of the others saw us, they didn't dare show themselves. Maybe they knew. Maybe they felt the shift.

Her fingers twitched against my chest, not quite holding on, but not letting go either. I tightened my grip, lowering my mouth to her ear.

"Don't think. Don't fight. Just breathe." She made a soft, wrecked sound, like she hated herself for obeying. My smile cut through the silence. Perfect.

I should've taken her back to her room. Left her in her own bed, let her lick her wounds and rebuild her walls. But I wasn't that man anymore. Not with her. Not after this.

So I carried her to mine. The door clicked shut behind us.

The dark swallowed us whole. I set her down on my sheets, tugging the blanket over her before she could shiver. She blinked up at me, dazed, eyes glassy with exhaustion and something sharper, something terrified.

Good. She should be scared. Because she wasn't leaving my bed. Not tonight. Not ever, if I had my way. I pressed a kiss to her hair, whispered against her crown,

"Sleep, Riley. I'll keep watch." Her eyes fluttered closed, lashes trembling, her body curling instinctively toward mine as I slid in beside her. I wrapped her against me, her head tucked under my chin, her breath feathering over my chest.

And there, in the quiet dark, I finally admitted it to myself: I didn't want her body. I wanted her soul. And if she tried to leave, I'd chain both to me before I let her go.

56

Two Weeks Left

Riley

Skinny Love – Birdy

The hall clock was smug about it. Two weeks left. Fourteen days. Three-hundred-and-thirty-six hours. Not that I was counting or anything psychotic like that. Tomorrow, Grant would probably clear me — or at least attempt to while giving me his usual "ease back into full activity" speech like I hadn't spent the entire morning throwing grown men around the sparring ring for fun.

Jaxon twice, specifically.

Which was why I was now stretched across the couch like a victorious Roman emperor after battle. Cole sat at one end with my legs over his lap, aggressively kneading the arch of my foot like he was trying to tenderise steak. Lucas sat behind me, fingers moving slow through my hair, nails dragging lightly over my scalp in a way that was dangerously close to narcotics.

"This is humiliating," Cole muttered.

"You lost," I reminded him lazily. "This is called consequences."

Lucas chuckled softly behind me. "The worst part is she's being nice about it."

"I'm conserving energy."

It should've felt harmless. Easy. Instead it felt dangerous as hell.

Because this was the kind of stuff people missed when they left. Not the sex. Not the drama. This.

Warm hands. Inside jokes. Someone remembering exactly how you liked your tea without asking.

The terrifying domestic horror of it all. Three months.

The memory slammed back sharp and cold — blood under me, Killian's hands pressing hard against the wound in my side while he leaned down close enough for only me to hear.

Stay with us for three months. Or we move into your apartment for six. Not a request. Not technically a threat either. More like organised crime-flavoured emotional blackmail.

Cole dug his thumbs deeper into my foot and I let out a traitorous little sigh before I could stop myself.

Lucas immediately noticed. Bastard. "There she is," he murmured.

"I hate all of you."

"No you don't," Cole said instantly.

That was the problem. Maybe I was starting not to. And that? Terrifying.

Because love — real love — felt like standing in the middle of the road waiting for headlights.

The crash took my parents in one second. Sophie died in a hospital bed while I held her hand pretending not to fall apart. Every person I'd ever loved had left eventually — one way or another.

I wasn't doing that again. In two weeks, Grant would clear me. And then I'd be gone before this house turned into something I couldn't walk away from.

"I'm not staying," I said finally.

Cole snorted. "Sure you're not."

Neither of them believed me. Which was cute. Delusional. But cute.

Jaxon

I heard Riley laughing before I saw her. Actual laughing. Not the unhinged "I'm about to commit crimes" kind either. Real laughing.

I stepped into the living room and nearly forgot how breathing worked for a second.

She was sprawled across the couch like she owned the place. One leg over Cole's lap while he rubbed her foot with the concentration of a man defusing a bomb. Lucas sat behind her with his hands in her hair, and Riley — Riley looked relaxed.

Soft. Not guarded. Not halfway to bolting. Not carrying the weight of the world like she usually did.

Just... here. Like she belonged here.

And Christ, that thought hit harder than it should've. I'd give her the moon if she asked for it.

Hell, I'd probably steal the damn moon. Cole would help. Lucas would somehow hack NASA. Killian would stand there pretending this was beneath him while absolutely funding the operation.

That was the problem with Riley.

She'd somehow become the centre of everything without any of us noticing it happen. Then her eyes met mine.

And there it was again — that flicker of panic she got whenever she looked too comfortable. Like happiness itself was a security breach.

"I'm not staying," she said.

Cole smirked without looking up. Lucas kept combing his fingers through her hair like he already knew she was lying.

I didn't argue. Didn't need to. Because Riley Morgan could talk all she wanted about leaving, but her body told the truth before her mouth ever did.

The way she melted into the couch. The way she let us touch her. The way she stopped looking over her shoulder every five seconds when she was with us. She was already halfway home. She just didn't know it yet.

Killian

Jaxon stood in the doorway staring at her like a man witnessing religion for the first time.

Honestly? Fair.

Riley was stretched across the couch between Cole and Lucas looking dangerously domestic. Like she belonged there. Like this had always been her spot.

Which was exactly the issue.

Because if she kept thinking this safehouse was the entire picture, she'd still leave when the clock ran out.

And she was absolutely still counting. I leaned against the doorway beside Jaxon, lowering my voice. "We need to make her want to stay."

His jaw tightened slightly. "She's still counting down."

"I know." My gaze stayed fixed on her. "This place isn't a home. It's a bunker with better furniture." Jaxon glanced sideways at me. "You're thinking about the house."

Of course I was. Not this concrete box full of weapons and trauma and surveillance cameras.

Our actual house.

Morning sunlight through the kitchen windows. Her boots kicked off by the door. Riley swearing at the coffee machine while Cole made breakfast and Lucas pretended not to watch her over his laptop.

A life. Not survival.

The memory hit hard and sudden — Riley bleeding out on cold tile while I pressed my hands against the wound trying to keep her here through sheer force of will alone.

Three months. Back then it had been about keeping her alive. Somewhere along the way it stopped being enough. Now I wanted her to stay. Permanently.

"She thinks she's leaving in two weeks," I said quietly. "So we stop treating this like temporary housing and start treating it like a future."

Jaxon looked back toward her again. Riley was smiling now, eyes closed while Lucas played with her hair.

"She already belongs with us," he muttered.

I nodded once. Yeah. She did.

The problem was Riley still thought she could grab her boots, flip us all off dramatically, and disappear into the sunset in fourteen days flat.

Cute. Deeply insulting, honestly. Because sex wouldn't keep her here. Riley had survived without pleasure before.

Gifts wouldn't do it either. She'd leave every single one behind out of pure stubborn spite.

No. What we needed to give her was worse. Safety. Routine. Belonging.

A place where she didn't have to sleep with one eye open waiting for disaster to kick the door in.

Once someone like Riley tasted that properly?

Good luck ripping it away from them.

And if she still tried to leave after that? Well.

Cole was already emotionally six minutes away from building her a personalised parking spot and Lucas had absolutely started memorising her coffee orders like a psychopath.

At that point, we'd probably just follow her home out of principle.

57

Permission to Bleed

Riley

Burning House – Cam

Grant's clinic always smelled like antiseptic and bad decisions. I sat on the edge of the metal exam table, shirt abandoned somewhere behind me, sports bra barely covering the angry curve of scar tissue cutting across my ribs. My fingers toyed absently with the hem while my brain ricocheted between caffeine and the very recent memory of getting railed across Jaxon's workbench hard enough to qualify as a workplace safety violation.

Not that I planned on mentioning that to Grant.

He stood across the room pulling on gloves with the same expression he always wore around me — halfway between medical professionalism and you are the dumbest patient I've ever had.

"Off," he said, snapping the glove against his wrist and nodding toward my bra.

I raised a brow. "Buy me dinner first."

"Riley," he sighed flatly, "if I had a dollar for every time I've seen your tits while digging bullets out of you, I could retire."

I groaned dramatically and peeled it off anyway, throwing it toward the chair with as much attitude as possible.

"You're no fun."

Grant ignored that completely, stepping closer to inspect the scar. I flinched. Not from pain.From memory.

"You're healing well," he said finally. "Scar tissue looks good. Mobility?"

I rolled my shoulder, twisted slightly at the waist. "Still pulls sometimes. Better than before."

"Nerve regeneration takes time. Ghost pain's normal." He glanced up briefly. "Doesn't mean you're broken. Just means you survived."

"Story of my fucking life," I muttered.

Grant hummed quietly. "Surviving isn't living."

I stared at the ceiling. "Jesus Christ, Grant. What is this? Grey's Anatomy?"

"No." His tone stayed maddeningly calm. "This is me telling you to stop letting your trauma choose your lovers."

That landed like a slap. I looked at him sharply. "Excuse me?"

He peeled one glove off slowly, tossing it into the bin. "You think I don't recognise the signs by now?"

"I don't know what you're talking about."

"Bullshit."

Not angry. Not judgmental. Just tired.

"You come in flushed, defensive, covered in bruises you pretend don't matter, and suddenly you're acting like getting attached is some kind of tactical error." He folded his arms. "I've known you too long for that act to work."

"I'm not attached."

"Don't lie to your doctor. It's embarrassing for both of us."

I shut my mouth. Grant stepped back toward the counter, grabbing gauze he clearly didn't actually need just to give his hands something to do.

"You want medical clearance? Fine. You're physically stable." His eyes lifted back to mine. "Emotionally? You're a live grenade with a loose pin pretending it's strategy."

"That's not fair."

"It's not supposed to be fair. It's supposed to be true." Silence dropped hard between us.

I stared at my hands instead. Scarred knuckles. Calluses. Tiny half-moons from my nails digging into my palms. "I didn't ask to feel anything," I admitted finally, voice quieter than I intended. "It wasn't supposed to get this far."

"It never is." Grant moved behind me again, pressing the cold stethoscope to my back.

"Deep breath." I inhaled slowly. Shakily.

"You trust them?" he asked.

"Sometimes."

"That's not enough."

"I know."

A pause. Then quieter: "Did he do this to you?" he asked, nodding toward the scar.

"No."

"Then why are you still acting like you're in danger?"

That question lodged somewhere ugly under my ribs. Because he was right. No one here had hurt me. Not really.

And somehow that scared me more than if they had. I looked down at my hands again. "Being wanted like that," I whispered, "feels worse than getting shot."

Grant exhaled through his nose like I'd just proven his entire point.

"I patch you up because nobody else gets close enough to do it," he said quietly. "You show up bleeding and laughing like dying's just another Tuesday."

I swallowed hard. "But I've seen your face when someone touches you like you matter." My throat tightened instantly.

"You don't need my permission to be okay," he added. "But if you want it?" He shrugged lightly. "You've got it."I looked away fast.

"You're allowed to let people love you without it meaning you lost something." God. That one hurt.

Grant finally stepped back, tossing the last glove aside. "You're cleared. Try not to nearly die again. The paperwork's annoying."

I slid off the table, tugging my hoodie back on. "Thanks, Grant."

"Anytime, kid."

Then, just as I reached the door— "And Riley?"

"Yeah?"

"If they hurt you, I'll kill them."

I snorted softly. "Get in line."

He waved me off immediately after that like the softness had never happened. Typical.

The air outside bit cold against my skin.

Bandages clean. Brain absolutely not.

Not because of Grant — dear God, no — but because of everything he'd said. You're allowed. Like softness wasn't a trap. Like wanting something didn't automatically mean bleeding for it later.

I shoved my hands into my hoodie pocket and my fingers brushed the chain Jaxon gave me.

Enough. The word felt almost mocking now. Because I didn't feel like enough. I felt like a disaster waiting for the right trigger.

The SUV idled beneath a flickering streetlamp like it was already irritated about existing.

Cole sat behind the wheel wearing sunglasses despite the fact the sun had fully fucked off hours ago. Lucas sat shotgun scrolling through something on his tablet. Jaxon lounged in the back seat, headphones half-off, already watching me the second I stepped outside.

And Killian?

Back seat corner. Hoodie up. Arms crossed. Pretending to sleep like the world's most emotionally unavailable assassin.

I hated that my pulse still jumped when I saw him. I climbed in beside Jaxon without speaking.

The silence settled easy around us. Nobody asked about the appointment. Nobody pushed. They just… made space.

Jaxon shifted slightly so I had more room. Lucas handed me a bottle of water without even looking up. Cole adjusted the heat the second I rubbed my hands together.

And Killian watched me in the rearview mirror when he thought I wouldn't notice.

That was the dangerous part. Not the sex. Not the fighting. Not the obsession.

This. The terrifying domestic horror of people caring quietly. "So," Jaxon drawled eventually, "you wanna pick dinner or are we pretending Riley won't hijack everyone's order out of spite?"

"I don't hijack anything."

"Bullshit," Cole muttered. "Last time you swapped my sushi with extra wasabi just to watch me cry."

"And it was hilarious."

"She's spiralling," Lucas observed calmly.

"Am not."

"You're always spiralling," Killian said from the back.

I twisted around instantly to glare at him. "Says the man who growled the safe word like it was foreplay."

Jaxon choked laughing.

"Wait." He pointed at Killian. "What's your safe word?"

Killian didn't even blink. "Swan." Silence.

Then Cole absolutely lost it. "Oh my God," he wheezed. "Your safe word is a princess bird?"

"Shut up." I should've laughed harder. Instead my chest hurt. Because sitting here — in this stupid SUV with these stupid men and their stupid little acts of care — felt dangerously close to home.

And nice things never stayed.

The diner glowed neon-red against the dark when we pulled in. "I can stay in the car," I offered automatically.

Cole scoffed immediately. "You'll march your hot ass inside and eat curly fries like a good girl."

Killian's eyes flicked toward mine. "Green?"

I swallowed once. "Green."

He nodded once in return. Nothing else. But somehow it still felt intimate. We slid into the booth like muscle memory. Lucas ordered.

Jaxon built tiny ketchup-packet towers. Cole flirted with me aggressively across the fries. Killian sat beside me like a shadow I couldn't outrun.

And for a terrifying few minutes... I relaxed. I laughed. I stole fries. I drank my milkshake.

I forgot about scars and contracts and countdown clocks and Sophie's hospital room and all the ways loving people eventually turned catastrophic.

I was just here. Alive. Warm. Fed.

Which was exactly when the mood shifted. Lucas's tablet chimed three sharp notes.

The entire table changed instantly. Killian looked up first. "Talk."

Lucas turned the screen toward him. Killian scanned it once and his jaw ticked. "Debrief in thirty."

Jaxon groaned dramatically. "You're ruining the vibe."

"I am the vibe," Killian replied flatly.

Cole drained the last of his milkshake like a barbarian. "Where we headed?"

"Northern industrial zone," Lucas answered. "Shipment interception. Could be clean. Could be a bloodbath."

"Love gambling with my cardio," I muttered.

"Pack for overnight," Killian added. "Movement before sunrise."

Jaxon leaned back lazily. "So no dessert?"

"You're dessert," Cole said immediately.

"That's the problem."

The last fry hadn't even made it to my mouth before Killian dropped the bomb. "You're not going tonight."

I blinked slowly. "Excuse me?" Around the table, everyone suddenly became very interested in avoiding eye contact.

"You're benched," Killian said evenly.

I laughed once. Sharp. Dangerous. "Oh, cute. You almost sounded serious."

"No joke."

Ice slid down my spine. "You said I was cleared."

"I said physically." His voice stayed calm, which somehow made it worse. "Emotionally? You're still bleeding everywhere and calling it progress."

"That's not your fucking decision."

"It is tonight."

I shoved back from the booth so fast the chair screeched. "You arrogant—"

"Riley," Lucas cut in quietly. "Don't."

I whipped toward him. "You knew?"

Silence. That answered enough.

"I've trained harder than all of you since the second I could stand again," I snapped. "I've run drills. I've fought. I've bled. But suddenly I'm the liability?"

Killian stood slowly. Deliberately. "This isn't punishment."

"Really? Because it feels a hell of a lot like control."

"It's protection."

I stepped right into his space, chest to chest. "You don't get to protect me like this."

His jaw flexed once. "You're a storm without a centre right now," he said quietly. "And I'm not dragging you into a bloodbath until I know you won't drown in it.

I wanted to hit him. Kiss him. Scream at him. Possibly all three simultaneously.

Instead I laughed bitterly. "That's rich coming from the man who growled swan at me while handcuffing me to his desk."

Cole nearly inhaled a fry. "Okay wow," he coughed. "We're really sharing today."

"Stay out of this," both Killian and I snapped simultaneously.

The silence afterward hit hard. Killian's voice dropped lower. Final. "You're staying behind."

I grabbed my jacket. "You think this conversation's over?"

"I know it isn't." I didn't look at him again. Didn't trust myself to. Because if I did, I might break. Or beg. Or kiss him.

And all three felt like losing. So I walked out of the diner without another word.

I didn't wait for the SUV. Didn't look back when it drove past me either. Fine. Let Killian think he'd made the final call.

When this mission inevitably turned into a disaster — because it always did — they'd need backup.

And I'd already be five steps ahead.

58

The Glitter Spiral

Riley

Animal - PVRIS

.

That weight in my chest. That cold certainty that if I didn't hear from them, they were already gone.

Were they alive? Dead? Bleeding out in some alley while I was stuck here pacing like a caged animal? Who the fuck knew.

And I was supposed to just... sit here. Wait. Be a good little girl and stay put.

Grant had cleared me. Fully cleared. My body was fine. My mind? Not even close.

The longer they were gone, the tighter it wound inside me — panic sharpening into something brittle and dangerous.

Day one, I kept it together. Mostly.

Cleaned the warehouse. Reorganised weapons. Rebuilt my gear loadout. Sharpened every knife I owned until my hands cramped.

Day two, I worked out until my muscles screamed, until my lungs burned, until my body was too wrung out to think. That bought me maybe half a day of peace.

Day three, the cracks split open.

Because the whisper I'd been ignoring turned into a scream.

They didn't trust you enough to bring you.Not strong enough. Not good enough. Not theirs enough.

And it shouldn't have mattered.

But it did.

Because no matter how many times I told myself I didn't need anyone, some traitorous part of me had started to believe in them. Started to want... more.

And now? Now they were gone. Ripped away without warning.

So why did it hurt like this?

Why did my chest feel like Sophie's heart monitor slowing all over again? Why did my hands shake like I was still sitting in that hospital chair waiting for the last breath?

Four days.

Four days of nothing but my own head for company.

And my head is a vicious fucking place. So I did what I do best. I burned it down.

Not literally — though God, the thought crossed my mind — but close enough.

First, I rewired Lucas's security feeds, looping the footage into a slow-motion replay of him tripping over the rug last month.

Then I stole Cole's knives and built an elaborate sculpture in the middle of the living room, each blade balanced just so, the title card reading: Overcompensating Much?

Jaxon's protein powder? Glitter. Every single container. Maximum sparkle apocalypse.

And finally, the crown jewel: hacked into Killian's private server, shut it down, replaced his desktop with a screaming neon-pink World's Grumpiest Daddy wallpaper.

By the time I was done, the warehouse was a shrine to my bad decisions. Glitter in the air. Knives in impossible formations. Screens looping humiliation.

It wasn't about payback. Not really. It was about giving my hands something to do so I didn't start clawing my own skin off. About drowning the ache before it drowned me.

And if I was being honest — the part I'd rather set myself on fire than admit — it was about missing them.

I missed Jaxon's dumb pet names, the way he grinned like we were both in on the same joke. I missed Lucas's quiet grounding touches when he thought I wouldn't notice. Cole's relentless teasing that somehow landed right between comfort and provocation.

And Killian's steady hand on the small of my back — like he'd claimed the space and I'd let him.

I wasn't supposed to want this. Wasn't supposed to want them. And that's why I wrecked the place. Because it's easier to wade through chaos than admit you want peace.

At exactly 11:47 PM, the warehouse door slid open.

Boots hit concrete. Low voices. They were home. Alive.

I didn't move. Didn't speak. Just stood there in the middle of my glitter-crusted masterpiece and waited.

One by one, they stepped inside.

Killian. Lucas. Jaxon. Cole.

They stopped dead. No one spoke.

Jaxon

I knew it the second I stepped through the door. The glitter hit first — floating through the air like some fucked-up snow globe. My boots crunched against it, leaving shimmering footprints across the concrete. Weapons were arranged like an art exhibit. Lucas's hacked screens played him eating shit on loop. The knife sculpture in the middle of the room was so precise it physically hurt to look at.

Killian froze. Lucas blinked once. Cole's jaw tightened.

And me? My stomach dropped straight to the fucking floor.

This wasn't mischief. This wasn't Riley trying to be cute.

This was Riley after four days alone with no calls and too much silence.

This was her drowning and grabbing at anything sharp enough to stay afloat.

I saw it in her eyes before she even spoke. That jagged, too-bright look that said she was running on adrenaline, rage, and whatever thread she had left keeping her together.

The kind of look you only get when the hurt is so deep you'd rather burn the world down than admit you're scared.

And then it hit me, cold and ugly in the gut. Oh, fuck. We might have actually broken her.

Killian

The glitter clung to her like it belonged there — little flecks caught in her hair, on her lashes, scattered across the sharp line of her jaw.

She stood in the middle of the destruction she'd made, but she wasn't smug about it. Not really. She looked like someone who'd built herself a barricade just to survive. And that was on us.

Four days. Four days of silence. Four days of giving her every reason to believe we'd left her behind like everyone else in her life.

We didn't just fuck up. We gutted her trust. Handed her every confirmation of the fears she'd never say out loud.

And for what? Some misguided idea of keeping her "safe"? Safe from the mission? Safe from seeing us bleed?

She's seen worse. Survived worse. Her parents — gone in an instant. Her sister — dying in a hospital bed while she watched helplessly. And now us — disappearing without a word.

We became another entry in the long list of people who didn't stay. That was the real damage. Not the glitter. Not the knives. Not the hacked server.

The silence. The kind that eats a person alive from the inside out.

I'd been there the night she was shot. Felt her blood under my hands. Heard the defiance in her voice even when she could barely breathe.

She agreed to three months in the safehouse because she had no choice.

But in her head? She'd already decided she was leaving the second the clock ran out.

Two weeks left. Two weeks until she walks. And if we kept her here — trapped in this concrete bunker full of cameras, steel doors, and ghosts — she would go.

So the plan became simple. We take her to the house. Not the safehouse. Our house.

Because that's where the walls drop. That's where she sees the life we could give her. A kitchen she can wreck at midnight. A couch she falls asleep on. Sunlight through windows instead of fluorescent warehouse lighting and security monitors humming in the dark.

I wanted her to feel it. The kind of safety nobody had ever offered her without strings attached.

Except these strings?

I had no intention of letting her cut them. She'd given us her body. Let us touch her, mark her, ruin her in ways I don't give anyone.

But she still hadn't given us her soul. And that's the part I wanted. We fucked up. But I wasn't losing her over our mistake.

I'd drag her into that house myself if I had to. Make her see she belonged there. Make her want to belong there.

Because two weeks from now, Riley Morgan wasn't walking away. Not because we chained her down. Because eventually she'd realise the truth. She'd been ours all along.

Cole

Riley's voice cut through the glitter haze sharp enough to draw blood.

"You left me alone." She said it like a fact, not an accusation, which somehow hit even harder.

Then she kept talking — words layered with that reckless, feral edge she used whenever she didn't want anyone seeing the cracks underneath.

I caught pieces of it. Four days. No calls. Don't pretend it was nothing.

But most of it blurred, not because I wasn't listening — because I already knew what she wasn't saying.

She'd been trapped here with silence. And silence for Riley wasn't quiet. It was a fucking graveyard.

Killian's head turned slowly toward me. One look. That's all it took.

Yeah. I'm in. Lucas got the next look. He barely reacted, just the smallest twitch in his jaw — his version of agreement.

Jaxon hesitated, because of course he did. Always thinking three steps ahead when it came to her. But eventually his eyes narrowed and his chin dipped once.

Done. Conversation over. Four guys. One decision. We keep her.

She still thought she was in control. Still thought she was pushing us away on her terms.

But she didn't see it yet — the way Killian's brain was already moving, the way Lucas was calculating logistics, the way Jaxon was quietly recalibrating his entire existence around her.

And me? I wasn't agreeing because it made sense.

I was agreeing because I loved her.

Yeah. I'd never said it out loud. Barely admitted it to myself. But it was there all the same.

I'd give her the moon and stars if she asked. Burn the world down if she needed it.

And I'd sure as hell make sure she never felt that kind of alone again.

Two weeks left on her clock. We were going to erase every single one.

59

Creative Crimes & Adult Consequences.

Riley

Parachute - Song House and JYNDALL

The warehouse door slammed shut behind them. Concrete. Boots. Glitter. Silence. For one suspended second, nobody moved.

Lucas's screens still looped him eating shit over the rug in glorious slow motion. Pink light from Killian's hijacked monitor washed across the room. Cole's knife sculpture glittered under the overheads like a serial killer had discovered modern art.

And me?

I stood in the middle of it all with glitter stuck to my arms and four days of panic rotting through my chest.

Killian looked around once before his eyes landed on me. Not angry. Worse. Controlled.

"You trashed the warehouse."

"You left me alone."

The words cracked out before I could stop them.

Nobody joked. Nobody smirked.

Jaxon's expression shifted first. Something tight pulling across his face like he finally understood what this actually was.

Not revenge. Not boredom. Not me being chaotic for fun. Damage control.

I laughed anyway because the alternative was probably crying and I'd rather die. "Relax. Lucas can fix the server. Cole can unstack his emotional-support knives. The glitter adds atmosphere."

Cole stared at the sculpture in horror. "One of those blades is worth more than your car."

"One of those blades now looks like modern feminism," I shot back. "You're welcome."

Lucas muted the security footage with a quiet tap. "You rewired three independent systems."

"I had time."

"Clearly."

The silence stretched again. Wrong. Heavy.

Because none of them were yelling.

That's when the panic really started chewing through me.

"You didn't answer," I said, quieter this time. "Four days and nobody answered."

Killian's jaw flexed once.

Jaxon stepped forward first, careful like he thought I might bolt. "Ri—"

"No." My voice sharpened instantly. "You don't get to 'Ri' me right now."

Something ugly climbed up my throat before I could stop it. "I thought you were dead."

There it was. The truth. Raw. Humiliating. Hanging in the air between us.

Cole's face dropped first. The amusement vanished clean out of him. Lucas looked away briefly, tension pulling through his shoulders. Even Killian looked like he'd been hit.

And suddenly I was furious they could see it.

"So congratulations," I snapped, arms crossing hard over my chest. "You win. I spiralled. Happy now?"

Killian moved toward me slowly. "Riley—"

"No, actually, let's talk about this." I gestured wildly around the warehouse. "Because apparently I'm good enough to get shot for you people, good enough to patch up, good enough to fuck—"

Cole winced. Jaxon muttered, "Jesus Christ."

"—but the second things get dangerous, suddenly I'm benched at home like some unstable fucking civilian?"

"That's not what happened," Lucas said calmly.

"Really?" I laughed sharply. "Because from where I was standing, it looked a hell of a lot like you left me behind."

Killian stepped directly into my space then, all dark eyes and terrifying stillness.

"We left you safe."

"And what if I don't want safe?"

"You don't get a say in that when you stop sleeping, stop eating, and start turning the warehouse into a glitter-based hostage situation."

"That was one time."

Cole looked around. "This feels like at least seven times."

I glared at him. "I'm serious."

"So are we," Killian said quietly.

That shut me up.

Because underneath the control, underneath the anger, there was something worse sitting in his voice. Fear.

Not for the mission. For me. The room went still again.

Then Jaxon exhaled hard through his nose and looked at Killian. "She can't stay here."

My head snapped toward him. "Excuse me?"

Lucas nodded once, already thinking ten steps ahead like he always did. "He's right."

Cole rubbed a hand over the back of his neck. "This place is making it worse."

"You don't get to decide that!"

"We do," Killian said. "And we already have."

Cold panic flooded my stomach. "What the fuck does that mean?"

Killian held my gaze.

"It means you're leaving the safehouse." The air disappeared from my lungs.

"No." "It's done."

"You can't just—"

"We can."

Something dangerously close to fear cracked through me then because I knew that tone. Knew what it meant when Killian Moretti sounded that certain.

"Where?" I asked finally, hating how small the word sounded.

The four of them exchanged a look I couldn't read.

Then Killian answered. "Home."

Not the house. Not another location. Not temporary. Home. And somehow that single word scared me more than four days alone ever had.

Killian held my gaze.

"Home."

The word hit wrong.

Not warm. Not comforting. Wrong.

Because all I heard was: We're done with the safehouse. We're done with this. We're done with you.

Something cold cracked open in my chest.

Oh. Oh, they were leaving me behind. Of course they were.

Four days away on a mission, four days of silence, and they'd come back to this disaster I'd made — the glitter, the hacked systems, the knife sculpture, the meltdown dressed up as a joke — and finally realised I was too much. Too unstable. Too fucking exhausting to keep around.

I laughed once, sharp and ugly. "Right. Cool. Makes sense."

Jaxon frowned immediately. "Ri—"

"No, honestly." I shrugged too fast, too careless. "I get it."

Cole's expression shifted. "Get what?"

"That you're done."

Silence. Real silence this time.

Not playful. Not sarcastic.

Dangerous.

I pushed past it before they could answer. "I mean, fair enough. I hacked your systems, redecorated the warehouse like a psychotic raccoon, nearly had a nervous breakdown because none of you answered your phones—" My voice cracked slightly. I bulldozed over it. "Which, by the way, super humiliating for me."

"Riley," Lucas said carefully.

"No, it's fine," I said again, and this time the lie sounded almost hysterical. "Honestly, this is probably smarter. You realised I'm not exactly..." I gestured vaguely at myself. "Girlfriend material."

Cole actually looked offended.

I kept going anyway because if I stopped talking I might actually implode. "I mean, what did you expect? I don't exactly scream emotionally stable. I scream at walls and commit cybercrime when I'm upset."

"You thought we were abandoning you?" Jaxon asked softly.

The softness almost killed me.

My throat tightened violently. "Well, you vanished for four days," I snapped. "No calls. No contact. Then you come back and immediately start talking about moving me somewhere else."

Killian's jaw flexed hard.

"You benched me," I continued, words spilling faster now. "You left me here like I was too broken to bring along, and then you disappeared, and I just—" My breath hitched. "I thought maybe you realised I wasn't worth the effort anymore."

Nobody moved.

That was somehow worse.

The panic in my chest turned vicious. "God, don't do that," I muttered. "Don't give me the pity silence."

Cole set his jaw. "Princess—"

"No." My voice sharpened instantly. "Don't princess me right now."

I wrapped my arms around myself hard enough to hurt. "You wanna know the really pathetic part?" I laughed again, smaller this time. "I missed you."

The confession sat there like a live grenade.

"I missed all of you so much I started losing my fucking mind in this place." My eyes burned hot. "And the entire time I kept thinking, there it is. This is what happens when you start wanting people. They leave."

Jaxon looked like I'd physically hit him.

Lucas exhaled slowly through his nose.

Cole's face had gone frighteningly blank.

But Killian?

Killian looked furious. Not at me. That somehow made it worse.

He stepped forward slowly, voice low enough to vibrate through my ribs. "You think we came back here to cut ties with you?"

I swallowed hard. Didn't answer.

"Riley." I hated when he used that tone. That steady one. The one that made me feel seen straight through.

"You thought we stopped answering because we didn't want you anymore?"

The humiliation burned so badly I wanted to crawl out of my own skin. "Forget I said anything."

"No." Killian's voice sharpened. "Answer me."

I stared at the floor. And that was answer enough. A horrible silence followed.

Then Cole swore softly under his breath.

"Jesus Christ," Jaxon murmured, devastated.

Lucas rubbed a hand over his face like he suddenly understood every single hacked screen and glitter bomb in horrifying clarity.

Killian just looked at me for a long moment.

Then he said, very quietly: "Baby, we disappeared because we were trying to keep you safe."

I laughed bitterly. "Congratulations. It worked. I felt super safe."

His expression tightened. "That's on us," Lucas admitted. "We should've checked in."

"We should've called," Jaxon said immediately.

Cole looked furious with himself. "Four days was too long."

The apology only made my chest hurt worse. Because I didn't know what to do with it. Didn't know what to do with people who came back.

Killian's eyes stayed locked on mine. "You're not too much." My throat closed. "You're not temporary."

Something inside me cracked violently at those words.

"And you are absolutely not getting rid of us that easily."

I looked away before they could see how badly that wrecked me.

That's when Killian finally nodded once toward the hallway.

"Now," he said, voice turning darker, steadier, "with that being said..."

Cole's mouth curved slowly.

Jaxon actually sighed. "Oh, here we go."

Lucas folded his arms. "Actions still have consequences."

I blinked. "Wait, what?"

Killian held my stare. "You still hacked my private server, Riley."

"...Allegedly."

"And," he continued calmly, "before we deal with the rest of this mess..." His gaze dragged slowly over the glitter-coated warehouse. "...you need to be disciplined for what you've done."

Before I could argue, Cole moved. Fast. One second I was standing there glitter-covered and emotionally flayed alive, and the next I was hauled clean off the ground with an offended noise ripping out of me.

"Absolutely not—put me down—"

Cole just slung me over his shoulder like I weighed nothing. "Nope."

"This is kidnapping."

"This," he corrected, smacking my ass once as he started down the hallway, "is consequences."

I twisted immediately, trying to glare upside down at the others while my hoodie slid half over my face. "Lucas, tell your golden retriever to release me."

Lucas looked entirely too calm. "I think the retriever has a point."

"Traitors," I muttered darkly.

Jaxon snorted behind us. "You turned my protein powder into a disco explosion."

"You looked magical."

"Ri."

"Okay, fair."

Killian said nothing. Which honestly was more alarming than yelling.

Cole carried me deeper into the warehouse, past the gym, past the armoury, toward the back corridor I'd barely paid attention to before. My stomach started twisting slowly.

"Where are we going?" No answer. That was concerning.

"Guys." Still nothing.

The panic I'd barely gotten under control started scratching again. Not sharp yet. Just enough to make my pulse skip.

Then Cole stopped outside one of the storage rooms. I frowned upside down at the door. "Seriously? You're punishing me with inventory?"

Cole grinned. "Worse."

He shoved the door open. The room looked boring. Shelving. Crates. Cleaning supplies. A rolled rug near the back wall.

I blinked. "This is anticlimactic."

Killian walked past us without speaking and crouched near the rug.

And then— He grabbed the edge and yanked it back.

My entire body went still. Because underneath it wasn't concrete flooring.

It was steel. A massive square hatch built flush into the ground. Heavy-duty hinges. Reinforced locking wheel. Industrial. Hidden so perfectly I would never have noticed it in a million years.

"What the fuck," I breathed. Lucas stepped forward and spun the locking mechanism. Metal clunked loudly through the room.

No. No, no, no. I knew this warehouse. I'd memorised this warehouse. I'd found blueprints online weeks ago when paranoia got bored and needed enrichment activities. There was no basement level on those plans.

My pulse spiked violently. "Why is there a murder hatch?"

Jaxon laughed outright. "Murder hatch."

"That is a murder hatch," I insisted. "That is serial killer architecture."

Cole shifted me higher on his shoulder when I started squirming again. "Relax, menace."

"I am actively being carried toward a hidden underground bunker!"

Killian hauled the hatch open. Cold air rushed upward immediately. Darkness below. Concrete stairs descending into black. My stomach dropped straight through the floor.

"...Oh, fuck." The words came out small. Genuine.

Because I knew two things instantly: One — this place was old. Older than the rest of the warehouse. And two — they'd hidden it from me deliberately.

My brain immediately supplied the worst possible options. Torture chamber. Interrogation site. Body disposal room. Secret sex dungeon. Honestly with these men it could've been all four.

"You have got to be kidding me," I whispered.

Killian looked up at me from the bottom edge of the open hatch, expression unreadable. "Still green?"

That question hit harder than expected. Not because he asked. Because he always asked. Even now. Even carrying me toward a literal underground nightmare staircase.

I swallowed hard. "...Green," I muttered. "But if there's a human skeleton down there I'm haunting all of you."

Cole barked out a laugh and started down the stairs.

The deeper we descended, the colder the air became.

Concrete walls. Low lighting flickering on automatically as Lucas hit something on his phone.

The staircase curved once. Then twice. Jesus Christ, how deep was this thing?

"This wasn't on the blueprint," I said quietly.

Lucas glanced back at me. "Correct."

"That's deeply unsettling."

"Also correct."

The final step opened into a massive underground level. And I forgot how to breathe.

Soft amber lighting spilled across polished concrete floors. Dark walls. Massive bed. Steel fixtures gleaming subtly from the ceiling and walls. Cabinets. Leather. Chains. Restraints laid out with terrifying neatness.

Not random. Intentional. Curated.

My brain short-circuited completely. "...Oh my God."

Jaxon rubbed the back of his neck, looking weirdly sheepish suddenly.

"So. Funny story." "This," I said faintly, staring around at the hidden underground dungeon beneath the warehouse I'd been living in for months, "is the exact opposite of a funny story."

My stomach dropped so hard it felt like my organs were trying to evacuate my body.

"Oh, fuck," I whispered.

Cole's grin turned slow and dangerous. "Oh, yes."

Nope. Absolutely fucking not. My brain immediately supplied seventeen worst-case scenarios in under three seconds. Great. Cool. Amazing

I was either about to get murdered, tortured, sacrificed to some underground sex cult, or emotionally manipulated into talking about my feelings, which honestly might've been the worst option of all.

"This," I said carefully as Cole finally set me on my feet, "feels illegal."

Jaxon snorted. "Technically—"

"Wrong answer."

The room stretched around me in dim amber light. Massive bed. Steel fixtures. Chains bolted into concrete. My pulse climbed higher the longer I looked around.

Because this wasn't random. This room existed before me.

My mouth went dry. "What the fuck is this place?"

Killian stepped closer slowly. "A room built for trust."

"Interesting," I said faintly. "Because right now it feels more like a room built for my inevitable Netflix documentary."

Lucas looked suspiciously close to laughing. Bastard.

I took another step backward instinctively. Nobody stopped me. That somehow made it worse. Because suddenly all the panic from the last four days came crashing back in at once.

Too much. Too emotional. Too unstable. Too hard to love. My chest tightened painfully.

"So," I said quickly, voice climbing slightly, "before we continue this deeply concerning tour, are you planning to murder me?"

Cole blinked. "What?"

"Because the hidden basement dungeon vibe is strong."

"Riley—" Jaxon started gently.

"No, seriously. You disappeared for four days, came back emotionally devastatingly attractive, and then dragged me into a secret underground room that wasn't on the blueprints." I pointed accusingly at the floor. "That is serial killer behaviour."

Killian's expression shifted immediately. Concern. Which somehow hurt worse.

"Colour," Lucas said quietly.

I swallowed hard. The question grounded me just enough to breathe.

"...Green," I muttered. "But psychologically? Vibrating."

Cole barked out a laugh. Then Lucas stepped in carefully and reached for my wrists.

"Trust us," he said softly.

Terrible phrase. Horrifying phrase. Absolutely not. But I still let him touch me. Metal clicked around my wrists.

My heart launched directly into my throat. "Oh my God." The chains lifted slowly, drawing my arms above my head until my toes barely brushed the floor. Not painful. Just enough tension to make me feel exposed. Vulnerable. Held.

Panic fluttered violently under my ribs. "Guys."

"Colour?" Killian asked immediately. I squeezed my eyes shut briefly.

Still green. Still safe. Still absolutely losing my fucking mind.

"Green," I whispered. "But what the fuck is happening?"

Cole moved closer, hands sliding slowly up my thighs in a grounding touch instead of restraint. "Punishment," he said lightly. "And maybe intervention."

"That sounds fake."

"Nope."

Jaxon brushed my hair back gently while Lucas adjusted the chain so the pull eased slightly on my shoulders. Small careful movements. Like they were handling something precious.

I hated how much that affected me.

Then Killian crossed the room toward a massive steel cabinet built into the wall. My stomach dropped instantly. "Oh no." Drawer handles. Metal compartments. Storage.

This was it. Knives. Scalpels. Pliers. Car battery. My eyes widened in genuine horror.

"Oh my God, this is where it ends."

Jaxon choked laughing immediately.

"I'm serious!" I snapped. "This is absolutely the point where gangs attach wires to people's nipples and electrocute them while asking questions."

Cole doubled over. "What?"

"I've SEEN IT HAPPEN."

Lucas was openly laughing now, shoulders shaking silently. Traitor. Meanwhile my panic had fully committed to the bit.

"The end is nigh," I informed them grimly. "This is how I die. Glitter-covered in a secret sex basement."

Killian pinched the bridge of his nose. "Baby—"

"No, because honestly?" I continued, spiralling harder. "You guys are nice, but also I would not put it past Killian to own jumper cables."

"That's hurtful," Killian said flatly.

"You literally have a hidden underground dungeon!" "For consensual purposes." "That somehow does not comfort me!"

Then Killian slid the drawer open. I braced for torture implements. Instead my brain completely stopped functioning.

Because it wasn't knives. It was vibrators. Rows of them. Different shapes. Different colours. Sleek silicone lined up with terrifying organisation like some deeply unhinged luxury tech display.

I stared. Then stared harder.

"...What." Jaxon folded over laughing first. Lucas pinched the bridge of his nose like he was trying not to join him. Cole looked unbearably smug.

Meanwhile I was still hanging from the ceiling having a full spiritual crisis.

"This somehow feels worse," I informed them weakly.

"Good," Killian said calmly, selecting one.

"Oh no," I whispered. Then, after one horrible second of realisation: "...Oh yes."

"There she is," Cole grinned.

"I hate all of you."

"No you don't," Jaxon said softly.

The words hit too hard. Too close. My throat tightened immediately.

Because that was the problem, wasn't it?

I didn't hate them. I should. God, I absolutely should. Instead I'd spent four days wrecking the warehouse because I missed them so badly it felt like my ribs were splitting open.

Killian stepped back toward me, calm and devastating. "Tell us the truth, Riley."

Instant panic. "No."

Lucas tilted his head slightly. "You know exactly which truth."

I jerked against the chains once automatically. "Absolutely not."

Cole's grin sharpened. "Princess—"

"Nope." I pointed at all of them as best I could while suspended. "I know what this is."

Jaxon looked delighted. "Do you?"

"This is emotional warfare."

"It's really not," Lucas said.

"It absolutely is! You've chained me up underground and now you're trying to force vulnerability out of me like Batman villains."

Killian stopped directly in front of me. His hand slid slowly around my throat—not squeezing, just holding steady. Grounding. "Riley."

I looked away stubbornly.

"You missed us."

"That proves literally nothing."

"You were scared."

"I was bored."

"You thought we abandoned you."

Silence. God, I hated silence. Because silence meant truth had room to breathe.

Killian's thumb brushed lightly against my jaw. "And now you're terrified we know exactly what this is."

"No, I'm terrified because I'm hanging in a sex dungeon while you hold a vibrator like a supervillain."

Cole made a choking noise laughing. But nobody let the subject go. Jaxon stepped closer, expression softening in a way that made my chest hurt. "Ri."

Nope. Nope nope nope. I shook my head hard immediately. "Don't."

"Why?" Lucas asked quietly.

"Because if I say it out loud," I whispered before I could stop myself, "then it becomes real."

The room went completely still. And that was the first moment they realised this wasn't about stubbornness anymore. It was fear.

Lucas

Riley looked devastating suspended beneath the amber light. Not because she was exposed — she wasn't, not yet. Still fully dressed in combat boots, hoodie hanging half off one shoulder, glitter dusted across black fabric like fallout from one of her catastrophes.

No. It was the contradiction of her that hit me hardest. The way she stood there chained above her head, breathing too fast, panic and trust fighting inside her at the same time. Mouth still sharp enough to cut us all to ribbons while her pulse fluttered wildly beneath Killian's hand. She was terrified. And still green. Still here. Still letting us touch her. That mattered more than anything.

I stepped closer slowly, giving her every opportunity to pull away. My fingers brushed the hem of her hoodie lightly.

"Colour?" I asked quietly.

Her eyes flicked to mine immediately. Suspicious. Breathless. Defiant. "...Green," she muttered. Then, after a pause: "Emotionally? Absolutely not green. But physically green."

Cole snorted behind me.

The corner of my mouth twitched despite myself. "Noted."

I slid my pocket knife free slowly enough she could track every movement. The metallic click echoed softly through the underground room.

Riley froze instantly. "Oh my God."

"Easy," I said calmly.

"You pulled out a knife in the sex basement, Lucas. You have to understand how alarming that is."

"It's for your clothes."

"That somehow is not better."

Jaxon laughed outright at that.

I ignored him, eyes staying on Riley's face instead. Always her face first. Her breathing. Her pupils. The tension in her shoulders. No fear response beyond nerves. No shutdown. No dissociation. Just Riley spiralling theatrically because she didn't know how else to survive vulnerability.

My hand settled lightly against her hip. "Still green?"

She swallowed hard. Looked at the knife. Looked at me.

Then nodded once. "Green." Only then did I move.

The blade slid beneath the fabric of her hoodie near the collar. Careful. Precise. I cut downward slowly while she sucked in a sharp breath. Not from fear. From anticipation.

The fabric loosened gradually beneath the knife, falling open inch by inch. Her breathing turned uneven while I peeled the ruined hoodie away from her shoulders and let it drop to the floor.

Cole groaned softly somewhere behind me.

Jaxon muttered, "Jesus Christ."

Killian stayed silent. Which somehow felt louder.

Riley rolled her eyes immediately despite the flush climbing her throat. "You're all being weird."

"You're gorgeous," Cole corrected.

That hit her harder than the restraints had. I saw it instantly in the flicker behind her eyes. Deflection. Panic. Feeling too much. So I grounded her before she could spiral again.

My fingers brushed her waist lightly. "Stay with me."

Her gaze snapped back to mine. There she was.

I hooked the knife beneath the waistband of her cargo pants next, slicing carefully through the fabric instead of fighting the buckles and straps. The sound of tearing material filled the room slowly while her chest rose and fell faster with every inch of skin revealed.

Not naked. Not vulnerable because of exposure. Vulnerable because she was letting us see her at all.

The cargo pants loosened and slipped down her legs until all that remained was black underwear and her boots.

Riley looked down at herself. Then up at me.

"This," she informed me shakily, "feels aggressively symbolic."

Jaxon nearly choked laughing.

I stepped closer again until I could lower my voice just for her. "Nothing happens unless you want it to."

Her throat worked hard. "You say that," she whispered, "but all four of you are looking at me like starving men at an all-you-can-eat buffet."

Cole pointed immediately. "In fairness, accurate."

"Cole," Killian warned.

"What? I'm being emotionally honest."

Riley barked out one startled laugh before catching herself. Like she'd forgotten she was allowed to laugh here.

I reached up carefully and brushed glitter from her cheek with my thumb.

"Still green?"

This time her answer came quieter. Smaller. More real. "...Yeah."

And that was when I knew the chains weren't what scared her most. It was the fact she trusted us enough to stay.

Riley

I was still hanging there in my underwear, wrists suspended above my head, trying very hard to pretend my entire nervous system wasn't short-circuiting.

Which was difficult.

Because Lucas had cut my clothes off with surgical precision while maintaining eye contact like some terrifyingly gentle psychopath, and now all four of them were staring at me like I was the centre of gravity.

My pulse was everywhere. Panic. Adrenaline. Want. Humiliation. God.

Killian stepped in front of me slowly, dark eyes dragging over every exposed inch of skin before settling back on my face. Always my face first.

That somehow made it worse.

His fingers curled beneath my jaw, tilting my head back slightly. "You know why you're down here?"

I snorted immediately. "Because apparently all rich emotionally unavailable men eventually build underground BDSM lairs?"

Cole lost his shit laughing behind him.

Killian's mouth twitched once. Barely. "Brat."

"Correct."

His thumb brushed slowly across my lower lip. "Your punishment isn't physical."

"Good," I muttered. "Because honestly I bruise like a Victorian orphan with tuberculosis."

Jaxon wheezed. Lucas actually looked away to hide a smile.

But Killian stayed locked on me, steady and devastating.

"No," he said quietly. "Your punishment is honesty."

Immediate horror.

"Oh, absolutely the fuck not."

Cole folded his arms. "There she is."

I glared at all of them. "No. Nope. Negative. Hard pass. I reject the premise."

Killian ignored me entirely. "You spent four days tearing the warehouse apart because you thought we abandoned you."

"I was decorating."

"You hacked my server."

"Artistically."

"You missed us."

"That proves nothing."

Jaxon grinned. "Baby, you literally built a knife shrine."

"It had structure."

Killian stepped closer until I could feel his heat against my skin. "And now you're terrified because you know exactly what this is."

"No," I lied instantly. "I'm terrified because I'm chained up in my underwear while you all stare at me like emotionally repressed wolves."

Cole pointed. "That's fair actually."

Killian's hand slid slowly down my throat, not squeezing, just holding. Grounding. Possessive in a way that made my stomach twist hard.

"Say it."

I stared at him blankly. "Say what?"

His expression went dangerously calm. "That you love us."

I barked out a startled laugh so sharp it almost hurt. "Oh, fuck off."

Dark satisfaction flashed across his face immediately. Like he'd been expecting that answer.

"There's the problem," he murmured.

"I am not having this conversation while suspended from your sex ceiling."

"Why?" Lucas asked quietly from behind me. "Because you don't love us?"

My throat tightened violently.

"No," I snapped too quickly.

Silence. Shit. Cole's grin turned smug instantly. Jaxon outright looked delighted. Traitors.

Killian leaned closer, voice dropping low enough to slide straight under my skin. "Liar."

My pulse jumped traitorously. "You can't prove anything."

"Don't need to."

Then he reached beside me calmly. And the vibrator in his hand clicked on. Bzzzzzz.

My entire body jerked instinctively. "Oh no."

Cole groaned softly. "Oh, she felt that one."

Killian's eyes never left mine while the soft hum filled the underground room. Calm. Steady. Completely in control.

Meanwhile I was one heartbeat away from spontaneous combustion. "This," I informed him breathlessly, "feels manipulative."

"It is."

"At least he's honest," Jaxon offered helpfully.

Killian lifted the vibrator slowly, the sound alone enough to send heat rushing through me embarrassingly fast.

"Here's what's going to happen, Riley." His voice was velvet wrapped around a threat. "We are going to stay right here with you until you stop hiding."

My stomach flipped hard. "Nope."

"You are going to tell us the truth."

"Absolutely not."

"And every time you lie"—the vibrator brushed lightly against my inner thigh, not enough, nowhere near enough—"I'm going to make it harder for you to remember why you're fighting us in the first place."

My breath caught violently. "Oh, fuck you."

His smile turned dark and devastating. "That," Killian said softly as the vibrator hummed closer again, "can also be arranged."

My stomach dropped. My pulse spiked. "Oh, fuck," I whispered. Cole chuckled dark. "Oh, yes."

They began to circle. Predators. Judges. Lovers. Gods.

The air itself felt heavier with them surrounding me, all heat and control and devastating focus. My pulse hammered harder with every slow step they took closer.

Oh, fuck.

Killian's palm settled against my throat, steady and possessive, his voice a storm rumbling low against my spine.

"Time for your punishment."

The first sting landed sharp enough to make me jolt.

The second burned hotter. Then came their hands. Their mouths. Their attention. Too much of it.

Lucas stepped forward with the knife still in his hand, calm and precise as ever. The blade caught the amber light as he hooked it carefully beneath the last pieces of fabric still covering me.

"Still green?" he asked quietly.

My throat worked hard. "Yeah."

The knife slid through the material with terrifying ease. Not rough. Not rushed. Controlled. Every movement deliberate enough to make my breathing uneven.

The final pieces fell away. A sharp breath left me instantly.

The cool air hit my bare skin, but it wasn't the temperature making me shiver.

It was them. Four pairs of eyes on me all at once. The room went quiet. Not awkward. Not hesitant. Predatory. For one suspended moment, nobody touched me at all.

They just looked. And somehow that was worse.

Heat rushed violently beneath my skin under the weight of their attention. My nipples tightened helplessly, every nerve in my body suddenly awake and oversensitive beneath the amber light.

I hated how quickly my body betrayed me.

How obvious it was.

The chains rattled softly overhead as another involuntary tremor rolled through me.

Cole's eyes darkened immediately at the reaction, his jaw tightening once like he physically felt it.

Jaxon looked openly fascinated now, gaze dragging lower before returning to my face with devastating focus.

Lucas looked the most dangerous somehow — calm, controlled, watching every tiny response my body gave away without permission.

And Killian— Killian stayed behind me with one hand at my throat, silent enough that I could hear my own breathing growing thinner, rougher.

The room felt smaller suddenly. Hotter. Like all the oxygen had burned away. Lucas crouched slowly in front of me, setting the knife aside before his hands slid carefully along my thighs. Not greedy. Careful.

Like he knew exactly how close I already was to completely losing my mind. His gaze flicked upward once, checking me again before he bent his head and pressed a soft kiss against the scarred initial on my thigh.

The contact hit like lightning. A violent shiver rolled through me instantly, my thighs twitching beneath his hands while my head tipped back on instinct.

"Oh my God," I breathed.

My body reacted before my pride could stop it. Every slow touch. Every look. Every quiet breath against my skin sent heat curling lower in sharp, humiliating waves. The worst part?

They noticed all of it. The way my breathing kept catching. The way my thighs trembled harder every time one of them stepped closer. The way my body leaned toward them instead of away.

Killian's thumb brushed slowly against my throat, grounding me before I could spiral completely. "You're shaking," he murmured.

"No shit." But my voice came out thinner than I wanted. Breathless.

The corner of Cole's mouth twitched slightly at that. Not mocking. Knowing.

Lucas rose slowly to his feet again, eyes steady on mine. "Do you want us to stop?"

The terrifying part?

The answer rising in my chest was immediate. No. Not because I wasn't scared. I was.

But because underneath the panic, underneath the vulnerability, underneath the unbearable awareness of being completely exposed—My body wanted them anyway. Wanted the heat of their hands. Wanted the attention. Wanted them closer.

The realization hit hard enough to steal my breath.

And judging by the look that passed silently between all four of them— They knew it too.

Which was horrifying. Because now they knew exactly how to unravel me.

Cole's mouth found my nipple nipping and sucking hard enough to pull a helpless cry from me, his hands gripping my hips like he was anchoring himself there. Heat curled violently through me where his hands held me, every rough touch dragging another helpless reaction out of my body. My skin felt too sensitive, every nerve ending awake and sparking beneath them while my breathing turned thin and uneven. The chains rattled softly overhead as another tremor rolled through me, my thighs shaking hard enough I could barely stay upright anymore.

Jaxon stayed between my legs, devastatingly patient, every touch deliberate enough to make my entire body shake with frustration.

This was how I died. God, I was so close.

Every nerve in my body felt lit alive beneath his attention, my thighs trembling harder every time he dragged me toward the edge only to hold me there. Cruel. Precise. Intentional.

A broken sound caught in my throat as pressure coiled tighter and tighter inside me.

Then— Just as release started crashing toward me, he shifted. His mouth dragged upward slowly before he sucked hard enough to rip a cry out of me, my hips jerking violently against the restraints.

For one perfect, devastating second, my entire body folded toward him on instinct.

And then he pulled away. Actually pulled away.

I stared down at him in genuine horror while he calmly pressed a soft kiss against my thigh instead.

"Oh, you absolute asshole," I breathed shakily.

Jaxon grinned against my skin, completely unrepentant. "There she is."

Jaxon stayed between my legs, devastatingly patient, every touch deliberate enough to make my entire body shake with frustration.

This was how I died.

God, I was so close.

Every nerve in my body felt lit alive beneath his attention, on my core, my thighs trembling harder every time he dragged me toward the edge only to hold me there. Cruel. Precise. Intentional.

A broken sound caught in my throat as pressure coiled tighter and tighter inside me.

Then—Just as release started crashing toward me, he shifted.

His mouth dragged upward slowly before he sucked my clit hard enough to rip a cry out of me, my hips jerking violently against the restraints.

For one perfect, devastating second, my entire body folded toward him on instinct.

And then he pulled away.

Actually pulled away.

I stared down at him in genuine horror while he calmly pressed a soft kiss against my thigh instead.

"Oh, you absolute asshole," I breathed shakily.

Jaxon grinned against my skin, completely unrepentant. "There she is."

The tension dragged tighter and tighter inside me until it felt unbearable, every slow movement keeping me balanced right on the edge of losing control completely. My breathing turned ragged, uneven sounds catching in my throat no matter how hard I tried to swallow them down. The worst part was how deliberate they were about it — like they knew exactly how wrecked I already was and planned on dragging it out anyway.

Lucas traced the cold edge of the knife lightly along my ribs, precise and careful, the sensation sharp enough to keep my pulse sprinting.

My entire body reacted instantly.

The cold glide of the blade should have terrified me. Probably would have terrified a normal person. Instead, heat twisted low in my stomach so sharply it almost made me dizzy. Fear and desire tangled together until I genuinely couldn't tell where one ended and the other began.

A shaky breath left me as my back arched instinctively, the chains overhead rattling softly while goosebumps erupted across my skin.

"Oh, that's deeply concerning," I whispered weakly to absolutely nobody.

Lucas's eyes darkened slightly, like he'd heard every panicked little thought anyway.

Killian held me from behind with one hand at my throat, grounding me while the other kept me balanced on the edge of completely falling apart. The low hum of the vibrator rested exactly where it ruined me most, held there with terrifying precision while my entire body shook around it.

Every pulse sent another violent tremor through me, my knees threatening to give out completely as heat coiled tighter and tighter beneath my skin.

Killian's mouth brushed my ear, calm and devastatingly controlled compared to the absolute war happening inside my body.

"There you are," he murmured softly.

Like he was watching me unravel in real time.

Like he knew exactly how close I already was to breaking.

His grip tightened slightly at my throat as he leaned closer, the heat of his chest pressed solid against my back while the relentless hum between my legs kept dragging broken sounds out of me.

I could feel every steady breath he took. Every controlled movement. Every tiny shift of his hand that sent another wave of sensation crashing through my body.

Meanwhile the others closed in around me again — hands against my thighs, mouths against my skin, praise and taunting murmured low enough to blur together into pure overload.

The room felt smaller. Hotter.

Like I was being surrounded from every direction until there was nowhere left to run except straight through them. Too many sensations. Too much heat. Too much of them.

"Tell us," Killian rasped against my ear.

My breathing fractured instantly.

My thoughts stopped making sense somewhere around the point my body started shaking hard enough to rattle the chains overhead.

Everything felt too sharp. Too hot. Too much.

The room blurred around the edges while sensation crashed over me faster than I could process it — hands, mouths, praise, pressure, the relentless hum keeping me balanced on the edge of completely losing control.

I couldn't think properly anymore. Could barely breathe properly. Every nerve ending in my body felt lit alive beneath them, my mind flickering uselessly between panic and desperate want.

God, this was bad. This was so bad.

Because somewhere underneath the overwhelming heat and the chaos in my bloodstream was a far more dangerous realization:

I trusted them. Completely. Enough to unravel like this in their hands.

Enough to let them see every ugly, needy, vulnerable piece of me I usually kept buried beneath sarcasm and violence and running away first.

And that realization hit harder than any touch possibly could.

The room blurred around the edges as their attention closed in on me from every direction, overwhelming and impossible to escape.

Every touch dragged another reaction out of me.

Every breath against my skin made my body betray me harder.

My thighs were shaking uncontrollably now, every muscle in my body tightening and trembling beneath their hands. The chains overhead rattled softly every time another wave of sensation hit me, my head falling back as helpless sounds kept slipping out no matter how hard I tried to swallow them down.

I couldn't stop reacting to them.

Couldn't stop my body arching toward every touch instead of away from it.

Heat coiled tighter and tighter inside me until it felt unbearable, my pulse thundering so violently I could barely hear over it anymore.

I was trembling openly now, chains rattling softly overhead while panic and want tangled together so tightly I couldn't separate them anymore.

"You already know," I whispered weakly.

"No," Lucas said calmly. "We need to hear you say it."

Jaxon laughed softly against my skin, like he already knew exactly how close I was to breaking.

Cole's hands slid over my waist, holding me steady while his mouth found my throat again, rough enough to leave me shaking harder. Lucas pressed closer at my side, grounding me every time my knees threatened to give out completely, while Jaxon kept murmuring praise that only made my pulse spiral faster.

And Killian— Killian stayed behind me like the centre of the storm, calm and devastating while the others slowly unraveled me piece by piece.

Cole kissed me again, rough enough to steal the rest of my thoughts. The pressure inside me wound tighter and tighter until it felt impossible to survive it, every touch dragging me closer to the edge while they surrounded me completely — hands against my skin, mouths against my throat, voices in my ears, nowhere left to run from any of them.

I was drowning in them. In the heat. In the want. In the terrifying realization that I didn't actually want to escape.

And Killian— Killian kept holding me steady while they slowly, relentlessly tore down every wall I had left.

My body convulsed beneath their hands, overwhelmed and desperate and completely undone.

The pressure inside my chest snapped first. Then everything else followed.

The release hit so hard it stole the air straight out of my lungs, my entire body shaking violently while broken sounds tore out of me faster than I could stop them. Tears burned hot at the corners of my eyes from pure overload, my forehead falling forward as every nerve in my body lit alive beneath them.

"My head—" I gasped shakily. "Oh my God—"

But even then, even completely overwhelmed, my body kept leaning toward them instead of away.

And that was what finally destroyed me.

"I love you," I gasped out finally, wrecked and shaking. "I love all of you, okay?"

The room went completely still.

Like the entire world had stopped breathing with me.

Jaxon

Riley looked like she'd just survived a natural disaster.

Still suspended between us, breathing hard, trembling so badly the chains overhead rattled softly every few seconds. Her face was flushed crimson, eyes glassy and unfocused while she tried — and failed — to pull herself back together with sheer stubbornness alone.

And holy shit. I couldn't stop staring at her. Not because she looked wrecked. Because she looked real.

Every wall she normally hid behind had cracked wide open for one terrifying, beautiful second.

The sarcasm was still there — barely. The attitude too.

But underneath it?

God. She'd trusted us enough to completely lose control in front of us.

I'd never seen anything like it.

Cole looked openly smug about the whole thing, hands still locked possessively on her hips like he thought she might vanish if he let go.

Lucas stayed calmer, but I caught the way his eyes tracked every tiny reaction Riley made — checking her breathing, her pulse, the tension still trembling through her body.

And Killian—Jesus Christ. Killian looked like a man staring at something sacred.

One hand still wrapped around her throat gently, grounding instead of controlling now while Riley struggled to catch her breath.

Her knees nearly buckled again. All four of us moved instinctively.

That hit me harder than it should have. No hesitation. No thought. Just hers.

Riley let out one weak, horrified noise. "Oh my God."

I lost it immediately, laughing breathlessly while she glared at me through completely ruined eyes.

"Don't you dare laugh at me," she rasped.

"Baby, you short-circuited."

"I did not."

"You absolutely did."

Cole grinned against her shoulder. "Pretty sure I watched her leave her body for a minute there."

"I hate every single one of you."

The words would've landed harder if she hadn't leaned toward Killian's touch while saying them.

She realized it about half a second later too.

The look of betrayal on her face nearly killed me.

"Oh, that's devastating for you," I said sympathetically.

"Jaxon."

"Ri."

"That tone makes me want to commit crimes."

"You already committed crimes. Lucas had to rebuild his security system."

Lucas spoke calmly without looking away from her. "Again."

Riley looked genuinely offended. "You're acting like I'm the villain here."

"You turned my protein powder into glitter."

"You looked magical."

I barked out another laugh before I could stop it, but it faded fast when I looked at her again.

Because underneath the chaos and smart mouth, she still looked overwhelmed.

Not scared.

Just... emotionally exposed in a way I don't think she knew how to survive yet.

Her eyes flicked between all of us uncertainly, like she still couldn't fully process the fact we were here.

Still touching her. Still looking at her like she hung the damn moon.

And then it hit me all over again: She thought we'd leave. Jesus. Something sharp twisted painfully in my chest.

I stepped closer slowly until she finally looked at me properly. "There she is," I murmured softly.

Her expression cracked immediately at the words. Not fully. Just enough for me to see the panic underneath.

The fear. Like she still expected this to disappear if she relaxed for even one second.

My hand slid carefully against her jaw. "You with us?"

Her throat worked hard before she nodded once. "Unfortunately," she whispered weakly.

That tiny broken attempt at humor damn near ruined me. I leaned forward and pressed my forehead gently against hers for one quiet second.

And in that moment — with Riley shaking between all of us, overwhelmed and stubborn and finally letting herself be held — I was completely fucking awestruck by her.

Riley

Riley

I was still trying to recover enough brain function to form coherent thoughts.

Which was difficult when my entire body felt like static.

My wrists hung limp in the restraints overhead, chest heaving while I fought to remember how breathing worked. Every nerve ending still felt oversensitive, my skin burning everywhere they'd touched me.

Surely that was it.

Surely the punishment was over.

I'd confessed.

Humiliated myself emotionally.

Had what felt suspiciously like a near-death experience courtesy of one vibrator and four emotionally repressed psychopaths.

We were done here.

Right?

I swallowed hard, trying to regain what little dignity I had left.

"I just want everyone to know," I rasped weakly, "that I handled that incredibly bravely."

Jaxon barked out a laugh immediately.

Cole looked downright delighted.

Lucas was still watching me with that terrifyingly calm expression that suggested he'd memorised every single reaction my body had betrayed me with.

And Killian—

Killian still had one hand resting lightly against my throat like he didn't entirely trust me not to disappear if he let go.

My pulse skipped stupidly at that realization.

Dangerous.

Very dangerous.

I exhaled shakily. "Okay. Great. Lovely emotional trauma bonding session. We can all go upstairs now."

Nobody moved.

The silence hit first.

Then Cole smiled.

Oh no.

Not his normal grin.

This one was slower. Rougher. The kind that usually preceded catastrophic life choices.

"...Why are you looking at me like that?" I asked cautiously.

Cole stepped forward.

Once.

Twice.

My stomach dropped lower with every step.

Because there was something different about him now — heavier somehow. More focused. His gaze dragged over me slowly enough to make heat curl violently through my stomach all over again.

Absolutely not.

I was already emotionally deceased.

"Cole," I warned weakly.

"Yeah, princess?"

The pet name hit harder than it should have.

I narrowed my eyes suspiciously.

Then my gaze dropped.

Oh.

Oh, fuck.

The very noticeable situation happening beneath his pants hit me all at once and my brain immediately blue-screened.

"You have got to be kidding me," I whispered in horror.

Jaxon actually folded over laughing.

Lucas looked away briefly like he was trying not to smile.

And Killian—

Killian's mouth twitched once against my throat.

Traitor.

I looked back at Cole slowly. "Absolutely not."

His eyebrows lifted innocently. "Not what?"

"You know exactly what."

"Do I?"

"Yes! Your entire—" I gestured vaguely downward while still hanging from the ceiling. "Situation."

Cole glanced down lazily before looking back up at me completely unapologetic.

"Oh. Yeah. That."

"That?" I repeated faintly. "That is not a that, Cole. That is a full-scale tactical problem."

Jaxon was openly wheezing now.

"I'm serious!" I snapped. "I just psychologically collapsed in front of all of you. My body can't survive another group activity."

Cole stepped closer anyway, grin darkening when another involuntary shiver rolled through me.

And the worst part?

My body reacted instantly.

Traitorously.

Heat curled low in my stomach again despite my very reasonable desire to pass away peacefully instead.

Cole noticed immediately.

Of course he did.

"There she is," he murmured softly.

"I hate this place."

"No you don't."

Unfortunately for me?

That was becoming significantly harder to argue with.

Cole was first inside me—thick, relentless, his Jacob's Ladder dragging sparks along every nerve.

Killian slid behind me, one hand in my hair, the other pushing lower, lower, until his fingers pressed against the last place I thought I could keep safe.

The stretch burned, pleasure tangled with despair.

Jaxon watched, grin feral. "Look at her. She loves it. She fucking needs it." Lucas pinned me with a surgeon's calm, brushing his hand over my cheek.

My pride wanted silence. My body betrayed me. Cole's piercing tormented me inside, Killian's fingers claimed me behind, Jaxon whispered filth, Lucas held me steady. Cole kissed me like he'd devour me whole. "Mine," he growled. Killian's lips grazed my ear. "Ours. Forever."

Jaxon's teeth grazed my jaw, breathless laughter breaking. "You'll never get away from us Riley." Lucas pressed his forehead to mine, whispering like a vow. "Always."

Surrounded. Owned. Loved. And in that moment—wrecked, filled, trembling—I had never been more theirs. Or more myself.

Killian

She thought she could hide. But when she said it—I love you, all of you—it cut through me like a blade. Final. Binding.

Cole drove her until she screamed. Jaxon forced truth past her lips. Lucas carved her open with precision.

And I claimed the places no one else dared. My teeth. My voice. My cock buried deep in the darkest part of her.

Her tears streaked down her face, her body convulsing with another climax she couldn't control.

And even broken, wrecked, trembling—she looked at me like I was the only thing holding her together.

Good. I was.

When the frenzy slowed, I pressed my mouth to her temple. "Look at me." Her glassy eyes lifted. Wrecked. Beautiful. Bound.

"You'll never run from us again," I told her, steady as a vow. "You belong here. To me. To them. Body, heart, soul." My hand curved over her throat—not to choke this time, but to feel the pulse that now beat for us.

"You said you love us. That means you're ours. Forever."

Cole

She trembled around my cock, milking me like she was made for it. And maybe she was. Her words still echoed: I love you—all of you. I bit her shoulder hard, branding her.

"Your mine," I growled, voice breaking. "Your mine say it." "I'm yours, Cole," she sobbed, raw.

That was it. I spilled inside her, owning her in the only way I knew how.

Jaxon

Her throat was stretched tight around me, her eyes wet and glassy, and still she'd confessed.

I fisted her hair tighter. "You love us? Prove it. Take every inch."

She whimpered, gagged, clung harder. Nails in my thighs.

Not pushing away—holding on. , watched her swallow my cock like the perfect filthy girl she was. "Ours," I rasped. "Every broken piece. And I'll kill anyone who says otherwise."

Lucas

Precision. Control. That's my world. But Riley destroyed all of it.

She was open beneath me, my fingers still stroking the place that made her body seize.

She gave me everything—no walls, no shields. Just Riley. Raw. Mine.

"You carved yourself into me the day you let me bleed for you," I whispered, pressing my palm to her scar. "Now I carve myself into you again. Forever." She broke apart on my fingers, sobbing her love into my mouth.

Killian

They'd each claimed her. Marked her. Filled her. And still she shook—not with fear, but from the weight of us. I thrust deeper, stretching her until her scream cracked the air.

My hand locked around her throat, my mouth to her ear. "Say it again."

"I love you. All of you. Please—" That was it. The last wall gone.

We fed on her together, predators at the kill, every thrust binding her tighter to us.

Until there was no Riley without us. No us without her.

Riley

I couldn't move. Couldn't breathe without their weight pressing me down. My body was wrecked—shaking, overused, undone. But my heart? My heart was on fire. Cole sprawled over me, still pulsing inside, kissing me punishing, then tender. "Mine," he whispered, rough breaking soft. "Not just to ruin. You belong to me, princess. I love you."

Jaxon's laughter was gone. He hooked my chin, eyes blazing. "You're not running, Ri. Not from me." His teeth sank into my throat, marking me. Then softer: "I love you, brat. So much I'd burn the world to keep you smiling."

Lucas traced my scar, lips reverent. "I marked you once. But this—this is bigger. You gave me your heart tonight. I love you. Every jagged piece."

And Killian, inevitable as a storm. He cupped my face, eyes burning. "You're ours. Not pieces. Not halves. Every breath, every smile. I love you. Forever." Four voices. Four vows. Four chains I didn't want to fight.

My tears spilled—not breaking, but healing. Their hands anchored me. Cole across my chest. Jaxon's thumb on my pulse. Lucas's lips on my scar. Killian's breath steady on my mouth. I wasn't alone. I'd never be alone again. "I love you," I whispered—not with fear this time, but with truth. With surrender. The air snapped, charged with their growls and broken groans wrapping me like vows etched into bone.

I was theirs. They were mine. Not just for tonight. Not until I ran again. Forever.

60

A soft place to land

Killian

To Be Loved – Sufjan Stevens

She was limp in my arms, her head tucked into my shoulder, breaths shallow and uneven. Not from fear—never from fear—but from sheer exhaustion.

We'd taken her past the edge, stripped her down to raw truth, until there'd been nothing left between us except honesty and need and the terrifying depth of what we all felt for her.

Now she was ours. Completely. I adjusted my grip, one arm beneath her knees, the other wrapped around her back, holding her carefully as I carried her upstairs. Like she was something precious.

Because she was.

Her skin was damp beneath my hands, her body loose and trembling faintly with aftershocks. Every now and then she made these tiny exhausted sounds against my throat that hit somewhere brutal inside my chest.

The others didn't need instructions. Cole was already in the bathroom turning on the taps, steam beginning to curl into the hallway. Lucas lit candles beside the bath with methodical precision because apparently emotional devastation now required ambience. Jaxon disappeared long enough to return with towels piled in his arms.

No one spoke. We didn't need to. Every movement said it clearly enough.

She's ours. We keep her safe. We take care of her now.

I stepped into the bathroom and lowered her carefully into the hot water.

Riley let out a quiet, wrecked sound the second the heat touched her skin, her head falling back against the edge of the tub.

Something inside me tightened painfully at the sound.

Cole moved in first, kneeling beside the bath while he wet a cloth and ran it slowly over her shoulders, cleaning away sweat and glitter and the remnants of chaos.

Lucas settled behind her, fingers sliding gently through her hair as he rinsed shampoo through the strands with slow, grounding movements.

And Jaxon— Jaxon dropped beside the tub near her feet, rubbing lazy circles into her calf beneath the water while staring at her like she'd personally rearranged his entire understanding of the universe.

"You alive there, brat?" he asked softly.

One of her eyes cracked open. "Unfortunately."

"There she is," he murmured immediately, relief flickering openly across his face.

Riley groaned weakly and covered her face with one hand. "I emotionally confessed in a sex dungeon. I can literally never look any of you in the eye again."

Cole barked out a laugh. Lucas actually smiled faintly into her hair. But Jaxon just stared at her for a second longer, something quieter and more devastating moving behind his expression.

Because she still didn't understand. Didn't understand that the terrifying thing wasn't her confession. It was how completely ruined we all were for her.

Jaxon leaned his forearms against the edge of the bath, eyes fixed on her. "Ri." Her gaze flicked toward him cautiously.

"You never have to earn this," he said quietly. "Any of it."

The teasing disappeared from her face instantly. And there it was again—that tiny fracture beneath her ribs every time one of us cared about her too openly. Like she was still waiting for the conditions attached. Waiting for the moment love turned temporary.

Something vicious moved through me at the sight of it.

Jaxon reached up and brushed wet hair back from her forehead carefully. "You scared the shit out of us too, you know."

Riley blinked slowly. "By redecorating?"

"By spiralling alone for four days while we were gone." His voice softened further. "Coming home to this place looking like a glitter bomb crime scene wasn't exactly comforting."

"That was one time," she mumbled.

"It was never one time," Lucas said calmly from behind her.

Riley slid lower into the water with a mortified groan. "I hate this family."

"Liar," Cole said instantly.

But this time when she looked at us—really looked at us—something softer cracked open in her expression.

Not fear. Not panic. Wonder. Like she still couldn't fully believe we were here.

Still touching her gently. Still looking at her like she hung the damn moon.

Lucas rinsed the last of the shampoo from her hair carefully before wrapping a towel around her shoulders the second she started shivering.

Cole pressed a kiss against the top of her damp head without a word.

Jaxon stayed close enough that his knee kept bumping lightly against the side of the tub like he physically couldn't help reaching for her.

And me?

I watched all of it while something dark and absolute settled deeper into my chest.

Because this—her exhausted in our hands, safe between us, finally letting herself be cared for—felt dangerously close to holy.

Riley's eyes drifted shut briefly beneath Lucas's touch.

"You're thinking too hard again," Cole murmured.

"I'm literally naked in a bathtub having an emotional crisis," she mumbled weakly. "Let me process."

Jaxon snorted. "Fair."

Her lashes fluttered open again, gaze moving between all four of us slowly.

And I saw the exact moment it hit her. We weren't leaving. Not after tonight. Not after her confession. Not after this.

The realisation cracked something open inside her so suddenly her breathing caught.

I stepped forward then, crouching beside the tub until she looked at me fully.

"You're ours," I said quietly.

Not ownership. Not possession. A promise.

Something in her expression shattered completely at that. Not in pain. In relief. Her eyes burned instantly.

Cole's hand tightened gently around her shoulder. Lucas pressed a kiss against her temple.

Jaxon leaned closer, forehead brushing hers for one quiet second before he whispered, "You're stuck with us now, menace."

A watery laugh broke out of her despite herself. And God. That sound alone would've been enough to kill for.

By the time we lifted her from the bath, she looked half-asleep already.

Lucas wrapped her carefully in towels while Cole dried her arms and shoulders with impossible gentleness.

Jaxon kept making quiet jokes under his breath just to keep her smiling weakly between blinks.

And when I finally lifted her back into my arms, she went willingly this time. No walls. No fight. Just exhaustion and trust.

Her head dropped against my shoulder immediately as I carried her toward the bedroom.

The hall blurred past in silence. By the time I lowered her onto the mattress, her eyes were barely open. Cole pulled the blankets over her carefully. Lucas brushed hair back from her face.

Jaxon caught her hand beneath the blankets and held it there loosely like he needed the contact as much as she did.

I leaned down last, pressing my mouth softly against her forehead.

"Sleep, little one," I murmured against her skin. "We've got you."

Her fingers tightened weakly around Jaxon's.

And just before sleep finally dragged her under completely, she whispered something so quiet I almost missed it.

"...don't leave." Silence filled the room instantly.

Then Cole climbed into bed beside her without hesitation. Lucas followed.

Jaxon muttered, "Not a fucking chance," under his breath while settling against her other side.

And I slid in behind her last, pulling her back against my chest while the others gathered close.

Surrounded. Protected. Kept.

Riley exhaled softly in her sleep, tension finally leaving her body completely for the first time since we'd returned.

And holding her there in the dark, with all of them wrapped around her too— I realized none of us were ever walking away from this again.

61

Hold It Together (Or Else)

Jaxon

Graveyard Whistling – Nothing But Thieves

In hindsight... yeah. It was a lot. Too much? No. But it was everything.

I sat on the edge of her bed, watching her breathe — slow, deep, steady. Finally still. Riley. Our hurricane wrapped in leather, glitter, and sharp edges. Our chaos incarnate. Our girl. We'd pushed her tonight. Not just physically. Not just until her body gave out. We'd pushed her heart. Her trust. Past the point she usually bolts. And she let us.

That's the part that destroys me. She let us. Not just with her body — though, fuck, that was a gift in itself — but with the pieces of her no one gets to see. The softness. The fear. The need she pretends isn't there. She handed it over like a live grenade. And we didn't drop it.

I can still hear her voice when she broke. "Please." Small. Raw. Real. It wasn't surrender — it was faith. And after... the silence. The panic flickering behind her eyes. Like she'd just stepped off a battlefield and couldn't tell if she'd won or lost. Killian caught it first — he always does.

That tiny stutter in her breath. The tremor in her fingers. Cole's hands were already smoothing down her skin, slow and steady, like he could iron out the doubt. Lucas leaned in and murmured something soft against her ear. I didn't hear the words, but I saw the way her jaw unclenched. Me? I just knelt there and took her hand. Because sometimes words aren't big enough.

What do you even say to someone who's just given you the most fragile part of themselves and trusted you not to break it? You say thank you. You say I've got you. You say it again tomorrow. And the day after that. Until it sticks. Because this wasn't just about sex. It never is with her. Riley gives like it's war. Loves like it's a battlefield. Trusts like it's a goddamn suicide mission.

And us? We'll keep earning it. Every fucking day. I might be the reckless one, the clown, the man who laughs at danger just to see if it laughs back — but for her? I'd burn the whole world down just to keep the shadows out of her head. She could slam those walls back up tomorrow. Hell, she probably will. But until then, I'll be here. Hands open. Heart bare. Ready to catch her, every time she lets herself fall.

Riley

The sun barely crept past the heavy curtains when I stirred. My body ached — deep, pleasant, and exhausting.

Bruised in ways that weren't all physical. For a few seconds, I let myself sink into the tangle of them around me.

Killian behind me, solid as stone, breathing slow and steady. Lucas's arm looped snug around my waist, his face buried in my hair like he belonged there. Cole draped across my legs like he *wasn't* a six-foot wall of muscle. And Jaxon curled up in front of me, his fingers still tangled with mine like he was afraid I'd vanish if he let go.

It was warm. Too warm. Comforting. Suffocating. Terrifying.

Because I knew this could end at any second — maybe by their choice, maybe by mine. I could shove them off, throw up my walls, and pretend this never happened. Pretend last night never happened.

But last night *did* happen. I let all four of them take me. Fully. Brutally. Tenderly. And it wasn't just my body they had. They'd gotten the pieces I keep locked down. The part of me that wants. The part that hopes. The part that's stupid enough to believe in "ours."

I told myself it was just sex. Just release. Just scratching an itch. But if that were true, my chest wouldn't feel this tight.

Then Killian shifted behind me. His hand tightened on my waist, pulling me flush against him, breath warm against my ear. "You're awake," he murmured. Lucas's fingers traced my thigh. Jaxon pressed a lazy kiss to my collarbone. Cole's low growl vibrated against my calf.

"You're not going anywhere yet, princess," Cole muttered. And just like that, the heat drowned out the fear.

Round two wasn't violent like last night. It was worse. Slower. Deliberate. Intimate. Like they were carving their claim into me with every touch. Killian's steady rhythm. Lucas's whispered praise. Cole's mouth mapping me like he needed to memorise every inch. Jaxon's grip, unshakable, tethering me when I wanted to drift.

Every orgasm felt like a confession I didn't want to make.

When it ended, I lay wrecked and wrapped in them — and that's when the panic crept back in. Because if I believed this was more than lust, I'd be ruined. I could walk away. Put the walls back up. Tell them it meant nothing. And I almost did. But then Killian brushed my hair back, voice low. "You're ours." For a second — just a second — I let myself believe him.

Cole

I knew the moment she woke. Not because she moved — she didn't — but because the air around her changed. She went still in that way soldiers do when they're waiting for the next hit. Not tense exactly, just... braced. Preparing for the fallout before it even comes. And I hated that I knew that feeling. I didn't move at first. Just kept my arm draped over her legs, pretending I was still asleep. Letting her think she had a second to breathe before we noticed.

Then Killian shifted behind her, hand locking on her waist like an anchor. "You're awake," he murmured, and she flinched. Barely. But I saw it. Lucas caught it too. His hand slid down her thigh, slow and grounding, like he could remind her she wasn't alone without saying a word. Jaxon pressed his mouth to her collarbone, easy and unhurried, like affection was the most natural thing in the world. And me? I couldn't hold back the sound that rumbled out of my chest. Not anger. Not lust. Just... refusal. Refusal to let her think last night didn't mean something.

"You're not going anywhere yet, princess," I said, voice low. She froze. "I can't." Wrong answer. Killian's voice was quiet steel. "You can." And she did. She let go again.

This time we didn't take her hard. We took her apart slow. Deliberate. Every kiss, every touch meant to remind her she was safe here — with us. She fought it at first, I could feel it in the way her muscles stayed tight under my hands. But then her breathing shifted, her grip on Jaxon's hand tightened, and the walls cracked.

When it was over, she lay between us like she didn't know whether to cling tighter or vanish. And I could feel it — the second the fear crawled back in.

Because that's Riley's way. She doesn't panic about what's happening. She panics about what it means.

I wanted to tell her it meant everything. That she's ours in a way none of us are going to take back. That she can throw her walls up all she wants — we'll still be here when they fall again.

But she's not ready to hear that yet. So I just stayed close. Close enough that if she ran, she'd have to climb over me to get away.

Cole

She'd gone quiet in that way that wasn't just sleep — it was peace. Her breathing even, her body warm and loose under all of us.

We didn't get this often. Hell, we didn't get this ever. I memorised it. The curve of her cheek against Jaxon's chest. The way her fingers were still tangled in mine like she'd forgotten to let go. She was here.

With us. Letting us in. And I didn't care if the whole damn building caught fire, I wasn't moving.

Then Killian's phone buzzed. Once. Twice. Three sharp vibrations, like an alarm. His body went rigid behind her. My stomach dropped. "Extraction point's compromised," Lucas said, voice already turning to ice. "Pavel's moving early." And just like that — the moment was gone.

Her eyes snapped open. The softness vanished. The walls slammed back into place so hard I could almost *hear* it. She was already pushing up, already gone somewhere I couldn't follow. From safe. From ours. Back to the Riley who survives.

Lucas

One second she was sunk into us like we'd always been here. The next, she was all fight again — shoulders tight, jaw set, scanning the room like she expected an ambush.

The warmth between us evaporated. Mission mode took its place.

She didn't even look at me when she said, "What's the call?" And I hated it — hated that I'd been stupid enough to think we could hold her there for longer than a heartbeat. That maybe she'd let herself *stay*.

Killian answered, but I barely heard him. I was still watching her, memorising the afterimage of what I'd just lost.

Riley

The warmth bled out of the room like someone had pulled a plug. One second I was wrapped in them, drowning in something that felt dangerously close to... home.

The next, Killian's phone buzzed, Lucas's voice turned to steel, and the air thickened with mission tension. I sat up before I could stop myself, the shift jarring, muscles screaming protest. Didn't matter. Whatever that softness had been, it was gone. And it needed to stay gone. "What's the call?" My voice came out rough, but steady. Good. "Docks," Lucas said without looking at me. "We hit hard, fast." "Fine," I said, already pushing to stand. "I'll gear up—"

"No." Killian didn't raise his voice, but it landed heavy enough to stop me mid-step. My spine locked. "No?" "You're not going." It was like a bucket of ice water straight to the chest. "The hell I'm not." "You're not cleared," Lucas said, still calm, still infuriating. "You're staying in ops." I laughed. Sharp. Ugly. "Ops? What, so I can sit behind a screen like a good little mascot while you four go play hero?"

Cole's tone was softer, but it didn't help. "You're still healing, princess." There it was — that word. That softness. That *claim*. My throat tightened and I hated that it did. "I'm fine," I bit out. Killian met my gaze, unflinching. "You're ours. And we don't risk what's ours." For a second, something cracked — just enough for the words to hit somewhere deep. Too deep. And that was exactly why I straightened, smirk locked in place like armour.

"Newsflash," I said, forcing the edge back into my voice. "I don't belong to anyone. And if you think you can sideline me—" "You're not going," Killian repeated, final. The wall slammed up so hard it made my skull ring. Fine. They wanted distance? They'd get it. Because if I let them protect me like this, I'd start to believe it meant something. And I couldn't afford to believe that.

62

Soft Enough to Bleed

Riley

Arsonist's Lullabye – Hozier

The room blurred at the edges, my anger bleeding out into something heavier.

Not forgiveness. Not calm.

Just exhaustion wearing a mask that looked a lot like surrender.

The boys were still talking about the mission in those low, deliberate tones, words clipped now, sharpened by the argument. My argument. The one I'd lost.

I should've gotten up. Should've kept pacing until my voice gave out and my blood stopped boiling.

Instead, I stayed exactly where I was.

Killian's lap beneath me, solid and steady. Jaxon's thigh pressed under my legs. Cole's hands kneading slow circles into my feet like I was royalty instead of the liability they'd benched. Lucas's fingers combed through my hair in calm, rhythmic strokes, smoothing something jagged inside me every time they passed.

Why the fuck am I putting up with this?

My brain kept asking the question, but my body had already betrayed me. My muscles kept sinking deeper into the warmth surrounding me. My eyelids kept growing heavier. I told myself I was gathering intel. Letting them think they'd won while I planned my revenge.

But that wasn't the truth. The truth was... I didn't want to move.

Not with Killian's thumb brushing slowly against my temple.

Not with Cole's hands grounding me.

Not with Lucas quietly untangling knots from my hair like he had all the time in the world.

Not with Jaxon's warmth pressed along my side, his quiet laughter rumbling through me every time someone on-screen said something stupid.

And then it came again—that dangerous, traitorous thought.

God, I might love them. I shoved it down instantly. Adrenaline. Trauma bonding. Emotional instability. Stockholm syndrome with extra steps. Definitely not love.

Except the word stayed lodged in the back of my throat anyway, heavy and terrifying and impossible to swallow back down.

Jaxon laughed softly at something on the television. My pulse stuttered. My jaw unclenched. My eyes slipped shut for just a second.

The conversation around me faded slowly into static, their voices turning into warmth and background gravity while my anger dissolved beneath the weight of their hands.

It should've scared me more than it did. Because somewhere in the middle of all of it—in the heat, the softness, the impossible gentleness—I slipped.

Fell straight into that dangerous place where I felt... Safe.

Jaxon

Her breathing changed first.

One minute she was all sharp edges and fury, every muscle tight like she was still halfway through the argument.

The next... she softened.

Not completely. Riley didn't know how to completely soften.

But enough.

Enough that her lashes rested against her cheeks. Enough that her shoulders sank into Killian instead of staying braced for impact. Enough that she stopped fighting the hands touching her like maybe, somewhere deep down, she'd forgotten she was supposed to.

Cole noticed first too. His hands slowed against her feet, expression going distant in that dangerous way he got around her.

Lucas kept running his fingers through her hair with slow, steady strokes, calm as ever, but I caught the way his eyes lingered on her face like he was memorising this version of her.

And Killian— Killian looked fucking gone.

One arm wrapped around her waist, thumb brushing absent circles against her hip while he stared down at her like she was something holy he didn't quite trust himself to touch.

That should've scared me more than it did.

"We're making a mistake," I said quietly.

Three heads turned toward me immediately. Nobody bothered pretending they didn't know what I meant.

"She's letting us in," Lucas murmured softly.

"Exactly," I shot back. "And we all know what happens when Riley lets people in."

Silence. Heavy silence this time. Because they knew. Knew about the crash. Sophie. The way Riley loved like it was something dangerous instead of safe.

Cole's jaw tightened. "We're not leaving her."

"That's not what I'm saying."

Killian's gaze never left Riley's face. "Then say what you are saying."

I exhaled slowly through my nose. Because the truth was ugly. The truth was I saw exactly where this was heading, and I was already too far gone to stop it.

"She's gonna break our fucking hearts," I muttered finally.

Cole barked out one rough laugh. "Bit late to worry about that."

And shit. That landed harder than it should have. Because he was right. It was too late.

The second Riley started sleeping with knives under her pillow because she didn't trust herself to need us? Too late.

The second she tore apart an entire warehouse because she thought we'd abandoned her? Too late.

The second she looked at us tonight like she couldn't decide whether to run or beg us to stay?

Absolutely fucking too late.

Killian slid one arm beneath her knees and the other around her back before lifting her carefully against his chest.

Riley barely stirred. Just made one small sound and curled closer instinctively, like her body trusted him even if her brain still panicked about it.

Something sharp twisted hard beneath my ribs at the sight.

Upstairs, Killian lowered her carefully onto the bed.

Cole pulled the blankets over her.

Lucas brushed hair away from her face.

And me? I stood there for one stupid second just watching her breathe. Because even asleep, she looked like she was waiting for the world to take this away from her. That wrecked me more than the confession had.

Killian climbed into bed beside her first. Cole followed immediately after. Lucas settled behind her quietly, one arm sliding around her waist.

Like none of them even questioned it. Like loving Riley was already instinct. I looked toward the doorway for half a second. Like maybe I could still leave before this got worse.

Then Riley shifted in her sleep, brow tightening faintly like she'd noticed the empty space beside her. And that was it. Game over. I climbed into bed beside her without another word.

The second I settled against her, she relaxed again instantly, sleep-heavy and warm between all of us. Yeah. We were absolutely making a mistake. And God help me— I didn't care anymore.

63

You Don't Get to Love Me

Killian

Run for your life - K. Flay

Her voice hit like shrapnel. "It's a trap," Riley snapped, jabbing a finger down onto the map spread across the table. "Look at this route. It's a fucking funnel. Two entry points. No clean fallback. You want to charge into that with your dicks out and pray they don't spring the cage?"

Nobody laughed. Because she wasn't wrong. And because underneath the anger, underneath the venom, I could hear the real problem: she was trying to throw herself back into the fire again.

"No," I said flatly. "You're not joining this op."

She went completely still. Slowly, Riley lifted her head. "Excuse me?"

"You're not cleared."

A sharp laugh broke out of her. Pure venom. "Bullshit. Grant cleared me five days ago. Full mobility. Reflexes normal. Stitches dissolved. I passed every combat assessment."

I looked toward the others automatically.

Lucas avoided her eyes.

Cole suddenly found the ceiling fascinating.

Jaxon winced.

"She's not wrong," Jaxon muttered carefully. "Grant signed off on everything."

Betrayal flickered hot in my chest, but I shoved it aside.

"She's still not going."

Riley leaned over the table hard enough to rattle it. "Why? Because it's dangerous?" Her smile turned sharp and ugly. "Funny. You're all apparently fine walking into a kill box as long as I'm not there."

I didn't answer.

Because that was exactly it.

I'd rather walk into hell myself than watch her bleed out in one again.

"Tell me the truth, Killian," she said quietly now, which somehow hit harder than yelling. "Is this about the mission... or are you just scared to let me off the leash?"

That landed like a knife straight through the ribs.

I stared at her — the fading bruises along her throat, the scar near her collarbone, the fury barely holding her upright — and all I could see was eleven weeks ago.

Blood on concrete.

Her pulse fading beneath my hands.

The sound of her trying to breathe.

"I watched you almost die," I said finally. "You think I'm gonna throw you back into another setup because Grant says you can walk in a straight line?"

"I'm not your fucking porcelain doll, Killian."

"No," I snapped before I could stop myself. "You're my responsibility."

Silence crashed through the room.

Riley's expression cracked for half a second before fury slammed back into place. Her hands curled into fists.

"You signed a contract," I reminded her quietly. "Three months. You're still under it. Until that clock runs out, you're mine to protect."

Shock flashed across her face first.

Then hurt.

Then rage.

"You're using the contract to bench me?" she whispered.

I nodded once.

"If I have to."

"Fuck you."

The words gutted me harder than they should have.

She turned instantly, storming toward the exit. Nobody stopped her. Nobody was stupid enough to try.

But at the door, she spun back around one last time, eyes bright with fury.

"You know what's funny?" she asked shakily. "You think keeping me out of the fight keeps me safe." Her laugh cracked. "But if you go in there without me... you're the ones walking into a grave."

Then she was gone.

The door slammed hard enough to shake the walls.

Silence settled over the room like smoke.

Cole exhaled first. "She's got a point."

I didn't answer.

Just stared down at the map while dread crawled slowly through my chest.

Because Riley Morgan didn't need a leash. She needed room to run. And I was the idiot still trying to hold the chain.

Worse? If I opened my mouth again, I'd say too much. That I couldn't think straight when she was in danger.
That every mission without her felt wrong. That every mission with her felt unbearable. That somewhere along the line, protecting Riley stopped being leadership and became something far more dangerous.

Love. And love got people killed.

Riley

I didn't walk out. I stormed. Boots hammering against concrete hard enough to echo through the hallway, rage burning so violently through my chest I could barely see straight.

No clearance. Not going on the op. The bastard actually used the contract. Not because I wasn't capable. Not because I wasn't cleared. Because he was scared.

And somehow that pissed me off more than if he'd just admitted he didn't trust me.

I shoved through the hallway door hard enough it rebounded off the wall behind me.

"Riley—" Of course Lucas followed me.

I spun so fast he nearly walked straight into me. "Don't." I pointed at him sharply. "Do not come in here with your calm therapist voice right now, Lucas. I swear to God, I'm one bad sentence away from felony assault."

His hands lifted immediately. "Okay. Noted."

"Good." I started pacing again before I exploded.

"He used the fucking contract." I laughed once, sharp and furious. "Do you know how insane that is? What is this, medieval ownership laws? Am I livestock now?"

Lucas exhaled slowly. "Killian's trying to protect you."

I stopped dead. Then barked out a laugh so humourless it almost sounded broken. "Protect me?"

"Yes."

"From what?" I snapped. "The mission? Or his own issues?" His expression tightened immediately. Bullseye.

"Oh my God," I muttered, dragging both hands through my hair. "You're all insane."

"Nobody thinks you're weak, Riley."

"That's not the point." My voice cracked harder now, anger bleeding into something uglier. "I almost died for this team, Lucas." His face fell.

"I bled for this team. I recovered for this team. I clawed my way back from being stitched together like a fucking crime scene because I knew I'd get back out there." I jabbed a finger toward the war room. "And now suddenly I'm too fragile?"

"You're not fragile."

"Then stop treating me like I'll shatter!"

The words echoed violently between us.

Lucas looked wrecked already, but I couldn't stop now. Not when the hurt was finally bleeding through the anger.

"You know what the worst part is?" I laughed bitterly. "I actually thought he'd understand."

"Ri—"

"No." My throat tightened painfully. "I thought after everything, maybe he'd finally see me as an equal instead of something he has to drag out of danger kicking and screaming."

Lucas rubbed a hand over his face. "Killian doesn't know how to lose you." That hit way too hard.

I looked away immediately before he saw it land.

"Well, congratulations to him," I said quietly. "Because this?" I gestured between us. "This is exactly how you lose me."

Silence. Heavy. Awful silence.

Then Lucas stepped forward carefully. "Riley."

I backed up instantly. "No." The word came out sharper than I intended. More afraid than angry.

Because suddenly I understood exactly why this hurt so much.

It wasn't the mission. It wasn't the contract. It wasn't even the betrayal.

It was the fact that some stupid, broken part of me actually wanted him to choose me as an equal instead of protecting me like something delicate.

And that realization terrified me more than the mission ever could.

Lucas saw it happen too. I watched the understanding settle across his face in real time.

"Oh," he said softly. I hated that sound immediately.

"Don't."

"You love him."

"I absolutely fucking do not."

The denial came too fast. Too loud.

Lucas just looked tired now. "Riley—"

"I said don't."

My chest felt tight enough to crack open. Because if I stayed here another second, I might say something unforgivable. Or worse — honest.

So instead, I shoved past him hard enough to clip his shoulder. "Tell Killian something for me," I said without turning around.

Lucas stayed quiet. Waiting. I yanked open the garage door hard enough it screamed against the tracks. "If he wants to bench the bomb," I said coldly, "he better pray the mission survives without it."

Then I walked away before he could stop me.

Lucas

The garage door slammed hard enough to shake dust from the ceiling.

I stood in the hallway for a second staring at the empty space she'd left behind, listening to the echo of her boots disappearing deeper into the compound.

Shit. That had gone catastrophically worse than expected. Which was saying something considering the starting point had already been catastrophic. I rubbed a hand over my face before heading back toward the war room. Voices filtered through the partially open door — low, tense, clipped sharp around the edges. Nobody joking anymore. Nobody pretending this was fine.

Killian looked up the second I stepped inside. One glance at me and his jaw tightened. "Where is she?"

"Angry."

Cole snorted quietly from where he leaned against the table. "Groundbreaking."

I ignored him. "Also threatening bodily harm."

"That narrows it down zero percent," Jaxon muttered.

Killian's expression stayed hard. "Is she calming down?"

I stared at him for a long moment. "No."

Silence settled heavily across the room. Because we all knew Riley didn't cool off. She detonated.

Cole pushed off the table first, dragging a hand down his face. "Man, I'm just gonna say it." He pointed at Killian. "This was dumb."

Killian's eyes narrowed instantly. "Excuse me?"

"You heard me." Cole shrugged. "You basically told the most stubborn woman alive she's grounded."

"She almost died."

"And now she's gonna make it everyone else's problem," Jaxon muttered.

Killian ignored him completely. "She's not stable enough for this op."

I laughed once before I could stop myself. Every head turned toward me immediately.

"What?" Killian asked dangerously.

"You keep saying that," I replied carefully. "But this?" I gestured vaguely toward the hallway Riley disappeared down. "This is exactly why she's spiralling."

Killian's jaw flexed hard. "I'm supposed to throw her back into combat after what happened?"

"No," I snapped. "You're supposed to trust her to decide if she's ready."

That landed hard enough the room went quiet again. Killian looked away first. Which told me everything.

Jaxon sighed heavily and dropped into his chair. "You know what the worst part is?"

Nobody answered.

"She's right." He rubbed both hands over his face. "The route's a kill box." Cole swore softly under his breath.

I looked back toward the mission map spread across the table. Riley's handwriting still cut aggressively across the edges in black marker — alternate exits, blind spots, sniper risks, fallback routes.

Warnings. All ignored.

"She mapped the entire thing in under ten minutes," I muttered.

Killian stayed silent. And suddenly the room felt colder.

Because underneath all the anger and control and fear sat the simple truth none of us wanted to say out loud: Riley would've made this mission safer. For all of us.

Jaxon leaned back in his chair heavily. "So what's the plan when she inevitably commits several felonies out of spite?"

"She won't," Killian said immediately.

The entire room stared at him.

Then Cole barked out a disbelieving laugh. "Brother."

"Killian," I said slowly, "she once escaped handcuffs with a bobby pin and pure hatred."

"She bit a man," Jaxon added helpfully.

Cole nodded solemnly. "Actually multiple men."

"She bit me," I muttered.

Killian pinched the bridge of his nose. "You're all being dramatic."

Right on cue, the security alert on my tablet pinged softly. I glanced down automatically. Then sighed.

"What?" Killian asked immediately.

I turned the tablet toward him. "Tracker's moving."

His expression darkened instantly. "Where?"

"Few blocks out." I checked the signal again. "Still moving away from the compound."

Jaxon groaned loudly. "Oh, she's absolutely out committing crimes."

Cole looked almost fond. "Good for her."

Killian looked like he was developing a migraine in real time. "Can you patch into comms?"

"I can."

"Do it."

I connected to the tracker signal quickly, static crackling softly through the speakers before the line stabilised. Nothing. No engine noise. No talking. Just movement.

"She either turned comms off," I muttered, "or threw the tracker into traffic."

Cole considered that. "Honestly fifty-fifty."

Killian crossed his arms tightly over his chest. "Keep eyes on her location."

"You think she's coming after the mission anyway?" Jaxon asked.

Killian answered immediately. "No." But the hesitation before it?

Yeah. We all heard that too.

Riley

I should've gone back. That was the truly pathetic part. Not the screaming match. Not the threats. Not the fact I'd nearly launched a chair at Killian's head in what honestly felt like a morally justified act of female rage.

No. The pathetic part was that half of me still wanted to turn around.

I sat on Larry outside an abandoned service station three blocks from the compound, helmet resting against the handlebars while adrenaline burned through my bloodstream like bad gasoline.

The city buzzed quietly around me — distant sirens, traffic somewhere further out, wind rattling old signage overhead.

And underneath all of it?

Them. Still stuck in my head like shrapnel.

I could practically hear Killian's voice again. You're not going.

The rage came back instantly. "Go fuck yourself," I muttered to absolutely nobody.

Larry remained neutral on the subject.

I shoved both hands through my hair hard enough to pull at the roots. My chest still felt tight. Too tight.

Because underneath the fury sat something far worse.

Hurt. Which was disgusting, honestly. I should've been angry. I was angry.

But there was something humiliating about realising the reason this cut so deep was because I actually cared what they thought.

What Killian thought. That man was going to send me into an early grave fuelld entirely by unresolved emtional constipation. I leaned forward against the bike with a groan.

"Not cleared by me," I mocked bitterly under my breath. "What are you, my emotionally damaged parole officer?"

Still nothing from Larry. Traitor. My arm throbbed sharply beneath the duct tape wrapped around it.

Courtesy of the alley cat currently trotting around somewhere behind the service station wearing Killian's tracker clipped to its collar like a tiny criminal mastermind.

The little bastard had objected violently to being recruited into espionage. Honestly? Fair.

I glanced toward the alley where I'd nearly lost a finger five minutes earlier trying to attach the tracker while the furry menace hissed at me like I'd insulted its bloodline.

"Hope you're causing problems on purpose, you tiny demon," I muttered.

The cat yowled somewhere in the distance. Good enough.

At least now Killian and Lucas would be watching a tracker move randomly around backstreets while I went the opposite direction.

Paranoia: useful.

Potential tetanus: less useful.

I flexed my aching hand with a grimace before checking my phone again.

Tracker signal still active. Perfect. I stared at the blinking dot for a long second before barking out one harsh laugh.

"Oh, you paranoid bastards." Of course they were tracking me.

Killian probably thought I was one emotional breakdown away from setting fire to a federal building.

Which — rude. Unproven. Mostly.

I looked down the street slowly, mind already turning over possibilities. Angles. Timelines. Routes.

The mission replayed in my head piece by piece. The entry points. The boxed exits. The sight-lines.

The trap. My stomach twisted hard.

Because the more I thought about it, the worse it got. They were walking into a slaughterhouse. And the idiots were still going anyway. I closed my eyes briefly. I could leave. That was the smart option. Walk away now before things got worse. Before Killian dragged me into another fight about safety and contracts and whether or not I had a death wish.

I could disappear tonight if I wanted. They'd deserve it too. The thought landed hollow. Because the truth was ugly. I didn't actually want to leave them. I wanted them to choose me anyway.

And that realisation hit like a knife sliding clean between my ribs.

"Jesus Christ," I whispered. Love really was a terminal illness.

I sat there for another full minute staring into nothing. Then my phone buzzed again. Mission departure alert. My expression went flat instantly.

"Oh, absolutely not." The engine beneath me roared to life with one violent twist of the throttle.

Anger flooded back fast enough to drown everything else.

Fine. If those emotionally constipated morons wanted to march directly into a kill box without their tactical analyst because Killian Moretti was having feelings about it?

Fantastic. Amazing plan. Ten out of ten decision-making.

I slammed my helmet on and kicked Larry into gear hard enough the back tire skidded sideways across cracked pavement.

"You know what?" I muttered as the city blurred around me. "I hope they're stressed."

The bike screamed down the street beneath me like it was equally offended by the situation. And somewhere deep down — underneath the fury, underneath the betrayal, underneath the terrifying ache in my chest — sat one horrible truth I couldn't outrun no matter how fast I drove.

If something happened to them tonight?

It would destroy me.

Jaxon

Riley was right. That was the first coherent thought I had as bullets ripped through the alley wall six inches from my head.

Concrete exploded beside me. Dust filled the air. Somebody screamed somewhere further down the street — maybe one of ours, maybe one of theirs. Honestly? Hard to tell at this point.

"This is fucked!" I shouted, ducking lower behind the overturned car currently serving as our extremely temporary shelter.

Cole fired two shots over the hood before slamming back into cover with a hiss. Blood soaked through his shoulder.

"Little busy, Jax!"

"No, because I need everyone to acknowledge something important before we die!"

Killian reloaded beside me with terrifying calm. "Now?"

"Yes now! Riley literally said this was a funnel!"

Another explosion rocked somewhere overhead. Glass rained down across the alley.

Lucas's voice crackled sharply through comms. "Left side! Left side!"

Three gunmen rounded the corner immediately after.

Killian dropped one.

Cole dropped another.

The third vanished back behind cover before I could get a clean shot. Which was deeply rude of him, honestly.

"We are getting absolutely cooked out here," I snapped, breathless.

Because we were. Every exit point Riley marked on the map had collapsed exactly the way she said it would. Upper-level shooters. Blocked fallback route. Blind corners feeding directly into crossfire. A kill box. Exactly like she warned us.

And now? Now we were trapped inside it. Killian slammed another magazine into place hard enough to crack plastic. His expression looked carved from violence and regret.

Which. Fair.

"Status," he barked.

"Bad," I answered immediately.

Lucas sounded equally thrilled from somewhere across the alley. "I've got movement on the east side!"

"More?" Cole groaned. "Jesus Christ, do these people reproduce asexually?"

Gunfire answered him immediately. We dropped again as bullets shredded the car windows above us. One clipped the concrete near my shoulder hard enough to spray fragments into my neck.

"Oh, cool," I muttered, pressing a hand against the sting. "Love that for me."

Killian looked over sharply. "You hit?"

"I'm emotionally hit."

"Jaxon."

"I'm fine."

Probably. Honestly there were bigger issues currently unfolding around us. Like the fact Riley Morgan was somewhere back at the compound undoubtedly plotting murder while we reenacted the tactical equivalent of stepping into traffic blindfolded.

Another grenade detonated close enough to rattle my teeth. Smoke flooded the alley instantly.

Cole coughed violently beside me. "Okay. Revised opinion."

"What?" I yelled over the ringing in my ears.

"She's gonna kill us when this is over."

Lucas's voice came through comms again, strained now. "Killian—we need to move. They're closing both sides."

No response. I looked over. Killian was staring at the upper rooftops with an expression I'd only seen once before. Fear.

Not for himself. For her. Because now he knew. Now all of us knew.

Riley hadn't been emotional. She hadn't been reckless. She hadn't been overreacting. She'd been right. And we left her behind anyway. A bullet slammed into the car door hard enough to make all three of us flinch.

"This was your plan!" I shouted at Killian.

"I'm aware!" he barked back.

"Well I'd like the record to show Riley would never let us die this stupidly!"

Cole barked out one rough laugh despite everything. "That's fair."

Then another wave of gunfire erupted from the eastern corridor. Too close. Way too close.

Lucas swore sharply through comms. "They're flanking us!"

Killian's expression hardened instantly. Command mode slamming back into place through the chaos.

"Fall back north side," he ordered. "Move now."

"North side's exposed!" I snapped.

"I know."

Which was somehow worse. Because there weren't good options anymore. Just survival. We moved anyway.

Smoke burned my lungs immediately as we sprinted across open ground. Bullets tore through the alley around us like hornets. One clipped Cole hard enough to spin him sideways with a curse.

I grabbed his arm automatically before he hit the ground.

"Move your giant emotionally unstable ass!"

"Trying!"

Lucas appeared through the smoke ahead of us, firing controlled bursts while backing toward the next section of cover. And through all of it — every shot, every scream, every explosion — one thought kept hammering through my skull louder than the gunfire itself: Riley warned us. And God help us all when she found out how right she'd been.

Riley

The gunfire started two blocks out. Short bursts at first. Then automatic fire.

Then the kind of explosion that rattled storefront windows and immediately upgraded my mood from furious to homicidal.

I twisted the throttle harder. Larry screamed beneath me as I shot through the intersection fast enough to earn several terrified car horns and at least one shouted insult.

"Yeah, yeah," I muttered, weaving around a delivery truck. "I'm aware traffic laws exist."

Smoke curled above the rooftops ahead. Too much smoke.

My stomach dropped instantly. Because I knew exactly what that meant. The operation had gone sideways. Badly.

"Fucking idiots," I hissed through clenched teeth.

I cut down a side street hard enough my knee nearly scraped concrete. The bike fishtailed once before correcting.

Gunfire echoed again. Closer now.

And underneath the adrenaline and rage sat something far worse clawing violently at my ribs:

Fear. Real fear. Not for me. For them. I'd spent the entire ride over trying to stay angry enough not to think about it.

About Killian bleeding.

About Lucas trapped somewhere with no exit route.

About Jaxon making one stupid joke too late.

About Cole throwing himself between bullets and everyone else like the reckless idiot he was.

Because for all my dramatic speeches about independence and contracts and walking away? The truth was horrifyingly simple. If one of them died tonight, it would break something in me permanently. The thought hit hard enough I almost missed the turn.

"Absolutely not," I snarled at myself. "We are not emotionally processing during a tactical emergency."

Focus.

I killed the headlights half a block from the engagement zone and slid Larry behind an abandoned loading dock.

The second my boots hit pavement, another explosion ripped through the alley ahead. Men shouting. Gunfire. Concrete collapsing somewhere higher up.

And over all of it?

Jaxon screaming: "THIS IS WHY WE DON'T IGNORE THE SCARY WOMAN WITH THE MAPS!"

I closed my eyes briefly. "God, I hate them."

Then I grabbed my gun and moved. Fast. The alley opened ahead in flashes of chaos.

Killian's team pinned behind shredded cover. Multiple shooters positioned along the upper walkways exactly where I predicted they'd be. East corridor compromised. Exit points boxed.

A textbook funnel. Exactly like I warned them.

A man stepped into my path from the side corridor before he even realised I was there. One shot. He dropped instantly.

I kept moving.

Another shooter appeared above the fire escape. Two shots. Gone.

The third mercenary barely got his weapon raised before I drove my knife straight into his throat and ripped it free without breaking stride. Hot blood splattered across my sleeve. Didn't slow me down.

Ahead, I caught movement through the smoke — Cole dragging Jaxon behind cover while Killian fired toward the upper levels. Lucas was pinned near the north wall trying to return suppressive fire without getting his head removed.

Jesus Christ. They were seconds from getting overrun. Rage flooded through me so violently it almost steadied the fear.

"You absolute fucking morons," I whispered.

Then I stepped into the open alley and opened fire. Everything happened fast after that. One rooftop shooter dropped before he even saw me.

Second took a round through the shoulder and disappeared screaming backward.

Third managed half a turn before I put him down clean through the chest.

The gunfire shifted instantly. Confusion. Good.

I moved again before anyone could track me properly, cutting across the alley low and fast while bullets sparked against concrete around me.

"LEFT SIDE!" Lucas shouted suddenly.

I already saw them. Three hostiles pushing flank position through the eastern corridor.

I slammed into the closest one hard enough to send both of us crashing sideways into the wall. Knife under ribs. Twist. Drop.

Gun raised. Two more shots. Bodies hit pavement. Silence cracked briefly through the alley.

Not full silence. Just enough. Enough for all four idiots to finally look at me.

Jaxon blinked first. Then loudly yelled: "OH THANK CHRIST."

Cole looked halfway between relieved and terrified. "Riley?!"

Lucas actually stopped moving for one full second like his brain needed to reboot.

And Killian— Killian just stared at me. Smoke curled between us. Blood streaked down one side of his face. His chest heaved hard beneath tactical gear, eyes wide with something sharp and ugly and relieved all at once. I pointed my rifle directly at him.

"You," I snapped furiously, "are never allowed to make tactical decisions while emotionally compromised again."

Jaxon barked out a hysterical laugh.

A bullet whizzed past my head immediately after.

"Oh, for fuck's sake." I turned and fired again.

Cole

The last gunshot echoed through the alley like a coffin nail.

Then silence crashed down hard enough to hurt.

Smoke drifted between the buildings in slow grey waves. Shell casings littered the ground. Blood streaked concrete. Somewhere nearby, a car alarm screamed into the night like the city itself had finally noticed the war zone sitting in its backstreets.

And in the middle of it all stood Riley. Breathing hard. Covered in blood that was only partially hers. Gun still raised. Terrifying. Beautiful. Absolutely furious.

Jaxon leaned heavily against the wall beside me with a groan. "I would just like the record to show," he wheezed, "that Riley saved all of our asses."

"No one's debating that," Lucas muttered, pressing a hand against the cut above his ribs.

Killian still hadn't spoken. He just stared at her.

Like he couldn't decide whether to yell, kiss her, or lock her in a panic room for the next six months.

Riley noticed immediately.

And whatever relief had cracked through her expression during the fight disappeared again just as fast.

There she was. The wall slamming back into place.

She holstered the gun with sharp, angry movements before stalking toward us through broken glass and debris.

Every step sounded deliberate.

Final.

"Riley—" Killian started.

"No."

One word. Flat enough to cut steel.

She reached into her jacket pocket and yanked out an envelope folded once down the middle. Blood stained one corner.

Then she shoved it hard against Killian's chest.

"Read it later."

Killian frowned immediately. "What is this?"

"Consequences."

Something cold slid down my spine at the tone in her voice. Because Riley wasn't yelling anymore. She wasn't angry. She was done.

And somehow that was infinitely worse.

Jaxon seemed to realize it too because the humor vanished clean off his face. "Ri—"

"Don't." Her voice cracked like a whip. "None of you get to 'Ri' me right now."

Killian looked down at the envelope once before looking back up at her carefully. "You're hurt."

"Oh my God." She laughed once, sharp and exhausted. "Are you serious?"

Blood dripped slowly from the scrape along her arm. Dirt streaked her cheek. Her braid was half falling apart from the fight.

And still she looked at all of us like we were the ones who wounded her. Maybe we were.

"You benched me," she snapped. "You ignored me. Then you walked directly into the trap I warned you about because apparently all four of you share one collective brain cell."

Cole winced slightly.

Fair.

Killian stepped toward her slowly. "Riley—"

"No."

She backed away immediately. Not far. Just enough. Enough to say don't touch me right now. That hit harder than the bullets had.

"You don't get to act relieved," she continued, voice shaking now despite how hard she tried to control it. "You don't get to look at me like that after deciding I was too broken to stand beside you."

"We were trying to protect you," Lucas said quietly.

Riley rounded on him instantly. "From what?"

Nobody answered. Because the truth sat ugly between all of us now. Not the mission. Not the danger. Loss.

Killian looked wrecked enough to finally admit it. "I couldn't watch you die again." The words hit the alley like another explosion.

Riley froze. Just for a second.

Long enough for the hurt underneath the anger to show through clearly. And Jesus Christ—that was somehow worse.

"You don't get to decide that for me," she whispered.

Killian's expression cracked open. "Riley—"

"No." She swallowed hard enough I saw the movement from ten feet away. "You made your choice already."

Then she gestured around us slowly. Bodies. Smoke. Blood.

"This is what happened without me." Silence swallowed the alley whole. Because she was right. Again.

Jaxon scrubbed both hands down his face hard. "Baby—"

"Don't call me that." Her voice broke on the last word.

That one landed like a knife straight through the ribs. Killian looked like someone had physically struck him.

But Riley just stepped backward again, walls climbing higher with every second. "You needed me," she said quietly. "And I still came."

Cole's chest tightened painfully at the exhaustion in her voice.

Because she had. No matter how angry she was. No matter how betrayed. No matter how badly we hurt her. She still came back for us anyway. And we repaid her by making her feel unwanted.

Riley looked between all four of us slowly before speaking again. "This partnership?" She tapped two fingers lightly against her chest. "Dead."

Every muscle in Killian's body went rigid instantly. "No."

"Yes."

"You don't mean that."

Her expression finally cracked fully then. Not anger. Pain. Raw enough it almost dropped me to my knees.

"That's the problem," she whispered. "I do."

Nobody moved. Nobody fucking breathed. Because suddenly this wasn't about the mission anymore.

This was about losing her. For real. Riley climbed onto Larry without another word. The bike roared beneath her instantly, engine vicious and angry and alive.

Killian stepped forward automatically. "Riley."

She stopped. Didn't look back. And for one horrible second, hope flickered through the alley.

Then she spoke quietly through the helmet visor. "You were supposed to trust me."

The engine screamed. Tires spun hard against broken pavement. And then she was gone. Just smoke. Noise. Empty street.

Killian stood frozen in the middle of the wreckage holding the envelope in one bloodstained hand like it might detonate.

Lucas stepped closer first. "Killian..."

He opened it slowly. Read once. Then stopped breathing entirely. I watched the colour drain out of his face in real time. Jaxon moved beside him carefully. "What is it?"

Killian didn't answer. Didn't blink. Just handed the letter over silently. I read it over Jaxon's shoulder.

Termination Effective immediately, I am withdrawing from all field operations, communications, and association with your unit.

All tactical support obligations are considered fulfilled.

All personal ties are considered void.

Do not contact me.

Do not follow me.

This decision is final.

— Riley Morgan

Nobody spoke after that. Because the worst part wasn't the letter. It wasn't the goodbye. It was the horrible realisation settling slowly into all of us at once: Riley Morgan had finally done the one thing we thought she never would. She walked away first.

Killian

Killian

The paper shook once in my hand. Only once. I stopped it immediately.

My eyes dragged slowly across the final line again. Do not contact me. A hollow laugh almost escaped me. Like Riley thought this was a resignation. Like she could bleed beside us, sleep in our arms, let us carve ourselves into her soul—and then disappear with a letter folded neat enough to pretend none of it mattered.

No. That wasn't how this worked anymore.

Smoke curled through the alley around us. Sirens wailed somewhere in the distance, growing closer every second, but the only thing I could hear was her voice.

You were supposed to trust me. The words lodged beneath my ribs like a blade. Because she was right.

And because even after everything—even after we hurt her, benched her, treated her like something fragile instead of lethal—she still came back for us.

She came anyway. Back into gunfire. Back into a kill box. Back to me.

That wasn't duty. That was love.

And Riley Morgan was about to learn exactly how dangerous loving us truly was.

Cole sat against the wall clutching his bleeding shoulder, staring blankly into the smoke. Jaxon leaned beside him unusually quiet for once, exhaustion and guilt written across his face. Lucas watched me carefully. Too carefully.

He saw it. The shift happening inside me. The exact moment heartbreak stopped being grief and became obsession.

"She's gone," Jaxon said finally.

I folded the letter once. Precise. Controlled. Then slid it into the inside pocket of my jacket over my heart.

"No," I answered calmly. "She's running."

Lucas's jaw tightened. "Killian."

"She thinks she can vanish because she's scared."

"She's hurt," Cole muttered.

"I know."

That was exactly why this had become dangerous. Because hurt Riley fought dirty. She disappeared. Cut ties. Burned bridges before anyone else could cross them first.

But this?

This wasn't a contract anymore. This wasn't temporary.

Riley belonged to us now. And God help me, I belonged to her too.

The realisation settled deep and ugly inside my chest. Possessive enough to make breathing feel sharp.

I pictured her somewhere out there alone—bleeding through duct tape and adrenaline, convincing herself she'd escaped us cleanly.

The thought made something feral rise in my throat. No. Absolutely fucking not.

"She gave us a termination letter," Lucas said carefully.

"I don't care."

"She explicitly told us not to follow her."

That almost made me smile. Almost. Jaxon finally looked up sharply. "Killian..."

"She can hate me," I said quietly. "She can scream. Fight. Put a knife through my hand if it makes her feel better."

Cole went still. Because they all heard it in my voice. The certainty. The promise.

"But Riley Morgan does not get to disappear from us."

The alley fell silent again. Heavy. Dangerous.

Lucas rubbed a hand over his face slowly. "You're talking about hunting her down."

"Yes." No hesitation. No shame.

Because if Riley thought she was walking away after tonight, then she fundamentally misunderstood the kind of men we were.

The kind of men she chose to love. Cole exhaled harshly. "Jesus Christ."

"She's terrified," I continued quietly. "Not of us. Of needing us."

The words tasted bitter. True.

"She thinks leaving first means she survives it."

Jaxon's expression cracked slightly at that. "And what if she doesn't want to be found?"

I looked toward the empty street where her bike disappeared into the city.

Darkness swallowed the road completely now.

But all I could picture was Riley underneath neon lights somewhere, hands shaking around a cigarette she probably wasn't smoking properly, pretending the hollow feeling in her chest wasn't killing her too.

"She'll run," I murmured.

Because that was what Riley did when something mattered too much. She ran before it could destroy her. My jaw tightened hard.

But this time? This time she ran from men willing to burn cities down to get her back.

A dangerous calm settled through me completely. Not rage anymore. Resolve.

"She knows how we track targets," Lucas said slowly.

"She trained us in half of it," Cole added grimly.

"Then she'll make it difficult," I agreed.

Jaxon laughed once under his breath. "Difficult? Killian, she's gonna turn this into psychological warfare."

Probably.

She'd change phones. Dump vehicles. Rotate safe houses. Hack cameras. Ghost identities.

Riley would make herself smoke between our fingers if she could. And still?

I'd find her. Every time. Because Riley Morgan made one fatal mistake tonight. She thought love made us weak.

But men like us?

Men like us became monsters for the things we loved.

I stepped forward slowly, eyes fixed on the dark city beyond the alley.

"She can run across every state line in this country," I said softly. "She can hide under six fake names and disappear into every underground network she knows."

The sirens screamed louder now. Didn't matter. Nothing mattered except the certainty hardening inside my chest.

"We will still find her."

Lucas stared at me carefully. "And then what?"

I thought about Riley in my arms. Riley furious. Riley laughing. Riley trembling while admitting she loved us.

Then I thought about her driving away believing she was alone.

Mine. The word landed dark and possessive inside my skull.

Not ownership. Something worse.

Devotion. Obsession. Need.

"When we find her," I said quietly, "we remind her she stopped belonging to only herself the second she let us love her."

Silence followed that.

Then Cole stood slowly despite the blood soaking his shoulder.

Jaxon pushed himself upright after him.

Lucas sighed like a man realising the situation had officially escalated beyond sanity.

And me?

I looked out at the city one final time before turning toward the extraction route.

Somewhere out there Riley Morgan thought this was goodbye.

But she forgot one very important thing.

Predators hunt. And she belonged to four of them.

64

I Didn't Want to Love Them

Riley

The Night We Met – Lord Huron

I didn't even remember stopping. One second I was a blur of headlights and asphalt, lungs burning with adrenaline; the next I was on my knees in the dirt like the earth itself had ripped me down by the spine.

The scream came first.

Ugly. Raw. Violent enough to tear my throat apart. It ripped out of me like I was trying to cough up my own soul, echoing through the trees until it broke apart into choking sobs. My fists slammed into gravel hard enough to split skin instantly, but I barely felt it.

I hurled my helmet. Not tossed. Launched.

Every ounce of rage and grief and poison inside me went into the throw. It smashed against the tree with a crack sharp enough to sound like bone, the shell splitting clean in half before the pieces disappeared into wet leaves.

A perfect mirror for the way I'd just shattered.

My jacket hit the mud next. Bag spilling open beside it. Nothing mattered anymore.

"FUCK!" The word ripped my chest raw.

"FUCK YOU! FUCK ALL OF YOU!" My voice broke apart on the last one, echoing back at me through the dark like even the night wanted distance from me.

I staggered upright, shaking so violently my knees nearly buckled. Larry stood nearby beneath the moonlight, loyal and waiting exactly where I'd left him.

And I kicked him anyway. Hard.

Metal screamed against concrete as the bike toppled sideways, crashing into the dirt. Gasoline leaked slowly beneath it like blood.

I kicked it again. And again. Until my boot hurt and my breathing turned ragged and none of it fixed the ache splitting my chest open.

My hands clawed into my hair hard enough to hurt.

"Why did you say it?" I sobbed into the dark. "Why the fuck did you mean it?"

Because that was the real problem, wasn't it?

Not the mission. Not the contract. Not even the betrayal.

Them. The way they looked at me like I was worth keeping.

I wasn't supposed to be loved. Wasn't supposed to want it either. And now the feeling sat inside me like infection, tearing through every wall I'd spent years building just to survive.

I punched the ground. Once. Twice.

Again and again until blood slicked across wet dirt and mud packed beneath my fingernails.

"I don't get to have this!" I screamed hoarsely. "Not after Sophie! Not after everything! Not when I ruin every fucking thing I touch!"

The tears blurred everything.

Trees. Road. Sky.

All I could see was wreckage.

The bike. My bleeding hands. My chest ripped hollow with something too big and ugly to name.

This wasn't crying. This was grief turning feral inside me. Rage clawing inward until there was nothing left but hollow bones and ruin.

And still I couldn't stop.

The cemetery gates groaned when I shoved them open. Iron screeched against stone like it hated me too. Rain had started falling properly now, cold and relentless, soaking through my clothes and stinging the cuts across my knuckles.

I barely noticed. Row after row blurred past beneath the storm until I found her.

Sophie Morgan. God. Even the letters mocked me. Clean. Ordered. Still.

Like Sophie hadn't been chaos wrapped in sharp smiles and stolen cigarettes. Like she hadn't been the only damn thing that ever made this life survivable.

My knees hit the mud hard in front of the grave.

"You should've been here!" I screamed at the headstone. "It should've been me!"

Thunder cracked overhead.

I slammed both fists against the stone hard enough to split the skin wider. Blood smeared across her name instantly.

"WHY DIDN'T YOU STAY?"

Another hit.

"WHY THE FUCK DID YOU LEAVE ME?"

The grave stayed silent. It always stayed silent. Didn't say funniest person I ever met. Didn't say only family I had left. Didn't say I let you die while I survived instead.

I ripped the photograph from my pocket with shaking hands. The beach. The stupid sunglasses. Sophie grinning so wide it hurt to look at now.

Rain warped the picture instantly when I pressed it against the gravestone.

"I tried," I choked out. "I tried so fucking hard to be okay without you."

My fingers found Jason's necklace next.

The chain snapped when I threw it at the stone, silver scattering through wet grass.

"But I can't!" The words broke apart into another sob. "I can't fucking do this anymore!"

My forehead hit the gravestone hard enough to hurt. My body shook violently while sobs ripped through me one after another, ugly and uncontrollable and years overdue.

"I let them in, Soph," I whispered brokenly. "I let them in... and now I'm ruined."

Rainwater streamed down my face, washing mud and blood together beneath me.

"I run. I always run." My voice cracked apart.

"But this time..." My chest heaved painfully.

"This time it feels like I left myself behind too." For a long time I just stayed there collapsed against the stone while the storm swallowed me whole.

Then finally—slowly—I dragged myself upright.

One last touch against Sophie's name. Blood and mud streaked across the letters like a final apology.

My goodbye. My punishment. Then I walked away.

Heart hollowed clean out of my chest.

And every single step away from that grave felt like I was leaving my soul buried six feet under beside her.

Riley

Medicine – Daughter

I was bleeding. Not gushing, but definitely oozing—the slow, hot bleed that makes your teeth ache and your limbs feel like borrowed meat. And I was probably concussed. Again.

The bell over the door jingled as I staggered into *Magda's Needlepoint & Notions*, which was a fucking lie of a name if there ever was one.

The shop looked like someone had exploded a doily factory inside a pastel war bunker.

Bolts of floral fabric lined the walls.

Quilting thread in every colour imaginable. Cross-stitched quotes framed in gold: *Live, Laugh, Love*—except I knew for a fact the "Laugh" part had once been "Load" before she sold it to a church lady.

And in the middle of it all, perched on a velvet rocking chair like she owned the building and the street it sat on—Magda.

Seventy-something. Tight silver curls. Pearl earrings. A cardigan the colour of faded mint leaves. And a teacup in one hand like she hadn't built half the black-market weapons network in this hemisphere.

She looked up from her tatting, eyes sharp behind rose-tinted glasses. "Well," she said. "You look like shit, sweet girl."

"Hi, Magda," I rasped, leaning against the counter before my knees remembered they didn't have bones anymore. She set her cup down with surgical precision.

"Didn't I tell you? No more dramatic entrances. Last time you kicked my door in, we had to replace the hinges and explain the bloodstains to the quilting club."

"I'm not kicking," I muttered.

"Just bleeding. Low impact." Magda rose, joints cracking but posture still perfect. She came around the counter, reached up, and patted my cheek with a hand that could've just as easily broken my jaw.

"Sit. Couch. Now. Or I'll put you there myself—and you know I'm still mean enough to do it." That voice left no room for negotiation.

I shuffled to the tiny floral loveseat in the corner, collapsed onto it like a half-dead Barbie doll, and immediately stuck to the plastic doily cover. Delightful.

Magda disappeared into the back. A second later came the click of locks and the unmistakable whirr of something that definitely wasn't a sewing machine.

When she returned, she had: A china teacup of Earl Grey. A tin of biscuits shaped like bullets. A trauma kit. And a gold-plated Glock tucked into her apron like it was part of the uniform.

She handed me the tea first—because priorities—then started cleaning my wound with the same precision she used for embroidery. "You want to tell me what idiot tried to kill you this time?"

"Could be a long list. Current front-runner's a militia boss in a too-tight vest." Magda snorted.

"Bet he compensates in more ways than one."

I choked on my tea. "Magda."

"What? I'm old, not dead." She winked.

"Besides, if you're going to risk your life over a man, I expect at least six-pack abs and a... generous endowment."

"Jesus Christ." She smirked, swabbing at the graze on my arm.

"Language. I'm practically your grandmother."

"You're practically my war crimes lawyer."

"Same thing." Her hands were steady, her touch gentler than her mouth.

She muttered under her breath about "shoddy stitching" and "children these days forgetting how to cauterise properly."

"Did you eat?" she asked suddenly.

"Does panic and vengeance count?"

"I survived G. M. Hutchison's 3 a.m. feral plot dumps and all I got was this emotional damage."

Thank you for:

Enduring 50+ unhinged messages that started with "okay BUT hear me out—" and ended with "...is this illegal?"

Being my emotional support goblins through every morally grey spiral and "what if the villain was hot though?" moment.

Offering enthusiastic feedback to questions like, "Would it be sexier if she threatened him with a knife or a frying pan?"

Never blinking when I said, "Do you think this is too much spit?" and instead answering like scholars.

Contributing memes, filth, and disturbing amounts of encouragement that I will absolutely blame you for in court.

TO THE REST OF YOU—MY READERS, MY GOBLINS, MY FELLOW MENACE-GREMLINS:

Thank you for reading. Thank you for raging. Thank you for letting me write the kinds of books that make your face do things in public you can't explain. I see you. I love you.

Now go hydrate, charge your batteries, and maybe clear your browser history.

Or don't. Live dangerously. Stay weird. Stay wild. Stay feral.

And may your morally grey love interests always come with emotional damage and abs.

With love, smut, and just enough chaos to be legally concerning,

G. M. Hutchison

Hi, I'm G. M. Hutchison — but if you've made it this far, we've officially been through enough together that you can call me Gemma.

I only started writing in 2024 after I was blessed (and mildly inconvenienced) with a benign brain tumour — affectionately named Brain Barnacle. She's still hanging out up there, medicated and monitored, living rent-free while I attend regular check-ins inside the giant Pac-Man MRI machine. Honestly? She's not even the weirdest thing about me at this point.

You, though? You're my favourite part of this whole mess.

You could've picked any book in the world. Something safe. Sensible. Emotionally stable. And yet, for reasons known only to you and possibly several concerned medical professionals, you willingly signed up for this feral circus of morally grey chaos.

That makes you my kind of person.

You are now an official member of the unofficial Goblin Syndicate™ — the readers who laugh at the wrong moments, cry over fictional disasters, and text their friends:

I know he's toxic, but hear me out...

You're the reason I write heroines who bite back, banter that lands like a sucker punch, and fictional love interests you would absolutely regret in real life but would marry instantly in fiction.

You're also the reason I sit at my keyboard at 2 a.m. cackling like a caffeinated cryptid while whispering "just one more chapter" as if sleep isn't a biological requirement.

By day, I pretend to be a functioning adult.

By night, I build worlds where you can lose yourself, laugh until your stomach hurts, emotionally spiral over fictional people, and maybe need to clear your browser history afterward.

You know.

For reasons.

So thank you — for reading, for feeling, for surviving the emotional whiplash, and for letting my stories take up space on your bookshelf and in your brain.

You're my people.

And I hope this is only the first of many beautifully unhinged adventures we take together.

With love, chaos, and at least three morally questionable decisions,

G. M. Hutchison

FINAL NOTE

At its heart, this book begins with sisterhood. Being a big sister has shaped every story I tell — the fierce love, the loyalty, the laughter, and the chaos of growing up side by side.

No matter how far the pages take me, you'll always be my first chapter, my fiercest bond, and my forever little BBQ chicken nugget.

www.ingramcontent.com/pod-product-compliance
Lightning Source LLC
Chambersburg PA
CBHW010452310726
48979CB00013B/2160/J

* 9 7 8 1 7 6 3 8 5 2 0 2 0 *